The
SECOND STRING

Book 2 of The God String series

By
MONTGOMERY THOMPSON

Copyright ©2020 Montgomery Thompson

All rights reserved

ISBN: 1979126291
ISBN-13: 978-1979126298

DEDICATION

For my Pauline, my home.
And to my father, for leading by example.

Chapter 1

Asunder

'Life is the hyphen between matter and spirit.'
-Hare Brothers

In the void there was nothing. No reality of the physical, no sight, smell or sound. Somewhere in that darkness emerged a light, permeating the nothing and stirring the senses as it grew. Rand came close to his thoughts, awakening through layers of awareness until he felt as if he were fully alert. It was only then that he realised he was unconscious. Suddenly his mind felt like a trap. He tried to claw his way out, but he just dug himself in - into the shell, back into his own head. Later he would liken the experience to putting on an old sock as he donned consciousness and burst back into the world, his eyes flickering to life.

Brightly coloured petals drifted down in flutters of white and pink, touching him lightly on the cheek. Vapour rose from his clothing; Special Forces night camouflage BDUs. *BDUs, that's what Elsie called them.* The name slammed his mind into the

"Elsie!"

Rand sat bolt upright and looked around frantically. She wasn't there. His head throbbed, making it difficult to concentrate. He was in an old forest sp
bright air smelled of flowers and ions. He felt a shuffling movement in his backpack.

"Spang! Buddy, are you okay?"

He shrugged the pack off and helped the little dog out of the protective rigging. Spang jumped to the ground, his nose working fitfully as he probed the air and the ground. He moved closer to Rand with the concentration of a scientist hot on the trail of a discovery. No dog had ever sniffed a scent like this – raw time.

"Yeah I know buddy, it kinda stinks." Rand said scratching the little dog's head. He clipped Spang onto the leash attached to his equipment harness then stood checking his compass. To his left the woods became sparse. He held still and tuned in to his surroundings, his grey-blue eyes steady and penetrating. Through the breeze and the rusting leaves there came the sound of heavy machinery and... *people!* Quickly and quietly he covered the ground to the edge of the trees with Spang running beside him. Crouching in the grass, he pulled the little dog close.

"Be quiet buddy, we don't know what's going on yet."

Beyond the trees Rand saw an old antique bulldozer and steam shovel working on something out of view over the hill. He turned up his earpiece. The sporadic throttles of the antiquated machinery rumbled over the sound of surf in the distance. Peering out of the trees, he recognised Montauk Point and the historic lighthouse. The Time / Space Shifter was far below him in a secret base accessed through the lighthouse keeper's house.

I must have appeared right above the TSS. He thought.

A figure rounded the corner of the keeper's house. He was armed and in uniform, walking a slow patrol around the lighthouse grounds. Other than Elsie it was the first human Rand had seen for over two years and he fought the urge to yell out. Remembering the SCAR assault rifle hanging from his harness, he brought the weapon to bear and used the scope to have a closer look.

The man was dressed in old Army gear, like he just stepped out of a World War II movie. Rand knew that the probability of them landing back in their own time was very low, especially on the first try. Now the truth of that became apparent.

"Jesus, we went too far back. That soldier's uniform, the construction equipment. I'd say we landed somewhere around the forties or fifties." He rubbed his forehead in frustration. "Dammit! We gotta find Elsie."

Rand turned and went back into the woods to where he and Spang had landed. Then, in ever-widening circles, he started combing the woods for signs of Elsie. Even if she had arrived before him he thought that he should be able to pick up some clues. He found nothing. Frustrated and a little frantic he tried to put the little dog's nose to work. His head continued to throb from the time shift experience.

"Spang find Elsie, go buddy!"

Spang just looked at Rand, tilted his head and shuffled his feet eagerly. He had no idea what the human wanted.

Rand sighed and started walking through the woods, quietly calling out for Elsie. As he came over a rise the trees suddenly ended at the edge of a cliff that plummeted fifty feet into the sea. To his left he could make out the construction along the shore. He suddenly realised what he was looking at.

"That's the base. They're adding on to the secret base."

A dump truck full of rock came up a steep road out of a large hole in the ground. The hole was only big enough for the one truck. A short distance away the bulldozer and steam shovel were excavating what looked like a parking lot. It began to make sense.

"They're turning it into a park. It used to be a base until forty-nine, then it became a state park. We read about this. It must be around nineteen fifty."

His powerful earpiece picked up a sound in the distance. It was a child's voice saying,

"Look daddy, look at the strange man!"

Rand scanned the shore and saw a boy and a man fishing down the beach from him. It dawned on him that he was totally exposed. He ducked quickly down into the grass and crawled towards the trees. He could still hear the voices.

"There's nothing there Donny, now pay attention to your line."

"But I saw him, he was dressed all funny in black clothes!"

"I don't see anything, it's just the woods."

"He was there! He was! Really!"

"Probably just someone out walking, now pay attention the fish won't catch themselves!"

Rand crawled deeper into the trees keeping Spang close to him.

"That was close. We better keep out of sight until nightfall."

***

As Elsie opened her eyes the earth shook. Dizzy inside her Kevlar helmet, she forced herself to move as her elbow pad struck something hard and sharp, she was on a rocky slope. As her sight adjusted to the bright sunlight she saw a large tire rolling just three feet from her head. Cursing, she rolled down the rocky slope and forced herself to a skidding stop where she caught her bearings. Her head swivelled as her eyes took in details. *Rocky slope going up. Dump truck driving away. Soldier on the far slope by the lighthouse. Sea behind. Navy battleship on the horizon. Forest up the hill.*

No Rand.

No Spang.

"Oh Jesus no, please." She had just found him, she couldn't lose him. Tears began to flood into her sky-blue eyes. She wiped them away angrily. Her mind swirled as the effects from being in the void left her woozy and disoriented. *Get a hold of yourself,* she fought back. *You're face down in the dirt on the side of a road in the middle of God knows when or where. Rand's here, you just have to find him.*

Keeping herself flat against the ground, she peered over a rock that was barely large enough to conceal her. The soldier walked strolled casually around the grounds of the lighthouse. He was on guard for sure, but hardly stressed about it. The guy was straight out of a comic book she thought as she tried to judge what time period it was. The plain drab olive uniform, old style helmet and M1 carbine told her that it could be any time between the nineteen forties to the seventies. *If anyone sees me they'll think I'm an alien in all this modern combat gear. C'mon Els, make a decision and move.*

Staying close to the slope she edged sideways away from the lighthouse, constantly scanning for anyone who might see her. Then it was up and up, scrambling until she had worked her way to a small stand of trees. She pushed her way farther into the trees keeping low and remembering her SERE

(Survival, Evasion, Resistance, Escape) school training: *be a ghost.*

She steeled her mind and moved quickly and silently forward. Pausing by a tree she caught her breath. Suddenly she felt like a complete idiot. She had forgotten about the communication earpieces. They were so comfortable she forgot they were there. They were in passive mode, ready to receive, but would not broadcast unless manually activated. She reached back to the control unit on her belt and flipped the small switch.

"Papa Bear tell me you're in here somewhere."

***

Rand was working his way deeper into the woods when his earpiece again picked up a sound, this time from off to his left. Suddenly his comms crackled to life, it was Elsie. He had completely forgotten about the radios.

"Elsie, oh thank God! Where are you?"

Spang barked and tried to drag Rand towards a shape moving at the edge of the woods.

"I think Spang found me." She replied with a relieved sigh.

They ran towards each other and wrapped together in a tight embrace.

"I was so scared I had lost you Elsie!"

She kissed him long and hard.

"Yeah, me too."

"We did it! We travelled through time and we made it together! The bad news is I think we landed somewhere in the fifties."

"Or the sixties or seventies. Did you see the soldier too?"

"Yeah, that and the old construction equipment was the tip off. There's no way to know for sure though. For now we have to lay low until it gets dark then we can explore."

They went deeper into the woods. Finally, Elsie could talk in a normal voice.

"It's really beautiful in here."

"You're really beautiful in here. I know we were only separated for a few moments, but the last thing I heard was you screaming for me. I felt so helpless. I was just floating in this black void. Then I woke up in the forest. I was so worried!"

"I came to by the side of that road and almost got run over by a dump truck, I was worried for me too. I didn't see you anywhere. Rand I'm so sorry. I have to tell you, I completely forgot about the radios. I was frantic to find you."

"Els, I was the same. I actually used the ear pieces to recon the shore but forgot about the radios."

"I was so fuzzy headed when I came to. It wasn't that I was afraid, I just had a hard time making any decisions at all."

"Really, you weren't scared at all?"

"Well, yeah for a second, but then I just knew you were okay. The time machine was kind of disorienting, we must have got displaced from it's location."

"Displaced? We just travelled through time, not knowing if we would ever see each other again. You're kind of nonchalant about it all things considering."

She looked at him with a confused look on her face. Then a realisation grew in her eyes.

"Oh Rand, I'm doing it. I'm so sorry, I can be such an ice queen. It's years of training, I just get really mission focused and shut off my emotions. I'm so sorry, I was really worried. When I'm stressed I switch into military mode to deal with it."

"It's okay, we'll figure it out. As long as we're together we can figure it out."

"But how do we get back? Where is the control unit? How would it even work if there's no power plant or collider built yet?"

"I don't know. There are more questions than answers right now. Why don't we chill out here. If we're anywhere before the nineties our night vision will let us own the night. We'll get our answers and decide out next move from there."

"Okay yes, that's a good plan." She resigned herself to wait it out. He handed her half of a power-bar from his backpack.

"Here, eat something and drink some water, you'll feel better."

The isolated spot concealed them well. Sunset filled the woods with a golden glow as they discussed their options.

"So you figure it's around the fifties because they're building on to the base under the guise of building the park. It makes sense."

"I think our first move would be to try and get back into the base. We know that the TSS is in there."

"No Elsie, even if we get in there and fight our way to the TSS, chances are we would still miss our time by a mile. We just don't know how to control the thing well enough to guarantee we can get back to RealTime or even the time we were last at, what did you call it again?"

"FirstTime, because we're the first people ever to have lived that far ahead on the time line."

"Right. I think it's smarter to stay in one time than to go jumping all over the place randomly in an attempt to get back. We have no idea what the repercussions could be."

Elsie nodded. "You're right hon. I think we have to find Remmel. He's here in this time."

"Isn't he be in the base? That's where we saw him."

"Remember the equipment in the control room said it was made in nineteen fifty-two. If it's before then he will working on the TSS somewhere else. We need to find out what time we're in to know for sure. But you're right about getting to Remmel. He is our best chance of learning how to control the thing.'

"So it sounds like our first target is the lighthouse. Maybe there is something there that can tell us the date. If nothing else we can recon it. If we have to venture further afield, we need to know how to get in there when we come back."

"Okay, sounds like a plan. If we do have to go further afield as you put it we won't get anywhere trying to hide out in the woods everyday. We will need to spend most of the night getting what we need to fit in around here. Plus, we need a place to stash our gear then get some clothes to blend in. Of course we'll also need money, transportation and eventually some kind of ID." The challenges seemed overwhelming, even to Elsie.

"It's okay hon, first things first; recon the base and find something to confirm the date. Maybe a newspaper or something. Depending on what we find we'll know how to go from there. It's either out into the world or down into the base. To tell you the truth both options kind of freak me out."

"Yeah, it's a different story with people around. We can't just go blasting our way into places. If it's fifty-two and Remmel is in the base we might have to impersonate military personnel. If it's not then we'll have to look elsewhere for him and that means blending in. Once we've procured clothes and cash we'll need a good stash spot to store our gear. This stuff would change the history of the world if someone found it."

"Well that's a bit dramatic." Rand looked at her like he wasn't buying it.

"Really?" She countered. "Think about Korea and Vietnam. Now add fully automatic waterproof shotguns, night vision, Gore-Tex, Velcro, teeny-tiny comms and ultra lightweight body armour."

"Oh." He realised she was right.

"Yeah. We need to be really careful."

"Okay, but remember what Dr. Remmel wrote about effecting history?"

"Yes, that if you interfered with events in the past it wouldn't necessarily create massive repercussions for the future."

"Do you still believe that?"

"I guess, but I'm thinking that only applies to little things. I would say that you can't kill people or interfere with yourself or cause major events."

"But what about the butterfly effect?"

"Remmel disagrees, but the only way we'll know if he's right is to get back home."

"So let's just operate on the principle that we can go about our business here as long as we don't kill anyone, meet ourselves or cause any major events that directly effect people."

"Agreed."

"Okay, then I have an idea where to get enough money that we won't have to worry about money if it comes to that."

She looked at him with renewed hope. "Really?"

"Yeah, but we would have to get to Chicago."

"Why? What's in Chicago?"

"The Lexington Hotel and Al Capone's vault."

The look of hope on her face soured. "What? Are you crazy?"

"Elsie listen, Capone died in forty-seven. His stash was reportedly found in nineteen seventy. So if we're between nineteen forty-seven and nineteen seventy no one has found his stash and no one ever knew about his secret room underneath the Lexington hotel. I'm just using history to our advantage."

"That is the wackiest plan -"

"And there's nothing wacky about our situation? C'mon Elsie. We're Mr. and Mrs. Wacky." He threw his hands in the air gesturing at them and their gear. "I mean, look at us. We're here years before we were born."

Her expression changed to a mixture of amusement and incredulousness. "It won't hurt to try."

The sun had been going down as they talked. The evening frogs came out to sing their songs as Elsie stood and took a deep breath.

"Have you noticed how fresh the air is. It's like it's thicker or something. I have so much more energy."

Rand agreed. "No hole in the ozone, pollution hasn't got out of control yet. If it were the seventies you'd definitely be smelling New York right now."

"So we're earlier than the seventies. Good. If it's the sixties we can dress like hippies and thumb our way around."

"Except I don't want to be stoned the whole time Elsie. People will look at you weird if you don't accept a joint they offer you."

"Oh, yeah. There is that."

"Let's find out which soup we're in before we go adding ingredients."

Rand tucked Spang back into his backpack harness. "It's time for night ops buddy. You gotta be really quiet okay?'" Spang rode with his head peering over the top of Rand's but seemed perfectly content. They made their way to the edge of the woods and checked for any guards. There was no sign of the soldier at the lighthouse.

Rand pulled the visor down on his night vision helmet and scanned the area. "All clear."

Elsie enabled her NV helmet. "Okay let's get down to that hole and check it out."

They went down the slope until they reached the place where the dump trucks had been emerging. It was completely covered up.

"What the?"

"It has to be a false cover. They'll be out here digging again tomorrow. That cave system had been under construction for many years."

"I wonder if the lighthouse still has it's access door?"

"Let's check it out."

They moved quickly back up to the trees and then towards the lighthouse.

"Elsie, on the back of your helmet are the night vision controls. Move the big selector switch all the way to the right."

'Roger. Hey there's the FLIR. I didn't know how to turn it on."

'Yeah, a heat sensor thing. What did you call it?'

'FLIR, Forward Looking Infra Red. Just what you said, it sees heat. Hey, check out the lighthouse."

There was someone moving around the building and light was coming from the windows.

"Must be the lighthouse keeper. I'll bet he lives in the place."

"So we can't get into the excavation and it's too much of a risk to break into an inhabited lighthouse just to find out the date."

"It's looking more like we should try and blend is for awhile until we can get more information and make a solid set of plans."

"Can you see how tall the light keeper is?"

"I'll switch to my scope." Rand's NV (Night Vision) helmet was synched to the scope on his SCAR rifle. He flipped the scope on and a small window popped up on his screen showing what the scope saw. "Looks like he's about five nine. Short old guy."

"Okay, you're not his size so you can't use his clothes. At least we know that it's manned."

They headed through the woods with their night vision on. They saw a lot of wildlife but no people. It wasn't long before they ran into a road.

"Let's try down this road. Stick to the woods to avoid traffic." Rand said as he scanned ahead with his scope.

They followed the road until they came to a gas station.

"Looks clear. I'm gonna move up and see if I can find a newspaper."

"Okay, I'll cover you from here. I'll keep Spang with me." She hoisted Spang out of his pack and clipped him to her harness. "Keep your ears turned up."

Rand moved across the road and approached the gas station from the right.

"Car coming from the south. Rand there is another road that joins with this one."

"Okay, I'm in the ditch. I'll wait until it passes."

A moment later a nineteen-thirty eight red Buick step-side pickup truck rattled by.

"Did you see that? A classic." Rand hissed a whisper over the radio.

"Let's just focus on getting some intel okay hon?"

"Right, sorry."

He made his way up to the station. A hand painted sign read 'Roop's Roost' on either side of a white circle with a 27' painted inside of it. A newspaper was folded on a chair that Rand guessed was the regular location of Roop's butt. He picked it up and tucked it into his web gear. Drawing his titanium crowbar from the side of his pack he carefully tried it in a crack of the locked door. The wood was soft and the hook of the crowbar found the latch. The door opened quietly.

"Rand what are you doing?"

"We're gonna need some resources if we're gonna get through this. Just hang on." He open the door and slipped inside. "Don't worry, I'm not going to clean them out."

Rand went to the cash register but it was empty. "Oldest trick in the book." He removed the drawer tray and sure enough, underneath was two fifty dollar bills. "Bingo."

"Rand come on back, it's been long enough."

"On the way." He quietly trotted back across the road and back into the woods.

"Good job baby," she kissed him, "what did you get?"

"Two fifties and a paper."

"That was a lot of money way back when. Just look at the sign. Seventeen cents for a gallon of gas."

"We need as much as we can get. Don't worry hon, I'll make sure he gets it back with interest."

"Yes you will." She scolded. "So, when are we?"

"Oh, right. It's…" He opened the paper. "April sixteenth, nineteen forty-nine."

"Jesus."

Rand stared at the newspaper, suddenly reality started to sink in. "Wow. We're really in nineteen forty-nine." Rand felt suddenly very alone. Elsie saw his face change and touched him on the elbow. It broke the spell. As long as she was with him, he would always be home.

"Baby lets get moving, we have to make the most of the night."

They put Spang back into Rand's pack and stayed along the side of the road for another thirty minutes until they started seeing the lights of a town. They stopped and let Spang out to stretch his legs and do his business then tucked him back into his protective backpack. As usual, the little dog took it all in stride.

"Let's try to get as close as we can. Keep to the shadows."

They crept off the road towards a group of houses.

"I see clothes on a line."

"Okay Els your turn. I'll watch, you steal."

"Borrow." She corrected then pointed a finger at both Rand and Spang. "You two watch for dogs."

"Got it."

Elsie scanned the area carefully with her thermal before going to the line and taking a dress. She returned to Rand.

"I saw people in that house. The men wear suits Rand."

"Okay. Maybe we can hit a dry cleaners or something. How did you do?"

"Good. I saw her. She looks close to my size but I won't know until I try it on. It'll do for now. Now let's get out of here. I hate being a criminal."

They made their way into the town as the evening deepened. The ocean appeared on their left as they followed their way along the road. Finally, the main road became a main street. They stuck to the shadows of buildings and carefully scanned ahead. It was getting late and the town was quiet. Rand set his watch by the clock tower in the town. It was eleven after two in the morning.

"Contact. Cop car eleven o'clock. See it?" Elsie said quietly.

"No. Where?"

Elsie used the infrared laser on her rifle to point out an old black and white.

"Sneaky bastards. Is there no such thing as entrapment in forty-nine? Man, I wish I had the Bugatti, I'd give em a chase they'd never forget." Rand chuckled.

Elsie elbowed him. "Use your scope to check out as much as you can of the town. We have be like snipers here, patience is key."

"Roger that."

He scanned the streets with the powerful night scope. About seven blocks away there was a large circular park in the middle of the town. The road cut right through it. Shops lined each side of the street.

"It's like Mayberry RFD."

"What's that?"

"The Andy Griffith show, remember? Mayberry? The town? Ron Howard is Opie. Oh come on, you have to remember."

"Lost me on that one hon, sorry."

"Hey, I think I found the dry cleaners. It's on the left just past the park."

"Would the cops be able to spot us from there?"

"Nope, not if we use the alley."

"Okay use the scope to pick a route, and watch for dogs. They are more of a danger to us than anything else." Elsie peeked into Rand's backpack to see Spang curled up and snoozing quietly.

"Yeah, little Spangler here would have a conniption and wake up the whole town."

Rand decided to cut through the big schoolyard and put the building between them and the police. Once they were on the parallel road they could approach the dry cleaners from the back. The plan worked and soon they were moving carefully up the alleyway to the back of the building.

"Okay, how do we get into this place?"

"There's a small pane of glass up there." Elsie said, "I could probably fit through without my gear."

"Glass is too noisy. I'll try the ol' crowbar."

He pulled out the crowbar once again and put it to the crack in the door. But this time the door was made of steel and wouldn't budge.

"Damn. Well, if I had a diamond I could cut the glass."

"Hang on."

Elsie put down her rifle, slung off her pack and dug into one of the side pockets. She produced a large diamond ring.

"Will this do?"

"Hey, that's your wedding ring!"

"I carry it with me, just in case… you know."

"We get the chance to finish the ceremony?"

"A girl's gotta be prepared."

"Nice one Els. Have I told you that I love you today?"

"Not for a couple of hours."

"Well I do. Now I just hope this works. I'm going to hoist you up. Stick some duct tape to it like a handle so it doesn't drop when you cut it."

Elsie stood on his shoulders as he held her up to the small glass pane above the door. She carefully peeled off several strips of duct tape and stuck them on the glass for handles. She traced around the frame with the diamond then tapped the glass with the heel of her hand. It didn't budge.

"You really have to press hard with the diamond."

"Okay."

This time she bore down as hard as she could. It was a bit noisy, but in the end the glass came loose.

"Hand me down the glass."

"Okay, you got it? Good, now push me up higher."

She hung halfway in the window struggling to get through. It reminded Rand of being stuck in the window of the armoured truck in Belfast. He still had the scars.

"Be really careful baby, that's glass."

"I know, it's okay the BDUs are tough and I've got good gloves on. There, I'm getting it."

She brought one knee through the hole and slid in. There was a bit of a thud when her boots hit the floor on the other side, but Rand saw no movement in the alley. With a click the door opened and Rand went in. It took little time to locate something for him. He settled on a khaki suit with a grey trench coat.

Elsie looked him over. "We're gonna need some kind of hair stuff to get your spiky locks to lay down baby." She handed him a fedora. "Try this for now until we can get some hair stuff."

"Pomade."

"Right, here's your shoes."

Elsie found a pair of shoes for herself though they were black and she would rather have something that matched her dark blue dress.

"We'll just have to go shopping."

"Hey, here's a bunch of military duffels we can use for luggage."

"Let's just use laundry bags and bury our gear in the woods. If we take those duffels those servicemen will be looking for their stuff. The less we take the better."

"You're right. Let's get out of here."

They put the white laundry bags and new clothes into their packs then carefully went back into the alleyway. When they reached the corner of the building they scanned for the police car but it had gone.

"Oh great, now we don't know where they are."

"Don't worry about it, I'm sure they got bored and moved on. We need to get somewhere and bury our stuff and get ready to do some hitch hiking."

They headed through back streets and alleys as much as they could. Soon they were clear of the town. Hiking with full gear through untracked forest and field was taking it's toll and they both laboured hard. Staying to the right of the road, they reached a treed area that led them through dense, marshy brush down to a thin beach. The water was still and reflected the brightening sky. Rand took a knee, breathing hard. They had been walking all night and it had been over thirty hours since they had slept.

"We can't bury it in the sand. Some kid will find it."

Elsie came up behind and collapsed next to him. "Hold on a sec, look at the water. This isn't the ocean, this is a lake. Use the scope, maybe we can spot some place on the banks."

Rand prayed as he scanned with his scope. They were at the end of the line. They would have to hide like rabbits all day unless they could find something. Elsie lifted her scope to help the search.

"There, I think I have something. It looks like a pump house. The only reason people go in there is if the pump breaks. We'll just have to try our luck."

They walked around the perimeter of the lake for another ten minutes, carefully scanning for dogs or people. The ground was soft and mucky and the woods were a dense tangle of branches. They finally arrived at the pump house tired and anxious.

"Okay, change quick and get the gear stowed."

They had to decide what to keep on them. They took the radios and earpieces and each packed a taser. Rand could keep his radio and taser in his pocket, but Elsie had to tape hers to her leg.

He hated to part with his .45, but it was just too big and heavy. He opted to carry his backup, a Walther PPK that he had in a pancake holster on his ankle. The Gerber multi-tool went into his pocket as well. He spooled a length of detcord into the liner of his fedora and tucked several radio igniters and the remote detonator into the breast pocket of his suit.

Spang had been sleeping in the cozy backpack. Now he was deposited out on the ground stretching and yawning. They fed him and gave him a little attention then Rand clipped him onto his leash.

"Rand that leash is way too modern."

He dug out a roll of parachute cord and cut a new leash. "That's better."

"So when we start talking to people what's our cover story?"

They both thought hard about it and exchanged ideas while they changed. The cold morning air cut through their tiredness as they pulled on the scratchy clothes of the period. Then they reviewed their objectives.

"Elsie, the one big technical advantage we have is our night vision. But there's just no way to take it along."

"It's okay, when we get a car we'll come back for the gear. That will be priority number one."

"I wonder what we can buy for a hundred bucks."

"Hopefully something that gets us to Chicago."

They stowed the gear in the laundry bags and hid it all in an old fifty-gallon drum in the pump house.

"Even if someone comes in here they'll probably think the barrel is empty."

They looked each other over.

"You look the part Elsie. I like that dress on you. These pants are incredibly high-waisted though. The belt is up to my ribs."

"I think you look rather handsome."

Everything was roomy and comfortable though a bit scratchy. Having no other option Elsie smoothed his hair down with a tube of Chap-stick she mashed into her hands. Then she stood back and looked him over

"I feel like a gangster."

"You look like a million bucks."

"Well this is the most authentic Halloween costume I've ever worn."

Elsie's dress had short sleeves gathered at the shoulder and a sash that tied around the waist. The dark blue dress widened as it dropped to mid-calf length.

"You have the figure for that dress babe, but given the choice I'll take the red motorcycle outfit."

"I like it." She said smoothing the dress and giving it a swish. "It makes me feel the part."

"Yeah well, we'll have to listen carefully for the way they talk. It's going to be a bit different than we're used to."

"And no cussing Mr. Carter. Any immoral behaviour will attract a lot of attention."

"Yes Mrs. Carter."

"Oh, that reminds me." She pulled out the diamond ring they had used to cut the glass, then she produced a platinum wedding band for him. "We should act like we're married." The look she gave him was a mix of sadness, anticipation and disappointment.

"I know you would have rather put these on officially. I would too, and we will… ah hell. We'll talk about all of this once we're safe and sound and can relax. Let's at least get food and shelter. Sound good?"

She nodded, handed him his ring and was about to slip hers onto her finger.

"Hey wait a minute." He stopped her. "Man that is one big rock honey." They looked at each other, both thinking the same thing. "This thing is worth a fortune."

"Rand your ring in made of platinum, that's worth a lot too. Especially in this time."

"Okay then that's our story. We're selling your mom's and my dad's wedding rings so we can get hitched."

"Very clever. We'll need to find a jeweller." She loved the idea, it meant they didn't have to pretend to be married.

In bare feet, they carefully picked their way out to the highway. It took fifteen minutes of hard and painful slogging through the undergrowth and wet ground. Finally, foot sore and exhausted, they reached the road. Spang, who had been carried through most of it was now deposited on the sandy side of the road where he commenced sniffing the road sign. They washed off their cut and bruised feet then put on their shoes and started walking. The April morning air was downright cold and a breeze from the ocean didn't help, but they felt better knowing that they were dressed for the time period. Rand wrapped his trench coat around

Elsie's shoulders. They walked for half an hour maintaining a quick pace to try and keep some kind heat up. Eventually the road became a thin piece of land that had the shore of the lake on one side and the ocean on the other. As the sun rose to a clear day they spotted a beige, wood-panelled convertible parked on the beach with a leg hanging out of it.

"Jesus, Rand are they dead?"

Rand went over to the car. "Hello? Are you alright?"

The leg twitched and a head full of dark hair looked up over the edge of the car. "Oh my!"

A young girl pulled a man's jacket up close to her neck. The young man next to her jumped back and looked at them terrified.

"It's okay, it's alright! I didn't know if you were dead or what." Rand assured them.

"You're not… you're not lookin for us?"

"No, not at all. We just saw you from the road. I'm guessing you had a late night and fell asleep?" Rand gave the boy a wink and smiled.

"Yeah, something like that mister. Say, where did you come from anyways?"

Elsie came up, "It's a long story. We sure could use a ride though."

Both kids looked at them, then each other. "Well sure, you bet. Just don't tell our folks."

The boy was clearly worried. The young girl stayed under the boy's jacket and tried to curl up against the cold. Elsie climbed in next to her.

"Poor thing, you're freezing." She put her arm around the girl. What's your name darlin?"

"Megan." She said nervously.

"Megan. I'm Elsie, and this is Spang." She had Spang curl up in Megan's lap. "He's only little but he'll help you get warm. Let's get moving boys, it's freezing out here."

"I'm sorry but the top got stuck when we tried to put it up." The young man apologised.

"That's fine son. We'll just take it slow." The boy offered Rand the opportunity to drive but Rand declined saying, "You're milking this cow son." He thought it sounded correct to the period. He reached out and shook hands with the boy. "Rand Carter."

"Avery Wilson, pleased to meet you Mr. Carter."

"Avery, we sure appreciate the ride. To tell you the truth we've had quite a time of it and now we just want to get to a hotel."

As the big convertible bounced onto the road, the cold morning air swirled around them. Elsie wrapped Rand's big trench coat over herself and Megan like a blanket.

"I don't mean to pry sir, but what finds you way out here at this hour of the morning?"

"Nothing under-handed I assure you, at least not on our part. You see Elsie and I are pilots and…"

"Really, no kiddin? Did you fly in the war?"

"Yes, B-17s. I was with the 92nd Bomber group out of England and Elsie…"

"Jeepers, a genuine war hero! Hey Megan didja hear that?"

"Yes, well the real heroes are the one's we left behind. Anyway -"

"I would have fought, but I was only thirteen. Some of the guys were getting in at fifteen, but they took one look at me and said no way son! But I worked real hard at the scrap drives and all."

"Well, we sure appreciated all that you did to keep us flying son."

The skinny young man's jaw kept running the whole trip. The way the kid went from one subject to another was mind-boggling. Spang, Elsie and young Megan fell asleep wrapped up in Rand's coat.

After about an hour, the trees parted and New York City came into view. Rand had never seen it before. To get his first view of it in 1949, the sight took his breath away.

He reached back and gave Elsie a small shake.

"Els, you might wanna see this."

She cracked open her eyes as the trees parted to let in rays of sunshine. The buildings gleamed in the golden light.

"Oh my G… goodness. Rand is that…?"

"New York City Ma'am. Ain't you never seen it before?"

Megan reached forward and thwacked Avery on the back of the head.

"Sorry, HAVEN'T you ever seen it before?" The young man rubbed his head with a backwards wince at his girl.

Elsie looked at Rand and they both chuckled.

"No Avery I have not. I mean, only from the air. I think it's spectacular."

Avery looked back at her with a big toothy grin. "Well, where would you like me to take you folks? I hotel I 'spect."

"Actually, could you take us to a jeweller?" Rand stealthily checked his modern watch. "They should be opening about now. We'll get a cab to the hotel from there."

"Sure Mr. Carter, it's no problem at all. Heck Megan an I was goin' to one of them too seein' as how we eelopin' an all."

Megan thwacked him on the head again, this time harder.

"Dangit Avery!"

"Sorry sweetie pie, it just slipped out."

Both kids looked at Rand and Elsie nervously. Elsie just gave Megan a big hug.

"Oh how romantic! Don't you worry, your secret is safe with us." Avery and Megan both gave big sighs of relief.

The big car wound into the early morning traffic. The sounds and smells of the post-war city were rich and vibrant. Fresh produce was being put out on the sidewalks, restaurants were opening for the day. A milkman went by in uniform. It was like walking onto the set of a Hollywood movie. Avery pulled up to a post on the sidewalk with a clock that read 'Fuller's Jewellery'.

"Now Avery listen. We have some pieces to sell then we'll be right back out. I know I told you that we would take a cab to the hotel, but I want to give something to you for all your help… no, no… I insist. Please promise me you'll stay here until we come out. And don't worry, this isn't some ploy to get you in trouble okay?"

"Okay Mr. Carter," Avery looked at him anxiously, "I trust you."

"Good, we'll just be a minute. Watch Spang for us please, he's like family to us."

Rand and Elsie climbed out of the car and went into the jewellers. A small balding man with a thin moustache greeted them from behind the counter.

"Good morning to you both, how may I be of assistance?"

"Good morning to you sir, I am Mr. Carter and this is my fiancé Elsie. We were wondering if you could help us with an exchange."

The clerk looked at them a bit suspiciously. "Exchange?"

"You see our parents, now deceased, each gave us their wedding bands. After we met and decided to get married we looked at the respective rings and decided they were… um, how shall I say…"

Rand took out the rings. The gigantic diamond filled the eyes of the little man. "…over sufficient I think would be the correct term don't you think dear?"

"Yes quite. Bordering on garish for my tastes. It is all that is left of mother's extravagance."

The little man was sweating as he eyeballed the diamond. "I see. Well we will most certainly be able to help you with all of your exchange needs. Fuller's International Exchange that's us. I was just going to have the sign changed. Please give me a moment while I fetch my appraiser."

He scurried into the back and Rand winked at Elsie who was giddy with excitement. The clerk came back in with another slightly taller man who was clearly his older brother. He wore a jewellers loupe headset and carried another loupe in his hand, which he flipped slowly from one hand to the next.

"This is my partner and appraiser Abram."

"Pleased to meet you both. I understand you have a…"

His eyes fell on the ring. He looked at his brother in shock "…ring. Yes, well let's have a look." After several minutes of examination he put the ring back down. "It's a very impressive piece. Unfortunately there is a flaw…"

Elsie stepped up. "It's a perfect 21 carat radiant cut. Flawless. It was mined at the Kimberley in South Africa. Have another look sir, I think you may have a scratch on your loupe."

The brothers just looked her incredulously.

"Madame knows her diamonds. Have another look Abram. And for goodness sake get another loupe!"

Abram reached around the corner of the door and brought out another loupe. This time he inspected more quickly.

Rand thought, *he already knows it's perfect, he's just going through the motions.*

When Abram finished he consulted with his brother in the back. After a minute of furious whispering they both came out.

"We're prepared to offer you... one hundred and seventy five."

Elsie's face flushed red and her finger went up as she took a deep inward breath getting ready to unleash a torrent. Rand had seen this once before, she was livid.

"Thousand madame, thousand." Abram said calmly. "Anything less would be an insult."

Rand almost burst out laughing as Elsie's face went through several colours before it changed back to normal, though slightly flushed. She smoothed her dress and put on her best demure look.

"I believe that, due to the informal nature of the transaction that should be sufficient." She turned to Rand for approval, he just nodded.

"Very well, which bank shall we use?" The Jeweller asked.

Rand stepped in. He had anticipated this problem and had worked it out while Elsie was dealing with the jewellers. "We will leave the piece with you in exchange for a promissory note and a small holding advance. We will send the details for the transaction of the remainder later in the day."

"That sounds very agreeable." The smaller brother said.

Abram drafted up the note and gave Rand $20,000 in cash. After Rand made some last minute arrangements, they shook hands and parted ways.

As they went through the small foyer Rand said, "Man I like the way they do business in this time." They walked outside to the waiting car. "Mr. and Mrs. Wilson to be, I… we have some instructions for you."

Avery and Megan leaned over the edge of the car excitedly.

"Elsie and I are indebted to you for your generosity. We now say farewell to you with our warmest wishes. We implore you to always keep your generous spirit and trust in God in everything you do."

"Oh we will Mr. Carter."

"Now get yourselves into that jewellers there and pick out your rings. It's all taken care of."

The Second String

They sprang out of the car. With a barrage of thank you's, Avery shook Rand's hand vigorously while Megan wrapped Elsie in a hug. They sent the two inside and hailed a cab.

"Where to folks?"

"The Waldorf-Astoria my good man."

The cabby whistled, "right away sir."

Elsie nudged Rand in the ribs. "Big spender."

Montgomery Thompson

Chapter 2

Star struck

'If I can make it here, I'll make it anywhere.'
~Sinatra

The experience of the Waldorf-Astoria in it's heyday was like no other. The opulence was off the charts. Service was given with a flair that modern hotels would have to hire actors to duplicate. The first thing they did after checking in was to have a bath, then he and Elsie caught up on much needed sleep. The amount of money they made on the sale of the ring was the equivalent of two-million dollars in modern terms. Rand knew they had no ID or social security number so he had left specific instructions with the jewellers to start an account in Avery's name. Avery would have to give them his information, so he would of course know that he had been given a considerable sum. Once the account had been created and the amount deposited, Rand had left a sealed note for Avery. It read:

Dear Avery, it may not make much sense to you why you are the recipient of this fortune. The only explanation I can give you is that kindness is rewarded, not always in this way, but this day it is.

Elsie and I have our own fortune that we will soon be reunited with so we wanted to share some of our blessings. It is with this in mind that I ask this next small favour:

The jewellers only had enough cash on hand for Elsie and I to get a hotel for the night. If you could leave $30,000 for us at the jewellers, we would very much appreciate it. It will get us down the road to the next stage of our journey. The amount will be returned to your account as soon as we arrive.

Please give Meagan a kiss from Elsie and accept our heartfelt hopes for you and your children in all the years to come.

Bless you both,
Rand and Elsie

Rand was certain none of this would be a problem. As he faded off to sleep he just hoped that someone wouldn't think he was money laundering.

They woke to a knock on the door. Spang huffed a little bark as Rand reached for his PPK.

"Turn down service, would you like your room cleaned?" Came a voice through the door.

He had forgot to put up the sign. "No thank you. Perhaps this afternoon."

"Very well sir." The maid left.

"Perhaahps this aahfternoon." Elsie giggled at him. "You're really good at this! Maybe you should have been an actor. Some of the stuff you were coming up with yesterday I was like… listen to this guy!"

"Yeah I know, I've seen too many old movies." He jumped out of bed and put of his hat. "Now look here see! Sharkey an da boys are getting tired of you flat foots nosin' aroun' see!"

"Bravo!" She clapped, "You're a natural!"

Spang retreated to the couch and promptly fell back to sleep.

"Your not so bad yourself sugar cakes."

"Come over here, I'll give you sugar cakes!"

They explored the room and each other from a variety of angles then collapsed, exhausted on the bed.

"I don't even know what day it is. How long did we sleep?"

"I'll find out." Elsie picked up the phone and ordered room service. Then she added the question at the end, "Would you be so kind as to tell me the date and the hour? Thank you so much, yes that would be splendid."

"Nice."

'We arrived yesterday around eleven thirty in the morning, April the fifth. It is now eleven in the morning on April the sixth, so we basically slept about twenty-four hours."

"That's a record for me."

"I only slept longer on Miracle Day."

"No wonder I'm starved."

They had just enough time to get showered and dressed when Room Service arrived. It took two people to bring in the whole spread. Rand tipped them well and sent them on their way, then they tucked in. They couldn't believe how good the food tasted.

"Oh my God Rand. Real civilised food! Is it just me or is everything… richer or something?"

"I was about to take offence but holy God… we haven't had anything like this since the happening." He swallowed his mouthful. "You're right. It's fresher, more vibrant. The tastes are bigger. If we stay here too long I'm gonna start putting on weight."

"We've been eating farm fresh for awhile hon, but we've had few spices and our herb garden was just coming in. I think that's the main difference."

"That and fresh baking. I can't get enough of these biscuits."

Spang busied himself with cleaning the crumbs.

Just then the phone rang. It was the jeweller. The front hotel operator put the call through. The jeweller informed Rand that the young man had left a package for him. Rand told him they would be there within the hour. He called the desk and made arrangements for a professional dog groomer to pick up Spang. He would be treated to the best vet service and pet pampering that money could buy. Half an hour later a portly lady came to pick him up. Rand though she was a bit over the top but felt assured that Spang was in the good hands.

"Well hon, ready to go shopping?"

"Oh yes dahling," she giggled.

They ordered a limo for the day. It was two hundred dollars.

"For the whole day?"

"Yes sir, until midnight."

They cleaned up as best they could and went downstairs. Rand just raised his eyebrows at Elsie as the 1931 Bugatti Royale Kellner coupe pulled up in front of the hotel. The chauffeur, complete with white gloves and a hat, departed the open cockpit, rounded the long car and held the door open to the luxuriously appointed cabin.

"After you my dear." Rand smiled.

In the lobby people admired the wealthy young couple. As the long car pulled away the gossip started to fly. They went to all the big shops, Tiffany's, Bloomingdales, Macy's and spent thousands. They worked out a strategy - when they got to a store they split up.

Rand got four suits tailor-made, a tux and a whole selection of casual clothes. After a haircut and a shave including a manicure, he looked like he had been born in 1949. At Tiffany's Rand needed a watch, but he knew that if everything worked out in Chicago they would be posing as some very wealthy people. The watch would help him play the part better than anything. The clerk at Tiffany's showed him a few high-end watches, but Rand acted unimpressed.

"This is Tiffany's, don't you have anything more exclusive?"

The Second String

The clerk went away and returned with the manager and two security guards. Rand's hand crept towards his taser until the manager presented him with a watch on a velvet pillow display. "Sir obviously has an appreciation for the finest things. Let me present the magnificent Rolex 4113 split-second rattrapante chronograph. It is the pinnacle of the craft, there are only twelve in the world.'"

"Outstanding. I'll take it." Rand paid over nine-thousand dollars for the watch, but was convinced that he had made a worthwhile investment.

By the time Elsie got done she looked like a movie star. She discovered a wide variety of period hairstyles. She went with a long and natural look. Most of the dresses she picked were tighter fitting and glamorous. She couldn't get over how all the bras tried to make her breasts look like bullets.

"Do you have something less… pointy?"

She was amazed to have several women attending to her every need. They even offered to bring her lunch from the hotel.

"Oh that won't be necessary, I'll be taking lunch with my fiancé." She twittered.

She was having the time of her life when without warning, the tape came off her leg and the taser rolled onto the floor. One of the girls quickly picked it up.

"I'll get that for you. Say, what is…"

Elsie snatched it away from her. "No that's okay, thank you."

The supervisor cut in, "Tracy don't you think you should be cleaning up all these tags? Get busy now chop chop!"

The supervisor hustled her away.

"Sorry about that, these girls can be so nosey." She leaned in close, put her hand up and whispered, "I have one too. Who needs a man around any more!"

Elsie just nodded and smiled.

Rand had stopped by the jewellers and picked up the money while Elsie was shopping. After he was done he had the driver take him to an upscale car dealer. He passed up a beautiful, green Jaguar XK120 and a Talbot-Lago T-26 with a heavy heart. The sleek two-seaters were just too small to fit all of their stuff. The runner up was a silver and white Delahaye 175S Roadster. The two-door had sporty lines, but also plenty of room. He had it delivered to the hotel like everything else.

The Second String

Elsie was completely wiped out after hair, make-up, nails, clothes, jewellery, accessories and luggage. When Rand found her at Bloomingdales she was lounging in a private room sipping lemonade.

"Well they've certainly got you looked after."

"I never realised how tiring this could all be."

"Well, tonight's our last night in New York. What do you say to dinner out, then we can pack and get plenty of rest."

"Sounds good."

They swept into the hotel like celebrities. At the front desk, the manager invited them to a special event that evening. Elsie told them that they would be delighted. Everywhere people seemed to be smiling at them and even giving friendly waves. When they opened the door to their room they could hardly believe their eyes. All of the day's purchases were laid out in an artistic display, like their own personal store.

"Wow, they really know how to do service don't they?"

Spang bounded into the room looking tidy and smelling as fresh as a daisy. Elsie put on the new collar and showed him the diamond studded leash she had picked up at Tiffany's. Spang was only mildly interested and climbed onto the bed where he promptly fell asleep.

Rand put on his dinner tux and Elsie slipped into a slinky, red evening dress. They stood looking at themselves in the mirror for ten minutes.

"We're in nineteen forty-nine Rand. Look at us. We're the real deal."

When they came out of the hall from their room they could still hear Spang snoring on the bed. An usher was there waiting to escort them.

"How did you know when we would come out of our room?" Elsie asked him.

"I didn't ma'am, I was told to wait until you did."

"Very good, thank you for your patience." Rand handed the young man a ten-dollar bill.

"Thank you sir. My name's Jenner. If you need anything else, I'm your man."

Jenner led them to a short line of people waiting to descend the sweeping grand staircase. A man was announcing the names as they came down. The press was at the bottom clicking away.

"Do we really want our picture in the paper?" Elsie said through clenched teeth.

"Not really honey, but there's not a lot we can do about it." Rand said back with a forced smile.

The Second String

Suddenly Jenner was at their side, "Don't like the press? I don't blame you. Follow me and we'll bypass this carnival."

He opened a door across the hall and motioned them to follow. Elsie went first with Rand behind.

The door lead into a dark hallway, Jenner was waving them past when Rand sensed something was wrong. He reached in his jacket for his taser as he passed Jenner, but just as he did he felt the barrel of a gun in his back.

"That's just fine right there Mr. Carter. Now Mrs. Carter don't you make any noise or your man here is gonna pay the price. Just hand over your wallet and nobody gets hurt."

Elsie tilted her head sideways. "Hand over your wallet and nobody gets hurt? Is that the best you could come up with?" She walked down the hall back toward them.

"Alright now Mrs. Carter, stay where you are. What are you…"

"Listen you sick little freak you better back down offa my man or I gonna bring da hurtin' down on your skinny ass!"

"What? What did you say? I…"

Rand spun in the disarming move he had practiced so many times with Elsie. In one lightening fast motion the gun was twisted out of Jenner's hand, his wrist broken and Rand's fist smashed into the bottom of his jaw in a powerful uppercut. Jenner went limp.

"Nice baby. I like the Jerry Springer touch. It totally threw him."

"It was all that came to mind."

"So it was a distraction, you weren't gonna take him down?"

"Hey, I'm in an evening dress here in case you haven't noticed."

"Oh I noticed." Her pulled her close and kissed her hard.

Jenner started to come back around, groaning and holding his jaw. Rand kept kissing Elsie as he pulled out his taser and put forty-thousand volts through Jenner's head.

Rand and Elsie stepped back into the hallway.

"Name sir?"

"Huh? Oh Rand and Elsie Carter."

"MR AND MRS RAND CARTER!"

There was applause and the cameras were flashing. Taking their cue, they walked down the stairs as gracefully as they could manage.

When they got to the bottom a staff member said, "Excuse me sir, your hand."

Rand looked at him confused. The man gestured with his head at Rand's hand that was dripping blood. He handed him a handkerchief.

"Oh, right. Thank you. I need to talk to security. Discreetly please."

"Yes sir, shall I send them to your table?"

"As long as it's within the next five minutes."

"Right away."

The man vanished. They entered a huge room with tiered levels that lead down to a broad stage where a big band orchestra played low-key music. They were escorted to a large round table on the third tier. Apparently, they were going to have company. They looked around, all the tables were the same. They sat where their name cards were. No sooner had Rand hit the chair when a large, stern man in a white tuxedo jacket was standing next to him.

"Security. How may I be of service Mr. Carter?"

"Well I don't want to alarm you, but one of your staff tried to mug us in the upstairs hallway just now. I knocked him out but he might be coming to. Here's the gun he held on me. You'll find his fingerprints on it I'm sure. I prefer not to make a scene or to get the police involved if it can at all be helped."

The security officer just nodded slowly. "I see. Would you like me to take... in-house security measures then?"

"Yes that would be fine. But don't hurt him, I did enough of that."

"As you wish sir. And Mr. Carter?"

"Yes?"

"Please accept my sincerest apologies. This has never and should never happen at the Astoria, and certainly not on my watch."

"It's okay, we can't control every situation."

"Enjoy your evening sir."

"Thanks."

Rand's knuckles were a bit scraped but it wasn't serious. Elegant couples filed in and were quickly seated. Champagne was brought around to every table.

"Rand, this is Dom Perignon." Elsie whispered.

All of sudden the lights went out and the band struck a note. The spotlight hit the stage where a man with a large microphone announced to glamorous fanfare, "Welcome to the Waldorf-Astoria celebrity charity ball!" The band started playing *Sentimental Journey*. Excitement ran like fire through the room.

"I get the feeling that this is a very special night Rand. How did we get invited to this?"

"I don't know hon, I…"

Just then a long black gloved arm reached between them and picked up the crystal lighter on the table.

"I don't know who you do or don't know, but I'm sure by the time the night's over everyone will know you."

Rand and Elsie's eyes followed the black glove up to a gorgeous short haired brunette in a stunning black velvet evening dress. The hand lit a cigarette in a long holder then put the lighter back on the table. Then it hovered in front of Rand's face in a relaxed droop. Both of them recognised the face instantly.

"Liz."

Rand, trying his best to remain unshaken, gave the hand a kiss and said, "Rand Carter, and this is my fiancé Elsie."

The woman leaned over Elsie and gave a glancing kiss to each cheek. It was like being brushed by a butterfly. She was a pro.

"So nice to meet you Elsie. I love your name, it has consequence."

Elsie was shocked. "Elizabeth Taylor? Thee… I mean, what an honour… pleasure to meet you. Wow."

Rand looked around Liz Taylor's backside, which was right in front of him, and made a *calm down* motion to Elsie.

"I mean, wow quite a night."

"It's so wonderful when everyone comes out to support the charities. We get so much from the industry and it's our chance to give something back don't you think?"

"Absolutely," Rand responded. "Though we're not in the movie business."

Now it was Elsie's turn to motion around Liz's backside for him to get her a chair. Rand quickly stood up and offered her his.

"Thank you, what a gentleman, so few of them these days." Everything she did seemed to be deliberate, even waiting for the chair.

Rand took the chair behind him to keep Liz between them.

"No no, you love birds must sit together so I can see what a darling couple you make. There, that's better. Oh my, you really are magnificent. Isn't love the best thing in the world? Now, you were saying about what you do."

"Well I'm…"

"Oh do let Elsie tell me, she's so intriguing."

"Well, alright. Rand and I are pilots and…"

The Second String

"Seriously? How amazing! You DO know who's here don't you?"

"No, not really. You're the first person…"

"Well there's Howard right over there talking to Rita and…"

Rand and Elsie looked around the room and started to get it. Howard Hughes, Rita Hayward, Montgomery Clift and on and on. The place was packed with celebrities. Elsie was star struck. But it wasn't until Louis Armstrong came out on stage and drove the band into a rollicking version of *Mack the Knife* that Rand joined her in her amazement.

As the night went on there were more spectacular entertainments from acrobats to famous singers to song and dance routines on a grand scale. They felt like the whole world had turned into Hollywood. Somewhere between Doris Day and Perry Como Rand decided he needed a break and asked Elsie outside.

"Can you believe this night?" Elsie looked radiant against the shimmering New York skyline.

"It's a long way from space stations and vegetable gardens."

She turned to him, her eyes tearing up. "But that's our world, our home. I would trade any of this in an instant to be back there with you."

"Then we have to try and get back. But the whole point of doing this in the first place was to try and get back to FirstTime."

"Wait, that's the time where our world is normal and where my kids are. And your... Moira is right?"

"Yes. But she's not my anything now. You're my everything. As far as she's concerned I just up and walked out one day. I'm probably the worst person in the world to her. It hurts yes, but in no way does it impact how much you mean to me. You're my now and my future. My heart truly belongs to you. I never gave it entirely to her."

"But you gave some part of it."

"Dammit, it's not a pie to dole out pieces to people. It's me. I'm yours, I want you forever."

"I guess we've never really worked this out."

"There's nothing to work out. It's you and me always."

Elsie just looked up at him, searching his eyes. A soft voice broke in from their right.

"If you want my advice, it's not too often in this life you hear a man speak like that."

She was terminally blonde, from her legs to her cigarette. A bombshell starlet, sultry and dripping with attitude. "I'd take him seriously." She turned and leaned back against the railing. "Hell if it were me, we'd be hitched and heading to Monaco."

Elsie looked at her sideways. "And you are?"

The woman was slightly taken back. "Listen honey, don't get your back up, I'm no threat. Hell, the way he's lookin at you I could be made of solid gold and he wouldn't bat an eye." She tossed the cigarette over the wall and started to walk inside. "Just thought that this being a charity event and all that I should do my part for the sake of love. Which, by the way, would have you wrapped up all warm and cozy if it wasn't for that chip on your shoulder."

The woman walked, or rather, flowed back inside. Elsie watched her go, realising she was right.

"Rand. I'm sorry. I have been blocking you because I wasn't sure that you had let Moira go. I see now that you have. I believe you. I believe you love me."

Rand held her. It was the one thing he wanted to hear the most. After a long while he let her go.

She said, "Now who was that incredibly wise and gorgeous woman?"

Rand laughed and said, "I believe that was Lana Turner."

"Hang on a sec." She went back inside. A few minutes later she came back out.

"What did you do?" asked Rand

"I thanked her and told her to quit smoking."

"What?"

"Well, she dies of lung cancer. Maybe I can help."

"Okay, let's get out of here my head is spinning."

Back in the room they packed all the suitcases and prepared for the morning.

"Rand, how are we getting to Chicago?"

"Not to worry, I have it all taken care of."

"Okay. I guess I'll wait to be surprised."

The next morning Rand was up and ready. He sent the luggage with the porters and they both went down to the front desk.

"Mr. Carter, we have a few messages for you."

The manager handed him a stack of letters. Rand looked at Elsie who shrugged. He opened the first one.

Dear Rand and Elsie, it was such a pleasure getting to know the both of you. Here's my address in the Hamptons. You absolutely MUST come up to see me and stay a week or four. Looking forward to it!

The Second String

Love Liz

The other letters were all similar. There was even one from Howard Hughes that invited them to stop by and look at some of his new planes.

They just looked at each other in disbelief.

"I wonder what he'd say if I showed him the design for the F-22 Raptor?"

"Shhh." Rand laughed

When they went to pay for the room the manager told him that it was on the house. The security supervisor had told the night manager what happened and it went all the way to the top. The hotel owners insisted that they stay for free.

"Nothing like it has ever happened at the Astoria and it never will again. We're just lucky that it happened to such a capable man and no one got hurt… except the offending party of course." He said under his hand.

They thanked the manager, sent their regards to the security supervisor and tipped all of them very well. It seemed everyone at the hotel knew who they were and admired them. They counted at least twelve people who said goodbye to them. The doors to the Delahaye were held open and two porters were polishing the chrome wheels.

"Oh Rand, what a machine!" Elsie gaped at the dramatic lines of the new car.

"You didn't see the Jag I passed up for this, but we needed the room."

"It's really something."

Elsie was wearing a glamorously tight black and white dress with a little hat that had a black net veil. Huge sunglasses, white gloves and heels finished the look. They climbed in and Rand tooted the horn at the taxi in front of him. They pulled away as the taxi moved but Rand stayed glued to the taxi's bumper.

On and on they went turning through the city.

"Rand do you know where you're going?"

"Yes dear."

"How?"

"I have a GPS."

"How is that possible?"

"He's right in front of us. I hired him to lead the way out of the city and to the highway to Montauk."

"I wondered why you were tailing this guy so hard. Very smart." She punched him in the shoulder.

The cab pulled off and waved after about twenty minutes and they followed the road back to the New Jersey peninsula. After about half an hour things began to look familiar.

"Hey, there's the spot where we found Avery and Megan."

"Okay, how bout we wait here til the sun goes down then back track to the gear."

"Sounds romantic."

They parked on the beach in the same spot where they had found the two lovers, watched the sunset and talked about the incredible night before. They had seen New York and all the stars in their heyday. Louis Armstrong young and live was a moment Rand would never forget.

"I don't mean to break the romantic moment hon, but what's the plan after Chicago?"

"Well, I was thinking about that. Ultimately we need to track down Dr. Remmel. He will be very interested to meet people from the future who have used his machine. I'm just not sure where he is."

"Yes it does seem to be the next obvious step. I suspect he's in Nevada at Area 51, or he might be in Alamogordo, White Sands. That's where they did all the nuclear testing. Either way it's going to be hard to get in there. Maybe our night vision gear will be enough to do it, but I doubt it. It will be dangerous."

They both thought it over for a while and decided to work it out when they had finished their business in Chicago.

After the sun was down Elsie changed clothes then they sped back down the road to a spot where they could enter the forest inconspicuously.

"Rand I'm going to stay on your six, about a hundred feet back just in case we run into trouble."

"Okay, you'll need this." He handed her the PPK.

"Radios on, full hearing."

They put in their earpieces and Rand pulled out his taser. Rand rolled up his trousers and Elsie hiked up her dress. Shoes and socks were left in the car and they prepared to take more abuse to their already sore feet.

"I had to tell the pedicurist that I got tangled in some reeds at the beach. It's not normal for a rich lady to have bruises and cuts on her feet in this time period."

They stood at the back of the car, feeling the asphalt on their already battered feet. Rand shook his head. "This is stupid. I have a brand new pair of tennis shoes in the suitcase. When the hell am I going to have time to play tennis?"

He opened the trunk and started rummaging around in the luggage. A minute later he handed

Elsie a pair of white canvas tennis shoes. "There are yours, now if I can just find mine…"

"Rand, there's a car coming."

"It's okay, we just look like a couple of people on vacation, digging through our luggage on the side of the road. It's nothing too out of the ordinary. There they are."

A black car whizzed by as Rand came out of the trunk. Elsie put on a bored face as she relaxed against the car. She had made sure she let her dress back down before the car had got into range. They finished putting the tennis shoes on.

"They're not Gore-Tex combat boots, but they'll still make a world of difference." Rand said. "Spang, you guard the car buddy. We'll be right back."

Spang huffed as he watched them from the car. They headed off into the woods. Rand got slightly off track and came to the lake from a slightly different route. Without night vision gear it was hard to navigate the pitch black woods. He decided to stay to the banks of the lake which would lead him right to the old pump house. The problem was that they were exposed and anyone looking out at the lake would spot the movement, even in the dark. So he had to stay into the trees a short distance which meant that the roots in the bog were tripping their every step. It was gruelling work. Finally they found the pump house and crouched down beside it, dirty and out of breath.

"Okay, all clear." Came Elsie over the radio. She stood back in the trees and scanned the forest for movement.

Rand slipped inside and pulled the first bag out. He had packed the helmets last so they were on top. He put his on and handed Elsie hers out the door.

"Much better."

He grabbed the two heavy bags and peeked out the door. "All clear."

Elsie was just switching hers on. "Boy that's so much better. Can you believe they won a war without this stuff?"

"No kidding, it's pitch black in these trees without it."

"Rand I have to get my boots on. Even with the sneakers my feet are taking a real beating."

"Me too. It's like a mangrove swamp in here."

They dug through the bags and found their boots. It only took a few minutes for them to put them on and lace them up.

"Much better! Let's get back."

The Second String

The heavy tread and thick leather and nylon protection of the boots made the return trip much easier. They climbed back into the car.

"I'm going back to the spot on the beach. We can wash off and change there."

"Good call."

The salt water washed all the muck off. In the car they went through the gear.

"It would be great to put some kind of false wall in the trunk, but we just don't have the stuff to do it and a mechanic will ask too many questions."

"How about luggage? We can buy matching luggage and put the gear in there. If for any reason somebody inspects the trunk all they'll see is luggage."

"And if they inspect that all they see in the first three cases is clothes."

"Yep, one remark from me about them wanting to play with my panties and the search will be over I'm sure."

"Anybody tries playing with your panties besides me, it'll all be over real quick."

"Oh your such a tough guy!" She teased.

To stick with the plans they had made at the hotel Rand had put on his black ops gear, Elsie stayed in regular clothes. She drove as they turned out and went back down the road. They headed back toward the lighthouse and found the gas station he had broke into the night of their arrival. Cruising by slowly, Rand scanned for dogs. There were none. They parked the car up the road and turned the lights off. With night vision on, Rand made his way to the station. Elsie covered him from the car with the night scope on the SCAR.

Rand had put a thousand dollars in an envelope and an apology note. He made his way to the door of the station, lifted the mail slot and dropped the envelope through. There was a screech and a bump from the inside like a chair tipping over.

"Rand! There's someone inside, get out of there!"

The front door rattled then swung inward, then the screen door banged open as a pudgy old man in overalls and a sweat stained t-shirt came out with a shotgun.

"Who do you think you are? You show yourself or I'll get the sheriff again!"

The old man saw no one. He swung the shotgun around a few more times, then went back inside.

"Damn raccoons. What the?"

He bent down and picked up the envelope, opened it and read the letter.

"Well I'll be damned! Martha! Martha come quick! Our prayers have been answered! It wasn't that brother of yours after all, it was a complete stranger! But they jes borry'd it!"

"Package delivered, return to base."

"Roger that." Rand said with a smile as he emerged from underneath an old pickup truck.

"Wait. Get back to cover, he's coming out again."

Rand ditched behind one of the pumps as the old man came back out and stood almost next to him.

"Whoever you are, thank you!" He hollered into the night. "I thoughtcha robbed me but I hadja all wrong. You jes saved ma lil boys life! You come back anytime!"

The station owner strained his eyes into the darkness, then turned and walked back inside. Rand had been holding his breath. He quickly and silently made it to the roadside ditch. He looked back to check if it was clear then he trekked up the ditch to a dark section of the road and cut across back to the car.

"Great job hon." She gave him a kiss.

"That was amazing! I wonder how we saved his boys life?"

"Guess we'll never know, but it feels good doesn't it?"

"It certainly makes up for acting like a criminal that night."

Rand stayed in black ops gear as they sped away back towards the small town.

As they approached the house where she had stolen the dress they slowed down, turned off the lights and switched to night vision. Rand hopped out while the car still slowly rolled forward and threw the dress on the grass beside the line. Then he ran back and got in the car as Elsie gently accelerated away.

"They'll think it fell off the line."

"Perfect."

"This next one is gonna be tricky."

"You leave that to me sugar. I've been psyching myself up for this all evening."

They kept the headlights off as they approached the town. It was now around midnight. Stopping in a dark place on the side of the road, Rand checked ahead with the scope.

"Sure enough, there they are. Same spot. Okay, get me up to the back side of the school."

The Second String

The car quietly avoided the main street and pulled up around the back of the school. Rand got out with a laundry bag full of the stolen clothes. Spang was tucked into his place in the backpack. The laundry bag was wrapped in one of Elsie's black ops shirts to make it less visible. He pulled the black night vision visor down and disappeared into the shadows.

Elsie kept the lights off and drove down the main road like she was just coming into town. Driving very slowly she stopped when she got to the center of town at the circular little park. Opening the driver's side door she got out and acted like she was trying to pop the hood. Then she pitched a little fit and kicked the tire, sat down and started to cry.

The police car pulled out slightly and watched her. She was a beautiful woman in distress. They turned on their lights and came rolling quietly up to her. The officer leaned out the window.

"What seems to be the problem little lady?"

"My boyfriend's stupid car won't work!"

"Why? It looks like a nice car to me. One of them new ones isn't it? What's wrong with it?"

"It's the lights! I drove all the way down the road with no lights on. It's so dark, I can't see a thing."

The driver looked at his partner and snickered. They both got out of the police car and came over to her, flashlights pointed at her eyes.

"So you're telling me that all of this is jes cuz you don't know how ta turn the lights on?"

She looked up at him, tears streaming down her pretty face.

"Darlin maybe that's cuz you've had too much to drink."

"No sir, I haven't had a drop. I'm just trying to get home."

The big officer bent down and took her by the arm, lifting her up to stand.

"Well let's see what we got here." The flashlight swept up and down her body, pausing at her breasts. "You ain't from around here are ya?"

"New York."

"Well slap me silly, the big city. How lucky are we to get such a lovely looking movie star from the big apple."

"Whatcha think Ronnie? You reckon she'd give us a turn?"

"Gee I dunno, pretty little thing all out here on her own just needin' a rescue. She might be grateful."

"Whaddaya say honey, you feelin' grateful?"

The Second String

Elsie looked at them, forcing herself to put on a scared and vulnerable face.

"I'll bet she feels real good!"

"I reckon you're coming down to the station with us."

Now Ronnie had moved around behind her. His light shining up and down the tight dress.

"Yeah, we definitely gonna have to incarcerate you for drunk driving."

"Don't you worry none, after a little what they call *sedative* it won't be so bad."

"Yep, won't remember a thing."

The man in front of her reached out for her wrist. She lifted her foot and stomped down on Ronnie's foot behind her, driving her heel straight through his shoe and breaking bone. At the same time, she slammed her taser in the throat of the big cop. With a lightning fast turn she whirled and tasered Ronnie who was standing holding his foot as he strained to scream out in pain. Rand came running up. Both men were unconscious on the ground.

"Are you okay?"

"Yes, never better. These bastards deserved worse."

She told him what happened as Rand's face grew grim.

"Take the car up past the dry cleaners and wait for me, I'll just be a minute."

"Rand what…"

"Trust me, I'm not going to harm them… physically."

She nodded and drove off. Rand still had his combat gloves on to cover any prints at the laundromat. He reached into the police car and turned off the radio. A quick search of the glove box revealed the sedative they had promised Elsie. After injecting both of them, he put the two cops into the police car then squeezed in and drove it to it's regular hiding spot. He dragged the big cop back into place behind the wheel with Ronnie a little too close next to him. Then, with a grimace, he opened their pants and put their hands on each others genitals. Grabbing a donut off the dash, he squeezed the custard out on their hands. The set up was even more believable when he found a girly magazine under the front seat. He propped it up on the radio, then taking the sedative with him, he returned to Elsie.

"What did you do?" She asked.

"Basically humiliated them for life." Then he told her the details of what he had done.

"Oh my God that's so disgusting but perfect! Besides, even if they try to tell truth, there's no way that anyone will believe their story that a little woman kicked their ass. Nice work baby… make sure you wash your hands at the first opportunity."

They made one more stop into the alley behind the dry cleaners, then they drove out of town. By sunrise they were flat out on I-80 heading for Chicago.

***

At eight in the morning Sid Macintyre pulled his car into the alleyway of his dry cleaning business. He had replaced the little window with a steel plate. At the base of the door sat a laundry bag bundle.

"Oh no, what now?"

He opened the bundle and found the missing clothes and an envelope. Inside there was five-hundred dollars and a note.

Dear Dry Cleaners owner. Please accept my sincere apologies for any stress I've caused you. I was in a desperate situation with my wife just having discovered me and my lover. I was running around completely naked and robbing your shop seemed to be my only option. I regretted doing it, and I will regret it until my dying day. Please accept this small amount as compensation for any grief I have caused you and the customers whose clothes I took. I am a wretched sinner but am turning my life around to get on a more righteous path. Pray for me as I will always for you.

With strongest regrets and all sincerity.

That morning Sid Macintyre delayed opening the shop for another hour to go to mass. He hadn't attended church in over thirty years.

The Second String

Montgomery Thompson

Chapter 3

Unlimited

*'If I ever get my hands on that dollar again,
I'm gonna squeeze it til the eagle grins.'*
~Jimmy Cox

The sleek little car performed like a dream. Spang rode with his head out of the window in the warm summer air. They watched their speed closely because neither one of them had a driver's license. As evening fell, they pulled into a little roadway motel and got a room.

"The rooms in these places aren't so clean in our time."

"I wonder how these people would feel to know that they aren't from FirstTime or RealTime."

"I don't think it matters. As long as they are in their own time."

"But to know that there's another time going on somewhere else is now a thought that I can comprehend. There was no way before."

"In FirstTime our Practical Magic house is standing, the goats are grazing, the trees blowing in the wind and things are rusting. Hopefully not too much."

"Yeah, just sitting there waiting for us to return. Once it's started maybe it doesn't stop. In RealTime your children are getting older, my guitar is… I dunno, probably in the fire." He laughed.

"Yes and in this time…"

"Yeah, how does that work? Were all these people here before us?"

"I remember that Remmel said that people would *snap* to their timeline. I'm still trying to figure out what that means."

"Wait a minute Els, I have a theory working it's way to the surface here. Maybe we *snapped* to this timeline because it's already been accessed by someone from our time, or the future at least."

"Remmel?"

"Exactly."

"So he's travelled back here? What about his nineteen forty-nine self?"

"Remmel theorised that if you met yourself, you would just replace yourself and start to forget about the things you knew about the future. You might even have a mental breakdown. He said that you would have to have someone from your original time with you to stay...yourself and retain your memories of your time."

"Well if that's the case with him then he might not be right in the head."

"Yeah but it would explain why we snapped to this time… if that's actually what happened. It's so confusing."

"Hang on, I think I'm following you. So we should, in theory be able to *snap* to our original time."

"Yeah, you'd think. It would be a pretty small move on the controls though. A nanosecond is very fast and to get here I turned the dial quite a bit."

"This is what we have to ask Remmel about. Controlling the Time/Space Shifter. We had to make some pretty big moves on the controls to even get the TSS to work. But when we did we went too far. I can only assume it's because we snapped to where he is - the only traveller besides us."

"How can you be sure that he'll be at one of those bases?"

"Where would you be as a theoretical scientist breaking the laws of space and time in post war America?"

"Yeah, I guess you're right"

"Skunk Works, Area 51. We know about it but in this time no one has clue it exists let alone what it's called or what they're doing out there."

He looked at her with a fading smile.

"Still, how are we going to break into Area 51? It's the world's most secret and heavily defended base. They shoot first and make up stories about it later. We're gonna need a plan."

She thought a minute then said, "Or maybe… add an *e* to that."

"We're going to need a plan E?"

"Plane Rand, we need a plane and a way to impress our way into Skunk Works."

"Hey, don't we have a standing invitation to check out Howard Hughes' designs?"

"Bingo."

After a restless night, they hit the road for Chicago. The April sun was heating up as they wound their way into the city. After asking directions several times they found their way to the Lexington Hotel and checked in.

"It's not the Astoria, but it's still very nice."

"Did you see that they are giving tours of Al Capone's rooms?"

"That will come in very handy for covering our tracks."

"Let's get some sleep, it could be a busy night."

They woke at midnight and put on their black ops gear. Rand made use of a small, flexible fibre optics camera he had in his pack as they made their way down the hall to the rooms that Capone had lived in. Across the doorway was a red rope with a sign that told about Capone's exploits. The door was open so people could look in.

"Are you sure about this Rand?"

"Yes hon I told you, there's a secret entrance behind his dresser that wasn't discovered until the seventies or something."

"Okay, just be careful with the noise."

"Keep your ears up and listen for foot traffic, I'll move the dresser."

Rand carefully eased the tall dresser away from the wall revealing what looked like a narrow door for a person under four-feet tall.

"What did I tell you." Rand said, clearly pleased with himself. He opened the door. A passageway, taller but only slightly less narrow than the doorway wound down the hall, then stopped at a set of steep stairs. Elsie stood at the stairway, scanning ahead while Rand quietly closed the dresser behind them. As he joined her, Elsie held her finger to her lips.

"There are people sleeping behind these walls."

As they took the stairs down, Rand had to turn slightly sideways to fit. The stairs continued down floor after floor. They passed a room where the headboard pounded the wall, shaking the plaster into a fine dust all over them. Suddenly a female voice groaned loudly. Elsie looked at Rand with a smile.

"Then again, some people might not be sleeping."

They kept going down until the stairs let out in a wet, dark basement. A large hallway, the width of a car, disappeared to their right. There were doors all along the wall.

"Let's check it out. I'll use the camera to map it all." Rand said.

Elsie agreed, "But we have to do this quickly, the more time we're down here, the greater the risk."

As they explored the passages they discovered an indoor shooting range, a pool hall, casino and several bars.

"It's like a world of it's own down here."

"Well, he had to spend his money somewhere. If he couldn't enjoy luxury in public, he had to recreate it in private."

Finally they reached the end of the road. The far end of a long passageway ended in a wall with no doors, just a round sewer lid at it's base.

"We're definitely past the footprint of the hotel. Who knows what we're under." Elsie said looking around. Her eyes came to rest on the manhole cover.

"Tell me we're not going in there."

"I'll look with the camera first."

The lid wasn't solid like a regular manhole cover but Rand still struggled as he pried it up with his crowbar and lifted it out of the way. A steel ladder led down into a round shaft lined with bricks, and further into darkness.

"I'm gonna have to shine my IR light down there, watch your eyes." She turned away from the light for a moment as Rand shone the bright infrared beam down the shaft. It was a straight drop, roughly three stories to a wet landing.

"At least it's not under water."

Step by step they climbed down the rusty ladder, testing each rung to make sure it would hold. Finally, Elsie's foot touched down on the cement floor. They stood together in a ten-foot diameter space in front of a heavy, iron door. It looked like the side of an old ship and the rivets were as big as Rand's thumb.

"Gee, does that door say 'vault' or what?" Elsie quipped.

"Okay. Iron door. Looks like we're gonna have to make some noise. I'm thinking detcord around the hinge area and all down the right side where the bolts should be."

"If it's a vault door it going to have bolts all the way around."

"Okay, I'll do the whole thing, but it's really gonna make a bang. I wouldn't be surprised if it woke the whole hotel."

"We're not under the Lexington anymore, besides, we've got to be at least fifty-feet underground and surrounded by concrete."

"Okay Els, you know more about this stuff than I do. We should be on guard just in case. If anyone comes, taze em."

"Gotcha."

"Let's do this. I'm starting to get a bit claustrophobic."

Rand took the spool of detcord out of his pack and they went around the whole door with extra cord where the hinges would be. Then it was back up the thirty-foot ladder. They were sweating by the time they were at the top. They backed off until they were in a small storage room down the hall.

"Ears on dampening."

"Roger that." They usually kept the radio earpieces at a notch or two above normal so they could whisper to each other clearly during ops. Elsie took out the detonator and flipped the safety off. Rand looked at her with a grin.

"Last time you blew a door this size what was it you said?"

"Gimme some sugar baby." She squeezed the trigger.

A sharp thud vibrated the floor and dust came off the walls. Their ear-plug radios did a perfect job of protecting their ears, but they could tell by the shaking of the ground that it was loud.

"I hope no one heard that."

"They probably felt it more. Let's get down there and see if there's anything at all. I'm praying we don't end up like Geraldo."

They quickly descended the ladder. Smoke rose up the shaft, burning their noses with an acrid smell. The door was flat on the floor of a room that was roughly ten-feet by eight-feet square. The walls and floor were thick cement. A stack of wooden gun crates was piled against the far wall. Rand moved across to the boxes and looked at Elsie.

"Now don't get your hopes up Rand, this was always a crazy idea…."

Rand smiled at her as he lifted the lid. He didn't even look.

"I don't know how to react Rand, I'm stunned." Elsie couldn't believe her eyes. The box was packed with cash. "I feel like a criminal again."

"But we're stealing from the stealer. History never found this money, why?" Rand grinned even bigger. "Because we found it first."

She looked at him wide-eyed. "We're the reason Geraldo came up blank? That implies that we've been here before."

"Well if we had, we would have left ourselves a note in one of these boxes." He looked around the box. "Nope. Geraldo must have looked in the wrong place."

"Okay. That makes more sense. But only if we leave ourselves a note." She flipped open her folding knife and carved 'E' and 'R' on the bottom of one of the boxes. "There, now if we ever do this again, we'll know we're in a loop."

"Freaky." Rand wrestled with the concept.

Elsie just took out one of the empty pillow cases they had taken from their room, "Fill 'er up."

There were four pillow cases total and they loaded them with cash. Most of the money was in hundred dollar bills. When they were done there was still five boxes left.

It was tough going, but they worked their way methodically back up to the dresser and carefully checked with a fibre-optic camera before pushing it aside. Elsie kept watch on the hallway while Rand restored the dresser to its original position, then they quickly and quietly made their way back to their room. Closing the door, Elsie breathed a sigh of relief.

"We did it, oh my God we did it!"

"Thank you Lord and thank you Capone."

It took the better part of an hour to roughly count all the cash and get a round figure. Spang sniffed the cash suspiciously. They both leaned back, exhausted and overwhelmed.

"Well, I guess it's the kind of lifestyle we're used to after having access to everything on the planet for free."

"Yeah, twelve million should do it."

"In 1949 terms, that's closer to a hundred and fifteen million."

"And there's a lot more than that still in the basement. What's the next move?"

"I think it's time to wire Mr. Hughes, more than ever we're gonna need some of his resources."

They hung the clothes in the closet, packed all the money into the suitcases and got some sleep. In the morning, Rand rang down to the front desk and had a Western union courier come up to the room. He sent a message asking Howard Hughes where would be a good place to see him for a visit. About thirty minutes later he received a knock at the door from the same courier with a return message:

Mr. Hughes will welcome you at his headquarters in Culver City, CA / STOP

"Not very personable is he."

"Elsie, he's the richest man in the world and an obsessive/compulsive germaphobic workaholic. He doesn't have time for pleasantries."

"I wonder if he's built the Spruce Goose yet?"

"I remember that he had some problems with the government. I wonder if that's all over and done with?"

"Keep in mind that we're going to be hanging out with a bona-fide wacko slash maverick. Watch what you say, stay sharp and whatever you do don't touch him."

"Great."

They went shopping for clothes that would suit the company they were about to keep and added a whole new suite of luggage. Now they had enough suitcases to hold the clothes, the gear and the money.

That evening, exhausted from the combination of shopping and their efforts the night before, they went to bed early and slept until midnight. Rand woke Elsie who looked at him sleepily.

"What are you doing?"

"Elsie, we have to get the rest of the money."

"Oh now you're just being greedy."

"Yeah maybe, but in truth it's not for us, it's for the taxes and…"

"What? How would the IRS know about the money?"

"When we start spending it they will, believe me. Maybe Howard Hughes knows somebody who can help us get IDs, you know, drivers licenses and stuff."

"Rand, we're not going to be here long enough to—"

"I don't know Els, we may have to be. It may take that long to track down Remmel. We still may have get the attention of the people in charge at Area 51 to get in. It's a lot to pull off. Now that we have the money we're gonna have to find a way to fit in legitimately."

"Oh Lord. Okay, I'm up. I hate all this sneaking around. If we get caught it could be real trouble. And what else were you going to say? What else is the money for?"

"Your kids."

"What?" She searched his face and tried to grasp what he was saying.

"We can stash some of it for them, for us, in the future."

"Rand that's just—"

"Weird I know, but I really believe that we'll get back to them. I'll leave Moira of course, right away and you'll leave Bob and I'll be a step-dad to your kids Elsie. How else did you think this was going to work?"

"I… I just never though it all through like that. You're right of course, but then…"

"But what Elsie?"

"What if we forget. What if, like Remmel says, we meet ourselves and forget all about each other, New River, all of it?"

"I don't think that's going to happen."

"How can you know Rand?"

"It's like Remmel says. We're here with someone from our own time. Because we're together we don't forget. Have you forgotten anything about New River or even the ISS or your life before the Happening?"

"No, I remember everything."

"See, we're fine because we're together. Remmel may be a different story. We have to move forward with the information we have and Remmel's theories are holding up so far."

'You're right. It's all we can do.'

"So let's get that money. Between taxes and our future it's going to come in handy. Besides, it's just down and back up again. Think of what you're getting paid for the effort."

Elsie looked at him with a smirk. "Alright, you win. Let's do it and be done with it so I can get some sleep."

They got into the gear once more and made the journey down into the vault. They saw no one as they went. In no time they came back through the secret door, closed the dresser behind them and quickly tiptoed back to their room.

Elsie sat on the bed and took a deep breath. "Thank God that's done."

"We're gonna need more suitcases."

They slept the rest of the night. In the morning Rand went to the car dealership and bought a gigantic wood-panelled Cadillac Ranch Wagon and more matching luggage. The porters helped him bring the luggage to the room. Elsie hid the money under the bed and in the bathroom until the porters were gone. Then they packed all of their clothes, equipment and money into the suitcases. Rand came up with a system of small scratch marks to identify what each piece of luggage contained. When they were ready they called the front desk to send up enough people to carry the fourteen suitcases down to the car. Elsie waited in the lobby as Rand walked with the line of porters.

"The missus certainly travels prepared sir."

Rand just shook his head and said. "You ain't kiddin' pal."

Under Rand's supervision they carefully loaded the huge car. The hand stitched pig skin luggage filled the back. Rand was careful to pack it so the clothes were the first cases he'd pick when the rear hatch was open. Two other cases with clothes were placed at the rear passenger doors in case someone decided to look into the cargo that way. The equipment cases could be reached by either Rand or Elsie from the front. Spang took his spot on a soft blanket in the middle of the expansive front seat. Rand had left instructions with the Hotel management about the Delahaye. They would store the sleek silver car and keep it in pristine condition until the courier came to pick it up. Rand issued a password phrase for the courier and took down the mileage.

"I'm the donut captain. I'm here for the monkey."

"Excuse me sir?"

"That's the pass phrase. Make sure they say it perfectly or they don't get the car."

"Certainly sir."

Rand tipped the staff and the management handsomely then climbed into the Cadillac and put the giant car into gear.

"I feel like I'm driving a fishing boat." Rand giggled.

"I think it's great. It's so big I can stretch out on the front seat and sleep if I want."

"Well baby, we're on a road trip from Chicago to LA in 1949. You're gonna have lots of time for sleeping."

"Wait, Rand I can't believe I completely missed this. We're going from Chicago to LA."

"Right."

"Before the interstate road system was built."

"Yeah, I think so."

"You know how to get to LA?"

"Well my first stop was going to be for gas and a map."

"You don't need a map, just get your kicks."

'What?'

"Get your kicks…" She acted like she was handing him an invisible package with one hand. Rand looked at her confused. "Come on! Get your kicks! On…"

"Route…Route 66?" He blanched, "Really?"

"Yeah, we get to drive the Mother Road in its entirety and in its heyday."

"Oh man, this just gets better and better! How did we miss that?"

They stopped for gas and got directions to the famous highway. Soon they were turning onto the hallowed tarmac, tooting the horn and whooping out the windows. The sun was out on a beautiful spring da. Chicago faded behind them as the big caddy floated along like a cloud. After several hours hour they checked into one of the many themed hotels along the way. As the days passed in similar fashion they enjoyed the drive like it was a vacation. They even sneaked pictures onto the iPad while no one was looking. In the evenings they cleaned the weapons, took care of the gear and talked about their plans. During the day, on the long stretches of lonely road, they charged batteries with the solar charger. They thought hard about what to do with Spang. Dogs weren't tolerated around Howard Hughes so they opted to get the very best pet care available.

After four days of driving they finally pulled into Culver City. The town was larger than they thought. It was essentially just West Los Angeles. The Hughes Aircraft Corporation was hard to miss. Smaller offices and a guarded gate surrounded a series of massive buildings. After they told the guard about the invitation and showed him the telegram, he gave them directions and let them through.

"Mr. Hughes is working in there. You can't miss him."

Indeed, as soon as they entered the building it was hard to miss the six-foot three Hughes standing atop a wing spar. He was discussing plans with several men. Rand and Elsie waited until he was finished. He hadn't looked their way or even acknowledged their presence, but before he had turned his head away from the plans he said, "Well Mr. Carter what do you think? Mrs. Carter, I trust you had an enjoyable trip?"

"Yes Mr. Hughes, thank you for asking. And thank you for your invitation, it was most gracious."

"I find it odd that two pilots such as yourselves, didn't fly. After all, I do have my own airport."

"I'm glad you brought that up Mr. Hughes, we'd like to talk to you about that if you can spare a minute."

He looked at Rand. He was clearly suspicious of them both. "Alright, after you've driven all this way it's the least I can do. I'm sure you want to freshen up." He kept looking at a spot on Elsie's dress when the fabric had a tiny snag. "Why don't you meet me at my office back here in an hour."

"That sounds perfect Mr. Hughes, thank you." Rand gave him a genuine smile and never broke eye contact. The man had to know he was in earnest. It was never more important. They left and checked into a little hotel a block away from the plant.

"We have to tell him Elsie, he's our only hope."

"What? Rand that man is highly unstable."

"The government trusts him with their secrets and this is a very paranoid time. I think if we prove it to him, he will help us. It's good for him and good for us, a win-win."

"It's really risky Rand. If he gives us up, we would be under serious scrutiny. They would eventually find out the truth and then we would be under a microscope, literally. I don't want to end up on some operating table."

"We can handle ourselves I think."

"I don't want to be on the run either, we'll never get anywhere."

"I think you're taking this to extremes. The man has a lot to gain by working with us, we could give him some useful technology."

"Telling him about us and then sharing technology? What has gotten into you?"

"Elsie, dammit! I want to get back home. We have to offer something, right now the only thing we have is technology. The man doesn't need money and he's the guy we need."

"There's got to be another way."

"What do we know about time travel?"

"Nothing."

"Wrong. We know more than anyone because Remmel and us are the only one's who have done it. There are many theories and opinions about how actions in the past may affect the future and rewrite history. Well, maybe it needs to be rewritten. Maybe we can give something small that will make a difference in people's lives. Life is hard, why should we not attempt to make it better?"

"But it would change people's lives. Say we give Hughes... I dunno, Velcro. The guy who invented

Velcro wouldn't. Then there goes his fortune. What about his family?"

"What about all of the things that Velcro makes better? Like the cuffs on the blood pressure taker thingy, and all the safety applications?"

"Yeah, but what about the guy who was supposed to invent it?"

"He's reaping the rewards of his efforts on another time line, another string. Listen, everything I do here everyday affects somebody. What about the gas station owner, Mr. Roop? He says we saved his son. Was he supposed to be saved? Apparently he was. What about all the money we spent in the stores? Was the car salesman supposed to make a big commission on us? I don't think so, but tonight he's taking his gal out for a nice dinner. And what about Megan and Avery, we certainly impacted their lives."

"Okay, I get your point."

"We have to live, no matter where or when we are. We're not going to do something evil. We just have to use what we're given to do the best we can. Like everyone else."

"Some might say we have an unfair advantage."

"Does a bear have an advantage over a rabbit?" He watched as she weighed the question. "Go ahead, wrestle with that for a while. I think you'll find that the playing field is even."

She nodded slowly and shrugged. "Okay. We'll see what he's like and if it seems like we should, we'll tell him."

After a shower and carefully making sure every stitch was in place, they went to meet Hughes again.

Howard's Office was spartan and very, very clean.

"Have a seat please." Howard gestured to the two chairs in front of his desk. Rand noticed from the impressions in the carpet that there had been more chairs there until recently. He's prepared for us, Rand thought, something's up.

"Now, before we begin I want to clear something up. Where exactly did you learn to fly Mr. Carter, and you as well Mrs. Carter?"

"We're both pilots, but we don't actually have licenses because—"

"Exactly. I did some checking up on you after we met. There are no records of a Captain Carter for the 92nd Bomber Group in England. Moreover, there are no records for you with the WASPs Mrs. Carter. So what's your story? I expect the truth."

"Okay." Rand looked at Elsie, she nodded.

"Is this room safe?"

"Pardon me?"

"We need to know that this room is safe for the dispensation of classified information Mr. Hughes, is it?"

Elsie had turned on her commander voice and now sternly looked Howard Hughes in the eye. It gave the big man a pause.

"Yes Mrs. Carter, we are quite secure."

"Good. Rand, go ahead darling."

"Mr. Hughes we're from"—

"Let me guess, the CIA."

"Uh… no."

"The FBI."

"No."

"Okay then, one of Truman's goo—"

"We're from the future."

Hughes' face went flat. He was not amused.

"Is this some kind of—"

"WE ARE from the future Mr. Hughes." Elsie stood up.

"Oh I've heard a lot of cockamamie stories in my time, but this is up there with the best. How much do you want?"

"We don't want any money."

"Oh really? Okay, okay I'll play along just for the sake of entertainment. What is it that you want? Why are you here future people?"

He sat down and stretched out in his chair.

"Okay, here's the whole story – this is going to take a bit of time so I need your full attention. When I'm done I'll prove it to you, irrefutably. Sound fair?"

Hughes slowly sat up. "You're really serious? You think you can actually convince me you're from the future?"

Rand looked at Elsie. "We should just show him now, I don't think he wants to listen to our long story."

"Mr. Hughes, do you mind if Rand goes and gets something out of the car? It will just take a moment and clear all of this up."

"By all means, anything that will save time."

Rand left the office and came back with two oversized, matching trunks. Rand carried one, a security man followed him and carried the other. After the man left he took the two Kevlar helmets equipped with night vision out of one of the cases. Hughes stood and scrutinised every move. His eyes lit up when he saw the helmets.

Rand handed one to him and said, "Put it on, like this." He put his helmet on demonstrating how to lower the night vision screen into place.

"Elsie, the lights please."

The office went dark and Rand reached up and closed the visor on Hughes' helmet, then his.

Hughes jumped, "Wow, I can see you!" He raised the screen then lowered it again.

"This is incredible! Where did you get these?"

"Elsie turn the lights back on please."

The lights came back up and Rand took off the helmet then motioned for Hughes to give his up. The man reluctantly did so. Rand returned the helmets to their case. Next, Rand fished his iPad out of the suitcase and showed Hughes the pictures of he and Elsie on their road trip on Route 66, then at their home in New River as he explained what had happened to them. More pictures followed of them standing next to, and flying the C-17 Globemaster and V-22 Osprey. Rand let Hughes hold the iPad while he explained.

"We're pilots, like we said. But we don't have any ID or licenses for this time period."

"We have loads of cash…" He kicked open the lid on the other suitcase revealing over three million in hundred dollar bills.

"...but we don't have any bank accounts or identity."

Elsie leaned over the desk. "We need to get legitimate. Driver's and pilot's licenses, bank accounts, birth certificates all of it. It needs to look like we belong here."

"In return," Rand picked up where Elsie left off, "we will share technology and aviation design information that will give Hughes Aircraft a strong edge over the competition."

Hughes leaned on a button on his intercom. "Miss Perkins, hold all my calls."

They had his attention. For the next five hours the questions never stopped. Food was brought in, couriers were sent out, stenographers and designers brought in and sent out. In the middle of the hurricane of activity, Hughes orchestrated and gleaned and calculated a mind-boggling array of details ranging from their personal history, the events of the time travel, their flying history, capabilities of modern aircraft, the significance of the computer, the world market and even their return of the money and clothes they borrowed. By the time they were done Hughes had a solid picture of who they were, what they had been through and what they were trying to accomplish.

"Well, I know all about Skunk Works. If they were military it would be no problem but they aren't, it's run by the CIA. Those bastards are so entrenched in there not even I can get in. Sure they toss me a few projects, but they feed me a pittance in contracts for flying boats while they're working on supersonic high altitude interceptors."

"We need to get in there and talk to Remmel."

"This Remmel guy is not on the charts. He doesn't show up anywhere."

"That's because he's like us, from a future ahead of now, but not the same future as our time."

"I thought you said his equipment was from 1952?"

"It is. He is of your generation, he got the machine running in 52 then he went back to now."

"Jeepers this stuff will make your head spin. No wonder all my physicists are so weird."

"Yeah, it hurts my brain too and I've actually done it."

"Okay, well we can only do so much in a day. We'll have your IDs and pilot's licenses by tomorrow then you can go and buy a plane, enough of this car business. As far as the money goes we'll hide it in some of my accounts and I'll slowly pay it out to your accounts in chunks, like I'm paying you as high-ranking business partners.

The IRS will have to have their piece of the pie of course."

"That's why we took the remainder of the money, for the IRS."

"Yeah well, they got Capone, they might as well have some of his money too. Say, what was your intention of grabbing all that loot anyway? Good old fashioned greed?"

"No, not at all." Rand shook his head.

"It was to step in as a financial partner with you on a design project that would impress Skunk Works enough to hire us." Elsie laid the last of their cards on the table.

Hughes looked at them appreciatively.

"So now we get to it. Well, it's a good plan if you two know anything that can help. What did you have in mind?"

"I don't know, what are you working on that could use our unique skill set?"

"Probably just about everything."

"What do you say we just sit on meetings and look around at your projects and see if there is anything we can offer."

Hughes looked a bit nervous at that suggestion.

"We're not spies Mr. Hughes. If we were, we wouldn't be showing you our technology, we'd be trying to steal yours." Elsie stepped forward.

"Here's an example of how we can help. You know that Chuck Yeager is flying the Bell X-1A trying to break mach two right?"

"How did you know about that?"

"Future, remember?"

"Jeepers. That is going to take some getting used to."

"Anyway, they are going to find out the hard way that they are dealing with something called inertia coupling. Basically it's caused by the inertia of a heavy and long fuselage that cancels out the forces that stabilise the aircraft's control surfaces. We can help with that."

"Okay Mrs. Carter we'll sit down with some engineers and see if you can help. If you can, then I'll do my best to get you into the Skunk Works to find your Doctor Remmel."

"At my expense, I insist." Rand knew he had to maintain the illusion of the dominant male role to engender respect. "Take that briefcase there to cover the costs."

Hughes finally seemed at ease. He walked briskly across the carpet and extended his hand to Rand.

"I like the way you work Mr. Carter, bold, very bold."

"Please, just Rand."

Elsie took a small, clear plastic container out of her purse and showed it to Hughes. He had never seen anything like either the container or it's contents.

"It's sanitiser. It evaporates after completely killing any and all germs. And, it keeps working even after it's evaporated for up to twenty-four hours."

She showed him how to use it. Hughes was fascinated and at Elsie's recommendation sent it down to his lab to be reverse engineered. After another hour of firming up details and getting more comfortable with being on a first name basis, they said goodbye for the evening and went to their hotel. Hughes sent armed security to transport the cash suitcases to his accountants. Rand and Elsie reunited with Spang and spent a low key evening relaxing and making notes about all of the things they could share that could make the world better. The list was long and included notes on subjects ranging from global warming to diet and exercise, automobile safety and earthquake proofing buildings.

"If we had access to the internet it would help so much more."

"Let's just stick with what we know Els. Oh, and add *internet* to that list." He laughed.

She came up and wrapped her arms around him from behind. "I really like the way you made sure he knew who wore the pants in our relationship."

"Elsie, I didn't mean to—"

"No, I really mean it Rand. You're the farthest thing from a chauvinist, but you had such a great situational awareness that you knew it would be important to Hughes. You trusted me to see it too and respond accordingly. We make a great team."

"Thanks Elsie, I think we do to." He turned to her. "Are you sure you know enough about aircraft design to help them solve the problems with the X2 thing?"

"Bell X-1A, lock it into your memory, you may need to show a level of competence in aircraft knowledge as well. And yes, I know I can help them with it."

"Bell X-1A got it."

The California sunset was low in the evening sky and had turned everything a golden orange.

"Anyway, I was really proud of the way you handled yourself in there."

"I just told the truth, that has a weight all of it's own. The man has quite a presence. All the legends about him don't do him justice. He's a powerhouse of a person."

"I have the feeling we're gonna be here for awhile."

"Probably. We can't let our guard down though. There will be people who want to know where Howard is getting all his good ideas. Eventually they might figure it out."

"We'll just keep it low key."

"Good idea. Let's start the day tomorrow by going plane shopping." She said laughing.

"The first thing I'm going to do is find some first-class care for Spang. Maybe Hughes can arrange someone."

They left Spang with the motel manager with promises of a healthy tip and started the day in Hughes' office. After sending a messenger scurrying to fetch a luxury Beverly Hills dog care professional he showed them their own offices and introduced them to their interior designers and architects. Then he left them alone for an hour to work out how they wanted their office space designed. The offices were on the ground floor with no windows. Rand took extra measures for security and asked Elsie to do the same.

When Hughes came back they let him know the drastic degree of their security recommendations and he never blinked.

"We'll have it done by the end of next week."

They switched the conversation to planes and Hughes suggested that they take his Sikorsky S-43 for a spin. It was a large seaplane that could land both in water and on dry land.

"I love the ability to land wherever I want. It's seaworthy enough for the ocean and holds quite a bit of cargo. But the thing I like most is that the engines are above and behind you, so it's quiet."

They made their way out to the tarmac and Hughes barked a couple of orders. The hanger was opened and the plane pushed out. It was ready to fly at all times.

"She's bigger than I expected."

"Ah but she flies like a gull!"

They climbed in and Rand let Elsie into the co-pilots chair. Howard quickly pointed out particulars about the controls and started the engines. Elsie watched, taking mental notes.

"It's not like the modern planes Rand, these old birds require finesse and feel. You should do fine."

"Hey whaddaya talking about old? This plane is brand spankin new!" Howard looked hurt.

"No offence Howard," Elsie shouted "she's only old relatively speaking of course. I think she's one of the most beautiful things I've ever seen."

"That's more like it." Howard chuckled as he applied power and taxied to takeoff.

The silver flying boat floated gracefully into the air. They sailed out over Los Angeles as Elsie took the controls and put her through her paces. Rand took over and dropped the plane to under a hundred feet, skimming over the waters just off the Santa Monica shoreline. Hughes directed him to a location along the shore about ten minutes north and told him to set it down at the pier.

Rand looked uneasy, "I'm sorry Howard I've never landed a seaplane before."

"Well then it's time to learn."

Hughes directions were simple and straight forward. In no time Rand was taxiing the big silver plane up on to a flat stretch of private beach.

"Now I see why you prefer seaplanes." Elsie said as she stepped out of the Clipper.

They took a set of stairs that wound up a fifteen-foot cliff and onto a perfectly manicured lawn that wrapped around a massive Spanish styled villa.

"I had some of my people look for houses for you two. What do you think?"

Rand looked at Elsie. She was beaming.

"It's stunning."

"I thought you might say that. Seeing how you're so far away from your home, I thought it might be nice for you to have one while you're here. So I bought it, fully furnished. I hope you don't think it too presumptuous of me." Hughes put his arm around Rand's shoulder. "Well old man?"

The physical gesture surprised Rand but he didn't let it show. "It's wonderful Howard, we can't thank you enough. I am assuming that you used our funds to purchase the house, I wouldn't have it any other way."

"Of course. What do think I am, rich?" He joked.

The house had ten bedrooms and as many bathrooms. The beach was theirs for four-hundred yards on either side but it also had three swimming pools. Hughes had the place already up and running with phone and servants. There was a maid, a butler, a gardener, a cook and two couriers. The couriers would shuttle papers between Hughes Aircraft and the house but were also available for any other jobs. They sat down to eat lunch in a cozy outdoor area next to the smaller pool. Rand told Hughes about the trend of hot tubs in their time. Hughes thought it was a rather Roman idea and decided to send somebody over to build one for them. Rand observed that that's the way it was with Howard Hughes. If you had an idea that he liked, there was no ground between thinking it and manifesting it. Elsie thought that between the three of them, they were a potent mix.

Over lunch they decided on two planes; a PBN-1 Nomad and a de Havilland DHC-2 Beaver. Hughes' Sikorsky Clipper was a bit too big for them and besides Hughes flew one. They didn't want to be seen as Hughes' clones. The Nomad was a specially modified version of the stalwart PBY Catalina, one of the best-loved flying boats in the world. The Nomad had a longer nose to help it cut through waves, a longer fuselage and had a redesigned tail in addition to a host of other important upgrades. All of these factors gave it significantly longer range, strength and load carrying capabilities. Both the Nomad and the Beaver were renowned for their reliability. Hughes seemed impressed by their choice and though he thought the Catalina was a bit too common he knew the Nomad was a rare bird.

"People will think it's a normal Catalina," Rand told him, "but she'll pack a punch that they won't expect."

They moved in that day and by evening they were settled in, watching Spang play in the garden as the sun set over their new home.

"What a whirlwind."

"No kidding, one minute we're scrambling through the swamp, the next we're in our new home in Malibu overlooking the ocean."

"There's so much to do Rand. I don't know how we're going to download all of our knowledge to Howard's team."

"I've been thinking about it. Let's start with carbon fibre, velcro and the body armour. Just give them samples of our gear for them to reverse engineer. I've watched *How They Make It* on the Discovery Channel enough to have a few helpful insights."

"I guess the best thing to do is just start writing it all down."

"Tomorrow I'm going to get started on making this place secure, like classified secure. There is likely to be some snooping once we start putting out information."

The next morning Rand called Hughes and had him send his security contractor out to the house. Rand envisioned something out of X-Men including underground bunkers and air defense systems. The contractor thought Rand's ideas were a bit extreme, but he got into the spirit of the thing and eventually had a few ideas of his own to add. In the end the security plan made the house a discreet disguise for a fortress. Rand sent his body armour to Hughes along with a carbon fibre grip off of Elsie's Beretta after having some of Hughe's gunsmith's make hardwood grips to replace them. Hughes got to work.

The de Havilland Beaver was delivered on the same day their new IDs arrived. The Nomad was to be delivered to Hughes Airport where it had it's own production facility. Rand and Elsie began to fly it regularly between the plant and home. When the Nomad arrived, Rand took Hughes for a night flight with the night vision helmets on. Hughes was elated.

"We have to start working on these."

"I'm afraid that the technology is way too far ahead. You have to develop not only the optics, but the silicon chip then the software development and all the other little bits. This stuff is at the peak of technology in our time. These two helmets are only two of twenty or so that exist. Believe me, our enemies would love to have them."

"Okay. But when you meet this Dr. Remmel and he shows you how to get back to your time, maybe you could bring me one."

Rand thought about the idea of seeding the past with future information and how radically it would alter the future. That future would then feed the past again. It would make a technological workhorse of the generations between the two times but the gains would be unlimited.

Chapter 4

Russians

'Whether you like it or not, history is on our side.
We will dig you in.'
~ Nikita Khrushchev

It was over a month since they had moved into the villa in Malibu. The security work was just finishing up and the labs were starting to gain some ground on the reverse engineering process. They had managed to create a bulletproof vest that would withstand a shot from most small arms and shrapnel. The carbon fibre was causing them some problems though. They could only produce strands of carbon that were twenty percent as strong as the fibres that Rand had given them. It was no better than fibreglass and twice as brittle.

"There are some things they are going to need," Elsie was telling him, "like an electron microscope for example. We're expecting them to build a calculator out of an abacus. It's just not going to work."

Just then the phone rang, Rand picked it up.

"Rand? Howard. The X-1A flew mach two point four-four. Your information did the trick. Congratulations, brilliant work."

"Thanks Howard but it was Elsie—"

"Listen, I've got a few people coming over to your house this evening around six o'clock for a little celebration. I think your going to like what I've got for you."

"I always do Howard but—"

"See you then old man." *Click*

He looked at Elsie, exasperated. "Call the staff together hon, Howard is having a party at our house at six." Rand shared all that Howard had said. "Apparently he credits me with the X-1A recommendations. I tried to tell him that it was all you."

"It's okay, that's how things are in this time. What matters to me is that it worked and now we can focus on getting into Skunk Works."

"Well I don't like it Els. You deserve the credit and I'll make sure that Hughes knows it."

"Just don't be too aggressive. We need him."

"Don't worry, I consider him a friend. I just want to nudge him towards a more modern way of thinking."

There was nothing to do but get everyone busy and get the place ready. It was eleven in the morning. The cook made some calls to caterers throughout Beverly Hills. The butler sent the couriers to get everything from candles to flowers and Elsie rescued the housekeeper by calling Howard Hughes' aide to get his personal cleaning staff over to the house to help. Spang was bathed and brushed within an inch of his life and in the end everything was ready just as the clock chimed six. Elsie fixed herself and Rand so they were free of flaws and instructed the staff in the foyer as the first limousine arrived. It was Liz Taylor. Rand watched with a smile as Elsie and Liz made girly noises and did the double cheek kiss thing.

"Oh you've been busy you two. I'm so glad that you and Howard hit it off. You know you're the talk of the town."

"Oh I hope not. We're private kind of people, not celebrities like you Liz. We don't know how to handle all the attention and certainly not with the grace that you do."

"You're so sweet but enough chit chat, where's the champagne?"

One of the catering staff was close at hand to meet the request. Elsie showed Liz to the main living area then returned to meet the next guest.

For the next thirty minutes people arrived. They could tell that the guest list comprised of everyone that Howard had seen them with in New York. There were only a few who couldn't make it. Finally, Howard arrived with a young brunette on his arm. He introduced her as Terry Moore, the two were obviously very amorous. After introductions Howard swept into the room and got the small group's attention.

"Alright everyone, I arranged this soirée for two reasons. First to welcome Rand and Elsie into their new home and into our little community…" There was applause all around. "…and secondly to celebrate something that I'm sure you will all be reading about in tomorrow's paper."

There were ooh's and aah's at this. Howard continued.

"When I met our two pilot friends in New York, little did I realize that I was talking to a pair of aeronautical geniuses. Now, pay attention because the tale requires a little back-telling."

The small group got comfortable and listened attentively.

"You see out in the desert somewhere there is a secret little project. A small team of propeller-heads built a plane that would fly faster than twice the speed of sound. Imagine that. To go so fast that if you spoke, your words would fall out of your mouth and tumble into the distance behind you."

Howard's dramatics captured the audience. "Now, imagine being the intrepid, brave pilot of this tiny bullet. You strap in, put your helmet on and whisk off to do the impossible, go twice the speed of sound. Mach 2. But as you get close to that breakneck pace, right on the edge of making history the little craft shudders uncontrollably. Fearing that you might disintegrate on the spot, you throttle down and bring her back, abandoning your hopes."

The audience sighed in disappointment.

"The engineers roll up their sleeves and send you out time and again, but every time it's the same thing. Finally, they have no tricks left in their bag. The impossible truly seems impossible. But then, a glimmer of hope! Through a chance meeting comes a random conversation. And in that conversation between, let's say, a debonair snob and a handsome genius of aviation..." Howard winked at them, *who was who?* "...the young hero and his gobsmackingly gorgeous fiancée offer a tiny suggestion. Just a humble tip to try and do their part to help these daring pioneers. A pinch of this and a dab of that they say. Just in the right places and that should fix your shuddering problem. Give it a try, we might be wrong, but we're not."

Now people were looking at Rand and Elsie with new respect.

Liz chimed in, "So, tell us what happened. Now that you've got us all worked up."

"What happened my dear is that I received a phone call this morning telling me that Chuck Yeager flew the X-1A prototype not only up to mach 2, but smashed straight through it without a hitch!"

Everyone was on their feet applauding with shouts of *bravo!* They were clapping Rand and Elsie on the back and shaking their hands. Rand had never had such a fuss made over him.

"Let's celebrate our two brightest new stars, Rand and Elsie!" The crowd joined in three robust cheers of "Hip hip, hooray!"

After that the champagne was poured, a man Rand had never seen started playing the piano and people set about taking turns with Rand and Elsie. Most of the attendees were actors and actresses so it wasn't long before songs were sung. Rand and Elsie found themselves star struck once again.

The Second String

Hughes didn't seem to mind Spang who received never-ending loads of attention as the magical evening sparkled on.

In a quiet moment off to the side, Liz talked to Elsie about Howard, "He's changed you know. I believe it's your fault, the two of you. I've never seen him so comfortable around people. You know how he is about cleanliness and germs and things, it's almost like he seems to be getting over it." They watched Hughes talking with people. It was true, he was touching people on the shoulder and shaking hands. He was even leaning on the piano and tapping his hands on the surface. Elsie continued to watch him throughout the evening. Several times she saw him disappear around a corner into the hallway, when he came back out he was rubbing his hands. It was the sanitiser.

Shortly afterwards she came up to him, "Howard do you have any of that hand lotion we were working on?"

Hughes looked surprised, "Hmm, what? Oh, uh… yes, yes here you are." He held out a plastic tube.

Several of the guests took notice. Elsie said, "Just a little something that Howard and I are working on. It's good for your skin and completely sterilises anything it touches. Don't eat it though." They all laughed as Elsie passed it around.

"Well, it's still in testing phase. I wasn't going to announce it for a month or so."

"Oh Howard is just being humble. It's more of a matter of marketing. We're hoping that it will make a big difference in hospitals and even surgery." She gave Howard a look.

Several people started making suggestions as to its application.

"What about public restrooms, it would be handy there."

"Or people in poor countries. Some of them have no sanitary conditions at all."

This started a whole conversation about humanitarian topics. Hughes pulled Elsie aside. "You know I am very used to doing these things without the help of others."

"You can't keep these things to yourself. When it's time for an idea to better the world we can't stand in it's way regardless of our personal feelings about it. No hoarding."

"I wasn't trying to keep it to myself I—"

"Did you know that pipes can be made from this stuff?" She held up a vinyl record of the Andrews Sisters *Rum and Coke-a-cola.* "PVC. No rusting pipes, clean water, no lead poisoning, lightweight, easy to install, lasts far longer than iron or cement. Check into it."

Hughes watched her walk away. He was unused to people dominating the conversation, it made him feel like a child. He went after her.

"Excuse me, Elsie?" She turned to him with a smile. "Does everything have to do with plastics?"

"There's the iron-age, bronze-age and steel-age. We need to get you through the plastics age so we can move on to the silicon age. So yes, there is going to be a lot of products that are based on a very wide variety of plastics; copolymers, vinyl's, acetals, polycarbonates, polyethylene and so on. You are already years ahead of what 1949 looked like in Rand's and my history books."

Howard's eyes narrowed as he gazed out at something far away. "I just want to see it, the future. I want to get past all of this and go faster and farther and know… more."

"It sounds like the most frustrating thing in the world, but no matter how far and fast we've gone it hasn't got us any closer to the answers. All there are is more questions."

"Here's a question that I've been wanting to ask, just for my own curiosity of what's possible."

"Okay Howard, I'll call these incidentals. They are curiosity questions about the future. We will answer them if we can, but keep in mind that the answers will change. We're changing them even now."

"Okay, I'll keep that in mind."

"What's the question?"

He smiled a mischievous grin. "How fast has man gone in your time? How fast is the fastest any man has ever travelled?"

"Oh, and there I thought it was going to something profound." She laughed. "Well, those records were set during space flight. The Shuttles reached around twelve-thousand miles-per-hour, but I think the fastest was the Apollo astronauts who went over twenty-four thousand miles-per-hour on their trip to the moon."

They were standing outside looking up at the moon as she said this. Hughes was dumb struck.

"The moon?' His voice was scratchy "And… did they… land?"

"On the moon? Yes, absolutely. It was amazing. July 1969, people went nuts. When they came back they had a ticker tape parade in New York."

He was looking at the moon and swallowed hard. "I'll bet they did. My God, twenty-four thousand miles-per-hour, we can barely hit fourteen hundred."

"To be fair, in space you have no resistance to overcome."

He started to ask her more questions, but then they decided it was probably best not be discussing such things with so many civilians around. She went off to be a good hostess and left him staring at the stars. Later, after quite a few drinks, a group decided to go skinny-dipping on the beach. Rand found himself standing with Howard on the lawn looking out at the sea. The sounds of squealing and laughing celebrities drifted up the cliff side.

"You know as well as I Howard that I wasn't the one who came up with the mach 2 solution."

"I assumed so, but I needed a reason for you to be here. Engineering genius and hero pilot are good cover stories. Besides, when you're in the spotlight it's easier to hide."

"Actually, in our time Chuck Yeager did a lot of amazing flying. I don't think it was him that flew mach 2 first, it was another guy."

"Well this time, it's Chuck."

"There'll be more in the next ten years. Man it's gonna get real trippy when all this new tech hits the street."

Howard looked at him strangely.

"What?" Rand looked back at him

"I'm not sure Rand, your speech took a strange turn there. Is that how they talk in the future?"

Rand laughed, "Oh dear, seems I've had a little too much to drink. Yes, I probably slipped into old speech patterns."

"Well it's okay around me, but don't let it happen in front of the rest of the gang. They'll think your funny."

"Understood. I'll be especially watchful from now on."

"Well, see that you are."

Rand was keenly aware how fast Hughes switched from casual to assertive. He made a note not to set the big man off again.

The next morning the papers said exactly what Hughes had predicted. *Mach 2 – Yeager does it again!* Elsie saved clippings from the events that were related to them and tucked them away. In the days that passed, Rand and Elsie continued to dole out every bit of information about the future that they could remember. Elsie made hundreds of suggestions and recommendations on topics ranging from the domestic to the scientific. Her input in the field of spaceflight virtually pioneered the field. From rocket development to communications and telemetry, she launched programs that would result in the development of a space program and far out pace the Russians in defensive capabilities.

Construction was completed on the security of the house and grounds and included an armoury and an underground garage that could hold over twenty cars. Hughes' companies were quickly gaining notoriety in virtually every field. Rand warned him against the dangers of monopolies and personally against the dangers of megalomania that could come from such global market domination. In short, Rand made it clear that he had to share if the information was going to continue to flow. With that in mind, Hughes set up a meeting with the leaders of industry throughout the free world. NATO was newly formed and encouraged countries to adopt a cooperative attitude towards each other in order to share in the technological wealth of the United States.

After four months of technological advances that so far out paced everyone else it became clear that no one could compete so they had better join in. After Elsie and Rand told Hughes about the Cold War and the Cuban missile crisis, Russia was given particular consideration and was invited to join in the wealth. It took some careful handling, but the Cold War thawed and the Soviet Union started to receive the benefits of the new tech.

It was the beginning of August. The weather was still warm and they had been spending time with Hughes and his girlfriend. With the encouragement of Elsie, Howard and his girlfriend Terry Moore decided to marry in an impromptu ceremony about Hughes' immense three hundred foot private motor yacht, the *Allene*. It was a soft evening sunset when Hughes announced it to Rand and Elsie.

"We're going to get married, Terry and I."

"Really?" Elsie was all a flutter. "Oh that's wonderful Howard when?"

"Now."

Her eyebrows went up. "As in, right this moment?"

"Yes as a matter of fact. Would you two be our witnesses?"

"I have a better idea." Rand stepped in front of Elsie. Then, getting down on one knee he said, "You've already said yes once. If you will permit the honour a second time I would love us to get married this very night, for all time. Will you?"

Elsie choked back the tears and wrapped her arms around him. "Yes, yes, oh yes a thousand times yes!" Then she looked up at Howard and Terry. "That is, if you don't mind it being a double wedding?"

Terry rushed over and hugged her. Howard just smiled and said, "I couldn't imagine a better way to do it."

Both couples said their vows under the starry vault of a warm pacific summer night sky. There was no sign of the strange occurrence that had affected their first attempt to be wed.

When the ceremony was over and the rings were on their fingers Elsie just said, "Thank God. We actually did it."

"Thank God indeed." Rand was so happy he had a permanent grin from ear to ear and couldn't keep his eyes or his hands off his new bride.

Terry was equally as happy. After a few glasses of champagne she said, "Let's share stories! How did you two meet?"

Howard interrupted saying, "Maybe we should each play like proper honeymooners and spend some romantic time alone."

Terry looked surprised and then a light bulb went off in her head. "Oh, I get it. They want to be alone. Good night you love birds!"

Hughes added, "You take fore, I'll take aft." His eyebrows did a Groucho Marx wiggle. "See you tomorrow around lunch time."

Hughes and his new bride went to the rear half of the ship. The crew continued to play romantic music and wait on their every need, quietly inconspicuous but always there when they were needed.

The next several months were busy with product releases. September of 1949 saw the introduction of Velcro, lighter and stronger fibreglass, advances in humanitarian aid and water and sewage treatment and food production. In the medical field, cancer had been associated with cigarette smoking and valuable discoveries were being made across the field in virtually every major disease.

The changes weren't all good. Technological advances sent a wave of fear through some religious groups claiming that the government was soon to enforce the number of the beast on everyone's forehead and that society was relying too much on technology and not enough on God.

"You can't expect people to just abandon their ways and accept the newest trend." Elsie explained. "Technology needs to be tried and tested over time in order to be trusted."

"I know Els, but there has to be a way for these people to understand that clean water is better than dirty water."

"They are going to stick with what they know. 'If it was good enough for my father then it's good enough for my kids' is the mentality we're dealing with here."

"Well, we'll see how long the kids want to do it the old way when they see how better life can be."

"What are we talking about here? Colour TV?"

"Well, sure."

"Rand, colour TV is hardly a major improvement of the human condition. We need to feed the hungry, cure the sick, stop overpopulation, get rid of fascism, promote democracy."

"How Elsie? How are we, as in me and you, going to do all that? Velcro?" He looked out to the sea. "It's just too big. We can't change the world."

"He's right." Howard came walking in from the main room. "You can't change the world. I've got all the resources a man could have and I still can't make a dent in it. Simple human stubbornness slows progress to a crawl. We're afraid of change. It's in the very core of our nature."

"But if we don't try—"

"You're right too Elsie. We have to try. That too is at the core of our nature, our very best quality."

Rand looked at them both, "But when we try, they deny."

Hughes looked back at him. "It's catchy, but untrue. Some welcome change, some ignore it and some rally against it. We're only interested in the ones who want it."

"And what, they pull the rest along kicking and screaming?"

"No Elsie, they leave the rest behind. I'm talking about a utopia; a place where people who are ready to embrace a new future can go to live in peace. A place that is so advanced that no outside nation could ever assail it. Complete peace and harmony, happiness and prosperity."

Rand looked at Howard with raised eyebrows. "That's all well and good, but let's work on being idealistic shall we."

"Cute Rand."

"No it's not, it's nuts! It makes a good novel for Ayn Rand but in reality it's doomed to fail. People are people and in the end, when you get them together someone always screws it up."

"Calm down Rand." Elsie came over to him and put her hand on his cheek.

"Now see here Rand, I'm not crazy, I'm just brainstorming is all. I have no intention of invading Australia and turning it into some Shangri-la. This train of thought needs to be chased all the way to the next station, as you're fond of saying, if for no other purpose than to see where it leads. Now, I'm sorry for setting you up like this, but I wanted to see what you two really thought about everything we've done and where it's going."

Hughes sat down, weary. "A man like me finds it hard to get the real thoughts out of the people around him. I just had to be sure."

Elsie sat down next to him. "We're the same people no matter what Howard. We have no ulterior motives."

"I can see that now. You'll forgive me for putting you to the test."

Rand sat down across from them. "I completely understand. As a matter of fact I'm glad we did this. It lets me know where you stand as well."

Hughes sighed. "We will have to give the world a break to catch up and then try introducing this technology at a more palatable rate. Oh, that reminds me of the real reason I stopped by. This came for you."

He handed them a letter. It was to Howard Hughes and Associates. The return address just read: *Safeway Foods Inc.*

"That's a grocery store chain isn't it?"

"Just read it old man."

Dear Mr. Hughes, in light of recent technological advances it has come to my attention that you have *two very capable new engineers / partners. We are at points on several projects where we are looking for a fresh perspective. If it pleases you to let them consult with us, we would be interested in partnering with various branches of the Hughes Industrial Enterprises to complete the projects. Of course there are always new projects in the works and, depending on the outcome of this proposed collaboration, we may be inclined to partner with you on those as well. Please send reply ASAP to the <u>exact</u> return address.*

Sincerely,
SW

"Well, there you have it. That's what you were hoping for isn't it?"

"If SW stand for Skunk Works then yes."

They looked at each other excitedly.

Howard looked at the ground with a frown. "It does. Listen, no matter how it goes from here I want you to know it's been really wonderful. I would ask that you stay, but that would be selfish. I would also ask you to come back, but it may not be possible. I only ask that if it is possible, you consider it. Not because I'm interested in the ideas and technology, though I am, but because you two are some of the only real people I know, and I value your friendship greatly."

Elsie approached him as if to ask permission to hug him, he embraced her easily. "Of course we'll come back if we can. We will miss you too."

Rand shook his hand and smiled, "You can count on it."

Howard said his good-byes. He was off to Germany for an industrial conference. They watched his plane roar off the water and fly south.

Two days after Rand sent the reply letter they received a telegram: *PRGM HYWK LNGS TFSN TING WLNG ITHG WOPI QSLK IHYT*

"What the heck is this supposed to be?"

Elsie took the telegram from Rand. "It's old code, well code in this time. We have no way to decode it though, it needs a key."

"Weird."

"There's not much we can do but wait to hear more."

That night they were having dinner with the staff in appreciation for all their hard work. A large meal had been prepared by staff hired to cover the evening and the next day. Amid the laughter and conversation, a whistle sounded from the beach below. Every one looked and several of the staff offered to investigate but Rand said he would check it out himself. He went inside, retrieved his

NV helmet then headed down to the beach via a secret stairwell. As he descended, he saw a small periscope breaking the water as it quickly headed out to sea.

By the time Rand reached the shore the sub was gone, but the evidence of the visitors were pressed into the wet sand around an ammunition can. He switched the night vision to thermal and swept the area for body heat but found nothing. Inside the ammunition box was a small book in a sealed rubber bag. Rand took the ammo can and waved out to sea then headed back up the cliff via the secret stairway. Once he put away the night vision helmet and the package he came back to the dinner table.

"Just boaters on the wrong beach. They were gone by the time I got there."

Elsie looked at him, he just smiled back at her knowingly.

Later that night he showed her what he had found. Handing her a little book he said, 'It's the key.'

The book was a cipher. In it was the key for the message which, once decoded, said: 36-37-38.838N / 116-01-39.114W 09/20/49 noon. They looked at a chart for the latitude and longitude.

"That's southern Nevada. It's got to be Area 51."

"Okay, this is it hon. I don't think we'll be allowed to bring weapons in."

"We'll keep them in the armoury. Let's take a few token gifts though."

Betsy was the Nomad. It had been undergoing major modifications to lighten and strengthen the hull and boost engine power. The interior was made quiet and comfortable by a lightweight sound suppressing rubber material that lined every surface. It was the predecessor to a crucial step in stealth technology, but at this point all it did was help to quiet vibrating surfaces. Rand and Elsie's conversion included room for up to six passengers, a private cabin with a queen bed and a fully functional galley and bathroom. The plane was kept ready to fly by Howard's personal crew.

They had breakfast, played with Spang for an hour then took the elevator down the inside of the hill to the Beaver's Dam, a small hangar dug into the cliff side at beach level. Rand had the inside painted flat black and the only light was infrared. The door matched the cliff face exactly. The project was headed by a Hollywood set designer with consultation from Hughes' head of security who was a sniper in the war. They used material saved from the excavation of the original cliff. Piece by piece the native rock and fauna had been removed and tagged like an archeological operation. Then it was all reinstalled onto a thick, armour plated door that swung open quickly, and closed even faster. The seam blended so perfectly that even a geologist, chipping away at the rock would have difficulty discovering the secret.

The Beaver and Nomad had also been modified for quieter operation. The single engine de Havilland rolled easily onto the beach and out into the calm surf where Elsie pointed it into the wind and took off for Hughes' airport. They touched down ten minutes later, Betsy was rolled out and waiting for them on the tarmac as they touched down in the little bush plane. They went from one plane to the other. Once the checks were done the two Pratt and Whitney R-1830-92 engines sputtered to life. Betsy lumbered as she taxied then, with a healthy roar, took off heading across the eastern mountains to the deserts of Nevada.

Rand and Elsie were always astounded at how unpopulated the 1949 landscape was. The desert was deserted and the mountains pristine. As they approached the secret base they were unsure whether to use the radio to announce their presence and decided to just fly across the airspace and hope they didn't get shot down. It was only a few seconds after deciding this that the radio crackled, "Unidentified PBY, you are entering restricted airspace, please identify."

Elsie responded, "Control this is PBN November Xray-179, here by invitation, requesting clearance to land."

The response was immediate. "November Xray-179 – control, you are clear to land on zero niner romeo. Taxi to tower ramp. Welcome to Groom Lake."

"Roger, runway zero niner romeo taxi to tower ramp."

"Elsie, look at the size of that runway."

Rand wheeled the Nomad around for their landing approach. The runway network loomed ahead of them. The largest was over six miles long. The big plane gracefully touched down and taxied over to the tower. The Nevada desert in September was very hot and dry as they stepped out of the plane. Two men in suits were there to greet them.

"Mr. and Mrs. Carter, we're delighted to have you join us. I'm Agent Adams, this is Agent Jefferson."

"Nice to meet you. I was hoping to be greeted by Abraham Lincoln but I guess he was unavailable, hmm?"

Elsie elbowed Rand in the ribs.

"Yes Mr. Carter, like everything at this site, even our identities are classified. Yours are as well."

He handed them security badges.

"John Buck and Jane Doe." Rand looked at Elsie, then at agent Adams. "You people need a creative department."

"This way please." The agent led them into one of the large hangars next to the tower.

Inside was the frame of a long plane. It appeared to be a large glider. Elsie nudged Rand.

"Doesn't that look like a U2?"

"That was in the sixties wasn't it?"

"There's a lot of years of development before that though. It might be the first prototype."

They passed it by and headed up a set of steel, lattice work stairs that wound up to an office overlooking the hangar. In the office was a large, oval conference table with high-backed leather chairs all around. One whole wall was a blackboard with aeronautical drawings and mathematical equations scribbled hastily. Elsie looked at Rand who had a wry smile on his face.

"Don't say it."

"What is it with secret bases and oval tables?"

"Rand, stay focused."

Agent Adams offered them a seat while Agent Jefferson poked his head into a door to another room and said, "Sir, our guests are here." A minute later a large man wearing a lab coat came out. He was the height of Rand at six foot two, in his late fifties with greying hair and a portly weight. He held out a heavy fingered hand to them.

"Welcome both of you. So sorry for the formalities but they are necessary in a place like this. I'm Louis McAllister, head of operations for this facility and my job right now is to brief you."

They exchanged pleasantries then got down to business.

"I mentioned that I'm in charge of this facility, but you have to understand that there are many facilities here at Groom Lake. The one you're in involves this hangar and an attached tool and machine shop behind us. At no time are you to leave either of these buildings, understood?"

Both of them nodded.

"Good, here's the basic operations of the place. You've met Agents Adams and Jefferson. They are CIA, I am employed by Lockheed. Those are the only two entities involved. No military, no federal or state authority, not even the FBI gets in here.

This installation does not exist. Never, under any circumstances are you to reveal anything that might lead someone to believe that there is anything out here but sand. Don't even tell 'em you've been to Groom Lake. If you need a cover story then we'll give you one."

"The place is Top Secret, we understand."

"Right. Well, no need to belabour the point. The reason you're here is—"

"We know why we're here Mr. McAllister. Please, just tell us how we can help."

McAllister ran his hand over his head and got up. "The project on the floor is for a high altitude spy plane. We have the cameras that can take high resolution pictures of the Soviets now we just need to get over their airspace undetected."

Rand broke in, "You need any ideas that might make your plane invisible to radar."

"Exactly."

"In the future Mr. McAllister we can do our job much better if you just get to the point."

McAllister was taken aback slightly. "I'm sorry, I thought you might need to be brought up to speed on the state of our achievements thus far."

Elsie took over. "Here are a few ideas for you to try." She picked up the eraser and looked at McAllister.

"Please, go right ahead." He said

She wiped part of the board clean then drew what was essentially a modern F1117 stealth fighter.

"Radar only sees what reflects back to it. So use hard angles and sharp lines to direct radar away. Explore radar absorbent materials that can be applied in lightweight layers to the exterior of the aircraft. Expect to cover every surface meticulously. We have some samples of a material we are working on that you are welcome to improve upon."

"But all of the sharp lines create drag and take away the aircraft's ability to fly."

"Good observation. The answer is to use the fuselage as a lifting body. In the war, the Nazis were working on a flying wing—"

"How do you know that?"

"If we're going to be working together we have to trust each other okay? As I was saying, all of your special projects can benefit from the use of titanium and carbon fibre as the primary materials. Lightweight and rigid is what every airframe should be. The sharp lines create drag, you're correct, but if you're invisible then speed is only a factor for impatient generals. Explore the use of guidance computers and fly-by-wire technology."

"Alright, thank you. We are having difficulties with the power plant as well."

"Yes, we're working on this at Hughes. Rand and I believe the answer is the triple spool high bypass ratio engine. Hughes engineers have been working on our designs for more efficient turbine blades and nozzle guide vanes as well as materials that can handle higher maximum operating temperatures. We can have the research sent to you. We believe we will gain much more ground if we are working in parallel."

McAllister was stunned. "That would be unprecedented. Will Mr. Hughes be willing to share such valuable information."

It was Rand's turn. "Absolutely. We have much more to discover in the years to come. Working in parallel saves us all time and money. Two heads are better than one after all. In the end it's the security of the country and the stability of the world that are at stake. It's not about control, but quality of life. That is what we are working for."

"Well I hope Mr. Hughes agrees with you."

"I can assure you that he does."

"Mr. McAllister as a sign of faith and in the spirit of cooperation I'd like to share with you something we are developing. I cannot disclose it's origin and I need absolute assurance that it will remain in your control at all times."

"Yes of course. We're very good at keeping secrets here."

"It needs to be reverse engineered. It's called an Integrated Circuit or IC chip for short." Rand produced the little chip and handed it to the scientist who took it gingerly.

Elsie explained briefly what it was meant to do, what they would find as they deconstructed it and what the challenges would be.

"But where did you get this? If, as you say, we probably won't be able to build one at this time then who built it? Is it alien?"

"No, it's man made, but unfortunately the man who made it is no longer with us and we have no idea how it was done. An IC chip on this scale is crucial to developing technologies that are small and powerful to get things like your airplane off the ground."

"Thank you. We will get to work on this immediately. Are there more, eh… just in case we accidentally destroy this one."

"No, we have one and you have one. That's it."

"Truly amazing."

"Now we're hoping that perhaps you can help us Mr. McAllister."

"Ah, yes of course for all of this wonderful new input what do you want in return?"

"We think you may have a friend of ours in your employ, we would love to see him again if it's possible."

McAllister's bushy eyebrows raised. "That's it?"

"Like I said Mr. McAllister, Elsie and I work for the benefit of the security of this country and the betterment of the world. That's not a line, it's an ideal that we strive for. It may sound naïve but other than an honest, open dialog, enthusiasm and good will, this is truly all we ask."

"His name is Doctor Remmel. Can you send for him please?"

McAllister's face changed slightly though he clearly tried to cover his reaction. "Remmel you say? Yes, he does work with us on other projects. How do you know him?"

"Oh we go way back."

"I'm sure he would be very glad to see us, it's been so long."

McAllister had a hint of suspicion in his eyes. "Certainly. I'll have him brought up here. Agent Jefferson could you ask Dr. Remmel if he could spare a moment for some old friends?"

The agent nodded, left the room and descended the stairs quickly.

Rand and Elsie waited under the watchful eye of Agent Adams as McAllister stood at the window.

"It doesn't look like much does it? The plane I mean. It's flimsy and awkward."

"It looks like a big glider." Said Rand looking down to the hangar floor, "It will stay aloft without spending much fuel. Of course the size of the wings have directly to do with the density of the atmosphere at operational altitude."

As Rand looked down on the floor all the engineers, mechanics and scientists left the hangar quickly as armed men began pouring through the door.

Rand shot a look at McAllister. "What's going on here?'

Elsie ran over to the window, but McAllister grabbed her arm. "Who are you, where did you come from? Or should I say WHEN did you come from?"

"Let go of me." Elsie spun under the grip of the big man's meaty hand. In an instant she was behind him as the big man crashed to the floor. He yelled out, "Help! I'm being attacked!"

"What do you know about us. Tell me or I'll cut your throat!"

McAllister felt cold steel at his jugular.

"I… I only deduced it from what Remmel has been saying!" McAllister stammered.

Elsie flipped him around and showed him the stapler that she had been holding on him. "I don't need a knife to kill you."

"It's true McAllister. Now call off your dogs before this gets messy." Rand stood over the unconscious Agent Adams holding his .38 caliber revolver.

McAllister, who had just been tossed to the ground like a roped calf believed what they said about their lethal abilities. "Okay, alright. Let's just be calm."

"We're calm. You tell those soldiers out there to stand down."

Elsie hauled the big man to his feet and lead McAllister to the door. He leaned out, "It's alright, false alarm people. Stand down."

The armed men stopped on the stair. "Are you sure sir?"

"Yes yes, there's no problem. The CIA got itchy about our guests and decided to call a security alert without probable cause."

Just then Agent Jefferson came barreling up the stairs through the ranks. "You gave me the signal. I called it on your signal. I need to inspect the pris… guests before we can stand down. You know that. It's protocol."

He looked up to start up the stairs when Agent Adams came out the door. "All clear Agent Jefferson. Everything's okay, just a misunderstanding."

"But Remmel…"

"THAT WILL BE ALL AGENT JEFFERSON!" Adams raised his voice to almost a shout.

"Yes sir. Men, stand down."

They all tromped back down the stairs

Rand stood behind Adams with the .38 in his back.

When all the men had dispersed Rand brought Adams and McAllister back into the room.

"Now. Tell us what you know. What did Remmel say?"

McAllister sighed. "Remmel has been a complete solo venture. He was put here because they didn't know what else to do with him. He claims to have some kind of theory about time travel and actually, his math works. But applied theoretical physics is my area. When he first came here he had occasional episodes where he would babble about losing his legs and his wife. Then, as the bouts became more frequent he went into long incoherent rambles. Once he said something about being followed through time by a couple of pilots… he described you two."

"So you knew this and that's why you sent for us. You wanted to find out what our story was, if Remmel was crazy or right."

"Is he?"

Rand was fuming. "We'd have an easier time telling you if you hadn't pulled that stunt just now don't you think?"

Rand opened Adams' .38, dumped all the bullets out and tossed it onto the table. "There. I'm sorry I had to hit you, but don't ever pull a gun on me again."

Adams just glared at him.

"Rand's right McAllister. We came here in the spirit of patriotism and cooperation and even proved it by sharing ideas and technology. So far all we've got out of it is manhandling and brutish suspicion. Now I suggest that you change your course here or you'll blow this country's best chance at that bright future everyone's always talking about."

McAllister rose slowly and in a thick Russian accent he said, "I'm sorry Mr. and Mrs. Carter I cannot do that."

The Second String

Rand sprang across the table at McAllister, but the big man suddenly exploded with speed. The last thing Rand felt was the giant hammer blow to the side of his head, Elsie's cries rang in his ears. "Raaa—" Not again, he thought.

Montgomery Thompson

Chapter 5

Rain

*'I am standing up at the water's edge in my dream.
I cannot make a single sound as you scream.'*
~Peter Gabriel, Red Rain

The cold. At the dentist? Jaw numb. Eyes, wake, wake.... Rand's consciousness scrambled towards the light. Blinking, he squinted against the pain. He was tied tightly, hands behind his back. The left half of his face was numb. There was blood covering the front of his shirt. He was freezing, soaking wet and had no shoes. The room echoed large, a warehouse. *Just like the movies,* he thought. *I'm tied to a chair in the middle of a warehouse floor with one light shining on me.*

"Are you kidding?" He mumbled as he spat out blood and part of a tooth. Anger rose in him, "ARE YOU KIDDING? A WAREHOUSE AND A CHAIR? IT'S SO CLICHÉ YOU IDIOTS!"

Without a sound a light came on in front of him, illuminating another figure about twenty feet away. They were in a similar state; tied to a chair, head slumped down.

"Elsie? ELSIE!"

"No I'm afraid not Mr. Carter. That one didn't make it. So sorry. We tried to save her after she talked so much, but the poor little woman couldn't take the strain of our... conversation." The big man stood next to the figure across the room.

"McAllister. You son of a—"

Rand was cut out by the big man's booming laughter.

"For being a genius you're not very smart are you? McAllister is a Scottish name. Do I look Scottish to you? I AM RUSSIAN!" He slammed his fist into the ribs of the person in the other chair. Rand could hear the echo of them cracking reverberate through the big room.

McAllister grabbed a fist full of hair and pulled the head back. It was Agent Jefferson.

"Useless CIA scum. He doesn't have the stomach for conversation either. Still. He served our purpose."

"Then let him go, he doesn't know anything."

"Ah but you do Mr. Carter. You have to, because nobody else has heard of this Dr. Remmel.

Who is he? Tell me and I'll let Agent Jefferson live."

"I don't know. He's just a physicist, like you said. We needed his help with our research."

"LIES!" McAllister came at him fast, much faster than he had ever seen a man that size move. He loomed over, putting his sweaty face a hairs breadth away from Rand's.

"You tell me what I want to know or I will tear you from limb to limb and have your parts sent back to Hughes!"

"Show me."

"What?"

"Show me her body."

"Oh, your beloved *"wife"*." McAllister made quotes with his fingers. "She was a spy, you were not married. We can tell, you only put on your rings recently that's how pathetic you are at your job. We are Russian, and we are very good at our jobs. When we create a couple for a cover they are one. They live for years together, even fall in love even though they know they will probably have to kill each other by the time it is over. That is how professional we are. We will do anything, suffer any pain, go through any hardship, make any sacrifice. You and your *'wife'* are not even in same the same league as us. You are outclassed, out smarted, out gunned and now you are out of time. Now, tell me who Remmel is."

This guy goes on like a b-movie script, Rand thought. "You can kill me, you can kill everyone, I still don't know."

A surge of electricity burned through his body. He screamed but it made no sound.

"Who is Remmel?"

"I—" again the searing heat shredded his veins. He felt like his blood was molten metal.

"You talk too slow. I said REMMEL!"

The third jolt sent Rand spinning into unconsciousness.

***

Elsie heard McAllister's Russian accent and immediately knew they had been set up. When Rand launched across the table, she spun on Agent Adams but he grabbed her and put her in a hold with her hand above her head.

Rand was laid out on the table, knocked out cold. McAllister threw him over his shoulder and barked orders at Adams. "Follow me. Stick to the plan."

Adams muscled her into the next room, right behind McAllister. Doors lead to the outside staircase that ran down the back of the hangar. McAllister checked to see if anyone was coming then headed down the stairs. Adams slammed Elsie's head against the door frame but she fought back. The man's face met the back of her head and he released just enough for her to break free. He faced her, drawing another pistol but his gaze followed the truck as it sped away into the desert.

"Chyort voz'mi!"

She swung a hard-hitting right hook but he just smiled at her.

"Bliad!"

His foot lashed out and kicked her in the stomach. The blow sent her sprawling across the floor. She vomited as she tried to rise but Adams was standing over her.

Suddenly shots rang out. "Adams back away from her!"

"Easy Jefferson, I'm on your side remember?" The Russian had slipped back into a perfect American accent.

"What the hell are you doing? Where is McAllister and the other guest?"

Elsie recovered her strength and launched herself up at Adams, grabbing his gun. They both flew over the table and rolled through the doorway into the next room. She stood and brought the gun around but he was too fast. The uppercut drove her sideways through the window sending the gun flying twenty-feet to the hangar floor. Elsie arched backwards through the broken glass and crashed onto the steel stairs six-feet below her. As she tumbled she blacked out. She woke up on the hangar floor. A woman was leaning over her with a cold cloth to her head. Medics were preparing bandages next to her. "Miss? Are you okay? She's coming around."

A man in a suit leaned in, "Mrs. Carter can you tell me what happened? Where are your husband, the professor and my two agents?"

She struggled to focus. "McAllister… Russian agent. Adams too."

"That's impossible!"

"No. It's true. They took Rand."

She was starting to come around fully. The nurse shoved smelling salts under her nose.

"Oh! Okay, okay, get that away! I'm fine." She stood with the help of the head agent. The medics rushed to put a bandage over the cuts on her back.

"Please Mrs. Carter, you're injured."

She stood still and let them do their work.

"No it's true." She quickly told the account of what happened. The agent sprang into action.

"Sound the security alert. Are you okay Mrs. Carter?"

"Elsie please, and yes I'm fine."

The man extended his hand, "Agent Washingt…" He paused, "No, I'm sure you've had enough of that. My name is Talbot, Agent Dave Talbot."

"Honesty. How refreshing. Now how are we gonna find our people?"

The loud speakers barked loudly: *Security alert, this is not a drill. Secure all stations. Lockdown code zebra, code zebra.*

Once she was cleared by the medics Talbot lead Elsie to a golf cart. "Don't you have something faster?"

"They're already gone and I can't see the ground from a car. I can see their tracks in this."

"Wait, so you're going to track them?"

"Yes ma'am, that is correct."

"Dave, my name is Elsie."

"Yes Elsie that's right."

"If you have a fast aircraft, I have a better way."

"We have the fastest."

"I know, get me into it right now."

Talbot whirled the golf cart toward one of the hangars. They whined to a halt as Talbot jumped out and ran up to a guard who yelled. "SMOKE!"

Talbot responded, "Foam. Have this aircraft prepped for immediate departure.' He turned to Elsie. "Where are you headed?"

"I'm going to get some very special equipment from the Hughes Aircraft facility in Culver City California. This gear is top secret."

"Everything is top secret here."

The hangar opened to reveal a long cylindrical plane that resembled a jet fighter from the 60's. It had no paint but look like someone had spent hours shining it. The result was a blinding mirror finish.

"Are you guys trying to get everyone to notice you? Flat light grey from now on, on everything."

Talbot looked at Elsie, "The F-94 Starfire, it doesn't exist. Think you can fly it?"

"Dave, I specialise in flying things that don't exist. Now do me one more thing, get me the head engineer."

The plane was rolled out and given last minute checks. As Elsie finished suiting up she talked with the head engineer. Dave Talbot watched as she intensely described something to the engineer by drawing on paper and waving her arms. In the end, they seemed to have reached an agreement about whatever it was. Then, with help from the ground crew she climbed the short ladder into the Starfire and familiarised herself with the controls.

Elsie gave the all clear and taxied the short distance to the runway as the canopy lowered.

"Hang on baby I'm coming." She said as she punched the throttle. The jet responded immediately and hurtled down the runway. She went full throttle and sped towards Culver City at over six hundred miles per hour. She was on approach at Hughes Aircraft Airport in twenty-three minutes. Elsie had radioed ahead to Hughes who forwarded instructions for her house staff to collect certain suitcases and deliver them to a courier flight that would be waiting at the beach landing area. Hughes' ground crew raced to fuel the plane as the courier landed behind the Starfire and taxied to a halt. Elsie had the suitcases tucked into the plane's bomb storage then climbed back in for the return run to Groom Lake. Twenty-five minutes later she was on the ground and taxiing to a halt.

Agent Talbot was there to meet her. "I've got teams on the ground tracking their location right now. We're closing in."

"Great work but don't attempt a rescue yet. It's too risky to both the captives and the assault force."

"Alright then what's your plan?"

"I'll brief you and your men at the same time, but first I'm gonna need a secure area connected to a ready room to gear up. Assemble a strike team of twelve men that you can absolutely trust with some highly classified technology secrets." She stopped and locked eyes with him. "I'm not kidding Dave, this is 'take to the grave' information you understand?"

"Understood."

"I know you're not used to working with females so factor that into your personnel choices. 'Ma'am' will do while we're on mission. As soon as you're done gathering the team meet me alone in the secure area. As a team leader you'll be wearing the same gear as me."

"You're going in as a combatant?"

"You bet your ass I am Talbot. Pay attention and you might learn a thing or two."

Dave Talbot had never encountered a female like her in his life. He called in his best agents and ordered them to combat readiness. All of these men had seen action as special forces in World War II. He had them assemble in the ready room to receive the briefing. Then he went to the adjoining secure room where Elsie was preparing.

When he walked in it was completely dark.

"Elsie? Hello?"

As soft voice sounded in his left ear, "Darkness."

He spun and drew his weapon, he couldn't see a thing.

The weapon was snatched out of his hands and Elsie's voice said. "It's terrible being blind."

Then the lights came on. She was standing in front of him dressed all in black and wearing a bizarre array of equipment including a helmet that made her head look like an insect. She handed him back his sidearm.

"Say, what's the big idea?"

"Take it easy. It's because I can see in the dark. Here."

She came over and placed a helmet with the same dark screen as hers on his head. Then she turned off the lights.

"Just lower the visor and the night vision will switch on."

"Night vision? Holy… you weren't kidding! How the heck?"

"Don't ask, just accept it and move on. These are the tools we're going to use to get Rand and your agent. But the longer we wait, the greater the chance that we won't find them alive."

She showed him how to use the night vision and introduced him to the silenced SCAR. Then she suited him up in Rand's body armour and harness. After an introduction to the ear pieces and communications radio she looked him over.

"Good?"

He nodded, "I have—"

"A lot of questions I'm sure, but remember what we talked about. Mission focus. The equipment doesn't matter, just the job at hand. Understand what the tool does and use it, never mind how it works or where it came from."

"The question I was going to ask was, how do I introduce you to the men?"

"Oh, right. I'm Major Carter, U.S. Air Force."

When all the men were assembled, they entered the ready room. All of them stood at attention as Talbot began.

"At ease men. As you all know we have had a top level security beach. Russian agents known to us as McAllister and Adams took two of our people. They are now two hours on the run. I'll turn the details over to the mission leader Major Carter, U.S. Air Force."

Elsie stepped in. The men were shocked. A woman.

"Thank you agent Talbot. That's right I'm a female. Get used to it, it's going to be a trend. But I'm a warrior first and I'll put any son-of-a-bitch in the ground who crosses me or my country. Right now there are two individuals who have done both. I mean to recover our people and make the enemy pay dearly. Are you with me?"

"Yes sir!"

"Ma'am will do."

"YES MA'AM!"

"As you see, Agent Talbot and I are wearing some equipment that you have not seen before. This is special prototype equipment that is classified beyond Top Secret. You have not seen it and there will be no comments or questions about it. If there is something about this equipment that I feel you need to know you will be told, is that clear?"

"YES MA'AM."

'Good, because if you fail in your mission to maintain secrecy, it is punishable by death. Now here's the plan. Split into teams of six each. Good. You six will be Team Alpha and you six are Team Golf…"

"Uh, ma'am? Sorry, why not team Bravo?"

"Ah, a thinker. Good question. What's your name soldier?"

"Nickelson ma'am."

"Well Nickelson, if the enemy intercepts any transmissions between us they will assume we have seven teams, A through G. It will scare the hell out of them and they will be looking for large numbers, subsequently enabling us to chew up and spit out their divided forces. Any more questions? Good.

Once we get intel back on our target location we will begin our attack, infiltrating from two separate entry points; Alpha on primary, Golf on secondary. I want all entries dynamic with…" The men were looking around at each other, confusion on their faces. "You don't know about dynamic entry?"

Talbot came up and whispered to her. "We have no idea what you're talking about."

"Okay then, I'll show you. Once you know the right way to do it, you'll never do it any other way."

She took them to the door and showed them how to stack up and enter a room with their weapons ready to assail any forces they met. Once they had this down she added the use of different fields of fire and modified the weapons they carried to compliment each other. After trying it three times each they had it down. It took just over an hour.

She talked with and got to know each of member of the team in the short time given. By the end of the short training all of them were impressed with not only the method of entry but in her ability to command.

"Excellent work teams. I can see why Agent Talbot selected you."

Just as she spoke, a runner came with the intel they had been waiting for. Elsie told the teams to run the drill another three times and then prepare their gear for night ops. Then she and Talbot looked over the information.

"A warehouse in Rachel, Nevada, really?"

Talbot looked at her. "What's wrong?"

"Nothing it's just so cliché. That's the best the KGB could do?"

Talbot looked at her surprised. "Do this all the time do you?" She continued as if she didn't hear him.

"The roof is just tin. It looks like there are rooms in the back."

"The scouts say that they heard the sounds of interrogation coming from the main area."

"Okay, it's a smash and grab. I want to be in and out of there in under a minute."

'But don't you want to take out the enemy?'

"I've got that handled. We just need to go in, lay down cover fire, grab our people and get out. Medical will be standing by in an ambulance behind the bus. Assign a medic for each team and leave them to provide cover on extraction."

"There are two medics already in, Nickelson and Wiley. Nickelson's a surgeon."

"Ah, the one with questions. Okay, good."

"Golf, that's you, takes the back." She pointed to two of the grenades hanging from his harness. "Flash bangs in the side windows here like we talked about, then dynamic entry. Sweep each room in one flowing motion. I'll count five after you enter. Alpha will do a quiet entry to the main room and retrieve the hostages. I will radio to you as soon as we've got them and are on our way to the exit. As soon, and I mean AS SOON as you get my call you high tail it out of there because I'm bringing the rain."

"What does that mean?"

"You'll see. Just get the heck out of there. You do not want to get caught in the rain." She was deadly serious.

Talbot looked scared. "Okay, we'll do a quick and orderly exfil."

"The medics will provide cover, but we can't see you until you are around the corner. So head straight out from the building at least fifty yards before you turn left back to the bus. Questions? No? Okay let's brief the teams."

Soon they were rolling towards the little town of Rachel, Nevada. The convoy consisted of a school bus and an ambulance. Elsie scanned ahead as night began to fall. The team's flashlights were given red lenses so not to ruin their eyes ability to see in the dark. They were encouraged to keep one eye closed at all times to condition their vision during the trip and not to look anywhere in the direction of the bus' headlights.

Rachel was a one road town. The warehouse was a half a mile down the road from the town center and surrounded by nothing but flat, unfenced desert. They departed the road and made a bee-line for the warehouse. As they came within sight of the building, they shut off the engines and lights and let the vehicles roll as close as one hundred yards. Elsie told the drivers not to touch the brakes in case they squeaked. While the attack was going on, the drivers were to start the engines and turn the vehicles around for a hasty evacuation. As soon as the vehicles slowed enough, the teams disembarked and headed for their entry locations. Elsie gave Talbot's team a minute to get into place.

"Alpha ready, copy?"

"Roger. Golf ready."

"Go."

***

Rand hung lifeless in the chair. He had returned to consciousness but didn't have the strength to hold his head up though he could tell that his interrogators had left the room. Thirst clawed at his throat and his body felt like it was in flaming ruins. He heard a small sound from across the room.

"She… live… sheees uh… live."

"I know. Be quiet, save your strength. They're coming for us."

Agent Jefferson made some more noises. Rand thought it sounded like crying.

"Stop it. Don't let them win."

The noises stopped. A door opened to his right.

"Ah, awake I see. Did you have a nice nap? I have considered your request and I will show you her body if you are willing to cooperate. What do you know about Dr. Remmel? What was he working on? How do you know him? These questions are easy. It's just like being at a dinner party having casual conversation. Just be polite, tell me and all of this miserable situation will go away. No more pain, no more suffering. Consider poor Mr. Jefferson over there. You don't even know his real name and yet don't you want to save him? You are not saving him, you are causing him to die!"

McAllister's giant ham fist pounded Rand in the ribs. Jefferson shrieked in pain at the same time.

"Ah such a beautiful symphony. The music of the soul." McAllister slugged Rand in the ribs again and again as Jefferson was electrocuted. This time he made blubbering noises as he mumbled.

"What's that?" McAllister went across the room to Jefferson. "Oh! Really?"

"Poor delusional bastard. She is dead. Isn't she Andreyev?"

"Da boss." A tall man in a black leather jacket loomed in the shadow. "I pushed her through the window and she fell down the stairs to the hangar floor below. Broke her little neck."

"If Andreyev says he killed her, then she is dead. Trust me, he knows his business—"

A loud series of pops shattered the air, blinding and deafening everyone. McAllister ducked while

Andreyev pulled out his pistol and ran to the back where the sound came from. Under layers of sweat and blood, Rand smiled.

***

Team Golf threw in flash-bang grenades then entered the first room just as Elsie had shown them; checking the corners first, each man covering their assigned field of fire as they flooded the room. Talbot, with night vision and the silenced SCAR assault rifle, came first. He shot a figure coming through the opposite door and kept moving into the hall. They continued through the doorway in front of them and entered into a hallway. Talbot held the hallway while his team cleared the four rooms.

"We've got a hostage here!" One of his men told him.

"Get the hostage out and back to the medic. Remember to stay clear of the building." Seconds later the rest of the rooms were cleared but he still hadn't heard from Elsie.

Elsie counted to five then gave the signal, "Go!"

The Second String

They piled through the door. Elsie's SCAR and night vision saw everything. McAllister stood over Rand. Elsie didn't hesitate. The SCAR quietly sent three rounds through his knees. The big man dropped like a bag of stones. Then she was next to Rand. He was a mess. She knew she wouldn't hold it together if she talked to him so she let the team recover him and went to McAllister. He lay on his back looking up at her.

"What are you?" Then a smile came across his face. "Remmel was right. You are from the future."

Elsie shot him in each shoulder then ordered the soldiers to drag him out.

"Golf this is Alpha, objective complete. We're running late. Get out now."

She sprinted for the front door. As soon as she made it out, the roar of a battery of heavy machine guns sounded in the distance above them.

Just as Talbot was beginning to wonder why he hadn't heard any shots from in front, Elsie's voice came over his radio. "Clear. All out"

He barked his orders. "That's it, we're outta here! Move, move!"

The team sprinted out the back door and ran clear of the building. Talbot covered their exit and made sure there were no enemy lying in wait. The bus was in sight when the distant sound of heavy machine gun fire reached his ears.

Suddenly the sky was alight with hundreds of glowing tracer rounds, ripping through the structure and reducing it to rubble in seconds.

He lifted his night vision visor. "Bring the rain. Holy shit, she wasn't kidding."

"Golf leader let's go!"

"Roger, on my way." Talbot sprinted the distance to the bus which was already starting to roll. Elsie was there.

"Alpha captured McAllister, did you get the agent?"

"I shot one person. He's dead in the warehouse."

"Shit! We have to get him. There will be a lot of questions if the locals find the body of an armed man riddled with bullet holes."

Talbot looked back at the warehouse growing smaller in the distance. He could already see the lights of the local sheriff's car.

"It's too late to go back, they're already there. I'm sorry Major, this is my fault."

Elsie tried to conceal her frustration from the men. It was her oversight and she was responsible. The convoy sped at top speed back to the base.

They were greeted by a few medical personnel, all ready to help. Elsie and Talbot stayed hidden in the bus until it pulled up to the ready room doors. They quickly made their way inside with the teams. The men were ecstatic.

"Now that's how you do a raid!" One of the soldiers was saying. They had been forbidden to speak in the bus so Elsie let them chatter a little bit to take the edge off of their nerves. After a minute she had Talbot sit them down for the debriefing.

"Alright men let's sit down and wrap this up so we can all have a shower and some chow. I'll hand it over to the Major."

"Thank you agent Talbot. Congratulations people, you have completed a delicate retrieval. Now I'm sure you all have questions about several points of the operation. I will explain only one of the things that you have seen and the rest you will be expected to forget. You will not talk about it to anyone, including each other. That means no whispering it to the guy in the bunk above you etcetera, etcetera. Zero tolerance will be given. If you are heard saying anything regarding this mission you will be shot on sight. No trial, no courts martial, just shot. And I hope it's me who catches the sorry SOB who would dare betray us. By us I mean everyone in this room. We did this mission as a team and secrecy is the ongoing part of the mission."

She looked at every one of the men in turn.

"What I encourage you to remember is a job well done. Three hostages saved, one enemy captured - the ring leader no less, and one enemy put down like the dog he was."

The men nodded proudly.

"Now, as to what you saw coming out of the sky, that is what I call 'the rain'. When we left on this mission there was a specially modified C-123 Provider covering our every move. This particular aircraft carries six .50 cals all pointing out of one side of the plane. At a specific time in the mission, it rolled into a slow circling turn and six gunners unleashed hell on that target. In the future, I will be pushing for close air support like this for all ground troops. How do you like the idea?"

The room erupted in applause, cheers and whistles.

"Good, it's unanimous. Chief engineer liked the idea too. I'm hoping Congress will approve. Now. ATTENTION!"

The men jumped to attention.

"Gentlemen it's been an honour to serve with you. I hope to see you again. If not, I wish you well in all of your endeavours."

She went down the line and saluted each man and shook their hand, calling them by name. Then she left and entered the secret room where she got out of the black ops gear and stowed it all neatly in the suitcase. A moment later Talbot came in and started removing the gear in silence.

When it was all packed away and they stood in civilian clothes he shook her hand. "I'll never forget you."

"You'll never forget that weapon." She joked.

"In the short time that I've known you, you have shown as much if not more courage and leadership than any man I've served with. Thank you."

"David Talbot, you're a rare breed. But we're not out of this pickle yet."

"Don't worry, I'm headed to the PR department to help them spin this. We'll blame it on fireworks for the cover story but then release rumours that the CIA had been tracking an illegal arms dealer through the area. He was hiding out in the warehouse when something set off his ammunition stash."

"Clever." She shook his hand, picked up the suitcases and turned to go to Rand. "Stop by the hospital if you get a chance. I'd like to introduce you to my husband." She said as the door closed. Dave Talbot's mouth dropped open.

A driver waited for her outside. When she arrived she was shown to Rand's room. The doctor briefed her before she went in.

"Agent Jefferson is in a coma, we're trying to stabilise him now."

"What are his chances?"

"It's about fifty-fifty right now."

"What about my husband?"

"He stable now. He was in shock from the beatings and electrocution. He has four broken ribs and his jaw has been dislocated. It will be at least a week before he can talk normally. Energy levels will be low and he should spend as much time as possible resting. That means he should only get up to go to the bathroom."

Elsie quietly opened the door to his room. He watched her come in and tried to smile. His face was black and blue and one of his eyes was red. His jaw and mouth were swollen. She came to him and held him softly, speaking words of love and tenderness. They both cried away the misery. After awhile she drew back and looked at him.

"We have McAllister, he's alive. They will be interrogating him now.

Rand winced at the word.

"Don't think about it hon, it's nothing to do with us now."

"I just want to go home." He murmured. His face was numb and he couldn't get his mouth to work properly.

"I know, so do I. We'll go as soon as the doctor clears you."

"No, I want to go home, to New River. Back to the life we built."

"Oh baby." Elsie started crying all over again. The sight of him so battered. They had been through so much. "We'll get there."

Just then came a knock on the door. Elsie sat up and wiped her eyes, then went and opened the door. It was one of the soldiers from the raid.

"I'm sorry to disturb you ma'am. Agent Talbot asked me to tell you that they have identified the unknown hostage as Dr. Remmel."

Elsie knew she had failed to disguise her shock.

"Are you okay ma'am?"

"Yes I'm fine. It's just good news that I didn't expect to hear. Where is he?"

"He's just coming out of ER, but he can be put in any room you like."

"Put him in the adjacent room to this one and please ask Agent Talbot to stop by here as soon as possible."

"Yes ma'am."

"Oh and Wiley, it is Wiley right?"

"Yes ma'am."

"Get some R&R, you've earned it."

The soldier smiled gratefully. "Yes ma'am."

The door closed. "Rand did you hear that?"

"You got Remmel." He said in a slur.

"Yes baby, soon we'll be on our way home."

After about half an hour another knock came at the door. Elsie answered it, it was Talbot.

"I heard you wanted to see me."

"David yes, come in. Rand, this is Agent David Talbot, his actual name. He was the leader of the second team on the mission."

"Thank you so much David." Rand said with a slur.

"It was my honour sir. Your wife has been one of the finest military leaders I've served under, and that includes Normandy."

"Normandy? Good Lord. Thank you so much for everything you did then and tonight." It was painful every time he tried to speak but Rand felt that his thanks was the least the man deserved.

"Thank you sir, I'm just doing my job."

Elsie bent down over Rand, "Get some rest, I'll be right back." She stepped outside with Talbot.

He lit into her as soon as the door closed. "Elsie, I had no idea he was really your husband!" He looked at her with renewed admiration and thought, she ran that raid like clockwork and the whole time she must have been dying inside.

"Yes, and now I feel that you are one of the only people we can trust. Is there a secure place we can talk?"

He nodded and lead her down the hall to a private meeting room.

"I think you've got a mole, at least one, maybe several."

"I am of the same opinion."

"If that's the case then we need to lock this place down. Remmel, Rand and I have different pieces of information that if put together could really be a game changer on a global level. Right now we're all in the same place and they know it. I expect them to make their play soon."

"Alright. Thanks for bringing this to my attention. I'll assemble the men from the team."

"Good. Let's get them in here in shifts. The gear is also a big piece of bait though I'm not sure if they know about it yet."

"Where is it?"

"Don't worry about it, it's safe. Right now get your home office to run thorough checks on everyone. Look for anyone who came in groups of two or more. Reissue security badges. Confiscate the old ones without warning and have them thoroughly inspected."

"No disrespect Major, but I can do my job."

Elsie sighed with resignation. "David, I'm sorry. Yes, of course you can. I have every confidence in you."

"While you are tending to Mr. Carter, write down any ideas that you have. Two heads are better than one."

"Will do. And David, thank you."

"We'll get this cleaned up Elsie I promise."

Two combat ready soldiers were placed at Rand's door and the hallway was sandbagged with a machine gun emplacement. The whole installation was on lockdown. No one was permitted in or out. Air patrols kept a tight watch on the perimeter. The CIA home office found three more suspects. All of them were with Lockheed and had entered the base with McAllister. The only CIA double agent so far was Adams, aka: Andreyev.

The newspaper from Rachel, Nevada read that a fire in a warehouse overnight had destroyed the building. The cause of the fire was unknown. No bodies had been found.

Montgomery Thompson

Chapter 6

Underway

'As is our confidence, so is our capacity.'
~William Hazlitt

The morning sun drew long shadows across the desert. Rand swivelled slowly out of bed and propped himself up. His body was weak from the electrocution and the doctor had told him that there was a lot of internal tissue damage. His legs shook slightly, but he could walk and made his way over to the cot where Elsie was sleeping and gently woke her.

"Hi."

"What are you doing? You should be in bed!"

"I'm gonna go talk to Remmel. Wanna come?"

"Don't you think we should wait a day or two?"

"We're talking, not running a marathon."

She rolled her eyes and tossed the blanket off of her, "Okay, as long as you feel up to it."

They surprised the soldiers in the hallway who snapped to attention. Elsie greeted them "At ease gentlemen, have you had breakfast? No? Nurse, could you arrange for some breakfast for these heroes please?"

Rand thanked them both for the rescue and continued to amble over to Remmel's room. Remmel was a slender man. He was balding with white hair and a large nose flanked by hollow eyes that were unusually close together. A pair of large, square glasses rested on the bedside table.

Rand tapped on the door as he opened it. "Hello?"

Remmel looked up from his newspaper and said in a thick German accent "Good morn… you!"

The doctor scrambled to get out of bed. His breakfast flew as he got tangled in the sheets and fell to the floor. The nurses came in the door with the soldiers close behind. Rand and Elsie got out of their way.

"You can't have me! What are they doing here? They want to kill me!"

The nurses were helping him up. The soldiers were helping the nurses. Rand started to leave but Elsie stopped him.

"No. We're going to wait this out. He'll see that we mean him no harm."

Remmel continued to rant but his strength quickly failed him and he grew quiet.

Elsie moved in. "Dr. Remmel we do not want to kill you. We don't mean you any harm at all."

One of the soldiers spoke up. "She's the one who lead the mission to save you. She's the reason you're still alive."

"No, no she just wants to interrogate me!"

"No I don't. I just need your help. Please! Please Dr. Remmel just hear me out then we'll leave you alone I swear."

Elsie was at his bedside now, holding his hand. The look on her face was pleading. He looked at her as realisation slowly creeped across his face.

"I… remember…"

Elsie turned to the nurses, "You have to leave now. Guards keep everyone away from this room. Stay within calling distance. And no one, I mean no one goes into our room."

"Yes ma'am."

"Thank you. Also, send for Agent Talbot."

Remmel looked at Rand "I remember now. You were there at the controls. I showed you how to use them. It was there, at Montauk."

"Yes, we saw you. But when was that?"

"I was in the TSS facility in 1966. All of my research had been moved there. We had just completed the installation when the control unit started to hum… and there you were. When I came here I started to forgot…I got confused and paranoid. That why…I thought you were sent from the future to kill me."

"No, not at all doctor. We were trying to get back to our time."

"When? When are you from?"

"Two thousand fourteen."

"Oh my sweet Lord! I had no idea it went that far."

"It's a long story. We just want to know how to control the TSS to get back to our time."

"So you have been looking for me?"

"Yes," Elsie said, "I have children. We have a life."

"I am so sorry. I cannot help you. The control unit is gone. I left it behind in another time."

"What? What do you mean?"

"When I saw you in 1966 I jumped on the controls that instant and tried to travel to 1943. It sent me here… to the same time as you."

'Yes, the God string.' Elsie interrupted, "it snapped you here because you were already here. Not only here in this time but here at this facility. You met yourself, that's why you couldn't remember." The whole picture formed in her mind, she knew what had happened now.

"Dr Remmel you met yourself, here at this base. Just like you wrote about; you merged. Your future-self merged with your 1949 self as soon as you got within range of each other. With no one from the future near you, you succumbed to the influence of this time and began to forget. It was almost a loop, but then we came looking for you."

Remmel scrunched up his face as he followed the train of thought. "And now that you're here I am starting to remember. Yes, yes! It's all making sense. My God! I thought I'd lost my mind and so did everyone else. That's why they sent me off base. That's when McAllister and that other… horrible man took me prisoner."

"You're safe now, don't worry."

"But you two did not forget, correct?'

Rand shrugged then immediately regretted it. "Yes Doctor. You're theory was correct. Elsie and I haven't forgotten a thing."

"You a couple?"

"Yes." Elsie beamed.

"That also make s big difference, love is very powerful. Were you a couple before you travelled?"

"No. We both woke up one morning and everyone on the planet was gone. We theorise that earth was stopped in time by a nanosecond and that we, because of some deep sleep state, kept moving forward. It created a new timeline."

Remmel's eyes went wide. "What? The whole Earth? That's impossible. You would need the energy from something the size of a star to create that kind of event. My device could never accomplish that. It would be ash if I used even a hundredth of that kind of power. But for you two, as long as you are together, since you are the only two people in FirstTime you can never forget."

"We have an idea what may have caused the event. We call it the 'Happening'." It definitely wasn't your machine. Your design is small and elegant. But we think that after you disappeared in 1966 they couldn't get it to work. So they built and built until they had an accelerator so large… well, you'd have to see it to believe it." Elsie changed the subject. "Listen Dr. Remmel, we need to find the controller. Right now they are building the facility you were at in sixty-six. You said they moved the controller there, from where? Is it here?"

Remmel took her arm in his hand, his eyes bright.

"No. I told you, it didn't come along with me. But it may be there in Montauk in the underground base."

"How? If you didn't build it then how could it exist?"

"Ah, but I did build it. I built it in fifty-two. Don't you see, you brought it back with you!"

"Oh my God Rand, he's right. It's probably still there, the room and everything right where we used it."

"Dr. Remmel, Montauk was a base in the war. From what it looks like in our time they have always been working on it. Could it be that they're building on it and don't know that the control unit is there? It's might even be fused into the rock... Elsie..."

"No, haven't you read my displacement theory? The Higgs field won't permit two units of mass to occupy the same space."

"That's how it got there. We brought it with us. They're excavating what they built…"

"Dr. Remmel in our time the TSS is a huge facility. The accelerator runs for miles and miles in a loop. The cooling tubes alone are over four stories high and the whole thing in underground."

"My word! That means that the main—"

"Yes, it's massive, but when Rand and I found it only a small section of it was revealed. It was completely embedded in the rock like it had been there since the beginning of time."

"So that means that we must have brought it with us when we came here, and the government excavated it later."

"That doesn't make sense. Again, the Higgs field won't—"

"Yes, you said that—"

"Stop interrupting me! I am trying to explain. Arriving to a time through a time/space conjunction will not allow for physical dual-occupation of matter! The only way that could occur is by a type 2 or higher civilisation as defined by the Kardashev scale. They could conceivably possess the technology to…how do I say…teleport matter over a distance. To translocate something that large it might even be bordering on a Type 3."

"Are you saying that aliens are responsible?" Rand was shocked.

"I'm a scientist, we don't jump to conclusions. I am saying that man does not have the capacity to build something that large, not even in two-thousand fourteen no matter what the comic books predict about the year two thousand and beyond. I am a idealogical futurist among my other pursuits and I have a keen interest in how society will grow. There is no possibility that we will come anywhere close to becoming even a type one civilisation in the early two-thousands. If what you say is actually there then I assure you, man did not make it and therefore man did not control it. Whatever created your 'Happening' was not a human endeavour." Remmel stopped., breathing heavily and pushed his glasses up on his nose.

"Fuck me." Rand muttered.

"That is not to say…" Remmel started up again. "that the event occurred as you experienced it. It may have been created on a different time string. Did you notice that the people you eventually ran into in your new time were different in any way?"

"No, there are no people. No one. The planet is completely deserted. It's like they just disappeared in the middle of what they were doing. We've been to the UK, to the States, it's all the same. No one. They all just vanished - poof!"

"Then it was you, the split was created to accommodate you. I wonder if the innocence factor..." He trailed off in thought.

"What do you mean?" Elsie pushed. "What is the innocence factor?"

"It is one part of my theory that a new string will be created only for those souls who are innocent, those souls who did not create the event. The event has to have happened 'to' you. Not to say that you are free of sin or anything like that, just that you were completely unaware of the event. Oh, also, you would have to have been astral travelling at the time. Were you?"

"Well," Rand looked at Elsie surprised that they might have been right all along. "We actually thought that might be the case. We each were sleeping so deeply that we markedly recall that fact."

"Well then I would say..." Remmel got a twinkle in his eye. "that the time line, the God string that we are in now is yours. The two of you were the first ones in it. God himself created it for you and now anything you do, even travel through time, will be done in this string. In this time the two-thousand fourteen that you know is devoid of people. Your 'happening' is destined, but anything before that will be populated. Be prepared that reality and history as you knew it might be radically altered."

"How could there be a TSS in both times?" Rand continued to struggle through the reasoning. "Besides, we hadn't brought it back yet. We would have found it in Montauk the first time either fully constructed or under construction with the excavation included. There would have been unbelievably huge tunnels everywhere."

"Ah, that one is easy." Remmel said. "It is because time happens all at once. To God there is no then and now, it is all happening simultaneously."

"So everything that happens, already is?"

"And anything that's going to happen—"

"Is already happening, precisely. You are very good at this you two. I can see why you are a couple." Remmel smiled and nodded.

"Elsie this is a good thing. It means that the ISS is in Montauk and up and running."

"Yes Rand, but it doesn't mean we know how to operate it any better than we did before."

"Then we have to bring Dr. Remmel with us." Rand turned back to Remmel. "You don't mind coming with us just to help us get back do you? Go whenever you like after that, just please help us get back to our time."

"Of course this must be done." The doctor agreed, "But I must bring my wife too."

They both looked at him.

"Your wife?"

Remmel told him his whole story. He came back to get his wife. She left him because he had lost his legs.

"She is a strong and proud woman. She did not want a cripple for a husband. I worked for the Nazis during the war but I lost my legs in a raid in 1943. The Americans captured me and brought me here. I had no problem working for them, I was never a dedicated Nazi. My wife however, is fanatical. She practically worshipped Hitler."

"I read some of your papers doctor. You used the title of Reverend as well, are you still religious?"

"Yes, all of my research depends on my faith. Science does not oppose God, it explains God's creation you see."

"The God string."

"Exactly. And now it seems that I wasn't very far off the mark."

Elsie stood. "Tell you what gentlemen, let's have some breakfast brought in and we can get this all sorted out and make some plans."

Remmel agreed. Elsie ordered food in then Remmel continued to tell them about his wife, her involvement in the Nazi party and her reasons for leaving him.

"She needed a man who was whole, not a cripple. The Nazis believe in a master race, strong and potent. She wanted me to be a soldier - an officer of distinction fighting for the fatherland. I just wanted to continue my work. I'm starting to wish now that I had listened to her."

"Doctor I'm sorry, but as a woman and a wife I have a hard time believing that a woman who loves you would abandon you in your hour of need. Lots of people lost limbs in the war came home to loving families and spouses."

"She is Aryan and still believes in the superior stock. But I love her, she is my everything."

"Where is she now?"

"As far as I know she is still in Germany. When I was taken to America after the raid she fled and would not come."

"Doctor they are still rounding up Nazis left and right." Elsie said. "I doubt she's still in

Germany. Are you sure she hasn't been captured by the Russians?"

"No, they would have used her against me when I was held captive. They don't know where she is."

Suddenly a light went on in Rand's head "I know where she might be!" He sputtered.

"Oh!" Elsie snapped he finger and pointed at him, nodding affirmation. "That's right Rand."

"Argentina!" They both said together.

"What? Why do you think that?"

Elsie explained. "In our time they discovered that the Nazis all fled to Argentina. The government there protects them."

"Then we need to find my wife before the Americans do… or worse, the Russians. That is the condition I have if I am going to help you." Remmel was suddenly very stern.

"Rand, can I talk with you outside for a minute?"

They went out into the hall just as Talbot arrived.

"Talk about timing." Elsie looked at him curiously.

"Good morning Carters. Wow, the nurses told me you were ambitious Mr. Carter, look at you up and walking around."

"Good morning David. Yes, he doesn't stay down for long, even under doctors orders." She gave him a teasing scowl.

"Call me Rand, please." Rand murmured.

"What can I do for you this morning?"

"Is the CIA still looking for Nazis?"

Talbot was surprised by the direct question. "Yes we are, but not as much as the Israelis."

"Well, I think we can help your search, but it's a trade. We need to recover someone who is with them."

"Let me get my boss on the phone. He has already been informed about you both regarding the raid."

"I suspect the CIA would know all about our dealings with Hughes."

"Yes, but as a friend I have to tell you that the FBI has been looking into your accounts and identities."

"I thought Howard had sorted all that out."

"Well Mr. Hughes isn't exactly popular with the current administration."

"True. Thanks David we really appreciate the candid attitude. Can I ask why though? Why the trust I mean."

"Well… I sort of… have a hunch about you two. I believe you are who you say you are, but there's more to it. I understand the need for secrecy certainly. Nevertheless, that gear was like nothing I've ever seen before."

"You think we're aliens or something?"

"No, the equipment was clearly made for humans. There is just a lot that is unexplained about the both of you, and Dr. Remmel too."

Rand gave her a look, "You showed him the gear?"

"We used it on the raid honey, he wore your stuff. Under the circumstances I didn't think you'd mind."

Rand put his face in his hand and thought it through. Elsie turned back to Talbot.

"David, I feel comfortable telling you about us, whether Rand does, I don't know. But your boss couldn't know. It would have to stop at you. Unfortunately I believe that would be a violation of your oath as an agent."

"I understand. You are correct in assuming that my loyalties are very strong and I take my oath seriously to be sure. However, in no way does it require that I divulge personal secrets to anyone unless it is a threat to national security. Is what you are proposing to tell me a threat to national security?"

"No. It's about who we are and where we came from. There are technology secrets attached to it but that technology is not a threat to anyone but me, Rand and Dr. Remmel simply because the Russians have a hunch who we are and they want the secrets."

"Okay then. You have my word, your secrets are safe. I will also add that because the enemy wants what you know then I am oath sworn to make sure that doesn't happen. So, assisting you appears to be in alignment with my oath."

"Rand?"

He had reached his resolve, "Alright, your trust and his word is all I need."

"Okay. Let's go back in and talk with Remmel."

They introduced Talbot to the doctor. He was tentative at first but as Rand and Elsie told their story he began to realize that the agent was trustworthy. Remmel contributed the parts where he was involved along the various timelines. By the end of the story Talbot only had a few questions to clear up some details. Then he sat back and put his hand to his head.

"That explains a lot."

"Well, it's the truth. Whether you believe it or not."

"Oh I believe you, I'm just... I don't know. This is a lot to take in."

Elsie left to fetch one of the large suitcases. When she came back she took out a small, plastic wrapped square package and handed it to Talbot.

"What's this?'

"MRE. Meal, ready to eat. It's like K-rations but updated. These were for US Marines. Look at the date."

"Keep until two thousand twenty four. Manufactured in April, two thousand twelve. U.S. Marine Corps... my God."

"Like I said. Rand and I live in New River..."

"Marine Corps Air Station, yes. Thanks. This really brings home the reality of your story." Talbot just looked at them both for a second, then he clenched his eyes shut and rubbed his face. "You poor people. What have you been through?"

"We're okay Dave, just want to get home." Rand assured him.

"Okay. Now. Dr Remmel is looking for his wife, who is still a Nazi in hiding. Where is she?'"

"Buenos Aires."

"Oh headquarters won't go for that at all. Argentina is strictly off limits. They have so many problems down there it's hard to even know where to start. An American would stick out like a sore thumb."

"Well, we could go. You have a strike team now right?" Rand suggested.

Elsie looked none too keen on the idea. "Rand, you're in no shape—"

"Hon, by the time you train your boys for this kind of mission I'll be right as rain."

A light went on in Elsie's brain. "Wait a minute - no darlin', not right as rain - you'll be the rain."

Talbot looked at him with a smile.

Rand looked at them both. "What? What does that mean?"

"Oh! She hasn't showed ya that one…you'll see." Talbot laughed.

She kissed him, "You're gonna love it."

Rand shrugged. "You two work out the details, I'm bushed. Dr Remmel, we'll get your wife back, but Elsie and I need to know how to use the controls on the TSS. It seems to just want to snap us all over the place."

"That is no problem Mr. Carter, they are very rudimentary. I'll write them down and give them to your wife."

Rand said goodnight and went back to the room to sleep. There was something in the way that Remmel said *your wife* that made gave him a creepy feeling. *Relax.* He thought as he drifted off. *An ex-Nazi Reverend Doctor that built a time machine, what's not creepy about that?*

Elsie sat with Remmel a while longer. He explained the controls briefly and made some sketches on a napkin. Then he abruptly said that he was tired and going to sleep. He was not to be disturbed by anyone. Elsie felt like he was saying: *There, that's what you wanted, now leave me alone.*

She looked in on Rand then went and worked out more details with Talbot.

"Argentina is a long way David. I'll need the C-123 for this raid, but there's no way it's going to us fly all the way down there."

"I was thinking about that. There's the XCG-20A which is essentially a jet powered version of the C-123. But it's too fast to jump out of, too loud to be stealthy and there's no way we can get a jungle landing strip long enough for it."

"Besides that, we'll need the C-123's ground support capabilities. This operation is going to require some over-the-top logistical planning. What resources do we have?"

"The agency has a lot of resources after the war, and I have a few of my own."

"Can we afford to tell them about the Nazis? Once they know, it will be practically impossible to get in on the operation. There's no way they would let us have Remmel's wife if she's down there."

"You're right. The CIA must be the same in 2014 as it is now, they're not keen on sharing."

"We have to do it ourselves. That means getting the team and the C-123 within mission distance of Buenos Aires."

"That's fourteen hundred miles round trip. I'm thinking we will need to fly to the coast, probably Texas somewhere. Then we have to get the plane on board a ship."

"It's got to be at night and in secret. No shipyard is going to have a landing strip next to it unless it's Navy."

"Too many questions and eyes to use the military, although I might be able to get a night refuelling out of Alamogordo. The base Commander works with us all the time on night test flights."

"Good, make it happen. Now, when we get to the coast we'll need a flat, empty stretch of beach to land and prep the plane for shipping. Then…" Elsie tugged on her ear in thought. "I'm thinking maybe rolling the plane up onto a big barge right from the beach. Do you think that's possible?"

Talbot thought it over for a second. "Yeah. We'll need a tractor and the sand will have to be really compact, but it can be done. The ramp design will be critical. We'll have to carry it on the plane. I'm sure that some of my contacts would know of a tug captain who would be willing to do it. But Elsie all of this costs money and I'm not talking about pocket change. How are we going to finance this operation?"

"Rand and I are loaded."

She said it so bluntly that he had to laugh.

"That's right, I forgot. Capone! But are you willing to blow your whole fortune on this?"

"We have to get back to our time Dave. We're not interested in taking a bunch of out-of-date money with us. So the answer is yes, whatever it takes. We'll blow it all if we have to, but I think your seriously underestimating what I mean by 'loaded'. I mean we're loaded by twenty-fourteen standards. In today's standards, we're billionaires."

"Great! Sounds like this is going to be the best financed mission I've ever been on."

"So, back on track – tractor, barge… David do they have oil derricks in 1949? I'm talking about the platforms out in the Gulf of Mexico that drill for oil."

"Ah, I see... yes there are some drilling operations out there. They just started doing that a few years ago I heard. There's some kind of drill platform that they tie barges and ships up to... I think I see where you're going with this: here to beach, beach to barge, barge to ship. You're a tactical whizz."

"Thank you. Any thoughts on the ship?"

"Leave it to me, I have one in mind. If it's available it would be perfect. We might have to modify the plane to fit in it though."

"I'm thinking of modifying the wings to fold."

"That should do it. Let me get the details on the measurements. I'll contact them when we're done here. Oddly enough, the ship and the plane have the same name."

"Provider?"

"That's right."

"There's that old serendipity again." Elsie just shook her head and continued. "The next items are about where to base ourselves in South America and locating a local resource for intel on the Nazis. As you said, white people are going to stick out like a sore thumb."

Talbot finished adding the task to his list.

"My contact down there will be perfect, if I can get him. How about we reconvene tomorrow morning with Rand?"

She agreed then went to talk to the Chief Engineer. She was going to need a few more modifications to the plane.

The next morning they briefed Rand on their plans. He was excited to help but realised the best thing he could do for awhile was to rest. Talbot told them that had contacted a friend of his in Uruguay.

"Gerardo De Leon, he's Panamanian intelligence currently living in Uruguay. If he can find a small strip in the northern Argentinean jungle, it will be out of the way of prying eyes but just close enough for the mission. We went through training together, he's a good man… at least he was. That area of the world is rife with corruption. Still, he might be able to help me out if he knows he'll come out on top."

Elsie knew what Talbot was getting at. "Would two-hundred and fifty thousand persuade him to our side?"

Talbot blanched. "For that much he'd buy us the whole country. Three dollars a week down there makes a man wealthy."

"Okay, then two-fifty's your budget. Get us good intel working around the clock in Buenos Aires."

Over the next week Rand healed rapidly. He still had a couple of weeks to full recovery but he could make his way around the installation. Talbot had made sure they had full access to every area. They began to get to know most of the people who worked on the base. The raid had done a lot for their credibility and they made many friends.

Talbot had to cover his bases with CIA headquarters. He made up cover stories to explain the Carter's continued presence at the secret facility. His bosses were told that Elsie, while waiting for her husband to recover, was training the new team in the techniques she had shown them for the rescue mission. It was a good story but the CIA made it clear that when Rand had healed enough to go home they wanted both of the Carters gone.

Knowing that all of their communications were monitored, they couldn't contact Hughes other than to say that all was going well and they would be going on a bit of a holiday after they were done with their business in *the west* as they called the base. In reality Elsie was training the troops to jump out of an airplane at high altitude and open the chute at the last minute, it was called a HALO jump for *High Altitude Low Opening*. It would keep the Argentinean military from picking them up on radar or hearing the airplane as well as limit the possibility of the parachutes being seen. They had the chutes died dark grey/blue with occasional specs of white to mimic a clear night sky.

The plane was fitted with a fire control station so one person could look down and fire a bank of three 20mm cannons. Rand was to be that person. He had the two night scopes from the SCAR assault rifles mounted and calibrated like binoculars. They served as sights for the guns.

Much to his doctor's disgruntlement Rand left the infirmary and worked with the engineers on the new system. Soon the guns were installed and they began test flights to try them out. After they worked out all of the kinks they practiced over the desert on daytime runs until he and the pilot, a man named Carl, worked in perfect unison. Rand directed the pilot where he needed him and used a traditional radio to communicate with the two team leaders; Elsie and Talbot who were using the earpiece radios that Rand and Elsie had brought. The three could communicate as far as twenty miles with Rand as a relay. One evening Talbot told them that the final arrangements were being made. He was just waiting for confirmation that the offshore oil rig was going to be available. The payoff was $104,000.

Elsie was slightly miffed. "Rand, that's about a million dollars in our time. We could have built our own oil rig for that."

Talbot also told them that the head office was wondering why they were still there. He did an impression of his boss at CIA headquarters.

"It shouldn't take that long to heal and do a bit of training Talbot. I don't want them sniffing around our sensitive operations. Use their vacation as an excuse to push them out but, don't let them go until they give up some more technology. We're counting on you Talbot, don't let us down."

Rand and Elsie laughed at the grumpy impersonation. Still it seemed they had limited time before the CIA would want them off the base.

Elsie offered up a suggestion. "We'll buy a little time with some more information. How about… fleece."

Talbot looked confused. Rand just smiled at him.

"Oh you're gonna love this. Especially when it's cold."

The engineers worked on the plane in two shifts, day and night. They used a design tip from Elsie that added faster engines to the plane, but had the propellers set to a gentler pitch. The result was that the props pulled the same load but the noise was cut by forty percent. When most of the work was complete they practiced every night both in the classroom and in the desert.

The C-123 would fly in at low level with Elsie at the controls using night vision. They hugged the ground until they got close to the target. Then they climbed steeply, levelling off at eighteen thousand feet. The teams jumped in two waves. Once the teams were on the ground the C-123 or the 'Spook' as Elsie named her, would then circle down to attack level to provide close air support and feed tactical information to the teams.

The teams were given silenced assault rifles, but Elsie and Talbot were always the first ones in. The soldiers complained a bit, but after they were told about the night vision, they understood why. Because of this the team started calling themselves the Vampires. The name stuck.

While this was going on Elsie gave Rand's night ops uniform to the seamstresses to cut up for patterns. Velcro had hit the market in September and was now in wide use. The whole team was fitted out in modern BDUs and web gear. Elsie also sent a request to the Hughes plant: '*Send twenty of your wonderful filo pastries. I have a little party planned.*' It was the code name for the bulletproof vest project because one of the seamstresses thought the layers of nylon looked like filo pastry. The message had two purposes; the first was ordering the vests for the team, the second was that it alerted Hughes that something was up. He raised the security level at his facility and alerted Rand and Elsie's staff at home.

The Hughes team had been working on perfecting the body armour for about four months. Because they had a working example, the research and development went quickly. They were heavier than the sample, but they were still effective. By the time Elsie's request came in they had made several hundred units and Hughes was getting ready to break the news to the world. He shipped the vests on a private plane the same day.

Elsie used one of the vests to prove to the team that they worked. The men couldn't believe their eyes. "We really could have used these in the war." It was a common statement among them.

The weapons division was put to work reverse engineering the 40mm grenades that the SCAR assault rifle fired from a launcher underneath the main barrel of the gun. They looked like giant, stubby bullets and they came in a variety of different types. One type acted just like a standard grenade, another would burst in the air and float down, lighting up the battlefield, yet another would shake buildings and blow through heavy doors, penetrating up to three inches of steel plate. As he would be shooting them from the C-123, Rand wanted his version of the grenades modified to fly considerably farther. They set about the task of modifying the shell and establishing an assembly line. At the same time, another team of engineers built a launcher based on Rand's requirements.

The Vampires continued to train and after three weeks everything was ready. A fully automatic 40mm grenade launcher had been fitted to the Spook and they went out for one final training run. Rand could switch from the twenty-millimetre cannons to the grenade launcher or both at once with a thumb switch. The system worked flawlessly and was utterly devastating. The engineers would monitor the training runs from the ground to make design adjustments. Old trucks, cars and even a tank were used as targets. Dummies were set up to determine the splash damage from shrapnel and the percussive force of the explosions. Chief remarked that he had never seen one piece of weaponry deliver such a barrage.

"It's like the apocalypse in a plane."

Under Chief's direction the engineering and special weapons team continued to tweak and enhance the prototype system until it ran flawlessly under heavy use. Rand became very accurate with the system, so much so that he felt like it was an extension of himself. He and Carl began to function as a cohesive unit, though outside of the mission Carl remained aloof.

Finally it was the night of the departure, the team assembled for one final brief then went to bed at five in the afternoon, it was to be an early morning for all of them. After the briefing Rand and Elsie stood at the railing of the mess hall and looked out over the desert. The sun would be going down in a few hours.

"God what I wouldn't give for the C-17 right now."

Elsie looked at him. "I know, it would be so much faster. All that hardware sitting there in New River and we can't even use it."

"I'm just glad we have what we have. The engineers have really done an amazing job."

They stood in silence as Rand put his arm around her. Elsie turned to him. "You know hon that there are never any guarantees." Her eyes shone with sadness.

What do you mean?"

"That we're going to come out of this alive. This isn't a movie or a novel where the happy ending is guaranteed."

"Elsie, don't say that."

"It needs to be said. The consequences need to be acknowledged. I want more than anything to live a normal life with you." As she looked at him she could see that he was in pain and withdrawn. "But I suppose that a crazy, risky, abnormal life with you is better than a normal one without you."

"Els…' He held her close to him. She pulled him tightly as if she could, by the strength of her will, keep anything from ever happening to them. It was a prayer given through action. *God please don't let me be without him.*

"I'm just saying that no matter what, it's all been worth it."

Rand held her tighter.

Talbot stood at a short distance and watched them. "You know you two make me want to settle down."

Elsie laughed, "But then where would you get your fix for all this action?"

"I think after this is over I will have seen enough action for a lifetime."

Elsie gave him a look that said *yeah right*.

"Okay, maybe not quite yet. Maybe after I get to play with that gear a bit more."

Elsie picked up her small daypack that she carried with her everywhere. "Speaking of which, I have something for you Mr. Talbot. Or, for your bosses rather." She pulled out a fleece vest, having carefully removed the tags earlier. "You're sure the barge and tractor will be there?"

"As sure as I can be about anything."

She handed him the vest. "Okay then, see you in the morning."

"If you call one minute after midnight 'morning' then I guess you will."

Sleep didn't come easily. Elsie tossed and turned with details of the mission flashing through her head and Rand hadn't slept well since the Russian incident. Morning came early and they showered and geared up in silence.

Rand was in his ops gear watching Elsie. His face was stony. "Els, when we get back from this we need a break. All of this military stuff is not good for us."

She looked at him, knowing what he meant. "I know. I have a difficult time switching from Major to wife and back again all day long. I tend to just stay the Major."

"I miss you. I miss Spang. I want to just be done with all of this."

For the first time Elsie started to realize just how much the Russian interrogation had damaged his spirit. He was grey, his eyes ashen. She came to him and kept his eyes locked with hers and said quietly, "You can't let those bastards continue to beat you, shock you and torture you. It's your life Rand, take it back."

Suddenly he blurted out, "But I'm jut a musician Elsie. I'm not a Special Forces hard case. I'm not a gun toting badass. I just live and let live."

She saw him retreating, withdrawing back into himself. It left her with a chilling flash of loneliness. "Jesus, no. Not here Rand. You will not abandon me here in nineteen frickin forty-nine with a stack of insanely difficult things to accomplish by myself while I become an emotional crutch! Fight it. You have to heal. Like you told me about, when you were in Belfast and had to climb in to that shower all cut up, you fought in that shower. Remember when it was just you and Spang? Fight it like you did in Belfast! I need you Rand. We need you, me, Spang and Henrietta and Bucky and the rest of our crazy little farm."

Rand was sitting on the bed sobbing. He could feel the electricity searing him, smell the sweaty breath of McAllister in his face as he sat bound and helpless. Then something in him snapped – like a chain under heavy strain. When it broke, both ends went flying apart from each other. One end was *live* the other was *die*, one end *no* and the other *yes*. He stood up shaking and pulled Elsie to him, kissing her hard, absorbing her strength and the strength of their love. *Yes!* His mind pounded, *this is what I am living for. I am so much more than anything I have been. I am love, I am truth and I belong to God! I will not wear this yoke anymore.* When he relaxed his hold on Elsie she lay in his arms, her head back, eyes closed. Slowly she opened them.

"There you are." She whispered, closing her eyes again.

"I'm sorry Elsie, I'll never you leave again."

They had very little time, but the ferocity of their lovemaking made up for it. He took her quickly, stripping her to the ankles and driving from behind as she grasped for something to brace herself. Finally she freed one of her feet, threw him onto the low cot and drove down on him in a powerful squat with her feet on the ground. The slow, stroking grind was made more intense when she arched her back. Their eyes locked on each other with the ferocity of a love that was clawing it's way to freedom, the pounding of their wet flesh finally yielded to the pulse of their hearts in heavy waves of elation. She finished him off with her mouth, milking every last drop of tension out of him.

Rand was completely revitalised. He didn't feel foolish for having been in despair. He knew how had got there and how Elsie and his faith had helped him get back. There was nothing to be ashamed of. They emerged from their quarters and headed across the tarmac to the C-123. Among the modifications made to the big plane the biggest was it's folding wings. The team had practiced rigging the aircraft to get lifted by crane with the wings folded and then stripping and stowing the rigging and readying for takeoff. It was a complex operation but each man knew his job and they did it with precision.

It had been painted in a night camouflage that was dark grey and olive green with a light grey belly. The paint was flat, not shiny. All reflective surfaces had been covered other than a large red V painted under the cockpit windows with the silhouette of a bullet and a knife in the middle. Rand thought it was a bit over the top but the team liked it, maybe because they had designed it.

Talbot was there to meet them. "Good morning. Rand, you look different. I think you've healed right up. Nothing like a daring mission to put a pep in your step."

Rand just looked at Elsie and smiled. "Here come the men."

The twelve men of the special squad trickled in one by one, stowing their gear on the plane and taking their seats. Rand joined Carl Capaldi, the pilot, in the cockpit. Elsie would be the navigator on this leg of the mission. She climbed into the cockpit when all the men were on board.

"It's all you Carl."

The big plane softly whirred to life. Extensive modifications had made her very quiet and much faster. She took off with surprising speed and pushed up to altitude quickly. When the plane had levelled off Elsie joined Talbot to brief the men.

"Alright Vampires, we warned you it was going to be a long trip. Any bets so far?"

Several men revealed that the bet pool was up to two hundred dollars. Antarctica, Saudi Arabia,

Thailand, Brazil, France, Germany, five for Russia and one guy who thought they were going to Las Vegas.

"Well, we're on our way to Argentina, specifically the Misiones province. It's just across the border from Brazil."

The man who had bet on Brazil did a small celebration dance while the rest gave him a hard time. Talbot and Elsie knew it was a long trip so they let the guys have a little fun.

"From here we stop in Alamogordo for a refuel then land in Texas on a strip of beach on South Padre island in the small hours of the morning. We have a barge and a tractor. You will prep the plane for shipping as we practiced then the tractor will push the plane up the ramp and onto the barge. Who's our tractor driver?"

McElroy raised his hand. "I've been driving them all my life sir. Never met a tractor I couldn't operate. Hell, I'll even plow that beach for ya. We'll have us a crop by the time we get back!"

"That's fine McElroy," Talbot said. "you got the job but keep that hayseed shit to yourself."

"Yes sir."

"We'll take the barge out to an offshore oil platform where a special cargo ship is waiting. They have a crane that will hoist the plane onboard with us inside. It is imperative that none of the crew on any of the boats or the oil rig sees us, other than the cargo ship of course. From there, we sail for South America.

"We'll be travelling on the good ship *Provider*. She's cleared for top-secret missions and has worked with the agency before. We will disembark at an abandoned pier at Itapoá, Brazil and ready the Spook for flight. I've been assured that there are no wires, poles or obstructions and we can take off directly from the pier. However, there's no such thing as perfect intel and we will have to be ready to deal with any problems as we go." He paused for a second and became very stern.

"I shouldn't need to tell you that all of these operations need to be done at record speed and in complete silence. The smoking lamp is out at all times until further notice. If we are discovered we will most likely be tortured and killed. Our presence might even incite a war. The United States will not claim us as they have no knowledge of this operation. We're on our own."

Talbot let that sink in and then continued. "When we take off from the pier at Itapoá it's a three-hundred and fifty-two mile flight to the LZ. If everything is going well it should take just over two-and a half hours. The LZ is a small abandoned air base in the jungle we're calling Vampire Zulu and it will be home for awhile."

The men liked the fact that the base was named after them.

"Don't get too excited, the place is hardly the Ritz. It's just a dirt airstrip leftover from the war. That's it. I have tried to get some conveniences in there for you but once again we have our C.O. to thank for any conveniences that we do have. I'll turn it over to her now."

Elsie had come down to listen to the briefing. Now she stepped forward. "Thank you Mr. Talbot. All of you must remember at all times that we are in Argentina. Perón would like nothing better than to catch the U.S. sneaking around in his back yard. Our presence must remain completely undetected for the entirety of the mission. We're ghosts people, plain and simple. That means we have to become one with the jungle.

"Vampire Zulu will be our base but like Mr. Talbot said, it ain't pretty. But that doesn't mean it has to be a shit hole. When the Roman legion camped every night after a long march they erected an entire fort complete with ditches and battlements. If they can do it so can we, but instead of ditches and battlements our efforts will go towards making our base invisible. The

Argentinean government won't know we're there. No one will, not even the CIA and it has to stay that way. You will be briefed on our final objective once we reach Vampire Zulu. Expect to be there for up to a month. That's it. Questions?"

"So you mean we're going camping for a month in the jungle?"

"If you call building an invisible base in a hostile environment using basic hand tools, rehearsing dynamic entry, hostage retrieval, sniping, survival, evasion, resistance, escape, mountain climbing, underwater insertion and jungle reconnaissance while maintaining proper military discipline, cleanliness and a fully functional special operations base deep inside enemy territory a camping trip then your answer is yes Johnson. Any more smartass questions? Good. We're gonna be living in tight quarters for up to a month. I will NOT start this mission with attitude problems. Anyone with an attitude problem can pack out at Alamogordo no questions asked. I'll even pay for the plane ticket home."

"Ma'am?"

"What Johnson?"

"Ma'am I'm sorry, I meant no disrespect. I'm with you all the way ma'am."

"Acknowledged. Now all of you get ready to take notes, I'm going to go over the plans for base construction."

Elsie had it planned down to the minute their feet hit the ground at Vampire Zulu. The men were broken up into four fire teams consisting of three men each. Each fire team had a pick, axe and shovel. There was a chainsaw for any really big jobs but it had to be used sparingly as gas and bar oil was limited. They had two large army tents, come-alongs with plenty of rope, and a cache of other necessary equipment. The majority of the supplies would be waiting for them, having been brought in on donkey by Talbot's contact.

After an hour and a half the plane landed at Holloman Air Force Base in White Sands, New Mexico (otherwise known as Alamogordo) to refuel. It was 1:46 AM and only two service men came out to meet them. The tower called them *Vampire one* and talked very minimally. The fuel truck pulled away after fuel was topped off and they continued on their journey.

After two hours, Rand called down. "All right everyone we're at South Padre Island. Touch down in about five minutes."

Carl had begun the approach. Their landing strip was nothing but a long stretch of hard beach.

They had timed the landing for a low tide. Elsie took over with night vision and guided the plane down with no lights, smooth as silk. While they were still rolling to a stop the rear hatch opened with only dim red lights illuminating the cargo area. The men poured out on to the beach. One team was sent to recon the area and turn back any late night beach wanderers. Talbot took a strong, hand-held signal lamp with a red light and flashed a code out to sea. A pinpoint of light flashed back at them. Talbot finished the exchange and said,

"He's on his way, about ten minutes out."

Slowly they could see a shape emerge out of the darkness. The barge and it's tug boat had no lights on. As he got closer Talbot used the signal light to guide the barge in. Finally, the massive craft slid gently onto the beach.

While the barge had been coming in the men were at work folding the wings in. The ramp on the barge was lowered and the tractor was rolled off. Then the inevitable sound of the tractor's engine crackled through the night.

"So much for stealth." Talbot groaned.

Rand looked at Elsie, "Wow, that's loud."

"Have you ever heard of a quiet tractor?" Elsie replied, "We were lucky to get one at all."

The team nervously hooked the tractor to the nose gear of the plane. The wheels dug into the hard sand and started to skid, but Elsie had the men put their shoulders to the plane and the tractor and slowly the big tires began to roll as they backed the Spook towards the barge. They gained momentum as the slope of the beach grew steeper. At last the rear wheels lurched up the ramp then over the crest. There was a brief moment when they thought the plane was going to bottom out on the ramp but it cleared by inches. It took ten minutes of relentless tractor noise. In the end the plane got onto the barge with the men and equipment.

They all kept their fingers crossed as the tug strained to get the barge off the sand. Finally, with a sudden jolt they broke free of the beach and chugged slowly out to sea. Elsie and Talbot kept watch with their heat sensor and night vision while Rand scanned the beach with his night scope.

"Nobody. Amazing. Half of Texas probably heard us."

As the shore receded to a thin line everyone breathed a sigh of relief and got busy rigging the plane to be hoisted. Talbot told Elsie that the tug captain gave about an hour and a half travel time to the oil platform. Rand kept scanning with Elsie. The sky was getting lighter on the horizon.

"You really trust Talbot?"

"Yes hon."

"I'm not sure I trust him."

"He's done quite a lot. He lead the team to—"

"I know, I mean I don't trust him with you. He has an eye for you, I can tell."

"Yes he does. But I am aware of it and I keep it professional."

"Okay, you know about it. That's the main thing for me hon. I completely trust that you got it handled." He gave her a kiss. "Now, let's just enjoy the cruise."

Elsie was just watching him. She couldn't decide whether he was being sarcastic or he actually meant what he said. After a minute she concluded that he was serious.

"You never cease to surprise me."

He could tell by the way she looked at him that her heart was on fire, he felt it too, but she couldn't be hanging all over him in front of the men.

"You better go do the rounds Major." He winked at her.

"Yes. I love you too." She whispered and then went around to the men.

Carl Capaldi, the pilot whom the men were now calling *Captain Carl* came up beside Rand and leaned on the rail. He was tall and well built, tan with blonde hair. He wore Khaki pants and a white short-sleeved shirt with the sleeves rolled up. This guy could have been a model, Rand thought.

"How in God's name do you keep control of a tiger like her? I don't envy you."

"Why is that?"

"She's a strong, assertive type of woman. I don't go for it. I'm more into the young, soft and easily lead kind of woman."

"Well I'm a firm believer that there is someone for everyone."

"I don't know, there's a lot of fish in the sea."

"Ah, a playboy pilot. Now there's something you don't see everyday."

"Yeah I know. Predictable, but they keep coming at me. It would be a waste to turn them away." Captain Carl laughed.

"I would spend my time getting to know the team better. We're going to be depending on each other in that jungle and on the mission."

"I don't need to know them, they just have to do their job. I have the Spook to look after, that's enough."

It was true. The big plane was his sole job. He was responsible for making sure it was transported safely, maintaining it, concealing it in the jungle and flying it on the mission.

Rand continued to keep a visual lookout. Then he noticed a small red light twinkling on the horizon. He radioed Elsie,

"Contact eleven o'clock."

"Roger, I'll notify the captain of the tug. Keep an eye on it as you scan."

"Yep."

No other contact appeared but as they grew closer the red light split into several lights both red and white. Soon the outlines of the oil rig and the cargo ship were visible.

"Okay everyone, load up.'

The men climbed into the airplane. Only Captain Carl and Rand stayed on the barge. Rand was in his night BDUs and body armour with his trusty .45 in a holster on his thigh. His face had grown harder since the Russian interrogation. His eyes had become a steely gleam that now swept over the approaching oil platform and cargo ship, searching for signs of deception. The tug captain swung the barge around slowly as men from the cargo ship prepared to receive the huge craft along side. The barge was about half the length of the cargo ship and not as wide. The ship towered over them even though she had a load on her already. A long stairway was swung out and lowered to the deck of the barge. The sea was completely calm and only a mild breeze blew as a single figure descended the stairs.

"Good morning, I am Raymond Delarosa, captain of the *Provider*. He shook hands with Rand and Carl. I have been instructed to tell you that I am only a cargo ship captain and I do not want to know anything about your mission or who you are. My crew and I welcome you to inspect any part of the ship at any time and question any crew members. They are all cleared by your organisation and we have worked with them several times already. Please tell your people to make themselves at home and enjoy the journey. If there is anything you need that we can assist with, you have only to ask."

"That all sounds very reasonable, thank you."

"Now, you have large and delicate cargo to load yes?"

He waved up to the ship and four men came down as a crane cable was lowered. The cable was massive and Rand had no doubt it could carry the weight of the loaded plane. Captain Carl watched as they connected the harness to the lifting straps they had prepared while Rand went up to the deck of the cargo ship. There were about ten crewmen standing around massive doors that had been slid open to reveal the interior. The cargo area was full of shipping containers, but a plywood platform had been constructed on top of the containers for the plane to rest on. Even with the big plane sitting on the containers there was still ample room for the giant doors to close, securing the whole cargo in a watertight hold. There were four men in the hold looking up, each held the end of a heavy strap that was tied somewhere inside the ship. They would use these to secure the plane so it wouldn't move in transit.

Rand watched as the plane rose slowly off the deck of the barge. The operation was very delicate but in end the C-123 settled into the hold and the crew began to secure it in place. As soon as the plane came to rest Elsie, Talbot and the troops climbed out and entered through the inside of the ship. The whole operation was done behind a large stack of shipping containers, completely out of sight of the working oil rig. Rand went back down to the barge, paid the tug captain ten thousand dollars cash, and thanked him. Then he rode the stairs as they were hoisted back up. The barge pulled away and the cargo ship made ready to get underway.

"Elsie where are you?" Rand asked over his radio.

"In quarters."

Rand made his way to the huge superstructure in the middle of the ship. A crewman met him on the way. "Can I help you find where you are going?"

"Si, gracias." It was the only Spanish that Rand knew. "Officers quarters please."

The man lead the way through the maze of passages, up several ladders and finally to an area where the walls were finished in wood veneer. When he told him that he was looking for the woman's quarters the sailor smiled a knowing grin. Rand smiled back and held up his wedding ring finger. The sailor suddenly looked apologetic. When he reached the room he was surprised by the accommodations.

"There you are!" Elsie wrapped around him as soon as the door was closed.

"Wow baby this place is impressive, it's like a cruise ship in here."

"It reminds me of Howard's Yacht." Elsie's eyes went completely soft, "The night we we're married."

The ship suddenly shuddered slightly, pushing her into to him. "Oh!"

Rand turned down the lights. "Next stop, the jungle."

Montgomery Thompson

Chapter 7

Vampire Zulu

'Don't go walkin' slow, the Devil's on the loose.
~Creedence Clearwater Revival, Run through the jungle

The giant cargo ship *Provider* steamed out of the Gulf of Mexico at top speed. Inside the superstructure the Vampires assembled in the briefing room. The uniform was jungle BDUs and olive t-shirts.

Talbot, Elsie, Rand and Carl entered as the men stood at attention. Elsie began.

"Be seated. The first phase of the operation is complete and so far everything has gone smoothly. You will continue to be passengers for the remainder of the sea leg of the trip. I expect you to be on your best behaviour. That means gracious and mannerly to our hosts regardless of their rank.

We are on our way to the abandoned pier in Itapoá, Brazil."

She pointed to a map on the wall behind her.

"Spooky will be unloaded the same way she was loaded. As soon as we hit the ground you will be unfolding those wings and readying the plane for takeoff. We will be on an abandoned pier. That doesn't mean it's devoid of people. Anyone could be there; homeless, or lovers parked, or the police on their rounds looking for trespassers. We need to be out of there before anyone spots us. If we're discovered, the cover story is that the Provider needed to make an emergency docking to check on a possible dangerous fuel leak. They chose the abandoned pier for safety reasons in case there was a fire or an explosion. Everyone clear on that? Good." She continued, "Once aloft we will be suiting up for a HALO jump into Vampire Zulu where we will secure the LZ. When you hit the ground you will form into fire teams as follows."

The men really perked up at this. The fire teams were groups of three. The assignment would be permanent and indicate whom they would be living, working, and fighting beside for the duration of the mission and most likely for the whole time they served in the Vampires. Talbot and Elsie had carefully assembled them based on personality, skill set, experience and even social background.

"From Alpha, fire team one is Johnson, Wiley and Baker. Fire team two is Rhodes, Taggart and McElroy. From Golf, fire team one is Sloane, Jeter and Paige. Fire team two is Nickelson, Pau and Reece. Everyone happy?"

"Yes Ma'am!" The men knew better than to answer any other way. In truth they were all very pleased with the assignments though they were professional enough to be happy with anyone from their unit. There was already some competition between Alpha and Golf.

"Now, because of the generous hosts of the good ship *Provider* we get to do some unique training. We will learn how to take a ship, deck by deck and room by room until we own it and everyone on board is either dead or captured... not literally of course. In addition, your hand-to-hand skills will be augmented and you will be going to school to prime yourself for the upcoming training in jungle survival. For now, excellent work, it gets harder from here. Mr. Talbot, they're all yours." She sat down and let Talbot brief the men on what was expected of them. Though the ship's crew stood watches, the Vampires would be keeping a watch as well.

The voyage went smoothly. Everyday was training. They were tested and ran drills that challenged them to their limits. Competitions were set up between the teams and they fought each other in scenarios set up by the officers. Carl would have spent most of his time reading in the plane, but he was brought in to participate and even then, he stayed quiet. One evening Elsie found him alone in the weight room.

"Carl."

"Major."

"I know your not a ground soldier, but it would only benefit you to get to know the men a little. The more they know you, the more they'll trust you."

"I don't need their trust. I'm getting paid to do a job and I'm doing it. Very well I might add. I'm not a part of your glee club Major."

"Right, it's as I thought. You've got an attitude problem. Somewhere you got a chip on your shoulder. What is it? Me? I'm a woman is that it?"

"My attitude is fine. I'm a pilot. I fly planes. I don't play footsy with a bunch of gun toting grunts or act like I'm one of the team. I don't do things in groups."

"Ah, the lone wolf. I get it. Listen I don't mind if you're the lone wolf type that's okay, but this is a covert operation. It's highly likely that we could get in the shit, and when you're in the shit your friends are all you have."

"There you go with friends and teams."

"I'm talking about allegiance, trust and loyalty Carl."

"Yeah I looked into those, they're a myth. What do you do when your precious friends get vaporised? Who's there when you're in the shit and your team is nothing but a collection of body parts?"

Elsie started to realize where Carl was coming from. "Where did it happen Carl?"

"What are you talking about?"

"Where Carl? Was it in France? Somewhere over England? Where are those body parts who used to be your friends?"

Carl's eyes started to get red. "Fuck you. You know nothing about it."

"Maybe I don't, but those men do. Those guys out there. They've seen it, been through it. They're your brothers Carl and you're turning your back on them."

"I'm not turning my back!" He said angrily, 'They turned their back on me. They left me there, alive. Them and their precious fucking Corps!"

"You're not there any more. No one on this team is going to leave you. No one gets left behind or forgotten. I will lay down my life for you, as will any man in this outfit."

"Yeah, I laid down my life for my guys too except I lived and they didn't." His eyes were watery now. "You can't make friends out here Major, they just die on you and your left feeling like this. It's too risky."

She wasn't relenting. "So what, you go cold? Humans aren't meant to be that way. I've seen it, they just fall apart. Lone wolves don't survive the winter Carl. We have to take the risk, that's real courage. We take the risk with you. We all take it together. You know Rand is the same. Every time you're up there flying with him, you're doing it for us. Hell, you're doing it already."

"That's my job. But my job is not to care or be friendly with these people."

"This is no job Carl. A job is going to work at nine and punching out at five. This is not a job, this is risking your life to change the world. If you didn't care you wouldn't be here. Stop the show, nobody's buying it."

"I can't just… I can't risk it. It's too much." His face was red and tears were welling up.

"It's too much for all of us. But these people are the only ones we can talk to. We're the only ones who will ever know. That's why they say *brothers in arms*. It's too much to bear alone. When your guys died on you they left you to carry it all. Now you don't have to. Tell them. Johnson, Paige, Nickelson - they all have stories. They tell each other all the time. That's how they deal with it."

"Okay, alright, you got me. I guess I just didn't want to have to deal with it again. I don't know if I can."

"Listen, you don't have to get married to them, just let them know that you've got their back."

Alright." He shook her hand

Come on, let's have some dinner in the mess."

"Don't—"

"Carl, I'll never tell a soul, not even Rand. But I want to tell you one thing that's a common saying where I'm from."

He looked at her. She could see a light beginning to form in his eyes. "A heart is like a parachute. It can save you, but it only works when it's open. Try to be open."

"Okay. I'll give it a shot."

They joined the rest of the team in the mess. Carl was more relaxed than he'd ever been. After dinner everyone went to get some well deserved rest. Talbot and Carl were assigned to one of the spacious officer's cabins. Talbot started talking to Carl about flying. Elsie had encouraged him to learn and he wanted to know some of the basics. He hit on the one thing that Carl loved to do more than anything else in the world and they ended up talking until early in the morning. The next day Carl joined Talbot on his run around the deck. Several of the men joined them. Elsie and Rand stood on the bridge watching them while they had their morning coffee.

"I don't know what's happened but Carl seems to have finally opened up to us. Must be the sea air or something."

"I've noticed it too. I think it's a good thing."

Rand studied her for a moment. He could read her like a book. "Elsie, what did you say to him?"

"Me? Why do you think it was me?"

"Oh that clinches it. It was definitely you."

"Okay, I can't deny it. But what we talked about is between he and I."

"Well… good job hon, he seems to be much happier."

"Changing yourself takes true courage. He's the one who deserves the credit."

The voyage lasted two weeks. By the time they spotted land they were fit, well-trained and more prepared than ever to take on their next challenge. It was the middle of the night as the ship pulled into the pier. All of them, including Rand and Carl, waited in the plane feeling like rats in a cage as the crane hoisted them up and then down onto the ground. Everyone was relieved when they felt the wheels touch the pier.

"Go." Came the short command from Elsie. The troops poured out and pulled the wings into position. Two men were on the wing struts reconnecting control cables, wires and couplings. Then they pushed the wings into their final position and quickly installed the massive pins that held them in place. A second team inspected all of the operations before they slid down the wings and into the aircraft as it powered up.

"All in." Elsie reported as she climbed into the navigator's chair.

Rand and Carl looked at her.

"Aren't you supposed to be piloting this leg?"

"Change of plans. Carl is a Vampire, he should be able to see in the dark too."

Rand nodded, "Yeah, definitely."

She smiled at Carl and put her helmet on him, and slapped down the visor.

"Holy shit! I can see everything, it's like day!"

"Yes, and you'd better get us off the ground before someone comes along."

"Roger that."

The plane whirred down the pier and onto a bumpy dirt section then jumped into the air. They stayed low to the trees, winding their way over jungle terrain.

"This is incredible." Carl lifted the visor for a split-second to make sure it was actually dark out. "Amazing, we're like ghosts. No one will ever see us or know what we are until we're on top of them. I think I finally understand what you've put together here Major."

After one hour and fifty-five minutes of flying Talbot gave the order and Rand hit the switch that turned on the red lights in the cargo hold, it was the signal for the teams to get ready. At the same time Talbot and Elsie went down into the cargo bay after she had retrieved her NV helmet from Carl. The teams put on parachutes and prepared to deploy. They had been through this drill many times. It took four minutes for the whole team to get seated and strapped in.

"We are ascension ready." Talbot said through the intercom to the cockpit. Carl throttled the engines to full and banked the plane up and at a steep angle in a spiralling climb.

Rand's job was to keep an eye on the climb rate. 'eight-hundred, nine-hundred' he called out how many feet-per-second they were climbing. 'One-thousand.' Carl kept the plane at that rate of climb until the reached twenty thousand feet. They levelled off and flew for another five minutes. Rand kept strict time, at five minutes he flashed the red lights three times. In the pressurised cargo area Elsie and Talbot had cracked chemical lights on each other packs.

"We're green. Vampires, are you ready?"

The men responded with a roar then strapped on their oxygen masks as the tail ramp opened and the frigid, high altitude air rushed in. Elsie stood with her back to the opening, facing the men. She saluted then fell backwards into the darkness. Talbot plunged after her then the men in fire team order.

The wind tore at Elsie's clothes as a calm voice spoke in her ear.

"Be careful baby. I love you."

"Soft landing honey, I'll see you on the ground."

They dropped through the air like stones. Head first, pointed straight at the earth. As they dropped in altitude they didn't need the oxygen masks any more. Elsie and Talbot both took theirs off and lowered the visors on their NV helmets. Talbot pulled up next to her, both of them scanning for the runway in the jungle as they tore through the clear night air at one hundred twenty miles per hour.

As time ate up altitude the ground got closer, slowly at first then faster and faster. Finally, Talbot spotted it. "I have visual of the LZ. No contacts, it looks all clear." He said over his radio.

"Roger that." Elsie replied. "Possible contacts on thermal, but I suspect it's just the local animals. Golf Zero take lead, I'll follow."

Talbot spread his arms and legs so the flaps on his jump suit caught the air, slowing him down. He steered towards the approach, feeling the wind. The rest of the team followed the little lights on their backs.

He slowly levelled out and flattened his body to slow down, then gave the command.

"Golf two-three deploy."

In Golf fire team two, the third man was Reece. He opened his chute first then, like a row of dominos all the chutes opened like a series of dark blue flowers against the night sky. Elsie and Talbot opened their chutes in the last ten seconds of the drop, scanning to identify all of the heat signatures. The forest lit up with images of so many small animals it was like they were landing in a zoo but there was no human presence.

"Alpha Zero clear on thermal." Elsie reported.

"Golf Zero clear on thermal." Talbot echoed.

They gently touched down on the old dirt landing strip five seconds later and moved to opposite ends of the clearing. The rest of the men followed them in succession, spreading out so they wouldn't get tangled in each other's chutes. They landed and rolled softly then stood and hit the quick release for their chutes. In seconds the fire teams located their teammates and headed to rendezvous with their team leaders. From there the four teams split the field into four parts while Elsie and Talbot searched for the cache drop made by Talbot's contact earlier. Each team entered the jungle then circled toward another team. When they made contact they changed direction and circled back, working their way deeper into the forest. When they had reached their designated waypoints they came back to the open area. When the teams returned Elsie radioed Rand.

"Vampire Zulu Secure."

Fire teams A2 and G1 placed infrared lights to designate the runway.

The Spook made a fast approach and slowed quickly using specially installed airbrakes. Rand used his scope to spot the infrared lights and directed Carl onto the approach and landing. The big plane touched down quietly in the forest clearing and taxied to the tree line.

As soon as the plane was parked, the rear door was opened and a flurry of activity began. The wings of the big plane were kept unfolded for a quick evacuation. G1 went on roving watch and assisted in locating the equipment caches left by Talbot's contact. A1 and A2 took a giant camouflage net out and draped it over the plane, staking it to the ground at the rear and sides but making it possible for the plane to slip out from under the netting. A sharp blade on the tail had been specifically installed to cut through the netting. Then they erected the large command tent in the trees at the edge of the clearing. Fire team G2 pitched everyone's barracks tents then went to sleep so they could take over as the other teams rested in rotation.

Supplies had been brought in and left in carefully camouflaged areas. Some were so hard to find that it took until the following day to discover them. The mess tent was prepared by sunrise and the leader of A2, a soldier named Rhodes, had

The Second String

breakfast ready. G2 relieved the next fire team in succession as they took over watch, and so it would go with three teams on and one sleeping at all times with the exception of training in which case Rand and Carl would take the watch.

By the time two days had gone by they had a fully functional little base; latrines, mess hall, command center and barracks. On the evening of the third day four armed men had made contact with the watch. One of them asked to be brought to Talbot by name. The watch stayed with the other three men under the surveillance of a second fire team hiding in the jungle. A third fire team escorted a large man into their camp.

Talbot recognised him immediately. "Gerardo you old so and so!"

"David you have a sighting of sore eyes!" The thick Panamanian accent pushed through his even thicker moustache. Rand thought the guy looked like a cartoon of a coffee bean grower. He had the stripy, rough cloth slung over one shoulder and a large brimmed straw hat. With his black hair, broad mouth, nose, and droopy eyes all he needed was the burro. The two friends greeted each other warmly then Talbot introduced the officers.

"You can thank Gerardo for the supplies as well as the location."

Elsie stepped forward and shook his hand. "Our thanks to you Mr. De Leon. Without you we would never be able to attempt this mission."

"Ah! I believe in what you are doing and I will help in any way I can. I myself have been attempting to make such a mission happen for several years now. I never had the financial resources not to mention the men and equipment. Now, you are all here. The Vampires! How exciting, welcome to Argentina."

"Gerardo my old friend," Talbot took on a somber look, "please tell me you have news."

'Yes, that is the main reason why I come.'

The officers headed to the command center while the soldiers went back to work.

"I have news from Buenos Aires. I have been there myself. It boggles the mind what goes on in South America while Europe and America dawdle about with their head in the clouds."

"So, what's the news?"

"It's big. Bigger than you can imagine."

He was building up to something. The man was about to burst from wanting to tell what he knew and his excitement was contagious.

"The man. He is there. I have seen him."

"The man?" Talbot was confused.

"THE man. He is a no dead. He is ALIVE." He practically whispered it.

"I'm sorry, which man are we talking about?" Elsie asked.

Gerardo stood up stock straight and raised the Nazi salute. "Heil… come on, come on." He beckoned to the group to guess.

Elsie took a stab, "Hitler?"

"YES YES YES! You are right senora! He is there, I have seen him."

"You've seen Adolf Hitler, alive?" Elsie was aghast.

"Bingo pretty lady! Yes, yes!"

There wasn't an open mouth in the tent. They sat gaping at him. Then a whoosh of "Holy shit, oh my God, is he joking?"

When they all calmed down Talbot asked, "How many others are with him Gerardo?"

"There are many of them. Over two hundred I say, maybe four."

He continued to give details about what he had seen. Elsie told him that they needed photographs of every Nazi they could identify. They needed to know what buildings they were staying in, if they had meetings, parties, everything about them.

"I have limited resources senora. I…"

"How much do you need?"

The glint in his eye could be seen from across the room.

"I think that—"

"I'll give you ten thousand a week."

Gerardo's eyes went wide, then searched from Elsie to Talbot, to Elsie again. It was clear he was looking for a way to get even more money. Elsie saw it too. Rand just watched her work, fascinated.

"Or, we can find another service. I'm sure there are a lot of mercenaries who would be more than happy to work for that kind of money."

"No! No I will do it." He covered quickly, "I was just thinking of who to get. The best, only the very best will do."

"And we'll need some experienced guerrillas willing to train my men in jungle warfare and survival. Send them to talk and I'll pay you ten percent of what I pay them. They must be trustworthy and able to keep their mouths shut."

"Yes, of course. Now, about the fee. How about —"

"Not negotiable."

"Yes, that's fine. I will arrange it tomorrow, but it will take several days for them to get here. Talbot my friend you keep hard company, but it makes me happy to see you are in good hands."

The Second String

"And you Gerardo." Talbot slapped him on the back. "You are the man who found Adolf Hitler and his Nazi criminals. You will be a hero."

"No my friend, I do not want anyone to know that it was me, it does not matter. I want to see them all die, then I want to live in peace with my children."

"Amen to that. Go get us that intel and let us be done with it then."

Rand went and got the money out of the safe in the plane. He handed it to Gerardo with a handshake, "Good luck."

"Yes. I will report back as soon as I have something worth reporting. It may be several weeks for me. Look for my men in a couple of days."

"Good, we can use the time to train."

"Farewell my friends, I will be back with the information you require."

The evening was coming on and the jungle was dark as they all said goodbye. Gerardo joined up with the three Argentinean guerrillas at the edge of the jungle as the officers regrouped in the command center.

"Do you trust him David?" Elsie asked.

"Don't let his greasy look and cheesy accent fool you. He's dedicated. The CIA struck a deal with Panama to cross train some of their agents, that's where I met Gerardo. He was chosen from among hundreds. He's tough, resourceful and a hell of a networker."

"Hey, anyone know where Rand got off to?"

They all looked around, and then went outside. He was nowhere to be found.

Rand had been eyeing Gerardo and decided that the man needed watching. He came in with guerrillas, they might have seen the plane and the layout of the camp including the number of men they had. Argentina had a problem with the United States. If they took the Vampire base, they could wave it front of the world press and say how the U.S. was sneaking around in their country with a military presence. The Argentinean government would pay a lot of money for an opportunity to get a leg up on their problem with America. The temptation would be too great, Rand knew he had to follow them and listen in.

After Gerardo had been paid and the others were watching him go, Rand quietly went to his tent and picked up his NV helmet and EAR comms. He exited through the back of the tent and skirted the edge of the camp, following Gerardo. Pau was sitting outside of his tent next to

The Second String

a little fire and spotted Rand approaching. Rand suddenly realised that he only had his .45 pistol on him and it would be wise to have backup. He motioned for Pau to quietly follow him. The dark haired Italian quietly picked up his silenced MAS 49 rifle and slipped into the jungle after Rand. Gerardo had joined his Argentinean guides and Rand picked the little group up on thermal as Pau caught up to him.

"What's up sir?" Pau whispered.

Rand kept moving as he watched the group. "I've got a funny feeling about Gerardo's companions. I just want to make sure they're on the up and up."

"It looks like they're going to come out by the intersection in the road over there. You want me to flank?"

"Good idea, you get ready to snipe if anything happens. Just make sure Gerardo stays safe."

"Yes sir." Pau headed off to Rand's right and quickly circled the small group. Switching to night vision, Rand turned up his ears. The small group marched noisily through the jungle for about fifteen minutes until they came into clearing where a rough, two track road forked. There they paused, lit cigarettes and drank water. Rand hung back in the trees and listened to the conversation.

***

Gerardo watched his guerrilla companions closely. They had fought with Perón during the Grupo de Oficiales Unidos coup in 1943 but after he became Presidenté in 1947 the man's shifting political agendas had caused them to lose faith. Added to that was his megalomaniacal wife Eva whom the people called 'Evita', who preached in support of her husband as he changed from being an advocate for the rights of the common man to promoting industrialisation and tighter government control of the people while also restricting liberties. He and his wife were rewriting the country's constitution and placing themselves as the ultimate authority. The men with Gerardo had fought on the side of the military when another coup attempt failed to overthrow Perón. Now they worked in the jungle, biding their time to see how it would all play out. They were an unstable bunch, but he needed them to navigate the jungle safely. The whole time they had assisted him in bringing the supplies to the old landing strip they had been jumpy. Now he was glad that this was the last night with them. He would get Diego and Luis to train with the Vampires, he thought. They were loyal and reliable and would be just returning from their mission in the high country. As they connected with the main road, the others stopped and lit cigarettes. Gerardo's sixth sense told him something wasn't right.

"So Gerardo, what do you think of your American friend, is he still a patriot?'

'Yes Carlos, he is as good a man as I remember." Sensing the tension, Gerardo's training kicked in and he subtly positioned himself to deflect Carlos' gun if he decided to raise it.

"What about the company he keeps?" The question came from a guerrilla named Juan. He was a small time dealer from a local village and had joined up with Carlos to make some extra money. Juan moved to the side of Gerardo and adjusted the grip on his weapon. "You like the fact that those Americans are camping out on our back door? I don't trust them, they smell like spies."

Gerardo didn't talk directly to Juan, it would take his attention off of the other two. As he stood, he could see all three. "They are looking for Nazi scum in Buenos Aires. They have nothing to do with politics."

Carlos went firm in his stance. "That is where you are wrong Gerardo."

Gerardo had underestimated Carlos. He didn't think the man would be smart enough to realize the political opportunity. He was wrong, now he was going to pay with his life. "Let me go, you don't know what you are doing."

"Those Americans are worth a fortune to Perón. He will pay us. We will be heroes of Argentina and the Americans will be driven out."

"No, they are no threat to us. We have nothing to do with this."

"You made your choice Gerardo. You are a traitor to your country, now you must die."

Carlos raised his gun and Gerardo reached down to block it. He had already planned his next three moves. Block the gun, turn and shoot Juan with Carlos' gun, smash Carlos' nose with the back of his head. When Carlos released the gun from the pain of having his nose crushed, Gerardo would shoot the third man, Thiago.

Before any of that could happen, half of Carlos' face vaporised in a pink mist. A sound like popping watermelons exploded all around Gerardo as he watched the faces of his enemies crumple into disfigured masks. Their guns clattered as they hit the ground and quiet settled over the jungle. He was alone with three corpses at his feet.

The Second String

Gerardo turned around fast, swivelling this way and that but saw no one.

"Gerardo, don't be afraid, you're safe." A voice came from behind him.

Two men stepped out of the jungle, one to his right and the other from behind. It was one of the American soldiers and the woman's husband... what was it? Carter, yes.

"Rand Carter, and this is Sergeant Pau. Are you alright? I followed you because I didn't trust you, but now I'm glad I did. I heard everything."

Rand was walking slowly towards him with his hands out and what looked like some kind of sleek black welding mask tilted up on his head. Gerardo felt disoriented and sat down at the edge of the road. Rand came and crouched next to him while Pau scanned the perimeter.

"You okay?"

"Yes, yes what happened? How did you—"

"The Sergeant is a good shot. We're not called Vampires for no reason."

"Yes, clearly."

"Sir, we should get rid of the bodies." Pau recommended.

Rand felt a bit sick. He had never seen a person die, much less head their head blown apart. He struggled to remain stoic as he clipped a strap on the NV helmet to his shoulder and slung it over his back. He didn't need Gerardo getting too close a look at it.

"Yes Pau, Gerardo can help you. I'll call and get the rest of Golf to come and escort us back to camp."

Just then, Elsie came over Rand's radio.

"Rand, where are you?"

"I'm in the jungle about half a click to your southwest. Gerardo was ambushed."

"Oh my God, are you okay?"

"I'm fine."

"And Gerardo?"

'Thanks to some excellent marksmanship from Sergeant Pau we're all fine. Send out the rest of Golf for an escort back. We're at the road intersection."

"Roger that, see you in a minute."

Gerardo and Pau were dragging the bodies into the forest. Rand left them and went into the jungle on the other side of the road to look for team Golf. Crouched behind a tree he fought the sick feeling from what he had just witnessed. Rand took the NV helmet off and took deep breaths until he heard team Golf approaching.

"Pull yourself together Rand." He hissed at himself quietly. As the team approached Rand squared himself and gave the challenge: "Armadillo."

"Wallet." Nickelson gave the reply instantly. Rand was the one who always made up the notoriously comical passwords called C&R (challenge and reply). Golf escorted them back to base and they regrouped in the command tent to debrief. Once the story had been told and all the details gone over it was decided that Rand's decision to follow Gerardo's group had been a wise one. Both Elsie and David Talbot asked him to please involve the chain of command before taking other such risky actions on the future. Pau was given special praise for his actions and received the undying gratitude of Gerardo. Afterwards Elsie and Rand retired to their quarters. When they were finally alone Elsie gave him a look that said she was furious that he risked himself, but after Gerardo's account of the events she had to admit that it was the right thing to do. Still, she scolded, he shouldn't have gone alone.

"I wasn't alone hon, I had you in my ears the whole time."

"What do you mean?"

He reached over to the earpiece control unit on her belt and changed some of the settings.

"Now just listen." He walked over to one of the barracks tents.

"Good evening sir." Rhodes stood at Rand's approach.

"As you were Rhodes", the soldier sat back down. "I wanted to tell you that you did an excellent job leading your fire team in drills today."

"Thank you sir."

"How are you finding jungle living?"

"It's hot as hell and sticky. McElroy says he's got the runs, but we're all in good spirits and ready for the mission sir."

"Glad to hear it. Send McElroy to see the medic, either Wiley or Nickelson. Dysentery is a serious concern out here."

"Yes sir."

"Keep on high alert tonight. We may have company."

Rhodes sat up straighter. "Yes sir, A2-can-do sir."

'That's catchy, you just make that up?'

"Naw, Taggart gets the credit for that one."

"Okay, get some rest before your shift… and see that deet on. Good night"

The Second String

Elsie watched Rand make his way back to their personal tent.

"I heard every word. I didn't know these things could do that."

"Yeah, I just discovered it. Hey, I wonder…"

Rand picked up the night vision helmets and carefully examined the controls. He had never spent much time with them and now he chastised himself about their maintenance. He should care for them like rare eggs. Looking over the controls at the back of the helmet, he found something that looked like a little Bluetooth symbol. It reminded him of his own time and a tinge of homesickness washed over him. It's always the little things that catch you unawares, he thought.

"Here it is." He flipped the small switch next to the symbol.

On the inside of Elsie's helmet, a small window appeared on the screen. It showed everything that Rand's helmet camera was seeing. He enabled the sharing function on both helmets.

"That's handy. I'm not sure how, but I know it is… hey, there's something else here." Rand squinted at the underside of the controls mounted to the back of the helmet. "We can record! This is a send to a high speed USB. Cool."

"Like you said, handy, just not sure how at this point."

"Oh I'm sure we'll find a use for it. Now come here. We've done enough for one day."

They slept next to each other in cots with one big net around them. Rand had horrible dreams about the men he had seen killed that day. They kept turning into people he had known. The corpses called to him from under their graves in the trees. The next day he went into the forest with a fire team to bury the bodies properly. Rand made sure that they had a cross over each of the bodies and said a blessing that the souls of these men, who had lived in such troubled times, rest in peace. On the walk back he talked to Talbot about the dreams from the night before. David assured him that it was normal and that it would get easier with the passing of time.

"Giving them a proper religious burial was the right thing to do, not only for them but for you too. Now when you have those dreams you can offer them up to God."

Gerardo stayed the night with them and then returned to his headquarters. He was going to find it difficult to find the people he needed for the mission in Buenos Aires. He knew he would have to hire mercenaries that couldn't know about the

The Second String

Americans in the jungle. Gerardo's men arrived at the camp three days later. There were two of them: Diego and Luis. Slight of build and hardened, they looked like villagers with Ak-47s slung over their shoulders. They spoke broken English but Talbot's translation filled in the gaps. Rand noticed that they weren't pleasant people; they didn't smile much or joke around and seemed to permanently be in a bad mood. Maybe, he thought, that's what happens to you when you kill too many people.

They started with survival training, showing the troops how to drink, sleep, eat and treat wounds with nothing but a knife. Diego and Luis lived like this everyday, they had no need of supplies or grocery stores. Wild game was abundant and when the Vampires were shown how, easy to catch. There were many poisonous insects, reptiles and plants to learn but there were no books, just the guides. Elsie had each fire team pick a note taker. One man drew the plants and recorded the information from the day. Over the evening meal the four fire teams would compare notes and make sure they all had the same information. Rand had specifically chosen to do it at mealtime so their subconscious would associate all the snakes, spiders and bugs with food in hopes it would be a cure for squeamishness. Face it, he thought, no one like the thought of eating grubs.

The note share became something everyone looked forward to. The officers insisted that the guides be there to listen and make corrections. Also, they thought it would help to integrate them into the little family. It worked. Slowly the guides opened up and started to see that the men were not interested in taking over their country. They were fascinated by it.

Rand watched as Diego looked through Wiley's drawings of the plants and animals.

"Good." Diego rattled off a few sentences.

Talbot translated, "He says you should have been an artist, you have captured the beauty of the forest."

"Tell him that the beauty of his land far exceeds my abilities to draw."

After Talbot translated, Diego just smiled and nodded his head. Rand was constantly impressed by how articulate and thoughtful the combat hardened veterans could be.

The training went on. Survival training gave way to evasion training as the men learned how to move through the landscape while being pursued without being detected. They used the jungle's rivers to hide in and travel quickly. Next came jungle warfare. Diego and Luis showed them how to set traps, ambushes, climb trees for sniper positions and use the terrain to their advantage.

The rivers now became a tool for sneaking up on an enemy. The teams would emerge from underwater, their rifles and ammunition sealed with condoms and a resin from a local tree, ready to attack. Elsie taught techniques on how to resist interrogation and torture and even how to escape from such situations. Rand threw himself into the training, openly talking about what he had experienced. It turned out that several of the men had also been captives during the war. It was a commonality that bonded the group even further.

After the training came a test in four parts. Each fire team had to survive interrogation, escape capture and survive for three days in the jungle with just their knives while trying to locate a guarded depot and access weapons. Then they had to assault a base manned by two fire teams and escape through the forest evading capture. It was practically impossible.

All of the fire teams passed the interrogation phase and managed to escape as well. All the teams also managed to survive for three days though some ended up a bit hungrier than others. Three of the four fire teams, the ones who decided to assault the depot at night, succeeded. The assault on the base resulted in mock casualties, most of the time three members of the assaulting team got whittled down to one who usually took off at a run into the jungle. This happened with three of the four teams. Fire team G2 got smart and surrounded the little base with traps then waited outside the perimeter of the traps and tossed grenades into the camp. Out of the two enemies that survived, both ran straight into the traps.

For the last test the fire teams had to escape with a head start while everyone else tried to track them. A1 split up and confused the trackers and only Johnson got caught. A2 stayed together and they all got caught. G1 tried to double back and assault their pursuers, but the plan backfired and they all ended up getting killed. G2 lost Pau and Reece but the camp medic / surgeon Nickelson ran so fast for so long that no one could catch him. Diego and Luis concluded that he couldn't keep that pace forever and the trail left by such a hasty retreat was easy to follow. The verdict; he would have been caught. That night they had a little ceremony in the mess tent. Fire team G2 was the overall winner. They all laughed hysterically as they recounted the events of the test.

"The best was Nickelson," Pau said, "I'm closed in on three sides, getting gunned down like a criminal and all I see is Nickelson's backside disappearing into the distance!"

They voted through the evening on things like who was most scared, worst camouflaged, worst tactics and most miserable death but in the end they all toasted Diego and Luis and made them honorary Vampires. They gave them a drawing of the Vampires logo, which they had changed to honour Diego and Luis. They had removed the crossed dagger and bullet and replaced it with the silhouette of a Hanwei V-42 Special Forces dagger. A single drop of red blood hung at the point while a pair of black, raised bat wings extended up from the hilt of the knife. A rough, red paint stroke of a 'V' made up the background.

Diego and Luis nodded and smiled in appreciation. "Just the knife, very good. But you are not also needing the knife."

"Yes, it reminds us what you taught us; that we can prevail no matter what we lack."

"Si," Diego nodded, "You have victory with this inside you. Your hearts beating, your blood alone."

Nickelson sat looking at the ceiling in hard concentration.

"In cruor unus." He said finally.

Elsie said, "Nickelson why are you speaking Latin?"

"If I have it right ma'am, it means *on blood alone*. Like Diego said."

Elsie raised he eyebrows and looked around at the officers. "Is that our creed?"

Both the officers and the men all nodded. Elsie stood and raised her canteen then they all stood, held up their canteens and made it so.

The next morning, about a half of a mile outside the camp, the watch found a boy calling into the forest for Diego. Luis and Diego met him and relayed the message through Talbot.

"Gerardo is coming back. He says be ready to go. He should be here by tonight."

Talbot assembled the men in the mess tent for Elsie. She addressed them informally.

"The time has come to leave Vampire Zulu. Take everything for combat, leave everything else. It all goes in a pile in the forest behind the command center tent. It's going to be a long night, let's go people."

They worked through the day quietly tearing down everything they had built. Any waste was buried in the latrine hole. The rest was made into a pile. The officers inspected everything that was put on the pile to make sure it couldn't be traced back to an American presence. The remaining supplies would go to Gerardo's people to help them. They finished just as the sun was setting. Elsie had the fire teams hide on the perimeter with Talbot at the entry point to the camp. After about an hour the call came in.

"Golf two has contact." Talbot radioed. "It's Gerardo."

"Let him come," Elsie replied, "stay concealed, we're gonna show him what we've learned."

Elsie waited until Gerardo came close to the airplane, still under the camouflage, then she stepped out alone.

"Gerardo, we got your message. How are you my friend?"

"Senora, you startled me!" He shook her hand. "Diego and Luis help you no?"

Elsie quietly gave the command over her radio, "Now."

The fire teams stepped out of the jungle. The whole airfield was surrounded and there were five men standing in a semi-circle around Gerardo. He threw his hands in the air, laughing. "You got me!"

The men burst into laughter as Rand clapped Gerardo on the back.

"Most impressive."

Diego and Luis came forward and greeted their comrade then they had a quick exchange.

"Diego told Gerardo that we were excellent students and are all like a family now." Talbot translated. "Also, that they would like to go with us on our mission."

Elsie and Rand looked at each other with a smile. "We are honoured to have our brothers join us. Can they do a HALO jump?"

Gerardo talked quickly to Diego and Luis.

"Sadly, no." Gerardo explained. "They have never had the parachuting, nor me. There is no time to learn. The time is now to strike!" He held up a meaty fist.

"Tonight?"

"Yes, tonight. I have all the plans, maps, names and pictures."

"Gerardo, a surgical strike is something that takes days, even weeks to plan. It is carefully rehearsed and only then do you go in. We'd be jumping in with limited knowledge and no backup. It's very risky and not the correct way to do it."

"But I tell you it is tonight, they are all in one building. A big hotel. They have a party. They are plan something."

Elsie called the officers together and let Gerardo make his appeal. He described the situation, detailed who was there and how the Vampire's could take the Nazis by surprise.

When he was done Elsie said to them, "Gentlemen I need your opinions. Go or no go. Talbot, what do you say?"

"Go. We'll plan on the way."

"Carl?"

"Go. The Spook can cover you in pretty much any situation."

"Rand?"

"Go. I agree with Talbot and Carl."

"So be it. Gerardo, you have your raid."

"Wait Senora, what was to be your vote?"

She smiled, "In cruor unus. Go."

The camouflage netting over the plane was stripped off as the teams loaded in. Gerardo, Diego and Luis stood by watching as Rand came up to them.

"Get on board gentlemen. You may not be able to jump but there's plenty to do."

All three sprouted smiles and hurried onto the plane, they were greeted by cheers from the men. Talbot had radioed the transport ship *Provider* to let them know that they would need them on standby. The big ship had been running cargo from

Rio De Janeiro to the port towns of Paranaguá and Antonina on the Brazilian coast. They were only a fifty miles away from the abandoned pier.

Rand was the last to board the plane. He lifted the ramp for take-off as they bumped along, taxiing to set up on the runway. The soft whirr of the engines disguised their power as the huge plane sprinted up to speed and leaped into the air. The dark jungle absorbed the sound of their passage until they were a whisper under the sliver of the moon.

Chapter 8

Bozo's last ride

'...the evil plan is most harmful to the planner.'
~Hesiod, 800 B.C.

They flew at treetop level again. Rand knew Elsie was going to have her work cut out for her as she combed over the charts trying to find the best approach.

"Gerardo, get up there and tell Elsie where we're going."

Gerardo jumped up and handed Rand the big square cloth bag he always wore. It was full of papers and photos. "Look Mr. Carter, all the information is here." He took a map out and climbed up to the cockpit. Rand looked through the documents with Talbot.

The list of Nazi names was three pages long. There were over fifty photographs, most of them showed three to five people, all wanted. Rand froze when he saw the picture of Hitler. He had no moustache, he wore a white short-sleeved linen shirt and sunglasses. He was stretched out in a chair on the beach.

"Son-of-a-bitch. The most evil man in history and he's lounging on the beach." Rand was incredulous.

"Well I hope he had fun cause tonight's the night that all gets set to rights." Talbot was grim. "We can't take them all, there are too many of them, but we can't leave them alive either. It's going to be a nasty bit of business." Talbot's face had turned to stone. "You stay out of it Rand. Leave it to us."

Rand knew that he wasn't capable of killing people in cold blood, no matter what they were guilty of. He wanted to protest but he knew it wasn't his place to do so. This was their time, not his. They combed through the intel and worked to get a grasp of the situation. Most of the men slept, laid out on the floor of the huge cargo bay.

"The return is too far, we have to find another place to get Spooky onto the Provider." Rand was pouring over maps. "Could you send Gerardo down here hon?" Rand asked over the radio.

"He's on his way."

Gerardo came down and joined them. "Your lady, she has one smart cookies."

Rand just laughed.

"Okay Gerardo, I know we're stretching your contacts to the limit but we've got to get this plane back onto that ship. We might be able to make it as far as Pelotas."

"Si my friend, I understand. You are looking for a place to land and have reach of ship's crane." He looked over the map. "Rio Grande. This place might have hope." He brought out a magnifying glass and looked at the sea chart. "You see the Ponte Don Franceses bridge? There is no…" He struggled with the word and waved his hand in the air like he was shaping a dome.

"Supports?"

"Superstructure?"

Gerardo pointed at Rand. "Structures, si. It has space for the wings."

"But it's a road. Aren't there lamp posts?"

"No, no lamps. It is no matter that it is a road. It will be late night, no persons there. Plane land, ship, bridge, is done."

"You might have something there Gerardo. I'll call the Provider and see if her Captain agrees." Talbot headed up to the cockpit and the communications station.

Rand smiled at the big Panamanian. "If the Provider agrees, you may just have figured out the last piece of the puzzle. We can post road block teams at either side of the bridge and pretend we're a construction crew."

"Si!" Gerardo tapped his temple. "If you put big cover over plane, it will hide it when you crane up."

"Once we get to the U.S. we can disembark at a pier in Galveston, Texas. It's a lot like the pier in Itapoá. We should be able to take off from there and make it to Alamogordo."

Talbot came back down. "We're on, Gerardo you did it. The captain will push like hell to get the Provider on station in six hours. There are plenty of old piers at Rio Grande where he can stay on station until we arrive. The bridge is low to the water and a perfect loading location."

"Great Dave. We can refuel on the Provider?"

"Yes, he's still got a full load of avgas."

"Okay, that settles it. Boy am I glad you decided to come along Gerardo."

Rand took a one hour nap then relieved Elsie so she could get a few hours rest. Carl had the cockpit well stocked with thermos' full of coffee. He was just emptying the second one into a cup for Rand. 'Hey Rand, got everything nailed down?'

"Yeah, with Gerardo's help we got an LZ at a place called Rio Grande, no relation to the big river up north."

"Is it another pier?"

"No, I think you'll like this even better. It's on a flat bridge."

"That'll be fun."

"I've got the charts on the navigation table whenever you're ready to do the needful."

Carl climbed out of the pilot's seat while Rand took over flying.

"Hold her steady on two-one-two."

"Roger that."

The tall blonde pilot combed over the charts for the next hour, asking Rand questions about particulars. He had to wake Gerardo and put him on the radio to get weather reports under the guise of being a cargo vessel. The ploy worked and after he got the information out of him, he let the big man go back to sleep. He poured a big cup of coffee then climbed back into the pilot's seat.

"Okay, all the navs are done." Carl smiled.

"We've got a serious operation to complete with no practice runs and very little intel. As far as we know the skies could be swarming with Argentinean Air Force and the Army as thick as ants on the ground. Talbot tells me they have

Gloster Meteor jets." Rand tried to keep Carl's mind on the complexity of what they were about to attempt.

"Bah! No problem." Carl waved it off. "We'll grab those krauts and be out of there before they know what hit them. Then all we do is high-tail it off the beach in Buenos Aires and stay low for two-hours, forty-four minutes to Rio Grande."

"The whole time avoiding military radar, pissed off Argentinean fighter jets and spotters from the ground."

"Then we're up the coast as a northerly off-shore breeze gives us the red carpet onto the bridge."

"Providing the ship doesn't run into any snags, there's no traffic on the road or hordes of ship or land based witnesses." Said Rand skeptically.

"Once we're on the ship we fold up the wings and put Spooky to sleep with a nice bed time story."

"Then pray that we can escape South American seas without running into the Argentinean Navy on or below the water."

"Kick back for the trip to Galveston, unload and bee-line to Alamogordo for the hand-off. Then it's home sweet home."

Rand gave Carl a wink. "I sure hope we're telling your version of the story when we get there."

Carl sat up straight in his chair, reached up and flipped the red light switch. "Ding, ding, we're twenty minutes out."

Elsie had just reached around Rand from behind. "How's it going up here?"

"Your husband was just giving me a lesson in optimism."

"Hey sleepyhead, ready for a busy night?" Rand tried to grin, "The plan is pretty straight forward, Talbot will fill you in."

Talbot came into the cockpit just then. "Yes I will. Okay, here's the scoop…" They sat behind Rand and Carl in the navigation and communications seats, drank coffee and went over the logistics. Then they went over the assault plan for the final time as the men assembled and prepared for the jump. Fifteen minutes later Elsie addressed them.

"I know you live for this part, I finally get to reveal to you what the plan is. Gentlemen, tonight we will make history. We are on our way to Buenos Aires, Argentina. Our primary mission is to recover a woman named Erna Remmel. Here is a picture of her." She handed the picture around.

"Our secondary mission is the capture of Adolf Hitler."

Elsie let it sink in. The men looked back and forth at each other. Baker raised his hand. Elsie already knew the question.

"Yes Baker, THE Adolf Hitler. We thought he was dead, Gerardo found out otherwise." She handed the picture around of Hitler on the beach. All of the men grew very grim. All of them had fought in Europe during the war. Many gave a gesture of appreciation to Gerardo. It was clear that the picture of Hitler lounging on the beach angered them beyond words.

"Get back in the game gentlemen, we start getting emotional and we start making mistakes. He's an objective, nothing else. You can feel something about it after we're done." She looked at each one of them. "Am I clear?" There were nods all around. She was right and they knew it. Faces changed expression and they got their minds back on task.

"There are three pages of names here that are all wanted Nazis." She passed around the list. "Write down the highlighted names, those are the ones we want to take with us. The ones in blue are alternates in case some of the primaries are KIA."

The men scribbled into their books as the list went around.

"Everyone got it? Okay, they are having a party at this hotel tonight." She passed around photos of the hotel from various angles. "The Argentinean government will be there to some extent but we give no quarter to Nazi sympathisers. We're going to hit fast and hard then get the hell out of there. Everyone has to do their job. If one person fails, it will mean failure for the whole operation, do you understand?"

She laid out a drawing of the hotel and the grounds. "Okay, here's how it goes: HALO jump into position; A1 on the roof, G2 with Mr. Talbot on the lawn in the front. A2 on the side entrance; you will cut the power and cover the exit. G1 will secure the beachside facility and set markers for the plane to land. Spooky will provide close air support and eliminate any reinforcements. When we get our quarry we will herd them all to the beach. Be prepared for hysterics, women in dresses crying, the whole charade.

"For all intents and purposes they are cattle, don't let one of them slow you up or get the jump on you. These people are fanatical and they will know this is their last stand. Shock and awe is the strategy. Keep them in shock until we have them bound and on the plane. Spooky will be on the beach. Diego, Luis and Gerardo will be binding, bagging and gagging the quarry. Once they are loaded, we're out of there. A1 and G1 will guard from the corners while A2 and G2 strap them into their seats.

'There will be no conversation. These people will not know what our faces look like nor what our voices sound like. I'm told it's a two-hour and forty-four minute flight to our rendezvous with the Provider. We'll be landing on a road bridge this time. The Provider will pull along side and hoist us from there. Because of the change in location we will be covering Spooky with the camo tarp in case we have any prying eyes. A2 and G2 will go to opposite ends of the bridge and put up road blocks. Your story is that the bridge is closed for late night maintenance. It will be open in a few hours. Debrief on board Provider. Expect security detail. Questions? Okay, sticks in the wind in…" She looked up the ladder at Carl. He flashed a 'two' and 'five' with his hands. "Twenty-five minutes. That will be all." Elsie went back up to the cockpit.

"Rand I am definitely expecting the military to respond. After the shooting starts they will probably come down the main road with troop trucks and armoured cars, you have to keep them from getting to the hotel."

Rand knew that this was where the rubber would met the road. "Elsie, I don't know if I can do it."

"What do you mean?"

"I mean taking lives; I don't think I can do it. In the forest, Pau shot the three guerillas. I still haven't gotten over it. I don't think I can do it, even from the air."

Elsie thought hard for a minute. "It's okay maybe you don't have to. When you see the reinforcements they should be far enough away. Just shoot forty millimetre grenades into the road in front of the approaching vehicles. It will blow holes big enough to stop them. From there, the soldiers will have to travel on foot. It should slow them down long enough for us to make our escape. Once we have Bozo and Bimbo I'll signal you."

"Wait, Bozo and Bimbo?"

"Yeah."

"So Hitler is…"

"Bozo."

"And Bimbo?"

"Erna."

"Did you just make that up now? That's good!" He chuckled. "Okay, that makes me feel better, but Elsie…" He looked at her very seriously. "Know that if you or any of the team is in danger I won't hesitate to shoot to kill. I don't want to and I'll do anything I can not to, but if it comes to that don't worry, I won't let you down."

She put her hand to his face and kissed him. "Let's hope it doesn't come to that." She cleared her throat and put on her serious face.

"Now stay focused. You'll land on the beach, just like Padre Island. Carl, if the sand is too soft you know what to do, just keep her rolling. Rand you lower the ramp but don't let it drag, it could get the plane stuck. You have to hit the beach with the stretcher and start loading in as many prisoners and/or bodies as the boys bring in. It's gonna be gruesome but it's gotta be done."

"David was thinking we'd only take the live ones." Carl interjected. "There are just too many of them."

"Okay, that makes sense. Let's go with that. So Rand, forget about the stretcher and just help Diego, Luis and Gerardo tag and bag. Carl when we're all in, hightail it out of here fast and low. I'm counting on this whole thing to take no longer than ten minutes. Any longer and we could be dealing with ground forces and fighter planes and that would not be good."

"Elsie?" Rand said with a worried tone.

"Yeah hon, what's wrong?"

"There are too many Nazis to fit onto the plane. What happens to the rest of them?"

Elsie cleared her throat looked away from him, she couldn't look into his eyes.

"I'm the one who answers that question. Me and me alone." Talbot stood on the stair. "Elsie you will have nothing to do with it, you either Rand." He turned and faced down the stairs. "We don't have room for all the Nazi bastards. I will take care of it. I will kill them. No one else need be involved.

"None of them can be left to spread the disease they tried to kill the world with. If we leave them alive, Argentina will be the cause of another war. The U.S. will come down here and try to find the rest of the Nazis and Argentina will refuse. The Soviets will back the Argentines and it will be World War 3.

"Now I know that what I'm saying is not right, believe me. I'm not the murdering type. However, it is less wrong than failing to administer any justice at all and less wrong than starting another war. I am grateful for the chance to do such a horrible service, what is saved will outweigh what is lost."

The plane was silent. Gerardo stood up and walked over to Talbot. "You will not bear this burden alone. I have enough rage to spend on them and never feel guilt. I will show them hell. Luis came and stood beside Talbot, then Diego and several other men. They didn't say a word. As they stood looking at the others they seemed to be grim angels, bent on a mission of reaping.

"So be it." Elsie said.

Rand tapped his watch, it was time to go. Talbot barked the order. "Alright, strap in for ascension." The cabin erupted into activity. As soon as everyone was in their chairs and buckled down for the ride Talbot gave the ready and Carl pulled the Spook into it's steep circling climb. Rand counted off the climb rate and after twenty minutes, she hit twenty thousand feet.

"At this point we will be on their radar." Elsie said as the engine throttled up to full speed.

"Three minutes to target." Rand called down then switched all the red lights off except one. Elsie waited for two minutes then put on her oxygen mask and opened the door. As always she stood with her back to the door, saluted the men and fell backwards into the howling darkness. Talbot followed as the rest of the men jumped in mission order.

Once the men were out Rand came down and closed the door. After a minute the cabin had repressurised and he removed his oxygen mask. As he lowered the banks of weapons, the plane descended rapidly and he strapped into the fire control chair. He flipped on the two night scopes that had been mounted on the sighting mechanism for the plane's weapons and began scouting the location for any military presence. He keyed his radio by a button next to the trigger.

"Comm check, Spooky."

"Spooky, Alpha Zero, check clear."

"Spooky, Golf Zero, check clear over."

"Golf one, multiple tangos in the gazebo on the beach. Alpha one, lone tango on roof…" Rand started calling targets as the teams began firing their silenced weapons before they even landed. Rand winced as he saw the figures drop.

***

As Alpha Zero Elsie lead A2 to the side of the building. She had switched from oxygen mask to her NV helmet at five thousand feet. The fire team hit the ground running, went straight to the electrical panel and cut the power. At the same time A1 landed on the roof. Johnson took out the guard sniper with one shot from his silenced MAS-49 as he descended. Fire team G1 landed on the beach side of the building and headed for the large beachfront gazebo. G2 took the front with Talbot in the lead, sniping out any lights that were still on.

As soon as the lights went out, the Argentinean security units scrambled. Elsie's team stationed at the side door leaned around the sides and started shooting anyone who left the building from the front, rear or from the doors on their side. Elsie and Taggart concentrated most of their fire on the front doors as people started streaming out. They shot low at the legs and caught the exiting Nazis in crossfire with shots coming from G2 flanking the front of the building. After the first few fell to the ground the ones behind them retreated back indoors, screaming and pushing.

G1 sent Reece down to the bar and gazebo on the beach. As there were no guards, he took the place by himself without firing a shot. Nickelson and Pau each took a corner and so managed to cover the side, rear and front from their end of the hotel. Team A1 worked their way through the interior from the roof, herding people out as they went.

All of their training on the ship now came into play as they cleared room after room. After five minutes, A1 signalled from the front hall. "Tango prime and secondary, I repeat, tango prime and secondary. Bozo and Bimbo secure and uninjured." They had found them together.

From above, Rand could see the action as they slowly circled. Faster than expected, military troop trucks were out on the road heading Southeast towards the hotel accompanied by armoured half-tracks. He could see the soldiers stacked in the back of the truck. He selected the grenade launcher and sighted ahead of the fast moving vehicles as he squeezed the trigger. Fourteen fist sized rounds chugged out of the sky creating an exploding line of devastation down the road.

The lead truck plummeted into the crater left by the explosion and immediately stopped the convoy. As the other vehicles tried to manoeuvre around the obstacle Rand created more craters, trapping the vehicles. The stunned soldiers couldn't tell where the fire was coming from and took cover behind anything they could find.

Rand shot a barrage of forty-millimetre grenades that landed in an open air market behind them to the Northwest. The soldiers, believing the fire was coming from the market, turned and began moving away from the hotel. They concentrated on setting up an assault on the market which was over six blocks away. Rand was elated. By the time they got to the market and figured out they had been duped, the Vampires would be long gone.

"Reinforcements have been diverted. You're all clear."

"That's great news Papa bear." Elsie sent back. "We're almost done here."

On the field below, the noise of Rand's handiwork convinced both the Nazis and the Argentineans that hundreds of troops were attacking the city. Rand continued to cover the Vampires below as Carl tried to line up the big plane for a landing.

"Bozo and Bimbo secure." Came Elsie's call over the radio.

"Okay Carl time to get down there." Rand radioed up to the cockpit.

"I can't line up, the wind coming off the ocean is too strong, I'm going to have to go around again."

Rand leaped out of his chair and bounded up the stairs into the cockpit.

"We don't have time. They'll have air support by then." He climbed into the co-pilot's seat and took the controls. Remembering Elsie's training in the C-17, he pushed the big plane into a steep climb, causing the plane to stall. "It's the best way I know to lose altitude fast. Hang on!" Rand yelled. Carl yelled something unintelligible back at him as the engines screamed. Rand squared himself and remembered what Elsie had shown him. He slowly corrected the fall and recovered control of the plane at a thousand feet over the beach. Then he let it drift in for a hard landing. Carl took over the controls, shaken and looking at Rand wide-eyed. Rand was already out of the seat as Gerardo stood ready with Diego and Luis to lower the ramp.

"What you doing up there crazy peoples?" Gerardo complained. "You fly drunk?"

As A1 signalled from the lobby, Talbot brought his team up to the steps and started going through the people. There were several leg injuries, but so far no casualties. Fire team G2 started identifying faces and pulling them out. They picked out the top names on the list and worked their way down. Elsie came around to the front and called out names from the list. Only a few stepped forward.

"You need to go now Elsie." Talbot looked at her grimly. "I've looked at them all like you requested."

She reached around and flicked off the recorder at the back of his NV helmet. They had documented the whole raid on video, every face of every Nazi, but what was about to happen didn't need to be filmed. With her back to the room she raised her visor and looked hard at Talbot. His eyes were steely under his balaclava. "You're sure about this?"

"Just go."

Elsie knew there was no talking him out of it. She lowered her visor, turned and followed the teams back to the plane with the prisoners.

"Where are the three amigos?" She asked Rand when she got back. He pointed towards the hotel. Gerardo, Diego and Luis had somehow passed her and now stood with balaclavas on, next to David in the distance. Elsie turned into Rand's chest and they both looked away. The chatter of four, silenced Thompson sub-machine guns introduced the remaining Nazis to the horrible reality of their final solution.

The teams made themselves busy securing the prisoners. Each one was the same: duct tape over the mouth, black hood over the head and handcuffs. They were made to sit on the hard floor of the cargo area while the soldiers secured them, starting from the cargo door and working up to the front. Elsie took off her NV helmet and adjusted the balaclava she had worn underneath as she worked her way towards the front of the plane.

Talbot, Luis, Diego and Gerardo returned and raised the ramp. The floor was covered in prisoners, some being treated by the two medics. She looked up to take the ladder to the cockpit and came face to face with Hitler. He was standing at the foot of the ladder, handcuffed but not yet hooded or gagged. They stared each other in the eyes for a long moment. Suddenly her elbow lashed out and smashed him in the face. He sprawled backwards, unconscious.

"Keep that piece of shit hooded and gagged." Elsie quietly ordered Baker.

Rand followed her up to the cockpit.

"All in." Paige reported quietly to the cockpit.

"Now Carl, let's leave this accursed place."

The engines revved to full as the plane lumbered down the beach, much heavier than it was when it had landed. They barely cleared the approaching waterline as the Spook took to the air and climbed hard. Carl and Rand pulled together and retracted the landing gear as it grazed the tops of the trees. Carl left the engines at full throttle, flying extremely low at top speed from the city. Behind them sirens wailed and searchlights began to stab skyward, desperately hunting for a target, but Spooky, faithful to her name quietly slipped away.

Under a strict 'no talking' order, the Vampires watched the Nazis like they were burning holes in them with their eyes. The plane reeked of cordite and adrenaline. Two and three-quarter hours passed like a blink. As they approached Rio Grande, Gerardo radioed the Provider and spoke only the code word that Rand had made him practice that told the ship that they were on final approach.

Gerardo keyed the mic looking hesitantly at Rand and said, "Wuhzaaaah."

Rand went into convulsions trying to suppress hysterical laughter while Talbot looked at Gerardo like he'd lost his mind. Gerardo just shrugged and pointed at Rand. Elsie meanwhile buried her head in embarrassment. The laughter from the cockpit broke the thick tension among the Vampires and everyone started to breathe easier.

Carl put on Elsie's NV helmet to land at the Ponte Dos Franceses Bridge at Rio Grande. The whimpers and crying of the prisoners had faded and the cargo hold was eerily quiet. With a soft bump, the plane touched down. Elsie couldn't believe that they had just landed on a bridge.

When she gave him a thumbs up, Carl just blew his nails and scrubbed them on his shirt. The teams mobilised in a flash, happy to have something to do to. The bridge seemed like it was in the middle of nowhere. They let the prisoners relieve themselves briefly though they had to remain hooded and cuffed. They gave them water one at a time, removing the gag long enough for them to drink then putting it back in place and moving to the next one.

At the same time the Provider quietly and gingerly pulled up to the bridge. The big ship practically spanned the channel and the engines rumbled sporadically as she struggled to hold position. Finally she was moored securely as the prisoners were herded back into the plane under guard.

With the wings folded, the camouflage tarp on and the harness rigged for the lift, the men scrambled to connect it to the crane. Under the watchful eye of Captain Carl, the job was completed in under a minute and everyone piled back into the cargo area as Rand closed the door. This time there was a lot of groaning and creaking as the giant crane hoisted the heavy craft into the hold. The plane settled on its rest and they heard the sound of the crew securing her to her moorings.

Rand opened the rear hatch when the tapping signal came on the fuselage and they herded the prisoners into the ship. In silence, the crew guided them to where the prisoners would be kept. Because there were so many, they were kept in various places all over the ship and never in groups. To prevent them from communicating to each other they would always be bound, gagged and hooded anytime they were around other prisoners.

Talbot went straight to the radio room and made a secure connection to his bosses at the CIA. They were shocked at the news and several times Talbot threatened to hang up on them and take the prisoners to the U.S. Military. In the end, the CIA wanted in on the already successful raid.

"Listen closely," Talbot said to his CIA boss. | This whole thing was a private operation. I was invited along, but by no means was I a representative of the CIA. Actually, I don't work for you any more. I work for Rand and Elsie Carter. This mission was conceived at Groom Lake, but was financed entirely by the Carters. U.S. military veterans from various branches of the service formed the whole of the mission unit. So the way I see it, you should be glad that we contacted you at all. Now do want a piece of this or not?"

"I see Talbot." Came the voice over the radio. "Well this is of course all very surprising, but then you are an outstanding undercover agent. What part of this are the Carter's willing to share?"

"What kind of question is that? They're not looking for credit, they're looking for justice."

"We are certainly interested in the same thing. What do you need from us?"

"Just a place to unload the cargo. We'd like to drop off all the clowns, including Bozo, to the fine folks at Alamogordo. We'll include a full report of the mission with photographs and recovered intel. We just need a refuel to get back to Groom Lake. Of course, a little celebration may be in order." He turned and smiled to Rand and Elsie who were listening to the whole conversation.

"Talbot you can count on it. You and your team, the… what did you call yourselves?"

"Vampires."

"Yes, well you and the Vampires, including the Carters of course, can consider Groom Lake your home base. You'll have your own facilities including R&D. You can continue working in your capacity there as cover. We will provide you with assistants who can take over in your absence, upon your approval of course."

"That's a very good offer. I will let the Carters know and we'll get back to you."

"Yes, well that will be fine. Talbot, are you sure you want to leave the company? With all of this there are some real opportunities here."

"Yes, I'm sure. I feel I can best serve the interests of the country by working with you on a less restricted basis."

"Well then, I'm sure that will be the case. We'll arrange everything as you requested. Thank you for your service, and I know I speak for everyone here when I say congratulations on your remarkable success. We truly owe the Vampires a debt of gratitude. Rest assured we will remember that. Gavel out."

"Well that went well." Elsie said. "Do you trust them?"

"Not as far as I could throw Spooky, but I know they will follow through on their deals. To them this is a new relationship. They are afraid of what we've accomplished without anyone's aid or knowledge. They know we are very, very dangerous and they will try to assuage their fears by trying to control us. I expect that Congress will start handing down edicts regulating our activities very shortly."

"That is assuming that we take them up on their offer to make Groom Lake our home base." Elsie smiled and turned to Rand, knowing that he had the rest of the thought already on the tip of his tongue.

"That is assuming that we even need a base, or that we are even forming an organisation." Rand smiled back at Elsie. "The Vampires will dissolve and fade into obscurity. As far as anyone knows, they were assembled for just one mission. Of course, at anytime they can be reformed."

"They can't control what isn't there. They can't issue edicts and laws that apply to only a few people." Rand assured him.

"Don't worry Dave. You will always have job with us, even if it's your job to relax and have some fun." She gave the man a hug.

They treated the captives in strict accordance with the Geneva Convention. Once the prisoners had been stowed, the Vampires were formally welcomed back to the *Provider*. There was a palpable excitement from the crew as they were briefed on the prisoners. Then Captain Delarosa addressed his crew.

"We have a policy not to get involved in our passengers missions, but the circumstances are different this time. We must assist in the care of these prisoners for humanitarian reasons. Not for the prisoners sake, but to make sure that our friends here do not get blamed for any mistreatment and tarnish their stellar achievement and contribution to all of mankind. So we must do our part."

The crew applauded this idea and the Vampires were all very grateful, once again, to the *Provider*.

Elsie did the debriefing.

"I know you're all tired so I'll make this fast. Once again the Vampires have, against all odds, completed the mission without a single friendly injury or casualty."

There was applause and cheers at this.

"I want to make something very clear to you all. We have changed history. We have made a difference. We have served on the side of righteousness and prevailed." As she scanned the faces she looked at Talbot, Gerardo, Ruiz and Diego. "Let your conscience be clean because tonight you were the sword of justice, wielded by the hand of Justice herself."

"We couldn't take all the trash with us. We left a few of them, where they left millions but be assured, their final destination is a bit different than those blessed souls. So, do not mourn. Do not wake with bad dreams. Know that what we did was in service to, as the good Captain said, all of humanity. I am proud of you all."

The men stood and applauded her. Some shed tears. She shook hands with and saluted each one, calling them by name. Then it was to quarters for a hot shower and sleep. Rand closed the door quietly as she stripped out of her night ops uniform.

"I know you believe everything you said in there."

"Absolutely or I wouldn't have said it."

"Still, I have a tough time with it."

"You know the reasons Rand. If you're going to look at it, then look at the whole thing. Don't search for evidence to convict and ignore the evidence in defense. Better yet, don't look for any evidence at all. The decision made at the time was the right one or things wouldn't have turned out the way they did."

"So you're saying just stop dwelling on it?"

"Exactly, let it go."

"Okay."

It sounded simple and it was. As the ship headed to Galveston, Rand kept busy. Any time guilt or remorse tried to find it's way in, he asked it to prove that it deserved to be there. Every time he challenged it, it had to back down and slink away. They pulled into Galveston at midnight, said good-bye to the crew of the *Provider* and met Gerardo, Diego and Luis on deck. The Vampires surrounded the three men, shaking their hands, patting them on the back and exchanging addresses and numbers. Gerardo extended an invitation for all of them to visit his home, but demanded a visit from Pau who saved his life.

"I have many children and several beautiful daughters. Who knows Pau, you may decide to stay down there." Gerardo gave a him a bear hug.

Elsie and Rand paid all three of them enough to take care of their families for the rest of their lives.

"This is not necessary Senora."

"No Gerardo, you have more than earned it. Since your names will not be known, at least you should have a reward to help you live a long and peaceful life from now on. Live it well, we will always remember you."

"You are always welcome in our homes. If you need anything please don't hesitate to call on us."

"Of course, the same goes for you - my three amigos."

She gave them all a kiss and went below.

The Second String

The ship unloaded the plane on to a large pier with the prisoners and the Vampires inside. Then the teams unfolded the wings and the plane taxied into position. A long road lead from the pier straight across a barren dirt flat where the shipping company stored freight until it was loaded.

"It's almost identical to Itapoá."

The Spook climbed into the sky and lumbered towards Holloman Air Force Base at Alamogordo (aka White Sands) New Mexico. White Sands was an apt description of the place. It was smack in the middle of a barren New Mexico desert and had been used as a test facility for the first atomic bombs. When they arrived this time there was a contingent of over a hundred Army soldiers and Air Force guards that met them. The commander of the base and his officers were there to greet them and supervise the prisoner transfer.

"Good morning, I am Colonel Ostrander. Who is in charge here?"

"I am sir." Elsie stepped forward and saluted. "Major Elsie Carter sir."

Ostrander did his best to conceal his surprise. Ranking senior Air Force officers were never female.

"Major, I'm not sure who authorised this mission or even who you are. What I've been told is that you and your team are heroes and it's my job to make sure you have everything you need."

"Thank you Colonel, just fuel sir and we'll be on our way."

"That's it?"

"Yes sir." She handed him the photographs and intel that had been gathered in Argentina. "I officially transfer these over to your care sir, top secret. I have more photos to send that will identify the Nazis killed in the raid but I have to develop them first." Talbot was to the side, taking pictures of the exchange for insurance.

"We have a state-of-the-art photo lab here Major, you're welcome to use it. My people can—"

"Not for these pictures Colonel. The means with which they were taken is beyond classified. There is a unique method for their development that I can only perform with special equipment at our base."

"Which is where?"

"I am not permitted to tell you sir."

The Colonel looked at her from under his bushy eyebrows, clearly frustrated at having no information about the team.

"Very well Major. Well done."

"Thank you sir, good bye."

Elsie returned to the back ramp of the plane. A black curtain had been drawn to hide the contents.

"Oh Major." Elsie turned back to the Colonel. "What do you call your outfit?"

"We're the Vampires sir."

The ramp closed and the plane, lighter after off loading the Nazis, quietly whirred down the runway and leapt into the sky.

The Colonel watched them leave. "Vampires. Now I've seen it all."

Just then one of the guards came running up. "Sir! It's one of the prisoners…you're not gonna believe this…"

After leaving Holloman AFB the soldiers had only one prisoner to take care of: Erna Remmel. It had become clear that she had gone into hiding with the rest of the Nazis. She was completely dedicated to Hitler and wept bitterly about his capture and her separation from him and Eva Braun. It was for this reason that she was treated as a prisoner. She was not told where she was going or that she was going to be reunited with her husband until the plane touched down at Groom Lake. When they finally arrived at Area 51, it was seven in the morning.

Elsie sat down across from her as the engines were winding down. She removed the hood and the gag. "Mrs. Remmel you are being reunited with your husband. He is outside waiting to see you. You will have to stand trial, but it is still possible for you to start a new life if you choose."

"I have nothing to say to you or him." The woman's face was as hard as stone.

Elsie lowered the big ramp as Rand and Carl came down from the cockpit.

"Will ya get a load of this!" Carl said as the ramp lowered to reveal all of the personnel on the base swarming to greet them. Elsie, Rand, Carl, Talbot and quite a few of the men were swept up and carried around as the crowd roared their congratulations.

The Chief Engineer, simply known as *Chief* shook Rand's hand until it was about to fall off.

"The message came in just after you left White Sands; Major Carter's Vampires coming home as heroes. Nazis captured or killed in midnight raid. Hitler and staff captured! We woke the whole base! It's like the war is really over!"

Rand was slapped on the back, shook hands, and hugged so many times his head was spinning. Somewhere in the middle of it all, he and Elsie were pushed together. He swept her up in a long kiss as someone popped a bottle of champagne and sprayed it all over them.

***

Across the tarmac, Dr. Remmel watched the celebrations. As he looked through the crowd his eyes came to rest on his wife standing at the back of the plane. He excitedly wheeled towards her, but as he got closer he slowed. She had seen him. Hatred and contempt etched across her face. He slowly came to a stop and slumped in misery, his tears hiding a rage that began in his soul. He listened to the cheering around him. The Carters, why did they come here? His plan would have worked. His Erna would have loved him again. It was all in the timing. He would be with her in Argentina taking long walks on the beach. He grasped his useless legs and thought again bitterly of walks on the beach. Slowly he turned and wheeled his chair away.

***

The celebration lasted into the small hours of the morning. It was a chance for the people at the secret base to relax for once. Many toasts were made and many of them to the Vampires. Most of the talk was about Hitler and that he was caught alive. Occasionally someone with too much drink would start to get a little loose-lipped around people from other departments. They were intercepted before anything was revealed and courteously but quickly ushered off by their colleagues.

Just after they landed, Elsie made sure that Erna Remmel was placed in a detention cell under tight security. She knew that the woman was a fanatic and may try and harm herself or others. It was two in the morning when Elsie and Rand went to check on the guard. They wanted make sure he got relieved so he could take part in the party. The cell was in back of the security offices adjacent to the armoury. Most of the security personnel were either on watch or at the party and the office was empty. They passed through the front office and made their way to the door that lead to the hallway where the cell was located.

"Man they must have cleaned the heck out of this place, it smells like a dentist office in here."

"Yeah it's strong. That man keeps a tight ship."

"Lewis, it's Captain and Major Carter." Elsie said as they approached the door. Rand spoke the password, "Mushroom." There was no answer.

The Second String

They looked at each other as they opened the hallway door. There was no guard.

"Private Lewis?"

"Wow, that smell is really strong in here."

"I don't like this Rand."

They drew their pistols and moved quickly to the end of the hall. Looking in the cell, they saw Lewis lying inside still armed. Rand's head started to throb and quickly developed into a pounding thump that went to his ears. He turned to retreat back up the hall but his legs were like lead weights. Somewhere at the edge of perception he heard Elsie collapse but couldn't see her, his sight was a blurred fog, then blackness.

The pounding returned with an intense pain in his head. It matched the sound of his heart that beat like a mallet high and piercing. Just when he thought it was going to drive him mad the pounding turned to throbbing then eased as it was slowly replaced by the beeping sound of an old-fashioned heart monitor. Light trickled into his vision that was foggy, but clearing.

"Rand? He's coming around. Rand? Can you hear me?"' It was Talbot standing over him, there were other faces too. "Your in the infirmary, what happened?"

"I… I don't know. Where's Elsie?"

"She's fine, she's right here beside you. She's coming around now too. Can you tell us what happened?"

"We went to the cell to check on Lewis. He was out cold, in the cell. Remmel's wife was gone."

"So is Remmel."

"When did this happen?"

"Um, about two in the morning." The fog was lifting but he still had a bad headache. "What knocked us out?"

"Our lab has been working on that since we found you around two thirty this morning. It appears to be an aerosol version of a fast-acting, powerful opiate called Fentanyl. The Russians have used something like it in the past."

"Russians again?" Rand sat up and leaned over to Elsie as she came back around.

"Rand we're working on it. It's priority one for the CIA now to find out what happened to her and Remmel. Just take it easy. You and Elsie just need rest for the moment or you'll be useless. Whoever took Remmel and his wife will be long gone by now."

The doctors insisted that they stay in the infirmary under watch until they were sure there would be no after effects from the drug. Then they went back to their quarters and slept for another twelve hours. When they finally woke, they felt much better. After a shower, they went to find Talbot.

"There you are, how do you feel?"

"None the worse for the wear I suppose. Now what's the update?"

"Do you remember Andreyev, aka Agent Adams? He's back."

"What? I thought you killed him."

"Well, I thought I did too, but the sheriff's report of the raid site found no bodies."

"Are they sure?"

"Yeah, they scoured the place when they cleaned up. It was our boys, made out to be a salvage crew."

"So he survived getting shot and a hail of fire from Spooky not to mention the building coming down around him. That's one lucky SOB."

"Yeah well, unlucky for us he's also violent and extremely tenacious. We still don't know how he got in."

"We were having a party David, what better time?"

"How did he know that? It would have to be an inside job and every individual was accounted for and has a bulletproof alibi."

"You two are forgetting somebody."

They looked at her. She had been listening, wracking her brain, then a light had gone on.

"Remmel."

Talbot looked confused. "Dr Remmel is—"

"Crazy in love with his wife. Elsie's right. He's the one who's motivated here. He would do anything to have her back. Yesterday, Rhodes was guarding her in the back of the plane. He said that when Remmel went to her she didn't want to have anything to do with him. He was completely rejected."

"In the middle of all that celebration, people laughing and cheering…" Elsie began to see the full picture. "…he was crushed. I'll bet he hates us."

"He'll do anything to get back with her."

"But how did he overcome the guards, take her and escape when he's in a wheelchair?"

"He didn't. Remember, he had Andreyev operating in the shadows."

"The enemy of my enemy is my friend. While we were gone he got in touch with the Russians. He's made allies with the people who held him hostage."

"Wow. That's twisted."

"Yeah, and he's got everything to gain by telling all."

"Rand," Elsie's face went white. "We gave everything he needed - his memory! He's going to Montauk!"

Talbot jumped on the phone and gave orders for a full security alert. He held the phone to his shoulder, "Montauk, what is that?"

"It's a secret base; it's where they have the time machine. He's going to use it to go back in time to get his legs back and then God knows what."

Talbot finished giving the order for a security alert and hung up the phone. "When?"

"'43 I think. He's joined the Nazis for her, he'll tell them everything he knows."

"Good Lord."

"David, he's from nineteen sixty-six. He invented the machine in fifty-two but he didn't make the first trip until sixty-six to go back to forty-three before he lost his legs. But he missed that time and followed us here. After meeting us he knows for sure there is a future beyond that."

Talbot looked confused. "Doesn't the future go on until forever… or the end of the world?"

"No, it only goes as far as people have lived. Elsie and I are from the furthest in the future.

We're actually a nanosecond farther in the future than the rest of humanity."

Talbot had his hands up in surrender. "So you're from a future that doesn't include mankind?"

"We told you already, we both woke up one morning and everyone was gone. Like, every human, gone."

"I remember you telling me, I guess it just didn't sink in until now. God that must have been horrible!"

"It was… it IS! We're trying to get back. Listen we don't have time for this David. Now that Remmel has interacted with us, our lives are linked. I'm pretty sure he can access the future with the machine. It wouldn't have been an option for him before he met us."

"But how did he get here to Groom Lake before you if he followed you here?"

Rand looked disappointed. "We didn't exactly make a bee-line straight here."

Elsie cut in. "We didn't know where to go. At first we had no clothes or anything for this time period so we needed money. The only free money we knew of was Capone's stash. That took awhile, then there was working with Hughes to try and get an invitation here. We knew there was no way we could get in to a guarded facility like this to get to Remmel. We needed an invitation.

In the meantime Remmel came here and met himself. They merged. It's what happens when your future-self meets your past-self. Then he started to forget everything about the future. The two selves get confused for awhile as they struggle for control. Eventually though the self with the most support wins. In Remmel's case the one who was from this time won out over the new comer. Remmel might have acted like he was going nuts for awhile but eventually he just forgot all about it."

"Say, I remember that. We escorted him off the base because he started babbling all the time and going into fits of rage when anyone told him to get a grip." Suddenly Talbot's face lit up. "Then McAllister cleared him again and set him up in private digs out at the sand piles. Come to think of it, that's the point of the weakest security around here."

"Can you take us there?"

"Absolutely, come on."

They got in a security car and sped out across the flat desert to what looked like a tin shed surrounded by broken down backhoes and dump trucks. There were mounds of sand over three stories high backed right up to the shed.

Talbot shot off the lock on the shed and kicked the door in. Inside was an array of chemical beakers and racks of old equipment.

"See, the old nut couldn't have been up to much with this stuff."

"Remmel's a genius. I'm betting there is more here than meets the eye."

Rand began moving the tables and lockers out of the way as the glassware toppled over.

"Be careful Rand,' Talbot said, 'you don't know what's in these flasks."

Elsie touched her finger to some of the spilled liquid and smelled it. "Water." She tried some more of the glass containers. "It's all water with food colouring. This place is a ruse."

Now they all started moving the furniture. Rand found a vent that had been covered up by a cabinet on small wheels. There were marks on the floor where someone had clearly gone in and out on their knees.

When they opened the vent and looked in they found a tunnel directly behind the shed. Talbot called several security units out as they continued to search. Rand went outside.

"What about all this heavy equipment?"

"Those were left here after they built the base."

"All of them?"

"I guess."

"David, every vehicle that's on this base should be registered and tagged."

"Well these were here before I got here."

"All of them?"

"I... I don't know!"

Rand was searching around them. He found a backhoe with a very large bucket attached to the arm. The bucket was flat on the ground.

"Get Chief out here and get this thing fired up."

In fifteen minutes the site was swarming with security personnel and engineers. When the backhoe bucket was moved they found that it covered a hatch that lead under the sand pile.

"He was able to hide the sand he excavated in the sand pile. They just kept getting bigger and no one noticed."

"No one ever came out here. They didn't want to deal with crazy Remmel." Chief said.

Talbot was clearly stressed out. "I can't believe I missed this."

The security team sent to check the tunnel came back. "The tunnel leads three-hundred yards past the fence and joins with a vertical shaft that goes down to some kind of lab. The top is covered by a hatch disguised as a rock sir." One of the guards reported.

Remmel's underground lab looked like a duplicate of the control station at Montauk.

"He was trying to build another one."

"Maybe he thought that the TSS would link up with it somehow."

"Well he seems to have left in a hurry. What papers we found were burned and there appear to be some components missing from the some of the equipment."

"He doesn't need anything. They are headed to Montauk to the machine there. If he's under the influence of his wife, he will go back to forty-three before the raid and save his legs. He'll give them all the technology he can." Elsie shut the door to give them privacy. "It means the Germans will win the war. Hitler will rule the world."

Talbot looked lost. "So, what do we do? They have a two day head start on us."

"I think we're gonna need a ride." Elsie looked at Rand.

Rand nodded. "I think we're gonna need the Vampires."

They split up - Rand to look for a plane, Elsie to assemble the Vampires and Talbot to contact the CIA.

The call to the CIA was to put out the alert that Remmel was working with the KGB and had escaped with his wife. Talbot reported that they had reason to believe they were headed to Montauk to rendezvous with the Russians.

"According to the CIA the Montauk base doesn't exist and there was no way I would be able to explain how we knew that it did. So, I had to make a cover story. It was the only thing I could think of at the time." He explained to Elsie. "They are discussing what to do. This is a major security violation on my watch."

"Blame has nothing to do with it. They can't fire you, you work for us now. We need them to put the clamp down on the KGB."

Rand went to the Chief. "Chief, I have to ask you and your team for anoth--"

"No problem, just slow down and tell me what you need."

"Something like the C-123, but really fast."

"Okay, follow me."

The big man took a golf cart across the tarmac to the far end of the large interconnection of runways they called 'the nest'. There, a collection of old hangars sat disused in the setting sun. He got out and went into the side door of a large one.

"Will this do?" Rand was looking at a C-123 with jet engines mounted to it. XCG-20A was written on the tail. "It's a C-123, but really fast. It's experimental but it's been very successful. I think they are about to use it as a passenger plane. It's the latest design by Chase Aircraft. They're from New York," He winked, "so it should get you to Montauk."

Rand vigorously shook the big man's hand.

Elsie rounded up the Vampires and had them gear up. Then she went to change into her combat gear. When she got to her and Rand's quarters she made a shocking discovery. She called Talbot on the radio.

"David, they got the suitcases."

She sat and stared at the wall. How could they have been so blind to let this happen. Remmel duped them all.

Talbot came skidding up with Rand who ran out of the car before it even stopped.

"Elsie! Are you okay?"

"Yes, I'm fine… as fine as can be expected. They got everything baby, the guns, the night vision, the radios, even the iPad."

"We have to catch them Talbot. I don't want nineteen forty-nine bullshit here. We need interagency cooperation on all levels. FBI, CIA, NSA, state and local law enforcement. I'm talking about a manhunt. The cover story is that they are serial killers on a rampage. Get a team out to the escape hatch with bloodhounds and track them down. Look at the tire tracks, figure out what kind of tires they are. Take fingerprint samples at the scene, the whole works."

Rand pulled Elsie to him. She was sobbing against his chest.

"Elsie, we still have a couple of things that can level the playing field. We've got two night vision scopes in the Spook. We'll put them on a couple of MAS-49s. We've got body armour and we have knowledge that they don't have."

She looked up at him with a little smile, tears running down her cheeks. "You're right, sorry hon. I just don't know how it all fell apart so quickly."

"It's okay, you're allowed to be human every now and then."

She laughed and wiped her face. "You forgot another thing that we have that they don't."

"What's that hon?"

She pointed over his shoulder, "Them."

The Vampires stood in a group geared up and ready to go. The men all gave words of encouragement:

"Don't worry ma'am, we'll get em."

"We're with you Major, all the way."

"I'll follow you anywhere ma'am."

Elsie thanked them all. When she turned to Rand she saw Carl standing beside him. "Hey you mess with one Vampire, you mess with the whole family."

Rand spoke loudly. "Vampires, looks like it's our turn again. Briefing in five minutes, ready room."

He called the Chief on the radio. "Chief we're gonna need that big toy you just showed me all ready to go in fifteen minutes. Is that possible?"

"No, but that's why they got me working in this God forsaken place."

"David, you should have all the comms you need on board the plane. Make your calls on the go."

Then he gathered Carl, Talbot and Elsie together in a tight circle.

The Second String

"Once again this is our baby, we've got the reins here. None of the agencies or the governments know what's at stake. Carl, you don't know everything, but I'm proposing that we tell you and all the Vampires." He looked at Talbot and Elsie. "They've all proven their quality and I feel that they deserve to know."

Talbot and Elsie were nodding. Carl just looked at them.

"I have the feeling I'm about to get my mind blown."

The Vampires were gathered in the ready room when the four walked in. Carl took a seat with the rest and Elsie stepped to the front while Rand and Talbot sat.

"I am about to disclose to you information that goes beyond classified. The CIA doesn't know, neither does the President, the government of any country or anyone in the whole of existence beyond the three people up here and two others. We feel that it is time we reveal to you who we are and what we are up to.

"They're from the future! I told you guys!" Johnson laughed. The men laughed along and gave Johnson a hard time before Elsie quieted them down.

"Alright you guys settle down. The truth is that we are indeed from the future. Two-thousand fourteen. Rand and I. We told Talbot before Argentina. Captain Carl, this is the first you've heard of it. Dr. Remmel is from nineteen sixty-six, he's the one who invented the time machine. The only other person who knows is Howard Hughes, a friend of ours who remains a very helpful ally."

She let the men react. After Johnson recovered from the shock he looked at Wiley and said, "You owe me fifty bucks."

Elsie wasn't surprised that the men seemed to take the news in stride. She continued to explain what they thought Remmel's plans were and about the Montauk base.

"We'll have to break into the site. It's most likely heavily defended by our troops so we don't want to kill anyone if we can help it. Even the thought of injuring one of our boys goes against my grain. But if we don't get to that control unit, Remmel could go back in time and give secrets to the Nazis that will certainly cause them to win the war and dominate the world."

Rand stood behind Elsie, "It's true. In the nineteen-fifties they learned that the Nazis were very, very close to developing their own nuclear bomb and a plane that could deliver it to any target in the US. Hitler's plan was not just Europe but the whole world." Rand sat back down. Elsie turned back to the men.

"Remmel is a mad man. He has to be stopped. Rand and I didn't know that when we came here. We came here hoping to find him and learn how to get back to our time. We don't know if we ever will, but right now it's more important to stop him from getting to either the KGB or the facility in Montauk. I… we would like to jump on Montauk and take the place as soon as possible. Rand and I are asking for volunteers."

The whole team immediately stood up. "IN CRUOR UNUS!"

Elsie choked back tears. "Thank you all so much."

Rand put his arm around her and smiled at them all. He had never felt so much gratitude. Talbot and Carl came up on either side and clapped them on the shoulder. Talbot turned to the men, "Let's go people, ten minutes to the flight deck."

Rand and Elsie went to get what was left of their gear together. There were four other suitcases with their clothes. Rand went digging through them to find some BDUs when he stumbled across the tasers.

"Elsie, Look."

"And they missed the solar battery charger. The batteries in the NV helmets and EARs haven't been charged since Argentina. They only have a half hour at the most."

Their sprits began to lift as they went out the door and made their way to the textiles lab.

"Edie, we need your help."

The old seamstress ran the show at the lab. If it could be sewn, her team could make something out of it.

"Yes, yes I know. Mr. Nickelson was just here and told me that the laundry machine tore up all your combat clothes. Well I said we'll just have to do something about that so I'm having the girls make up a set of those BUDs or DBUs or whatever that you're so fond of. They'll be ready in a couple of minutes if you just want to wait over there. Would you like some lemonade? Margaret just made it fresh."

They both took a glass of lemonade which was so tart that it made them pucker as they sat down. It was exactly two minutes and two sets of fresh, folded BDUs were given to them.

"You can change in there dears."

They thanked her profusely and headed out to the tarmac. The Vampires were all geared up. As

Elsie and Rand pulled up Talbot handed each of them a french made MAS-49 silenced assault rifle.

"I'm gonna miss that SCAR rifle of yours Rand, but these should do alright."

"We need the Chief to mount our scopes. It's mission critical that we have night sight."

A familiar noise reached Rand's ears. "Elsie, do you hear something?"

At the same time someone said, "Is that the Spook?"

Elsie looked through her scope and a smile spread across her face. "Rand, did you know about this?"

"It's all the Chief's fault."

As the big cargo plane rolled towards them they decided to retreat to the ready room. The engines wound down and Chief came in the door.

"Well what do you think?"

Elsie gave him a hug. "It's beautiful!"

"I thought it would fit the bill. Besides, I heard that you specialize in things that don't exist, and it doesn't."

"You've done so much for us already, but there's one last favour we have to ask Chief…" Rand held the gun and the scope up. "Could you?"

"It's no problem. I've had so much fun with all the new ideas and stuff you've brought us… but here now, you're talking like you won't be coming back."

"I don't know if we will Chief, you never can tell about these things."

"Well anything I can do to increase the chances of your safe return, I will do. Just give me half an hour with these scopes and I'll have them back to you."

"Okay everyone, thirty minutes to departure." Talbot called out.

"Turn them on here and sight them in the dark Chief." Rand showed the man how to activate the scopes. The Chief thought they were just really nice scopes, he had no clue about their night vision capabilities.

"What? Are you serious?"

"Just trust me, but keep it under your hat, under your hair and—"

"I get the idea. I'll take it to the grave, on my honour." He said and headed off to the armoury. Exactly thirty minutes later the Chief pulled up and handed Rand and Elsie their assault rifles back with the scopes on. He was wide-eyed and sweating more than usual. He leaned in to Rand and said quietly; "That is by far the most incredible thing I have ever seen. Any chance you can leave one with me?"

"Maybe some day you will have the chance to tear one apart, but right now we need them both."

"I look forward to it Mr. Carter. Best of luck to you." Then the big man looked over Rand's shoulder and yelled with his fist in the air, "Go Vampires!" like he was cheering a college football team and drove off.

The plane was configured almost identical to the Spook's cargo area. The Vampires strapped in as Carl and Elsie headed to the cockpit with Rand. The plane roared to life as they lined up on the runway. Once the engines had wound up to speed they were airborne in less than ten seconds.

Montgomery Thompson

Chapter 9

Three of a kind

'You can discover what your enemy fears most by observing the means he uses to frighten you.'
~Eric Hoffer

Oskar Remmel leaned his head against the window of the big black Desoto, watching the stars in the winter-blown desert night. Erna slept in the back seat and the Russian agent drove. She would love him for this. He would see that stone façade crumble back into a magnificent flower or he would dash himself against that rock trying.

Right now he was just tired - tired of hiding in his underground lab, crawling through the sand and getting manhandled by this coarse thug.

"What is your real name Agent Adams?"

The Russian didn't look at him.

"You don't need to know."

He was too tired to be afraid of the man any more. He'd had enough.

"If you think I am going to give all of my secrets to the KGB while you treat me like a pile of baggage you have another thing coming. I have plans of my own and I will not tell anybody anything until I get what I want."

The Russian was handsome in a weathered way, thin and tall but very strong. Remmel still had bruises in the shape of the man's fingers. His dark hair was straight and a bit long with flecks of grey. The man looked hollow; hollow cheeks, hollow eyes, even his mouth when he spoke was a dark hole with very few teeth showing. He took a deep breath and relaxed his hard face into a smile.

"Andreyev Grozny, that is my name. Okay?"

"Reverend Doctor Oskar Remmel."

"Do you think I came all this way and don't know who you are? For a genius you're not very smart." Andreyev chuckled to himself. He had held the old man captive in the warehouse for days. Even though he had been unconscious most of the time, the old fool still didn't remember him.

"Of course you know who I am, but there are things that you don't know about me."

"I know all I need to know for my mission. Rescue you and your wife from the American pigs and bring you to the beautiful Soviet Union where you can work in peace with plenty of funding and make the world a better place."

Remmel looked at him grimly. "Nice speech. How long did you practice it?"

Andreyev just shrugged.

Remmel's mind was ticking, he had to get this man to take him to Montauk. "You don't think I remember you but I do. I remember the American raid, you were laying on the floor bleeding when they drug me out of there."

The Russian shrugged again, "Could be. It is not the first time I have been shot."

"You tortured me."

"I was my job. Look at all we have done to help you build your little laboratory. Good men, digging in the sand, for what? But now all that is over. Now we are friends. I am bringing you to meet the heads of operation. It will be civilised and nice, you will see. Russian hospitality is famous."

Remmel knew about Russian hospitality. Their cruelty to the Germans after the war was horrific. He thought hard, he would have to play his trump card.

"Do you want to know why the Americans want me so bad?"

"I already know. It is because of the stuff in the luggage."

"No, it's not."

Andreyev looked at him. For a moment Remmel thought those eyes could pierce his skin. He fought off a shudder.

"It is cold for you old man, I will turn on the heating." He flipped on the heater and a rush of warm air blew into the cabin. "So what is the big deal? What is it that the Americans want with you? Nuclear secrets I'm sure."

"I'm from the future. I built a time machine and used it to come back here."

The Russian looked at him again. "You expect me to believe such fairy tales?"

Remmel knew it wouldn't work. He was going to Russia. No legs, no Erna. He should have stayed with the Americans.

"But let us say for the sake of conversation that what you say is true. Why would you come back here?"

"I tried to get back to nineteen forty-three so I could escape the raid in which I lost my legs. My wife thinks I am weak now, she wants nothing to do with me."

"That old hag? She has face like marble." Andreyev saw Remmel's hurt reaction. He needed the old bastard to spill his guts. He hadn't time to torture him properly. Now, it seemed like being friendly was the best way to get the man to talk. The problem was; being friendly was torture to Andreyev Grozny. He grimaced a smile.

"I'm sorry Doctor. I didn't mean that, I am just an old sailor. Sometimes my words can be a little crass."

"No, it's okay. She has grown hard. She wasn't always that way. She used to love me."

"So you say you are from the future. Do you know where your time machine is?"

"Yes, it's in the hands of the Americans in a secret underground base in Montauk, New Jersey."

"Right in New Jersey? That is a very unlikely place for a base. How do they build such a thing without everyone noticing?"

"People think the base was closed after the war, but the whole time they were excavating underground. They have been digging since they first laid the foundations."

"And supposing you were to infiltrate this base, get through their defences and reach your time machine, where would you go?"

"The plan is still the same. I would go back to nineteen forty-three to save my legs and win back the love of my life."

"And then from there where would you go, or should I say *when*."

"I… I don't know. I suppose I would…" Remmel suddenly remembered the Carters. Two thousand fourteen, what a world! Nuclear power, everyone free, cars that flew. "I would go far into the future to two-thousand fourteen."

The Russian made a surprised face. "Why not three-thousand or four-thousand?"

"It doesn't work that way. You can only go as far forward as man has lived."

"And you know that man has lived up until two-thousand and fourteen? How do you know that?"

"Because the two Americans, the Carters are from that time."

Grozny slammed on the brakes. The car skidded to the side of the dark, deserted road. He sprang out and went to the trunk. The tall man rummaged through the trunk and hauled out the suitcases. Remmel rolled down the window to watch Andreyev. The Russian looked from Remmel to the pile of equipment in the cases. Then he reached down and picked up one of the two rifles.

"I am familiar with guns. There are not many that I have not used." He inspected the weapon.

For a moment Remmel thought, *did they lie to me? Are they not from the future? How could they have known about me?*

Then the Russian said, "I have never seen anything like this. Even the materials it's made from are strange." He brought the silenced rifle to his shoulder and fired of a burst of automatic fire, sawing a one hundred year old Saguaro cactus in half. "Incredible." He lowered the rifle and looked at Remmel. "I am starting to believe you Doctor."

'Good, because you have to take me to Montauk. I have to get into that base and -'

'And how do you propose to do that Oskar?' Erna Remmel was leaning across the back seat. 'Are we going to wheel you in the door? Everyone get out of the way it is the famous Doctor, hero of the hour come to save the world? No. You have nothing. As usual, you have no plan, no solution. Because of you, the greatest man that ever lived is a prisoner, and I am being taken to live in Russia, a place where even pig shit is insulted to touch the ground!'

Andreyev levelled the rifle at Erna's head.

'Wait! You are wrong Erna. I am not without a plan. I am not nothing. I was there in nineteen sixty-six, I know a secret way in. I have to do it before I forget.'

There was a long pause when the three just looked at each other. Then Erna sighed and said, 'Good. Then we go there.' She slumped back into the back seat. Andreyev, surprised by the woman's complete lack of fear, shrugged and put the gun back in the suitcase.

'What do you mean forget?' Andreyev started the car.

'If I am near someone from my time I can remember things from my time. When I am alone I only remember future events in a limited way, like catching glimpses of dreams.'

'Sounds confusing. So who is it that you need to be around to remember things?'

'"he Carters, they are the only ones from another time, the only ones who have ever used the machine." He couldn't remember it's proper name, a name he had given it. He thought, *I'm already starting to forget.*

The black Desoto sped across the desert as the sun began to rise. Andreyev had driven the entire way.

"Mr. Grozny you need to sleep, you will get us all killed." She had been silent, listening and even rolling her eyes when they talked of her. Now, in light of this new information, it was time to be heard. Erna leaned over the seat and looked at the Russian in the rear view mirror.

"I will sleep when I'm on the plane."

"And how do you think we are going to take a plane. They will ask for identification. By now I'm sure they have notified all the authorities to look for us."

"Hey, you leave the logistics to me. I did not get here by accident. I can go anywhere in the world and they cannot find me. I am a ghost. If you do what I tell you we will go completely unnoticed."

"Okay, okay settle down. You see Oskar," She tilted her head towards Andreyev, "This is how a real man behaves. You cower like a dog."

Andreyev rolled his eyes in disgust. "Please." He pushed her by the face back into the seat.

"It's okay Mr. Russian, I like it rough."

Remmel looked at the both of them and moved closer to the window. As they rode in silence through the early morning a small town came into view. The Golden Nugget Casino sign dominated the Las Vegas strip and the Hotel Apache was one of the tallest buildings at three stories high. Except for a few drunks wandering in the street, the little town was quiet. They pulled into the Hotel Apache for breakfast and to wash up.

"Let me do the talking. I'm the only one who can do a perfect American accent." The Russian said in a perfect American accent. Then he looked at them both sternly. "Doctor put on a smile, you're on vacation with your wife. And you, stone face, lighten up and try to look like you're enjoying yourself. I'm an old friend from the war showing you two around my part of the country. Got it? Good."

They went inside and took a booth as the waitress came over. "Say doll can you tell me where the nearest airport is around here?"

"Leaving so soon? You just got here handsome." The waitress flirted back. "Well, okay I'll tell you if you tip me real nice. It's McCarran Field just outside of town." She gave him directions then took their order.

After breakfast they drove to the airfield, it was easy enough to find. The field was populated with large, prop-driven passenger planes. Most of them read *Bonanza* on the side.

"We're going to charter a private flight out of here to Montauk, then we'll see if you're either crazy or telling the truth Doctor."

"Mr. Russian, Oskar may be a weasel of a man but he is neither crazy nor a liar. I would believe him if I were you."

"Sorry lady, I have to see if for myself." He said, continuing in his flawless American accent.

It took no time to find a charter. Charters were for big spenders and big spenders got fast service.

Remmel took Andreyev aside. He was so stressed he was sweating. "How are we going to pay for this? We don't have that kind of money!"

"You're a nervous old guy aren't you? You obviously didn't look too deeply into those suitcases, they're loaded with cash. We have over a hundred thousand dollars Doc."

Remmel went as white as a sheet. "Oh they'll be after us for sure."

"And we'll be long gone. Now calm down…" He opened his jacket and revealed the top of a syringe. "…or I'll calm you down."

They boarded their own private DC-3, a large propeller driven plane normally used for up to 32 passengers. This one had been converted for the big spenders of Vegas. It was equipped with couches, beds and a bar.

"This is more like it." Erna inspected the cabin. The pilot told them they would have to stop in Chicago to refuel, but it wouldn't take long. The motors coughed smoke as they came to life and soon they were airborne over the Nevada desert. Andreyev tucked the suitcases into a closet and then went to sleep on the couch next to it. Neither of the Remmels were going to try and get to the guns anyway. They slept as the old plane lumbered across the continent.

Chapter 10

Return

'I am not your Autumn moon, I am the night.'
~Audioslave

"The sky is clear all the way to Montauk." Carl finished talking to the tower as the four jet engines shot them up to altitude.

"At four hundred and fifty miles per hour we'll be there twice as fast as the Spook."

Talbot got on the comms and started placing calls.

The jet made good time and had a considerably better range than the C-123 as it was able make the trip to Montauk without refuelling.

"What do we do when we get there?" Carl asked.

"We do a HALO insertion and land at the entrance to the facility and—"

"No, I mean what do I do with the plane?"

"Oh."

Elsie looked at Rand. "I didn't think about that. You'll have to find a place to land it."

"Mitchel Air Force Base right on Montauk." Talbot said from the comms chair. "I've already contacted them. They'll have an armed convoy ready for extraction complete with medical."

Rand smiled at him, "You rock dude."

Talbot looked confused. "Is that good?"

"Yes." He said as he climbed past. "I'm going back to check on the guys."

Rand settled in for the long ride. The men had a lot of questions about the future, how they got there and particularly about Elsie being as astronaut.

"So who wins the world series in nineteen-fifty?"

"I have no idea, I wasn't even born yet."

"Wait. Captain, how old are you?"

"Well I suppose I'm around thirty-four somewhere. I don't know, what kind of question is that?"

The questions kept coming in a lighthearted way as the laughed and ribbed each other. Rand told them life wasn't that much different. There were technological gadgets sure, but people were basically the same.

"I guess the biggest difference would be families. They don't stay together as much in the future. Now people raise their kids in the same house they were raised in and the kids take care of their folks when they get old. Children inherit the family business and they follow the morals and ethics of their parents. They stick together no matter what."

"It's not like that in the future?"

"Well, yes, but not as much. There is a lot of divorce. Kids spend all of their time distracted by gadgets like computers, phones and video games. Parents both have to work to make ends meet so they don't see their kids. Companies don't care about retiring people who stay with them. They want their employees young and fresh; cheap pay and full of ideas. Believe me guys, progress comes at a price."

"Yeah, but the cars must be incredible."

"Well yes, some of the cars are cool, but mostly only the expensive ones. Here, I got something to show you guys. It's called a taser. Be careful with it, it hurts like hell but it's non-lethal."

He passed the little device around. They wanted know what it was made of and how it worked. He explained as much as he could. Then he showed them the solar charger and the batteries for the tasers. Of course the MREs with the stamped date and the official US Marines seal was the thing that really brought the truth home. The questions kept coming and he answered every single one as best he could. Eventually he had to bring the session to a close and had them get as much sleep as possible.

Rand stayed up awhile, looking out the window and thinking about all they had been through. Then he said a prayer and went to sleep.

Up in the cockpit Elsie had Talbot contact Howard Hughes.

"Howard?"

"Elsie, good God! How the hell are you? Where are you?"

"So much to tell you Howard but right now we're in the race of our lives."

She filled him in about Remmel, his wife and the Russians. When he learned about Montauk and what they were trying to do he promised to use every contact he had to help out. Elsie gave him special instructions about their money and the house in Malibu. He said he would contact them in an hour with a progress report then signed off.

"Was that really Howard Hughes?" Carl was amazed.

"Yes Carl, would you like to fly for him?"

"Would I? That's a dream job!"

"I'll do my best to arrange it. But know that you will never need to worry about money for the rest of your life Carl. When we leave, we are taking care of all of the Vampires."

One hour later, to the minute, Hughes called back.

"Okay, I've got Spang and some of your things on an F-94 to Montauk. She'll be hitting mach 1.2 so they'll probably be waiting for you there."

"He'll be the fastest dog in the world."

"Indeed. As for the other matter don't worry, I've got it all taken care of. I'm sure Mr. Talbot and I will be talking soon."

Talbot looked at Elsie and mouthed *me?* She just nodded and put her finger to her lips.

"Howard, thank you for everything. When we're done here our head pilot needs a job. He's the best and he knows all about us. His name is Carl Capaldi, I'll send him to meet you."

"Sounds great Elsie, I can sure use good pilots. Give Rand my best. I will never forget you."

"Neither will we Howard. Say hello to Terry for us."

"Oh..." There was a pause. "We are no longer together."

"Oh Howard what happened?"

"Well, turns out that she was seeing some football star. Glenn Davis I believe his name is. Anyway, I immediately had the whole thing annulled. I even tore out the page in the record logs of the yacht. Don't worry though, I saved the part about you two."

"We're so sorry to hear that Howard. I guess it just wasn't meant to be."

"Howard? Rand here." He woke when he heard her say Howard's name. He took the mic from Elsie. "When one door closes another one opens okay, just remember that."

"You're good friends. I miss you two. Bye now." Hughes cut the connection off. He was never comfortable talking about personal matters, especially over a radio.

Elsie put down the radio mic and sat with her head in her hands. The news was depressing. She wanted to be there for the man. How many more times would she have to say good-bye? She got up and went down with Rand to get some sleep. They curled up in a corner of the plane on the floor using their parachutes as padding and tried to rest.

After two and a half hours they woke up and went to relieve Carl and Talbot. Initially the two objected but they finally conceded when they were told that they if they didn't get some sleep they would be up for the whole mission and then they would have to fly everyone back themselves.

"Understand that if we succeed, Rand and I will be gone."

"That is not exactly motivation for success. We've become quite used to you two being around. Frankly, I can't imagine Groom Lake without you. It has become a close-knit family and you two are at it's core."

"David it's the hardest thing to have to leave, but it was hard for us to leave our time too. It was like we died to everyone there."

"Now, it will be like that here."

"But we're not dead, we live, just as our friends do. Just in a different time. At least there is the comfort in knowing that."

Talbot scrunched his face in thought. "So we're all living at the same time, in different times?"

Rand sat down in the pilot's seat. "Yeah I believe that's how it works. Time is only linear to us, not to God. To Him and Heaven there is only creation, all at once. That's why the big bang looks like it does; one second nothing is there, then all of a sudden, it just *is*. Growing and changing, evolving… it's life."

"You know what the creation of the universe looks like? Wow! The future sounds like where I want to be. Everyone must be very enlightened."

"Hardly. The knowledge leads to more questions than answers. Most people think that science cancels out God and vice versa. The more enlightened folks understand that science validates God with every discovery."

"We have a long way to go don't we? Maybe the future isn't all it's cracked up to be."

"It's very much the same as now. But we're getting ahead of ourselves. We have to infiltrate this base. If, and I mean IF we survive that then we have to find out if the TSS is working and then IF it is we jump through time again. Then who knows where we'll end up. We could end up on your door years later to you and days later to us."

"Rand's right," Carl said, "We have a lot to do before we say good-byes so let's keep our head in the game. Rand and Elsie, you've been through this place before. Sketch out what you remember and let us know what we might be getting into. We'll try to get some shut-eye."

"Sounds like a plan."

Rand was relieved to have something to do. He drew out the whole facility as they remembered it while Elsie flew the plane.

"Shit Els, I have the map of the place in my gear. If they find it, they will know their way around it and the pass codes."

"Those codes won't be any good to them in this time. The base probably looks nothing like it did when we were there. Remember the section that was decorated like Goldfinger? That was obviously built in the seventies."

"And the automatic defense systems won't be there either. Come to think of it we really didn't see anything in there that was from this era."

"Right, even the TSS control was from nineteen fifty-two."

"But remember, we don't know how much of the place came with us. Maybe it's only the functional TSS and all it's components, maybe it was the whole facility in a certain radius."

"Yeah I've been wondering about that. The first time the TSS it was Remmel. The second time was the big machine that Remmel thinks is alien."

"That's our theory. The second one is what sent us on our little nano-second, life-changing trip."

"But the one we took here was with Remmel's little machine, yes? Or did they manage to connect Remmel's machine to the big supposedly 'alien' one as a controller?"

"That's a really good question. I don't know. Let's just hope that whatever the situation it was enough to bring the TSS with us."

"Pray that's the case."

"As long was remmel's small machine is there we'll have a chance. We need to get back to our string at the ver least, even of the time isn't right."

"I see what you're saying but Remmel seemed to think we were back on the original string, rewriting it as we go. The second string that we were on in New River won't continue."

"Unless of course we go back there—"

"Or Remmel does."

"That's it Rand, I bet that's his plan."

"His own sting in time to do with what he wants. Now that it's been created he can snap to it, especially because we met him. But he's got to get his legs back first."

"Then he'll start feeding future tech to Hitler."

"Honey I want to get us back to our original time so I can see my kinds and we can be together properly, but I don't want that fucking psycho taking over our home in New River either!" Rand was riled. "Els, get more speed out of this thing."

"Right, get Carl up here to find out where the jet stream is. If I can get us into it we can make serious time."

Rand woke up Carl who understood immediately and started working his contacts for weather information. Elsie climbed to the plane's highest service ceiling to get directly in the path of the fast flowing, west to east winds of the jet stream. They instantly doubled their speed.

Carl took over the captain's chair while Rand continued working on the map, filling in as much detail as he could remember. By the time he was done double checking everything with Elsie they were convinced they had the layout complete. Just as they set their pencils down Carl's voice came over the intercom.

"Twenty minutes to yellow everyone."

They looked up at each other over the map, "Here we go."

As they suited up to jump Elsie went over the procedures with Rand. "I'm sure you're nervous but don't be. You're surrounded by a whole group of professionals who have done hundreds of jumps. They will all be looking out for you."

"I've only done this once before and that was out of a Cessna at fourteen hundred feet. The thing might have been going seventy miles per hour."

"Not to worry hon. Just follow the procedures and just like flying, stay calm no matter what."

This time Rand and Elsie operated as a team on their own. The Vampires operated as two squads; Alpha lead by Johnson, and Golf lead by Reece. Carl had to stay with the plane and Talbot was needed to rendezvous with the CIA at the airstrip and coordinate the extraction. The Vampires would follow Elsie and Rand down. They attached red-lensed flashlights to Elsie and Rand's packs to be able to track them in the air. Elsie directed Carl over the radio.

"Do you have visual on the lighthouse?"

"Roger that, just on that point there."

"We'll try to land right in front of it, in the parking lot."

"Okay Vampires remember, avoid use of lethal force. As far as we know those are our boys down there. If we're successful, everyone gets to go home at the end of the day."

The Second String

Rand opened the ramp doors to a loud swirl of wind. The plane had slowed as much as possible for the jump.

Elsie reached out and touched Rand's face then ran off the edge and fell away into the blackness. Suddenly his heart was in his throat. Johnson grabbed him by the harness. "This way sir." The large black man carried him backwards out the door.

When they hit the air they were tossed and tumbled by a powerful wash from the jet engines. Johnson hung onto him until they stabilised then turned him around and pushed away slowly. Rand watched as the man gave him a thumbs up and beckoned him to follow as he put his head down into a dive. Rand tried to nod but the force of the wind was so strong on his oxygen mask that even moving his head was difficult. After a second he managed to nose down and follow Johnson.

The speed came on quickly and soon he could see the light on Elsie's pack. He raised his rifle up and looked through the night scope. It was a struggle in the high wind but he managed to bring the image to bear. He saw the lighthouse and the parking lot but the site was swarming with soldiers. He tried to pull up next to Johnson who was slightly ahead of then but the big man was too fast.

Rand concentrated on making himself as streamlined as possible and slowly began to gain speed. Edging up just ahead of Johnson he hand signalled to him as Diego had taught them.

Men – many – ambush

Johnson flipped over on his back and slowed down so rapidly that he disappeared behind Rand. Rand's radio crackled. Suddenly each one of the Vampires slowed and flipped over, Rand awkwardly copied the manoeuvre.

As the wind in his ears died down to a dull roar Elsie came over his comms.

"Papa Bear just spread yourself out and try to slow down as much as you can."

"Elsie, the parking lot is an ambush!"

The rush of the wind took his breath away, he wasn't sure if she had heard him.

"Minx come back, over!"

He struggled as he plummeted through the air on his back, the stars mocking his vulnerability to gravity.

Chapter 11

Alligator dreams

'I'm not bad. I'm just drawn that way.'
~Jessica Rabbit, Who Framed Roger Rabbit

"This is taking too long." Andreyev looked out the window of the old DC-3 as is droned through the Midwestern clouds.

"Relax, it will take days before the Americans can pick up our trail. By then we will be gone." Erna said as she looked over the Russian. Then she slid closer to him on the couch. Her husband was asleep on the bed down the aisle. "Besides, I have something to talk to you about."

Andreyev looked at her suspiciously. The German woman was in her fifties with greying hair and a face that was drawn and creased. She had the look of someone who had done nothing but worried and sneered her whole life. She carried her head too high for her height he thought. It made her look down her hooked nose even at people who towered above her; people like Andreyev Grozny. He was afraid of nothing, but for some reason was uneasy with her. He could sense her capacity for cunning and deception, it was a mutual trait.

"I will let you in on a little secret." She said quietly to him. "I am not planning to go very far with Oskar, he slows me… us, down."

"But he is the key to operating the machine."

"Yes, but once we know how to use it we can go anywhere. Imagine the opportunities."

He had been thinking of little else. Going back in time and changing world events, investments and his fortune was the principle focus of his thoughts. Now Erna leaned in very close to him, making sure her body pressed into his. It was like dancing with a hissing alligator.

"We could rule the world!"

Repelled, he backed away. She had come to the same conclusion as he had. He was about to say: *why the hell do you think I would need you,* when he stopped himself. Without her, the Doctor wouldn't cooperate. He had to wait and play this one out. The fox had to play the alligator at her own game. She thought him a dumb brute, so be it.

"How would we do that?"

She took the bait and leaned back in.

"He wants to get back to save his legs. I say, let the worm die as a cripple. Once we know how to use the machine – kill him. He is useless to us."

She was more savage than he had thought. At least she had the stomach for what had to be done.

"Then," She continued, "we go to the future. You keep me safe while I learn everything about the next decade or so. We return with this knowledge and make investments, change events, kill people. The Fuhrer had a bold plan but his vision was not as long as mine."

"And how long is your vision?" He said putting his face close to hers.

"As long as time itself." She locked her thin lips onto his and clawed at his groin. He grimaced, then reluctantly, he joined in the dance with the alligator.

It was a quick and messy business. Remmel listened to them grunting quietly as he pretended to sleep. Worst of all, he could smell them. Afterwards he couldn't hear what they were saying but he knew they were whispering secrets. Though he loved Erna, he knew better than to trust her. Her interests were not his. For Grozny he had nothing but mistrust. The man had proved himself a sadist and a cold and cruel killer. However, Oskar had a plan. As soon as he got his legs back he would get rid of Andreyev. They didn't know how to work the machine. Once he had his legs he would leave the Russian stranded somewhere in time. Then, once he was whole, his Erna would see what kind of man she had married. He would bring her the world on a silver platter. She would respect him, admire him and even adore him. Then it would be him she would be riding in the back cabins of airplanes.

The captain announced their arrival into Chicago and inquired if they would like a gourmet meal brought to the plane while they refuelled. Remmel pretended to stay asleep as Erna and Andreyev made their way into the main cabin.

"A meal to celebrate." Erna collapsed on the couch.

Andreyev shot her a look. "Yeah, to celebrate the last leg of this boring flight. Can't we make this crate go any faster Captain?"

"This old crate won the war sir, she'll get us there safely and in style. Besides, it looks like we've got a tailwind out of Chicago. We should be touching down in New Jersey ahead of schedule.

Once we refuel, I'll have enough extra gas in the tanks to push her faster for the rest of the trip. Sound good?"

Andreyev just forced a smile and nodded.

The food was brought on as the plane took on fuel. The Chicago winter was setting in and it was blowing cold outside. Soon the snow began to fall. Andreyev shouted up to the cockpit.

"Captain, get us out of here before this storm grounds us!"

The Captain went outside and stopped the refuelling. They were back in the air in fifteen minutes, Chicago fading into the swirling white. It was two and a half hours to New Jersey. Remmel continued to pretend to sleep, trying to listen to the small bits of talk between Erna and the Russian but the engines were too loud.

"Okay folks please fasten your seatbelts as we begin our landing into New Jersey." The captain announced.

The wind buffeted the old plane and she touched down hard on the runway. Once they were off, Andreyev hailed a cab to Montauk. It was three in the afternoon and the sky was cloudy and cold, no snow had yet fallen, but he knew the storm was on its way. The cab dropped them at the Flamingo Hotel, the pinnacle of luxury for the time. Andreyev checked into the suite and got on the phone as the Remmels inspected the room. Erna locked herself in the bathroom right away, Oskar just crawled out of his wheelchair and lay down on the bed.

"Haven't you slept enough old man? Jesus, how much can one person sleep?" Andreyev muttered as he waited on the phone. Remmel just lay on the bed feeling like a piece of luggage. Andreyev began talking in very fast Russian. The phone call lasted about two minutes then he hung up.

"Get up. We're leaving in ten minutes." He went and knocked on the door of the bathroom. "We're leaving in ten minutes. Don't make us late or I will come in there and drag you out." Erna replied something fierce but unintelligible through the heavy oak door. The Russian threw the large, heavy suitcases onto one of the beds and began to sort through their contents. He put the helmet on and lowered the visor. "I don't understand, why put this thing down when it blocks your vision?"

Remmel looked at him and said, "There appears to be some sort of apparatus in the back. Perhaps it needs to be turned on."

Grozny inspected the back of the helmet. "Ah, here." He switched it on and put the helmet back on his head. He just stood, moving his head from side to side for several minutes. Then said, "Doctor, turn off the lights."

"I can't, I'm crippled you fool!"

Irritated, Andreyev stomped over to the wall and switched the lights off. He flipped the visor up, then down. Up, then down again to check that the lights were really off. Then he just started laughing. Remmel looked at him like he was crazy but Andreyev just laughed.

"Zaebis!" He took off the helmet. "I believe you now Doctor."

"What? What is it? What does it do?"

Grozny put the helmet on him.

"Oh my Lord! I can see in the…" The helmet was snatched from his head. "…dark."

"Be quiet old man! If your wife learns of this she will kill us in our sleep! This is worth a fortune alone, and who knows what this other stuff does. With this helmet and rifle I could take out an entire regiment by myself."

He turned the lights back on and packed the suitcases again just as Erna came out of the bathroom, her hair in a towel.

Grozny picked up Remmel and dropped him into his chair, then grabbed her by the arm and pushed her towards the door.

"We don't have time for this woman. We're leaving, now. Push him, I'll take the luggage."

They left the room and met a large, black Desoto out front. There were two men in the front seat, they said nothing as they climbed in. The car took off east as the last of the sun's light dimmed under the darkening sky. The clouds had broke but Andreyev knew there would be more coming from Chicago. He spoke to the two men in Russian.

"What is the news?"

"Good to see you comrade Grozny. We have been tracking two fast moving planes across the Midwest. They can only be jet planes, nothing else could move as fast. Since the only jets we see are for testing in limited areas, we are assuming it is your pursuers. One comes from Nevada, the other is moving faster than mach one and a half coming from California. The fast one will be here in an hour, the other is right behind it."

"What is the plan?"

"Plan? You are the one running this turkey chase, what is YOUR plan comrade?"

Andreyev felt a chill. He knew the price for failure, especially on high-level missions, and it didn't get much higher than this. If this went wrong it could blow the lid off of every major operation they had going in America. But then, he thought, what did he care? He would be gone soon. Suddenly a plan started to form in his mind. He would let his pursuers be the distraction they needed.

"We ambush them. There is a secret underground base at the lighthouse on Montauk Point. Not even the President knows about it. We have to officially alert the base that there will be an attack by air tonight. They will end up firing on their own people." The men looked at Grozny like he had lost his mind but they said nothing. They would follow orders as directed, let Grozny hang himself with his own noose.

Remmel sat in the back and listened to the rapid flow of Russian between the three men. The man in the passenger seat directed the driver to pull off the road and into a wooded area on the beach then went back to a radio in the trunk and began to send instructions. After fifteen minutes and what appeared to be a lot of explanations, he put down the radio and spoke to Andreyev.

"Well? What was that about?" Remmel was beginning to get impatient.

"Shut up old man or you'll find yourself in a KGB prison!" Grozny hissed quietly. "You're supposed to be my prisoner."

The two men saw the exchange and walked from the car a bit. Grozny joined them. There was a heated exchange and a lot of pointing at the car. Remmel started to sweat uncontrollably. Erna just sat, staring straight forward with her defiant, stony gaze fixated on something far away. The three came back to the car. The driver got in and the other man went back to the radio. The call was short and concise then the trunk closed. There was a small clacking pop, then a figure moved quickly up the side of the car. The sound duplicated itself and Remmel felt something warm and oily splatter on his face. The man at the wheel slumped over sideways.

"Erna." came Grozny's voice. "Get out here now."

Andreyev, with Erna's help, drug the bodies into the woods and quickly hid them. Then they came back and got in the car. Without a word they drove back on to the road, east again.

"What was that?" Asked Remmel.

"Unnecessary baggage." His wife replied. He looked at her wide-eyed. When had she become so accustomed to death?

"Don't worry about it Doctor," Andreyev looked at him in the rear view mirror. "Those men wanted to take you to a KGB prison to interrogate you. We could not let them do that."

"But won't their bosses be looking for them? What about the radio calls?"

"Relax, they made the calls I needed them to make. Now the Americans at Montauk think that the American's who are looking for us are really KGB. They will be lying in wait for them and their parachuting tricks at Montauk. Just the distraction we need to get into the secret base."

"Very clever Grozny. Now we just need scuba gear."

"What?"

"There is an underwater entrance to the secret base. That's how we get in."

Andreyev stopped the car and looked at him. "You're joking."

"No. That is why I have been sleeping so much, so I can dream. I am forgetting but in dreams I catch glimpses of the future. It's the best way."

Erna glared at him, growing angrier by the second. "You fat, decrepit fool!" She rose up, looming over him. "We're chasing all over America to follow pieces of hallucinations from your feeble dreamland?" She shook her bony fists, "You are useless! You lost your mind in the desert and now you are useless! Worthless sack of meat on wheels!" She threw a barrage of punches at him but Grozny pulled her back into the front seat.

"Enough!" He slapped her in the face, she recoiled to come back at him put stopped short as he pointed a single muscular finger between her eyes. Then he looked at Remmel in the mirror. "You idiot. Can you even swim?"

The doctor was calm and confident as he put his bent glasses back on his face . "Yes actually quite well."

"Okay, even if you can swim it is winter-time and the Atlantic ocean is freezing cold. We will die."

"That's why we need the diving gear. The suits will protect us from the cold and—"

"Listen you stupid, stupid old man. Diving is a highly technical skill. Do you know how to run a dive rig? For three people it would require someone topside on a barge supplying air. There is one person per diver to tend the hoses. Your idea is… tupoy, you… tupoy svoloch!'" Andreyev was beyond frustrated. He got out of the car and stomped out on to the road with his fists lifted to the sky, growling and barking Russian.

"You fail once again Oskar. How are we going to get into the base now? How are you going to get your legs back?" Her face changed as she switched strategies. "How are you ever going to have me the way you want me? Come on, think Oskar, there is a genius in there I know it." She leaned over the back seat and turned her voice into a husky plea. "Come on Oskar, you can think of something. Get us out of here and we'll ditch that Russian bastard. I want to go home, like we used to be."

"Yes, yes Erna, like we used to be." Remmel's mind went into overdrive; *solution, solution, where's the answer, get in, get in…* "I've got it."

Five minutes later Andreyev, leaning down into the open window of the black Desoto had been listening to Remmel's plan. Erna, from the front passenger seat, was staring angrily at the old scientist.

"That's your plan? You have come up with some stupid ideas Oskar but this one takes a cake." Erna was incredulous.

Andreyev shrugged, "It could work. Big rewards take big risks. This one could work."

"Yes," Remmel urgently explained, "We would only be exposed for a short time."

She glared at him. "I hate getting wet."

"Psh… women. You hate everything unless it's made of money. We will do it." Grozny got back behind the wheel. "But you'd better be right Remmel or they'll be finding your body washed up on the beach in the morning."

He gunned the car, they had already lost enough time.

Chapter 12

Over the edge

*'Man cannot discover new oceans unless he
Has the courage to lose sight of the shore.'*
~Andre Gide

"LZ is compromised, LZ is compromised, seek alternate with cover." Johnson was repeating over the radio.

Then Elsie's voice crackled in, "Roger that, Vampires on me."

Rand was on his back, falling like a stone. He felt like the ground was going to hit him any second. He was looking up at Johnson who rolled back over. The big man unlatched his oxygen mask and gave him a smile and a thumbs up. Instantly Rand felt much better and rolled himself over. He could see Elsie's light and silhouette, she was still flattened out to slow her descent. With a glance over her shoulder she went spread eagle. Instantly the wind caught the wings on her jump suit and she shot away towards the woods. Rand followed the team as they silently slipped away from the ambush. He briefly brought his scope to bear and spotted Elsie. She was next to Talbot and pointing down at a small pond. Water landing, he thought.

He felt a hand on his boot and looked back. Johnson was there smiling at him *watch me* came the hand signal. Johnson pushed him away gently and glanced back. When the man behind him had opened his chute, he yelled unintelligibly at Rand, gestured and nodded then pulled his chute. Rand took the hint and pulled his ripcord. In quick succession the parachutes opened and they gracefully floated down into the pond. They landed mostly in the swampy edges though McElroy managed to splash directly into the middle and discovered that the water was only shoulder deep.

They rounded up their chutes and quietly moved into the forest. Rand and Elsie scanned with their scopes. No one. Off in the far distance was the faint sound of a jet passing to the north. Their jungle training kicked in immediately and they fanned out in an advancing formation. After fifteen minutes they passed a farmhouse next to a gas station. It was Roop's Roost, they had approached it from the rear. Suddenly a hound dog started howling. The team sat down in the grass as the sound grew closer.

"Barney! Get back! Alright who's there? I'm warnin' ya, I got me a shotgun an I ain't afraid ta use it!'

Rand recognised the voice and replied from the cover of the deep grass, "Just a couple of raccoons Mr. Roop, come to make sure your little boy got the money we left you. Do you remember, it was in April."

"Sweet Jesus!"

"Blessings be to you and your family Mr. Roop if you would kindly just let us pass, keep your dog quiet and never tell anyone that you saw us."

"Who… who are you? I can't see in this dark. What—"

"We're night angels Mr. Roop and we prefer it if no one ever saw us. You are the only one who has heard us and now we ask you to keep it a secret."

"I will sir, as you say. No one will ever hear of it though it's pure torture to sit on such a tale."

"You may be able to tell it in time, but not for many years."

"Yes sir."

"Good night then, and tell Martha that it was just the raccoons."

"How did you know her name?"

"We know a lot of things Mr. Roop, we're always watching over you all."

The station keeper hastily crossed himself and departed without a word. When he was gone Elsie gave Rand a look.

"Night Angels? We're always watching? You're gonna give that poor man nightmares for years."

"No, actually I think he'll sleep better." Rand was satisfied with himself.

***

The big black Desoto's suspension creaked as it sponged over the road. Andreyev had the car up to ninety miles per hour as they drifted through the wide bends in the forest road. The lighthouse suddenly loomed over the trees and the Russian briefly tapped the brakes to make the turn into the parking area. There were over twenty men, all armed and looking at them as the headlights cut across the ranks of surprised faces. They shouldn't be there, he thought, they should have been shooting it out with the Carters by now! He floored it and the big car accelerated towards the lighthouse a break-neck speed. One soldier glanced off the side of the car as it burst through the wooden gate and onto the broad sidewalk leading to the huge tower.

The soldiers watched in shock as the black Desoto roared off the path, across a patch of lawn and straight off the short cliff. The splash was drown out by the waves as the men sprinted to the edge to see if anyone swam out, but the big car had already started to drop to the bottom, it's lights flickering in the deep.

Inside the car it was mayhem. Remmel screamed, Erna slammed her head on the front seat, smashing her lip in a shower of blood and Andreyev's head hit the windshield. He rebounded, unconscious. Water flooded the car instantly. Andreyev had made them roll the windows down so the car would flood and sink fast. It was an important part of the plan. As the cold water rushed in he woke up just in time to take a gulp of air.

They dropped quickly. It was deeper that he thought. Already he was wanting a breath. Andreyev shouldered open the heavy door as the car fell. The Remmels pushed the door open on the same side causing the car to roll so open doors to pointed upward. So far so good, everything is according to plan he thought. Now they just had to swim, steady and smooth, conserving breath. His lungs began to burn. He looked back, the Remmels were beginning to pass him. The Doctor really could swim. Then Remmel headed up. No! Thought Andreyev, he's giving up! But then Remmel just disappeared into the rock. Erna followed. His lungs burning, Andreyev kicked hard and found he was swimming through a cavernous gap that appeared out of nowhere. He broke the surface trying, but failing, to keep quiet.

The young soldier had the Remmels at gunpoint. Both of them were on the stone floor of the cavern wheezing and dripping wet. As soon as Grozny's head broke the surface the soldier pointed his Tommy gun at him.

"Alright mister just come out of the water nice and slow."

"You have it all wrong private, we're the good guys. I'm Agent Adams, CIA." Andreyev slowly reached into his jacket and took out an ID. The soldier approached slowly, turning his head to keep an eye on the Remmels.

"Come on now hurry up, I'm freezing!"

The young soldier leaned over the small pier to take the ID. The silenced SCAR ripped a burst from under the surface, punching three holes into the soldiers chest. The man was a corpse by the time he hit the water. Grozny climbed out onto the pier as Erna stood and looked around. The cave was over two hundred feet long with ceilings well over twelve feet. It was lit by a string of loose hanging bulbs on the wall opposite the water. A small wooden shack made due as an office.

"This is how they get supplies in." Remmel said through chattering teeth.

"Good, let's see if they have anything dry to wear." Erna truly looked like an alligator now, shivering with her vibrating teeth bared and blood flowing from her lip.

The Russian shoved a supply cart at the doctor. "We don't have much time before this place fills up with soldiers. Get on, and you…" He pointed a dripping finger at Erna. "Push."

***

The Vampires silently reached the edge of the woods and scanned the parking lot. It was full of soldiers spaced evenly every six or seven feet. Several of the men reported back the exact count; twenty-six armed with Garand rifles, BAR machine guns, Tommy guns and shotguns.

Elsie quickly formed a plan. "We can't kill them. Alpha you take left, Golf right. Flashbang the whole lot of them, then move in and knock em cold. Rand and I will clean up with the tasers. Ready?"

"Wait!" Rand grabbed her shoulder, "car coming."

"Vampires standby."

It was a car alright, and moving fast. It came barreling around the corner, through the gate and straight off the cliff.

"What the?" Rand looked at Elsie. Her eyes were searching – suddenly they went wide.

"That's Remmel and company, they're going for the underwater entrance. Vampires, now!"

Twelve Flashbang grenades came flying into the ranks of soldiers. The Vampires shut their eyes and clamped their hands over their ears as they detonated, completely disorienting the soldiers. The men burst silently from the trees in a dead sprint. They closed the distance and took out the soldiers with the butts of their rifles. Not pleasant, Rand thought, but they would be alive and have no permanent injuries. He didn't even need to use the taser.

A handful of soldiers had run to the cliff edge to watch the car. They wheeled at the sound of the flashbangs and started back towards the parking lot. The smoke cleared as they charged to a halt and saw all of their comrades laying unconscious.

"What in the name of—"

Another volley of flashbangs came from the woods and the soldiers joined their companions. Elsie breathed a sigh of relief. So far so good she thought.

"Good work teams, let's get into that base."

Elsie and Rand lead the Vampires to the lighthouse entrance. Elsie gave the hand signal, *Alpha, dynamic entry.* The men stacked up at the door. A nod confirmed they were ready and McElroy stepped back and shot the hinges, Baker kicked the door open and spun out of the way leaving McElroy the first in. As soon as the door flew inward a shotgun blast from inside splintered the frame. McElroy staggered back and cried out. The team piled in anyway. There were no other shots fired. Nickelson was at McElroy's side immediately, searching him for damage.

Elsie looked down, "Sitrep." Nickelson looked at her. "That means Situation Report soldier!"

"Yes ma'am I know, it's just that he's fine. He just got knocked down. The vest saved him."

"That's what they're for Nickelson. Can you go on McElroy?"

"Yes ma'am, just a bruise. Sorry ma'am, I didn't mean to be the first casualty in the team."

"McElroy are you speaking to me?"

"Yes ma'am."

"Then you're not a casualty. Let's go."

McElroy felt where the buckshot had hit his vest and smiled and he joined his fire team. They all clapped him on the back. Inside they had the old lighthouse keeper in a chair, sans the shotgun. Rand came forward.

"I'm Captain Carter of the U.S. Air Force. Why in sam hell are you shooting at us old timer?"

"You don't look like any Air Force people I ever seen."

Rand knelt down and looked the man in the eyes. "I'm sure there is quite a lot that you've seen, but you've never seen us. Understand? We're special ops sent here to keep some really bad people from taking this base."

"I don't believe you and I'll never tell you anything!"

"That's okay, we know the way in. I salute your dedication. Just try to look before you shoot next time, you almost hit one of our boys."

"What do you mean almost? I shot him square in the chest, saw him fall myself."

McElroy stepped forward, "No sir, you just grazed my shirt. I dropped cause I thought you got me. It's my lucky day I guess. No hard feelins'." He held out his hand.

The hard expression on the old man's face softened. "By God that's a true Kentucky accent to match a true Kentucky gentleman, I'd bet my life on it." The old man rose and shook McElroy's hand.

"You got me figured quite rightly sir, but me and my team, well, we got a job to do. Maybe after we're done we can chat a bit if'n ya have a nature to."

"It would be a pleasure, now you boys go get em!"

Rand rolled his eyes at Elsie and went over to the stair, lifted it and found a key under the false bottom. He held it up to Elsie. "If it ain't broke, don't fix it." They both smiled.

As they went to the door under the stairway Elsie said, "Do you realize that's the first time you introduced yourself using your rank and service?"

"Huh. How bout that." Rand sneaked a quick peck on her mouth then leaned around the corner and asked the old man, "Is there still the old dropping elevator trap on this thing?"

The old man looked at him slyly, "That's right son, you've been here before."

"Yep, more than once. Thank you sir."

A set of metal stairs going down unfolded underneath the wooded staircase that lead to the second floor of the house. The rickety stairs were narrow and only one person at a time could descend. At the bottom was a door with elevator buttons on the wall, one pointed up the other down. Rand pushed the UP button and the door opened.

"Going down?"

Suddenly his radio crackled, "Captain Carter sir there's a package up here for you."

"Say again?"

"A package sir, for you and the Major. You need to come up here and see this."

Rand turned around and sent everyone in front of him back up the stairs. Johnson stood by the door of the Lightkeeper's house and pointed outside.

"Now what?"

Carl stood on the lawn next to a large black car, Spang was closing the distance fast. The little dog was at top speed and jumped into Rand's arms. Elsie joined them as the team stood around. After a minute they got up, Elsie held Spang and

Carl stepped forward. They welcomed him with their thanks.

"Mr. Hughes thought you might need this."

He held up Rand's AA-12 full-auto shotgun and ammo belt.

"Your timing couldn't be more perfect."

The team was intrigued by the stocky looking weapon.

"What is it?"

"A full-auto shotgun with very little recoil, plus standard, armour-piercing and explosive rounds."

"Oh baby, I got to get me one of those." Rhodes said appreciatively.

Rand transferred his night scope to the shotgun with a click. Then Carl gave Rand his pack that was specially built for Spang. 'There's other stuff in there but I didn't look.'

"Are you coming?" He held out the silenced MAS-49 assault rifle to Carl. The pilot took it with a smile.

"Absolutely."

After Rand secured Spang in the pack he headed back to the elevator. They went down, one fire team at a time. Rand, Elsie and Carl were first.

The door opened on a large cave with a cement floor. It was well lit and clean. A young woman in an Army uniform sitting at a desk that read 'RECEPTION' looked up, surprised.

"Don't sound the alarm corporal. I'm Major Carter, this is Captain Capaldi and Captain Carter of the US Air Force, special ops. Ring upstairs and your door ward will verify. There has been an incursion into this facility and we are here to stop it. Sound a full security alert and send responder teams to all of the TSS sections. We are headed there now."

"Yes Major, I'll need your passcode."

"Peter Moon and Preston Nichols." Rand stepped up. "This is Captain Carl Capaldi, he's never been here before. We're in a real hurry soldier."

Just then the elevator door opened and team G2 piled out.

"They're with us and there will be more, just hurry!"

"Regulations sir, I'll be quick, pick a passcode for him."

"My flight handle, Matador." Carl said without hesitation.

Rand and Elsie looked at each other with wide-eyes.

"It's the first loop we've seen Els."

Carl looked at them, "What? I like that handle."

"No Carl, it's perfect, trust me."

"Thanks Corporal, we're officers in charge of these men, sound the security alert now."

The young woman got on the intercom, "Security Alert, security alert. This is not a drill. All units report to battle stations…"

The elevator opened and team A1 pried themselves out of the small door.

"This is taking too long." Elsie handed the map to Nickelson. "We'll be here." She said pointing at a spot on the map. "Catch up when you've assembled everyone."

Elsie, Rand and Carl sprinted down the hallway.

"It's all coming back to me. Rand, do you hear that humming sound?"

"Yeah, it's probably the power plant. Man I bet they're scratching their heads over that thing."

Carl looked at them, "I don't hear anything."

The passageway ended in a 'T'.

"Right."

They continued at a jog. At the mess hall they encountered the first security station. There were four armed soldiers, one of them behind a mounted thirty-caliber machine gun. They held up their passes and moved down the hall to two doors labeled 'Executive Briefing'.

"This is the Situation Room."

Inside was a large oval table with wood paneling on the walls.

"It hasn't changed at all. Still with the oval tables, oi vey." Rand cruised past the table and up to the guards at a station showing them the badge. "You're looking for a German man in a wheelchair and a hard looking German woman, both in their fifties. They will be with a very, very dangerous man about my height and build, Russian in appearance, though he speaks with a perfect American accent. He might try to tell you that his name is Agent Adams with the CIA. He's not, he's KGB. Do not try to detain him, shoot to kill on sight. Oh, he may be wearing a strange looking helmet with a shield covering his eyes. Pass on this information to every station you can. Stay frosty people this is the real thing."

They headed down four flights of stairs to a door at the bottom.

"Rand."

"Oh I remember this." Rand took off his pack, pet Spang and reached in to pull out his goose neck camera. He inserted it under the door. Sure enough, the minigun batteries that had been there before were replaced by soldiers with thirty-caliber mounted machine guns poking though armoured ball mounts in the wall

"That's amazing." Carl said, impressed by the little camera.

"Yeah, it's pretty handy." Rand cracked the door and waved his ID through, "FRIENDLIES, COMING IN!"

He peeked his head through and made eye contact with very stern looking machine gun crews. "Captains Carter and Capaldi and Major Carter followed by our special operations response team. ID check please?"

One of the soldiers came out and looked at the IDs.

"Their clear."

Rand gave them the same descriptions of who they were looking for and cautioned them they could be coming from behind.

"They infiltrated via the sub docks. You should redeploy for better coverage. If you hear gun fire, hold station, they might be headed your way."

They worked their way to the end of the hallway and another T-junction.

"Wait." Elsie said then picked up her radio. "Vampires, Carter, do you copy?"

"Roger, all units on approach to waypoint one. Over."

"Good they're almost here. Just wait for them. It's better to be careful—"

The sound of a short burst of automatic gunfire echoed down the hall to the right.

"That was a thirty-cal or I've never heard one." Carl said and took off at a run.

"Wait, Carl!" Elsie called but he was already half-way down the hall.

"I'll get him hon." Rand sprinted down the hall after Carl, as Spang barked from the backpack. Elsie stood alone in the hallway. This isn't good she thought. She keyed her radio, "Vampires what's your cur—" She felt what was unmistakably a large, round, silenced barrel against the back of her head.

"Drop the radio and the gun." Andreyev stood behind her like a tower.

He was wearing the helmet, the earpieces dangled from under the black Kevlar. *Good,* she thought, *he doesn't know about the EARs.* She dropped the machine gun and the radio.

"Impressive toys you have Major." He gloated, "But I'm more interested in—" In a blink Elsie spun on him, knocking the SCAR aside and drilling her gloved fist into the bottom of his jaw.

Her combat gloves were weighted with sand and hard plastic knuckles. Grozny felt like he'd been hit by a sledgehammer, but he was used to being hit. She reached to draw her Beretta but just as quickly he raised the SCAR.

"STOP!"

She froze. A smile crossed his lips. Blood gushed from his mouth where he had bit through his tongue. "Quite the feisty little one aren't we. Did they teach you that in two thousand and fourteen?"

A piece of his tongue was flapping loose as he spoke. He took the pistol from her and ground the barrel into the base of her throat where she couldn't push it aside. Then he bent down into her face, opened his bleeding mouth and bit down on the rest of his tongue, chewing it off inches in front of her. She closed her eyes at the grisly sight.

"Now I see how squeamish and weak you are. MOVE!" He shoved Elsie down the way that Rand and Carl had run.

"Where is it bliad?"

"What's a bliad?" She was already following her SERE training; *torment your captors*.

"Your name, whore. Now where is the time machine?"

"Oh I understand now." She said in voice that sounded like a ditsy girl. "Well, we have to go down this hall. It's been while; I was having a hard time remembering. I think we're looking for a chemistry lab." Elsie had already profiled him. The Russian tough guy from the forties assumed a woman was completely incapable, so she would play into his expectations.

"Just keep moving."

They reached a room labeled *Coolant Storage*. The sound of the sea was getting louder.

"I think this is it." She said in a cheery voice. "Now we, um… lets see."

"Bliad! I've already been here."

Every time she moved Andreyev had his pistol in her throat.

***

Rand caught up with Carl at the end of the hallway. There, a guard station protected two doors to the right and left. The mounted machine gun still smoked as it rested between sand bags amid a stack of crates. The men were tending to a woman who was sitting on the ground, That must be Remmel's wife, Rand thought. Remmel lay on the cement floor next to a supply cart in a puddle of blood.

Carl just stood and looked.

Rand flashed his ID. "Captains Carter and Capaldi, where's the third one?"

"We saw him sir, he headed down the other way."

As Rand started to run back down the hallway he turned to Carl, pointed at Remmel and yelled, "Make sure he doesn't die!"

He disappeared down the corridor labeled with a big '2'. As Rand crossed the path of hallway 'C' he caught a glimpse of the Vampires coming out the door from upstairs. He keyed the radio.

"Friendly, don't shoot!"

Talbot spotted him first. "Rand, where's Elsie?"

"I think she's in trouble. The machine gun emplacement down there got the Remmel's." He turned to the team. "Nickelson, Wiley, go save the doctor, he's down." Turning back to Talbot he said, "I think the Russian has Elsie. We have to clear this hall fast. Go."

***

The two medics ran to the end of the hallway where Carl was trying to treat the doctor. A group of soldiers gathered and watched as Nickelson and Wiley took over. The woman looked like she was handcuffed, but then her hands came around to the front as one of the soldiers from the base handed her a tissue. She was crying? Carl thought, that stony bitch had no love for her husband.

"Secure the prisoner!" Carl shouted but it was too late.

She dropped the tissue, pulled the pistol from the soldier's holster and put it to his head. "Stay back! Nobody move. You!" She pointed the gun at Nickelson. "Will he live?"

Nickelson calmly leaned back, "Yes, it's just a graze—"

The gun went off knocking Nickelson flat on his back. Erna giggled maniacally. "Now I see why you men like to shoot each other. It's exhilarating!" The smile disappeared as fast as it had come. "I asked a QUESTION!"

Wiley held up his hands and said, "Yes ma'am, I'll just stitch him up and he'll be fine."

"NO MORE STITCHING UP! Put him in the cart!"

Wiley hauled the heavy man onto the cart just as Nickelson began to stir. Wiley shot him a look and mouthed, '*Stay down*'. Nickelson just closed his eyes and played dead.

Erna waved the gun, "Now, all of you. Run down to the other end of the hall. Go!" She fired several shots over their heads and the men took off running. Only Wiley remained. Dr Remmel was coming back around. "You are going to open the door and wheel him in there, then I will let you go."

"Okay ma'am, whatever you say." Wiley opened the door then wheeled Remmel inside then came back out.

"Thank you young man. Your parents will thank me for killing off their weak, snivelling little brat!" She pulled the trigger but nothing happened. The round was stuck in the slide, sticking up like a stovepipe. Wiley took off at a run as Erna pulled the slide back again, clearing the stuck round.

"Oh, that's how it works. So easy." She levelled the gun at the back of Wiley's head and squeezed.

***

The Vampires cleared the hallway as several shots came whizzing down in a series of ricochets from the other end. A second later Rand watched as a group of soldiers came running around the corner.

"The crazy lady's got my sidearm!" A young soldier told Rand as flattened himself against the wall.

They didn't have time for this. "Alphas, secure the hallway to the west! Take the Remmels into custody. Golf, clear the eastern passage, go GO!" The Vampires sprang into action, sweeping down both corridors and sending civilians and base personnel back to safety. "You men follow behind." He barked at the base soldiers. "Re-man your stations as soon as my men clear them."

Rand followed team Golf down the hall towards the sea as shots rang out at the western end of the hall. They must have took out Remmel's wife, Rand thought.

"We're clear in here Captain." Sloane reported as they swept through the scientist's living quarters. Rand nodded and continued down the passageway. The rough, stone walls became damp as the smell of the sea grew stronger. Rand rounded the corner into the underground pier and froze. Andreyev had his back to him. He was holding Elsie with the 9mm Berretta at her throat. Rand switched to his .45 and crept up slowly behind them. Elsie was buying time.

***

"There was a submersible here last time. Now there's nothing."

"The submarine leads where?" Andreyev spat blood.

"The time machine."

"You're lying bliad!" He was angry now. Her incessant stupid act frustrated him to no end. He lifted his pistol to smash her face in with it, but as soon as raised his arm she broke free. Elsie twisted and stepped away, her feet went sideways on the wet rock floor and she crashed to her side. Andreyev had his gun raised over his head, grinning with rage when half of his face exploded in a red mist. Elsie sat paralysed, then she heard Spang bark. Looking past the gruesome figure as it collapsed on the floor, she saw Rand running towards her. In one fluid move he dropped to his knees and cradling her head.

"Elsie! Are you alright?"

"Oh my God Rand that was too close!" She clung to him, breathing him in.

***

Wiley anticipated the bullet, he could almost feel it burning into his back as he ran for his life.

Erna Remmel's finger began to squeeze the trigger, but it never completed the task. Nickelson had been feigning death after being painfully shot. While she had been moving the doctor his hand found his rifle. He pictured the shot in his mind then raised the gun quickly and shot, but it went high. She ditched into the door as a second shot smashed into the doorframe. Out of the corner of his eye he saw Captain Carl kneeling with his assault rifle raised to his shoulder. In the chaos of everyone running he had ditched behind a crate. Nickelson looked again, but the Nazi hag had vanished just as team Alpha came storming up.

"Are you alright?" Wiley returned and dropped to a knee to help Nickelson. He had some broken ribs but Nickelson was already standing up to go after the Remmels. "Easy there buddy, you'll puncture a lung." Wiley made him sit back down.

Rand came over Carl's radio.

"Carl, sitrep, do you have the Remmels?"

"Negative Rand, they got away. We're in pursuit."

"I've got Elise, wait for us."

Rand lifted Elsie up. She was none the worse for the wear. They retrieved their gear from the dead Russian, joined team Golf and ran down the hall to the other end. Rand was focused like he'd never been.

"Vampires stack up. Johnson on point. This opens up onto a catwalk. Johnson watch for fire from below the rest of you check those corners." Rand instructed.

The teams stacked up on the door and burst through. The door opened onto a steel latticework catwalk that widened after twenty feet into a forty-foot square landing that supported a thirty-foot square room made out of glass. Inside the room were an array of computer cabinets and rows of desks stacked with modern flat screen monitors, laptops and workstations. From the landing of the catwalk, a steel staircase went down four stories flanked by an open elevator. The car was at the bottom.

"Would you look at that." Pau gawked at the modern equipment.

"Easy Pau," Rand said, 'They're just computers. They control the systems that operate this giant gizmo."

"How did Remmel create all of this?" Paige asked.

"He didn't." Elsie started down the stairs. "He invented a small one in fifty-two. When he used it, he vanished. Without him there, the government couldn't get the one he built to work, so they made it bigger. Over the years they kept building on it until it became what you see now in the twenty-teens." She used their old understanding as a cover story.

"You mean we're in your time now?"

"No Jeter, when we came here the whole apparatus came with us. Unfortunately, there was no cavern for it to pop into, so it warped right into the rock. Rand and I didn't warp into anything. The theory is that, because we have a soul we can't come into existence in the space of dense matter. We popped in at the surface, in the forest above this place." *This lying business is tricky with so many smart questions coming at me.*

"What does having a soul have anything to do with it?' Wiley asked.

"It's the God string." Elsie explained. *At least I can stick to the truth on this one.* "We are bound to our physical dimension in time and space by, what is essentially God's love. It's like a cord that attaches us to everything. Remmel's theory is that humans have never existed beyond a certain time. We are essentially living this time first. That is to say, no one has ever occupied this time before. Apparently this is the case with twenty-fourteen. It's as far along the time line as mankind has ever reached. Remmel says that if an individual disconnects with his physical dimension in time and space and transcends the time line further, then all of creation comes with them. Rand and I got to experience this first hand when this big gizmo as Rand likes to call it, had a hiccup and paused the whole world for a second. Rand and I, for some reason, continued on for that fraction of a second. Since we were the only humans travelling forward, we were the only humans that ended up in that time. To Rand and I it seemed like everyone just vanished. It was especially disorienting because we were asleep at the time."

"So you woke up and everyone had vanished."

"Yep."

"Wow." Wiley shook his head, incredulous.

"But dogs don't have a soul." Pau said scratching Spang in the backpack.

"Well, apparently they do because Spang came with us and didn't materialise into the rock."

"So you're saying that none of this was here before you showed up?"

"Correct."

"Will it be here when you leave?"

"I don't see why not."

They reached the bottom of the staircase that descended next to a massive bluish grey pipe that sprouted from the wall. Bundles of cable came straight out of the rock and ran along on the cement path that headed off through a tunnel.

Rand broke in, "Enough Q&A for now, we've got to move. Remmel is on his way to the control station. This is where the golf carts were. He must have taken the only one." They began to jog on the path that followed the four story high blue cooling pipe.

"It's a long way guys, pace yourselves." Elsie told them.

Rand reached back and pulled Spang out. It was better to let him run along beside them than to get shook up inside the backpack. Bright construction lamps lay on the floor, shining up at the walls and bathing everything in an eerie yellow glow. The tunnel was several hundred yards then sloped steeply down until it ran underneath the huge cooling pipe. Suddenly they emerged into a massive cave as large as a modern coliseum. The sound of bulldozers and excavators rang through the huge chamber and workers in coveralls dotted the landscape. The group stopped and took cover.

"I count about forty men." Johnson reported.

"I have three guards by that group of white buildings over there." Reece added.

"They should be at battle stations." Rand stood up and motioned for the men to follow. He climbed off the path and trotted over to the guards.

"Halt!" They raised their weapons. Rand already had his card out.

"What is the meaning of this? We're in security alert! Secure your stations, clear the workers and call ahead to TSS control and have them lock it down! No one in or out!" Rand shouted as the guards scrambled. He grabbed one guard by the arm.

"Did you see a man with no legs and a woman drive by in a cart?"

"Sir, there are people driving everywhere in carts."

"Well these people are dangerous. Didn't you hear the security alert?"

The guard looked at his companions. "No sir, we haven't heard anything!"

"They must have cut your comm lines. Send someone to fix it and get more men on station down here on the double!"

"Yes sir!" The soldier ran off in a panic.

"There are more carts parked by that building." Elsie pointed.

Rand scooped up Spang and put him in the backpack. The teams took ten carts and drove up the path. Elsie was with Talbot while Rand and Carl sat together.

"Together again co-pilot." Carl quipped.

The convoy of carts plunged through the cave system. After twenty minutes they entered into a cavern that was so large the whole convoy slowed down to gawk. It stretched over five miles long, two miles high and over five hundred feet high.

The men were shocked. "We're outside."

"No Reece, look again." Elsie pointed

Huge stadium lights shone up from the floor and reflected off a crystal ceiling, creating the illusion of a night sky. The large pipe was joined by many others, but across the cavern another blue-grey pipe was exposed in the rock face. This one was over ten stories high and only part of it was exposed.

"Let's go people!"

Talbot nudged Elsie and she stepped on the gas. The path led towards an elevator that climbed the cliff face that held the section of enormous pipe. The top of the elevator was parallel with a large window that looked out over the cavern. A single golf cart was parked at the bottom.

The Second String

It took an agonisingly long time to finally reach the foot of the elevator. The box was glass on three sides and rode straight up the cliff face on a single track. They climbed out of the carts and Elsie pushed the key to call the car back down.

"We can only fit about eight at a time. Dave, you lead the first group up to secure the room, we'll catch the next ride up."

Elsie knew that the Vampires had to go first. Her and Rand were like VIPs now, the mission was to keep them safe and get them to the TSS Control Room. Talbot loaded in with Carl and team Golf. A moment after the elevator reached the top the call came down.

"All clear up here."

They all climbed into the elevator. The air condition system kept the glass box cool and comfortable. Rand tapped the black touch screen controls and the elevator silently slid up the rock face. The men marvelled at the futuristic controls.

"Their still just buttons guys." Rand said. "Someone designed a sensor that picks up body heat. They made it turn a switch off and on. It's no big deal."

"When you put it that way I guess it's not. It just looks… you know, neat."

"Don't touch it Taggart." McElroy pulled the man's hand back.

The elevator opened on a small, pine-panelled landing. A stainless steel door that resembled a bank vault dominated the opposing wall.

"Remmel must somehow already have access." Elsie ran over and put her hand on the imprint scanner at the keyboard station next to the door. The screen read: *ACCESS GRANTED Peter Moon.*

"That's me." Elsie gave Talbot a silly smile and went through the door.

Inside was a row of modern desks stacked with multiple flat screens and computer workstations. A large, thick glass window looked over the gigantic cavern. To the right they could see the large tube, partially exposed in the rock. The mining equipment appeared minuscule down on the deserted cavern floor. The Vampires all huddled at the window looking at the incredible view.

Rand turned to Elsie, "Everything's the same hon, just like we left it."

Elsie was looking past Rand to the far end of the room with a grimace. "I knew I shouldn't have left those there." Rand turned to see what she was looking at.

"STOP!"

The Second String

Everyone spun around at the sound of Erna Remmel's voice. She held a grenade in one hand, the pin in the other.

"Those." Elsie said to Rand. The two grenades she had used to explain their time travel situation before they had come to nineteen forty-nine were still sitting on the table.

"You know what this is. Drop your weapons!" Erna held the grenade up high for everyone to see.

Elsie held up her hands. "Erna, wait, you don't know what you're doing. Just let us go back to our time, then you and your husband can go back and save his legs. You don't have to do this." Elsie stalled.

"Ah, little miss army girl always running around doing good. What a joke! You may have been smart enough to capture the Fuhrer, but not me. We will take the time machine, we will erase you and all of the perversions of the human race. Only the pure will be left."

Rand followed Elsie's lead .'Not without your husband. You don't know how to run the machine, it will send you into oblivion. I know, I've seen it.'

"It is too late for you to stop us." Erna seethed, "He is already in there and we will be leaving to change the world forever. Now, drop your weapons and go back outside."

To Rand's astonishment Elsie suddenly relaxed, cracked a smile and strode straight towards her. Erna took a step back and raised the grenade higher. When Elsie didn't stop, her face danced in a confused mix of rage, confusion and finally resolve. She threw the grenade at them, grabbed the other grenade off the table then bolted down the little hallway at the back of the room. Elsie just kept walking quickly after her. The grenade bounced off the table and rolled at the feet of the Vampires as McElroy dove on it. Rand finally understood. He grabbed McElroy and lifted him off of it as it started to smoke and sputter.

"Careful there, you don't want to give yourself a burn on that smoke grenade."

Rand took off after Elsie. Behind them, the room filled up with smoke as the Vampires pursued Rand and Elsie down the passageway. They found Elsie at the door to the control room, slamming into it with her shoulder.

"They've blocked it from the inside."

"S'cuze me ma'am." Johnson pushed his way to the front, his huge frame spanned the hallway. Elsie shot at the lock then moved out of the way. Johnson put his back to it, hauled back with his foot and smashed the door open with mighty kick.

A heavy thrumming noise spilled out of the room. Remmel was at the controls and Erna was behind him.

"NO! Oskar don't let them in here!"

"Carters!" Talbot shouted as the thrumming noise got louder and began to rise in pitch. The whole room began to divide into colours. To the Vampires, Rand and Elsie were flashing in time with the sound pulses and splitting into hundreds of separate images. To Rand and Elsie it was everything else that was doing the changing.

"I have done it Erna!" Remmel shouted. The sound reached a fevered pitch as static electricity flashed off of the metal cabinets. Reece leapt at Erna Remmel as she pulled the pin on the other grenade, but he went right through her and flipped over the railing that surrounded the control unit.

"We leave you to die!" Erna threw the grenade but it was too late, it vanished with them.

The Remmels were gone but the TSS continued on. Colours spun and electricity sparked in an ever-increasing frenetic storm of sound, light and energy.

"Rand, we're leaving whether we like it or not!" Elsie yelled.

Rand took the controls. "We still don't know how to use this thing."

"We have to try!"

Elsie looked at them all. Then she stood tall and gave them a salute.

"Vampires! Attention!" Talbot brought them to ranks.

"I expect amazing things from each of you." She yelled. "You will never be forgotten!"

"David," Rand yelled as loud as he could, the room was becoming a hurricane of light and sound. "There's a bunch of our gear in the trunk of that car lying at the bottom! Take the little submarine and get it before someone else finds it! Give it to Hughes."

"Yes, I'll take care everything!"

Elsie pulled a manila envelope from inside her web gear, threw it to Talbot, and blew them all a kiss. The colours dazzled and blurred their sight as the room began to fade.

"Elsie! I don't know where we're going! It's doing it by itself!"

"I don't care as long as we're together! Now hold on to me this time!"

Rand wrapped his arms around her as they both reached out and touched the control panel. The air slapped and seemed to go inside out as blackness took them both. They drifted in the silent void but he could feel her in his arms and her voice in his ear.

"I'm here."

Montgomery Thompson

Chapter 13

One

'To know thyself is the beginning of wisdom.'
-Aristotle

He was aware. It was awareness unto itself – self-awareness. I am, he thought. Love…I am love, my love has her, he reached out and knew she was there. Then he saw. The golden strand, like a fiddle string was vibrating down the vast distance, pulsing to his tempo. He reeled it in, keeping her close, travelling the golden strand until he could see where it pierced the void in a brilliant speck of light. He pulled harder and even though he thought it was so far away, the speck burst upon him. In a dull, ringing flash he was back.

"Hey, he's coming around. Rand?"

"David?" Rand mind swirled. He should have been somewhere else.

"It's alright, Elsie is right here. You didn't go anywhere."

Rand looked over to his right. Elsie lay on the floor of the control room, she was just blinking and rubbing her eyes.

"Rand? Where are we?"

"You're still here." Talbot said. "You never left."

They sat up and looked around. "Where's Spang?"

Carl let the little dog go to them.

Elsie's head was clearing. "Rand, Erna threw a grenade."

"I know hon, it—"

Talbot chuckled "Wherever they landed, they got a face full of smoke!"

"Hey McElroy, we can send you there to go jump on it."

"Funny Taggart." McElroy punched him in the shoulder.

"Not so funny for them," Elsie said, "the second one was a frag grenade."

"It probably exploded as soon as they arrived. It would have destroyed the control console and most likely killed them." Rand helped Elsie up. "That has to be why we got stuck in limbo." As

Rand explained what he had experienced in the void and how he had followed the golden thread back to the light, tears ran down Elsie's face.

"I knew you were there, but I didn't know where to go. I just felt your love all around me and then I woke up. You saved me, you brought me back." She threw her arms around him. They stood that way for a long moment.

Talbot broke the silence. "After the machine did it's flashing thing we found you two out cold on the floor. We thought you were dead but Wiley checked you out."

"You were completely stable, but it was like you were in a coma." The medic explained.

"Talbot talked to the base commander. He sent some frogmen to get your gear out of the car. They should be here in a little while."

Elsie dusted herself off. "Well it all seems a bit anti-climatic doesn't it?"

Rand looked at her incredulously. "After all we've been through? Besides, we're not home yet."

After they gathered themselves up they returned to the main conference room of the base and sat down with the base commander. Talbot explained who they were and why they were there, going through events step by step.

The tall base commander rubbed his greying temples and said, "There are several positive things that have come from all of this. One is that we finally understand why everything just appeared here last April. Another is that we saw the time machine actually operate and that we now know that it's more uncontrollable than we anticipated. However, what is most important thing to me is that we uncovered a network of moles that had infiltrated our operations at the deepest level. Despite promises of cooperation, the Russians will stop at nothing to get the upper hand on us."

Elsie spoke up, "We are the only ones who remain that have used the machine. We will only use it to return to our time and feel that after that, it should never be used again. We are fairly certain it has been destroyed in our time, so we will have to try and return a few weeks ahead of the event that started this whole thing in the first place."

"You're confident you have that level of control?" The base commander asked.

Rand nodded, "It took Remmel several minutes of operation to get the machine dialled in. After that it operated for a minute or two more. Now that I know how long I have to fine tune the settings, I'm pretty sure I can get us close. After all, the controls are currently set for the twenty-fourteen destination."

"Assuming Dr. Remmel also knew how to control the machine."

"It is his creation, he knew much more than he let on."

"How can you be so sure?"

"Because Commander, when he departed here, it was the second trip he had made today. I know this because he was standing at the controls."

One by one, faces at the table lit up with understanding.

"Oh my God," Elsie finally understood. "While we were having our little standoff with Erna, he went back and got his legs."

Rand nodded. "Then he came back for her. It all happened so fast and everything was so chaotic I almost missed it."

"But for him, it could have been years! All he had to do was return to this moment." Elsie looked at Rand. The implications were frightening.

The base commander stood up. "So you are unwilling to give us the knowledge to use this machine? Do you understand that you are taking away greatest tool mankind has ever known? What's more you are refusing to help your country insure peace and democracy for the whole world."

"That's where you're wrong commander." Elsie stood and met him eye to eye. "By shutting down this operation we are saving the country we love from becoming a dominating beast that tramples the free will of the world. Remmel built it small, but the power mongers of the coming decades built what you see, a world warping monstrosity. Do you think they won't go there again? It's human nature commander. Who is going to control such power, you? The President? How about the man after him or Congress, the Senate, lobbyists from big industry or the military?"

The commander sat back down, digesting Elsie's words.

"Yeah, you start to see how quickly this goes down the crapper. In twenty-fourteen we're still scared as hell about the nuclear bomb because it threatens us all. In our time some nut job can carry one inside a briefcase. We have to monitor uranium and plutonium very closely to make sure it doesn't fall into the wrong hands. The TSS is much more dangerous than a nuke. You have to stop looking at it as an opportunity. It's not. It's a death trap and it has to be shut down."

"So you refuse to participate in the program?"

"Not only do we refuse to participate, we'll shut it down ourselves if we have to." Elsie and

Rand stood, braced for the commander's response. The Vampires tensed.

The commander sighed. "That won't be necessary. Knowing that even in twenty-fourteen we won't be able to figure out how to operate the TSS, it doesn't make any sense to pursue the project any further. Still, knowing that it is possible will encourage others to try. Clearly such undertakings need to be regulated, in much the same way as the nuclear programs are, maybe even more so." He looked around the table. "You can relax folks, I'm not so blind as to see, nor so deaf as to hear. Wisdom must and shall prevail. I will convene with the President and Congress immediately to discuss the fate of the TSS program. I would deeply appreciate your attendance Captain and Major Carter."

Everyone breathed a sigh of relief. "Certainly Commander, we will be happy to assist in anyway possible, provided that our ticket home remains intact until after we're gone."

"Yes, of course. I fully intend that you will be returned to your proper time. It's the only way to fully repair whatever damage might have been done. Furthermore, Mr. Talbot, in the interim period I would like to place the security of the TSS base in the hands of you and your unit... the Vampires is that right?"

"We'll keep her buttoned up."

"Captain and Major Carter, I expect that your equipment has been recovered by now. If you'll come with me I'll get you to sign a receipt to take delivery of it."

"And so it goes. Military and paperwork, the inseparable pair" Carl rolled his eyes as they all got up and walked to the reception area of the base. They signed for the soggy luggage and said their goodbyes to the base commander.

"Talbot, I'll need you back here by the weekend to start locking this place down. The Russians will probably try to get in here again. They'll certainly be attempting surveillance by sea, so be prepared to deal with the Navy on this one."

"No problem Commander. I've dealt with inter-agency relationships at Groom Lake, it won't be a problem here."

"Groom Lake? Isn't that what they call Area fifty-one? Is there really a base out there?"

"No Commander, nothing but sand."

"I suspected as much. See you in a week Talbot."

They went up the elevator and stepped out of the lighthouse into a sunlit day. An offshore breeze filled the air with a salty sting and the distinct smell of winter.

"Well, where does that leave us?" Elsie asked Rand.

Talbot put his arms around their shoulders. "Listen you two. It's been a long day. The bad guys are gone and the base is secure. Why don't we get you home and you can take it easy for awhile. Nothing has to be decided right away."

"You're right David." Rand took Elsie's hand. "Let's go home to Malibu and take a little time for ourselves."

***

It was a quick trip in the XCG – 20A and they landed back at Groom Lake to an enthusiastic reception. The Vampires regrouped in the briefing room for a wrap up. Rand and Elsie assured the men that they would see them again before they returned to their time. The men dispersed with leave to go home and visit their families for a week before they had to return to Montauk and take over security duties at the base.

"Don't feel bad for us," Johnson reassured Elsie, "all of the civilians will be gone by then and we'll be staying in those luxurious scientist's apartments."

After saying goodbye to the base personnel they flew the Nomad back to Hughes' airport.

"So you stuck to the story that humans in twenty-fourteen built the big TSS." Rand said to Elsie over the comms as the big plane cruised at altitude.

"I didn't know what else to do. I mean, time travel was already enough of a mind-fuck for these people. I didn't want to add Remmel's theory that aliens are somehow involved as well."

"As much as an unstable guy as is was…is, Remmel's theories have been pretty spot on. If he says it's aliens then I tend to believe him."

"Well, if it is then we'll leave it to them to announce their presence or not. But if they do show up I'm going to definitely let them have a piece of my mind."

"Aw baby, just remember that we wouldn't be together if the Happening wouldn't have happened."

"I'll be in a more forgiving mood when and if we get home." Elsie grumped.

When they arrived back in Culver City Howard met them personally and assured them that he would leave them alone for a couple of days before he came over to hear the story of everything that had happened. They left the Nomad at the airport and flew the Beaver back to the house in Malibu. It was twenty minutes before sun down and the staff had the house glowing with candles and soft lights for their return.

In the days following, Rand made a tour of the property with his security designer. He and Elsie made up plans for another house on the estate. It was equally secure and large enough for a family of six with luxurious appointments including a gym, offices and an art and music studio. Rand purchased as much of the land around the house as possible and then had his attorneys negotiate right of first refusal to purchase even more of the properties adjoining his. These rights were bought from the highly agreeable owners for large sums of money. If, or when they ever decided to sell the property, he promised to purchase it at top market value in cash, no questions asked. Several of the property owners took him up on the offer immediately. With the additional space he and Elsie built six more luxury houses, each carefully designed to blend into Malibu's landscape.

With the knowledge that California had wildfires and earthquakes in its future, all of the buildings were built to unheard of standards of tolerance with steel frames and walls of inch thick steel plating between layers of reinforced cement. The fire suppression systems were equally robust and included high volume sprinklers spread throughout the grounds and mounted on the rooftops. Massive underground pumps brought seawater up at a rate that doubled what the Malibu fire department could generate. Rand made sure that extra couplings were provided for the city outside the walls of the estate. Elsie set up funding for education, care for the homeless, the poor, and a variety of other philanthropic projects to insure that the future of the local community remained bright.

By the time Howard paid them a visit they had a laundry list of things for him to work on after they left including environmental issues, terrorist watch lists and political issues. It would all take a lot of money and time, but each item was a battle in a crusade for a better world. They caught him up on Remmel's alien theory and the three of them decided it was best to keep it to themselves.

"We have an opportunity to build some strong allies in congress and the senate," Hughes told them, "especially if you appear in front of them to appeal the closing of the Montauk base. We'll give the story that you gave the base Commander, that the large TSS was build in two-thousand fourteen. But it will be the only things we conceal."

"You're right Howard, We must build those relationships strong. These convictions to change need to last if there are to be any real gains."

"You're starting to sound like a politician Rand." Hughes gave him a wry smile.

"Yeah well, this is important stuff. Unlike current issues, Elsie and I possess the facts about the consequences of our actions over the last... I mean next sixty years. It's likely to be one of the only cases where twenty-twenty hindsight can be used in our favour. I would love to have access to the internet so I could recall every issue we have faced in that time, but I have to just try and remember what I can."

"You can't take responsibility, that's the main thing. You've done enough already. Any insight you two can offer is just icing on the cake. Remember, you have a right to life, liberty and the pursuit of happiness just like the next guy."

"It will be amazing to see if anything we do has any effect."

"Indeed, I'll have to wait a lifetime, you'll get immediate gratification. Kind of makes me jealous." Hughes scowled.

"Don't be jealous," Elsie sat next to him, "You get to live in this wonderful time and help make the world a better place. We'll be there to see your efforts bear fruit. I've been in the void Howard, I know there is a light on the other end. We'll meet there, in that light and be together again. There is no doubt in my mind."

"Well, we're not gone yet sister. There's still much to be done. When are you two thinking of leaving?" He said it like they were just going on a vacation.

"We have to meet with the President, the Senate and Congress. Once we have been assured that the TSS will be shut down and dismantled then we'll go."

It was a week before they heard from base commander. "Major Carter, General Jenner Dodson here."

"I'm sorry, who?" It was the second 'Jenner' that she had encountered in this time, and the first one hadn't left a very good impression.

"I'm the base commander you spoke with. We never formally introduced ourselves forgive me. My name is Jenner Dodson, I hold the rank of General, one star. Major I'd like to talk to you and Captain Carter if I may."

"Yes General. I assume you would like more secure conditions?"

"You are correct Major."

"May I suggest we meet at our home. There is hardly a place in all the world as secure."

"Are you sure?"

"Yes General, by any standards modern or otherwise, the Carter estate is practically a fortress."

"Very well then. How does tomorrow evening sound, around eighteen hundred hours?"

"Wonderful General. We'll be looking forward to your arrival."

The General arrived by staff car at exactly six in the evening. The house and staff were prepared and he was met with decorum to match that of a high-ranking dignitary. Rand wore a suit and Elsie a smart business dress. They were going to talk business after all. The General was relaxed and very impressed. Rand took him on a brief tour of the house, explaining only enough of the security measures that were in place to make the man feel at ease. When the tour was over they settled into the living room.

"I must say I am very impressed with the steps you have taken to create a secure facility."

"Yes well, we have had some very unpleasant encounters with enemy intelligence. We're not going through that again."

"The main reason I wanted to meet with you is to prepare you for the upcoming meeting with the President and Congress."

"We are meeting with all of them together?"

"We are. The whole thing is very unusual and I might add, very rare. Unprecedented is the word that has been used. Of course it all has to do with the two of you and who you are. The TSS facility is unknown to all but a handful of people in Congress. The President himself is only aware of the base because of plans for it to double as an emergency facility in case Washington is attacked."

"Yes, it was used for that in our time as well. Listen General, we have a list of issues from the future that we feel need to be brought to the attention of Congress. These issues concern not only the United States, but all of humanity. If they are addressed now, they won't become a problem in the future and the likelihood of a more peaceful and prosperous tomorrow should increase dramatically."

"It's as if you read my mind. That is what I am here to find out, if there is anything else we should know other than the closing of the base and the dismantling of the TSS."

"Well sir, the answer is definitely yes."

They spent the evening going over some of the things on the list to give the General an idea of how to organise the time. It seemed that many members of Congress had limited attention spans, so it was important to be concise and to the point. At midnight, the General departed. "I'll meet you in D.C. on the tarmac. As you have no twenty-fourteen uniforms and we have no coinciding Air Force ranks yet, wear what you wore tonight. The Air Force is still officially a branch of the Army."

"It won't be that way forever sir." Elsie saluted him and nudged Rand. He snapped a salute to the general who returned it and departed.

When the General was out of earshot he said, "That's the first time I've ever saluted a superior officer."

"Really?" Elsie turned and pressed up against him, "Well I know more than one way to get you standing at attention." She pulled him inside and locked the door.

Three days later Rand and Elsie climbed aboard Chase XCG-20A. With Carl piloting they off from Hughes airport with Hughes himself in the co-pilot's chair.

"Now that is power." Hughes remarked about the twenty thousand pounds of force generated by the four de Havilland Ghost 5 jet engines. The experimental plane was the only jet-powered craft of its size in the air. Hughes knew that in England the Comet, a jet powered passenger liner, had made its first test flight that past July. But it would be several years before it would be in regular service. In contrast, the Chase XCG-20A was a one-of-a-kind experimental aircraft that received all of the research and development that Hughes, Chase aircraft and Groom Lake could throw at it. Coupled with Rand and Elsie's input it was quickly developing into a fast, efficient and safe airplane. They rocketed through the sky at five hundred miles per hour, just one hundred below the plane's top speed. They would traverse the twenty-three hundred miles to D.C. in about four and half hours with a tail wind. It was a noisy ride in the back of the big cargo plane, but Hughes had a few couches and beds strapped in at the last minute. What seemed like eccentric extravagance at the time was one of the only things that made the trip enjoyable. Elsie took some time to walk Hughes around the airframe and tell him about how the modern AC-130 gunships were set up.

The sun went down and after a short nap that seemed like minutes rather than hours, Carl came over the radio to tell them that they were on approach to Washington National Airport. No one knew what to think of the plane as it touched down on the runway in the cool DC night. The tower had no idea a jet powered plane was supposed to land and it drew some attention as it taxied to its designated hangar. The area was cordoned off by a military and police escort and a limousine cavalcade waited for them as they descended the ramp. A soldier confiscated an airport worker's camera as the military ground crew quickly scrambled to get the plane into its hangar. Carl decided to stay in the plane and catch a nap while Rand, Elsie and Hughes climbed into the limo and met General Dodson who was waiting for them inside. He briefed them as they sped off towards the Capitol Building.

"Mr. Hughes, delighted to meet you finally. Captain, Major, I trust your flight was satisfactory?"

Howard Hughes looked at General Dodson like he was an idiot. "General we just flew from

Southern California to Washington D.C. in under five hours. How could that not be satisfactory?"

"Yes, I see your point." Dodson was clearly perturbed by the spectacle of the plane. Or maybe, Rand thought, he was jealous.

"General, there are a number of ways we plan to assist the United States in becoming world leaders of peace and prosperity. One of them is the technology in that plane. Our little publicity stunt did exactly what it is meant to do; stir up excitement and hope for a brighter future." Rand began.

Elsie picked up where Rand left off. "In our time the military used a tactic called 'shock and awe'. The basis of it was to demonstrate to the enemy that our military capabilities were so overwhelming that they might as well not resist at all. This is similar tactic but with a more positive focus. We want to create excitement and hope on a similar level. If people believe that the path to peace isn't a pipe dream; that we can achieve a harmonious coexistence with other nations, without power struggles, they will choose to support that, rather than a path of conflict. If we can cause that perception to, as they say in our time, 'go viral' then life will certainly improve around the globe."

The Second String

Soon they stood in front of the whole body of Congress. General Dodson had told their story and introduced them. They began by repeating what they had told him on the ride over. Now Hughes took the reins.

"Of course it's an ideal. Of course, it sounds flowery and maybe even silly. But it's because we've never tried it. We never had the opportunity to even perceive how it might be done. Now the Carters bring us the proof of our current efforts. They can truly say what the result of the next sixty years will be on the course that we have set. And that insight gives us the opportunity to change that course, to alter it for calmer seas, warmer more fertile waters. Take their advice. This is the moment. There will never be another chance. So Rand, Elsie, what would you have us know? What would you have us do?"

To a rapt Congress, Rand and Elsie spent two hours covering every issue on their list. They emphasised that in the future, no one cared what party laid claim to what discovery or motion. The only thing that mattered were the results. The political legacies that stood the test of time were those of the bold and the honest. Those who worked for their own gain were revealed and their lineage often paid the price. Though some of it wasn't entirely accurate, Rand wanted to do everything he could to ensure that the Washington politics of his time might somehow be set on a straighter course. All he could do was try to scare them a bit. After they had finished, the questions came.

There were some who doubted that Rand and Elsie were form the future at all. Rand had come prepared and went around to each one with the iPad and it's pictures, the NV Helmets and the MRE with the date on it. Afterwards they took a short recess while Congress debated the legitimacy of their claim. They were led back in and stood before the room.

"It is with a solemn heart that we, the Congress of the United States of America do, through examination of the evidence given both by legitimate military observation, special agency testimony and overwhelming witness thereof, attest to the validity of the claim that Captain Rand Carter and Major Elsie Carter are indeed from the future from which they claim to originate. And by this conclusion we are honour bound to observe and pursue all means necessary to heed such insights as they have provided for the benefit of all mankind."

The Congress erupted into applause as Rand stood next to Elsie and Howard feeling like his heart would burst. Elsie squeezed his hand as she fought back tears. When the applause subsided Elsie stepped forward and address the assembly.

"And the truth shall set you free. Indeed, with you now lies our greatest hope. Share it freely, inspire with it and lead with it, for it is divine and shall not fail you."

Rand joined her. "We will stay with you for the next several weeks, but then we must go home. We've been trying to get back for so long…" He couldn't finish, the emotions rolled through him like a wave. Hughes took over. "They have been through more than any of us can imagine. Thank you for your time. God bless." Hughes put his arms around them and led them out to the limo. The General met them at the limo and leaned in to door to offer his hand.

"I have never, nor will I likely ever again, be so inspired. Thank you."

Hughes shook the man's hand. "You know where to find us General, the door is open."

They sped off to the airport. It was nine in the evening and the police and military escort pulled onto the tarmac. Rand climbed out of the limo, refreshed and less emotional. "I'm sorry hon, I don't know what came over me, it just hit like a brick." He told Elsie on the way. Now he strode up to the military guard. "Salute son, I'm an Air Force Captain." The soldier snapped to attention and saluted. "Sorry sir."

"No apologies son, how would you even know? What's your name?"

"Corporal Sato sir."

"And who is your superior on duty here?"

"Lieutenant Gerard sir." The soldier nodded towards the hangar. "He's with the plane sir."

"Thank you, and keep your eyes peeled, the Russians want that plane."

The soldier's eyes went wide. "YES SIR!"

Rand walked back to Hughes and Elsie with a smile. "Bright kid, wish they were all like him."

They met the Lieutenant at the bottom of the stairs leading up to the plane's main door. "I want you to make sure there is no press lurking around here waiting for us to pull out."

"Yes sir."

"Good job here tonight. It's not often you see such alert soldiers on plane guard. Special notice to Corporal Sato, consider a promotion. We will await your all clear before opening the hanger for departure."

The young man took off at a run and started organising his men as they boarded. They found Carl snoring on one of the couches. "Let him sleep," Elsie said, "I'll get us in the air."

"Ten bucks he'll running for the cockpit when the engines startup." Hughes whispered.

"He's a good man Howard, a good leader and a hell of a pilot. You should consider taking him on." Rand said quietly as they climbed the stairs into the cockpit.

"Way ahead of you old man. I'm going to offer him a position as my head of flight operations. He'll hire and train all my pilots, help build my airports and be an integral part of anything at Hughes that has to do with aviation."

"He's the perfect man for the job."

"Say, what did he do at Groom Lake?"

"Test pilot, one of their best."

Elsie turned to them. "I've got the all clear from the Lieutenant."

The hangar doors opened as the lights switched to red. The tug pulled them out to the tarmac then turned them. The flagman gave the signal to start the engines but Rand had to lower the ramp and tell the man that they needed significantly more clearance to start the big turbines. The tug pulled them out farther as Rand kept waving them on.

He could tell the ground support crew thought they were crazy for leading them out so far into the taxiway. In the cockpit, Elsie was arguing with the tower.

"Negative tower, no traffic on our six, the jet wash is too powerful. You'll have aircraft tipped over on the taxiway. We need a lot of room here."

Eventually the tower gave in and Elsie throttled up the big engines. She gave them an extra push just to show the watching crews what they were dealing with. One man thought he'd be smart and stepped into the wash. Before he could realize his mistake, he was thrown ten feet before he tumbled through the muddy grass and came to rest up against a fence. Elsie saw none of it as she began taxiing to her assigned runway. People crowded the terminal to look at what was making all the noise. Elsie put in full power as she lined up against the wind.

"Very funny you guys!" Carl had woke up and was hanging on to the stair railing.

Hughes just laughed. "Hold on!"

The plane smoothly accelerated and climbed into the air. Carl's arms were aching by the time they began to level off and Rand had to reach back and help him up.

"Boy! You just don't know how much force that is until you try and hold yourself up against it." Carl rubbed his arm and sat down. "Well, how did it go?"

They excitedly told him all of the details of the session with Congress.

"So, exactly how I expected it to go." Carl said with a satisfied smile.

"Really?"

"Yeah, you take you and Elsie and add in Howard Hughes? Are you kidding me? Who's gonna tell you guys no?"

"I like your style Carl. You're a good man, I can tell. What do you think about coming to work for me? I want to put you in charge of the aviation side of my operation."

For the first time since Rand met the man, Carl was honestly dumbfounded. He reached forward and shook Hughes hand enthusiastically.

Hughes just laughed, "Don't you even want to know what it pays?"

They touched down at Hughes airport at two-thirty in the morning. Rand had slept for three hours so he would be fresh to fly the Beaver to the house. A small tidal surge kept him on his toes as he brought the plane up to the beach at Dume

Cove. Rand pulled the plane onto the sand as the rock face lifted to expose dark hangar. One of his two-man ground crew hauled out a tow cable and hooked it onto a specially installed hook. The other man winched the plane in while the first man swept over the tracks with a wide broom built for the task. T

he men had come from Howard and now enjoyed a luxury lifestyle at the estate. Their only job was the care of the planes. Rand also made sure they had their own planes in his collection and would buy new planes based on their recommendations.

One of the men was Polish and had flown against the Germans in the 1938 invasion of Poland and again in the battle of Britain flying Spitfires at first, and later Mustangs with the 308th squadron. Unlike a lot of his countrymen he spoke very good English and decided to come to the U.S. after the war. His flight experience earned him a coveted spot on Hughes flight line where he volunteered to go to work for Rand and Elsie. Rand trusted the man implicitly and planned to offer him life long employment including a house and education for his children if he would take charge of the whole aircraft collection, seeing to their preservation and continued operation.

The second man was British and had fought by his side. They had profound respect for each other and Rand was inclined to make him a similar offer. Later that week he did just that. Both men happily accepted and, though it was the last thing Rand expected, swore solemn oaths to do their duty until their deaths.

Rand in turn swore to take care of them and their families even into retirement, old age and death. If the family managed to create an heir who wanted to take over the duties of the father, then he would extend the agreement to them as well. He knew he would most likely be meeting those heirs soon.

Similar arrangements were made with all of the staff that had become very dear to both of them. The property that had come available made it possible for the construction of enough fine homes for them and their families to live quite comfortably.

As the week went by Rand and Elsie spent every minute arranging for their absence. Rand purchased a large warehouse in town and had extensive security measures installed. Then he began hunting down collectables. From automobiles to weapons, military vehicles and planes to baseball cards and seeds, he created a museum of items. For a sizeable yearly contribution he engendered the services of the California Academy of Sciences to curate the collection in secret. Select pieces could be shown, but their source had to remain anonymous.

They made special instructions on what stocks to invest in and when. It was the ultimate in insider trading, but they also concentrated on bolstering the markets in future times of trouble. The Wednesday after they returned, Rand called Talbot.

"How long are you guys stuck in Montauk?"

"It's going to be a long haul. They don't know what they have to do to break the thing. They have started trying to tear out the big pipe, but it's going to be awhile."

"For cryin' out loud, why didn't they just ask us?"

"Nobody wanted to bother you."

"That's what we stayed on for! Just tear apart the control unit. That's the part they never figure out how to rebuild."

"Are you kidding me? Here, talk to the General."

"Dodson here, what's the secret?"

"The control unit, that's all. Blow it up then secure the doors. You'll need engineers to shut the reactor down then it's a matter of removing the fuel rods and storing them safely. No cutting corners there."

"I see. Anything else?"

"Yeah, I need Talbot. The Vampires are action men, they're not cut out for lounging around. Get a new security team and send me my guys. Ask for Lieutenant Gerard & Corporal Sato. They were our plane guards in DC, they did a great job."

"Copy that. I'll send Talbot and the Vampires to you as soon as I get Gerard out here. Two days I expect. Anything else?"

"Yeah, take a break and try to enjoy yourself."

Laughter came over the line. "Yeah, I'd like that."

"Come out to Malibu and play awhile. Bring the family, I'll send the jet."

"Really? Sounds great! How about Wednesday next week."

"Perfect, stay for a couple of weeks. We've got everything."

The General handed the phone back to Talbot who said, "You're learning a thing or two from Hughes I see. Can't wait to see you my friend."

"Ditto, see you in a couple of days."

Rand hung up and immediately called Hughes. "Howard? I need the best private eye in the business."

Howard knew the man by name. "Delgado, Paul Delgado. He's a crafty little Spanish guy, hard as nails and sharp as a tack."

Rand contacted Delgado and hired him to track down Avery and Megan Wilson. It was probably the easiest job that Delgado had ever done. The couple were living on the Avery family's ranch in upstate New York. When they had returned from eloping, married and rich, the families had forgiven them. Unfortunately, the relatives kept hounding them about money and though they were generous, it didn't stop people from being greedy. Eventually disagreements happened and then the family fell out, first with each other, then with Avery and Megan. A number of lawsuits were pending with a host of grievances that the family members had against them ranging from the petty to the ridiculous. All of the suits were targeted at getting money from the couple.

Rand told Delgado to contact Avery and Megan on his behalf and ask them if they would like to take a five-hour plane flight to visit, all expenses paid of course. While he was waiting for an answer he contacted his attorneys and explained that he wanted the best legal team possible to get to New York and get those vultures away from Avery and Megan once and for all. The couple sent the word back that they would love to come and see them. Rand sent the XCG-20A to pick them up that day and then return to take the lawyers to New York. The plane would wait a day then pick up the Vampires in Montauk and bring them to Malibu. Carl loved it. "This coast to coast run is fun. Plus I'll get to visit New York for a day and an evening."

"Yeah," Rand laughed. He had made special plans for Carl. "You get to see New York, and in a way you're not going to forget. Here are your only instructions, 'Just get in the car.' Can you remember that?"

"Yeah, just get in the car, no problem."

Rand contacted the Waldorf Astoria and arranged to give Carl the star treatment. He also purchased the 1931 Type 41 Bugatti that he an Elsie had been chauffeured around the city in. Carl would take it with him when he was done with it, sans the chauffeur of course.

Rand added more cars to his collection including a 1938 Bugatti 57SC, the 1949 Cadillac Ranch Wagon with all of the original Route 66 paraphernalia, a 1929 Type 40 Bugatti, a 1934

Rolls Phantom II Continental and a brand new Spohn Veritas. The cars would be kept in immaculate running condition in a sealed, heated warehouse for the next sixty years.

Rand left instruction for more to be added through the years; a Hudson Italia in 1954, as many Ferrari Testa Rossas from 1957 as could be bought including the prototype, a Ferrari 250 GT California Spyder in 1961, another Ferrari 250 GTO in 62, five 58 Corvettes, and one of virtually every rare muscle car from the sixties and seventies. He asked Hughes to make arrangements with his contacts at car companies for the rights to purchase the concept show models each year.

Delgado called Rand and told him that Avery and Megan were on their way. Later that evening Elsie and Rand received the young couple at the house. They were excited to see each other again and the two told them about everything they had done since they had left them in New York.

When they got to the part about their family woes it was worse than Rand had heard. Not only the Avery family, but Megan's family had essentially abandoned them both when they didn't give over all of their money to their parents. By this time they had already moved into Avery's family's farm land. They were harassed and even threatened at gun point to disclose where the money was hidden, but Avery never told them.

After Avery contacted a local lawyer, the man charged them exorbitant fees for very little service. They learned later that the lawyer had hired a private investigator to try and learn the exact whereabouts of the money. Again, Avery stuck to his guns.

Rand told the young couple that he had sent out a crack team of lawyers to put a clamp down on the fiasco. Even though these people were family, he just couldn't abide them trying to take advantage of the two good-hearted youngsters. They would be put in their place and by the time the lawyers had their way, they would be on a tight leash regarding Avery and Megan's money.

Rand and Elsie invited the two of them to stay and explore the area. They suggested that perhaps the best thing for them would be to build a new life away from the greedy grasp of the philandering families. The young couple agreed that it wouldn't hurt for them to explore their options.

The following day General Dodson showed up with his family. Jenner's wife Mona was a graceful, dark haired Mexican woman. Their children were extremely well behaved though Rand thought the General held the reins a bit tightly. Elsie reminded him that it was nineteen forty-nine and parenting styles were very different in comparison to how they were raised.

On the following day, Talbot arrived with the Vampires and Carl. The Bugatti was taken to the warehouse to be serviced and detailed. Elsie had never seen the Vampires in civilian clothes. She never realised how large they all were. It was like having a football team in the house.

They all lounged by the pool and played with the General's kids. Avery and Megan were shy at first, but when it became clear that Rand and Elsie really wanted to open the two up a bit, the Vampires engaged them like peers. Soon they were chatting away like old friends.

Avery had an affinity for vintage farm equipment and Rand had the thought that he might be able to expand the young man's appreciation of antique machinery. While Elsie and Megan played with the kids on the beach Rand took Avery and some of the Vampires to see the car collection. Avery fell in love.

"I love cars. We still have the Chevy Styleline, but it's nothing like these."

"Avery have you ever thought about an education? Maybe going to college?"

"Not really. I didn't like school that much."

His comment intrigued Nickelson, who was an educated physician. "What kind of stuff do you like Avery?"

"I like vintage farm machinery, like from the turn of the century."

"What is it that you like about those machines?" Nickelson probed further. Rand guessed where he was going.

"I don't know. All the wheels and pulleys. You can see how they work, they're not all enclosed."

"And that intrigues you."

"Yes, exactly, I can see all the parts in action. I think about how I would change it, or adapt it to work better."

"Avery, I hate to break it to you but you're a born mechanical engineer."

"But I'm not that interested in buildings and bridges."

"That's a structural engineer. There is a lot of focus on architects and structural engineers these days. Cities like New York are growing upward faster than outward. All the hubbub is about the guys who make the bridges and the buildings, not the engine builders, the watchmakers and the people who design printing presses."

Avery perked up at the mention of engines.

"Maybe you should go to a school that shows you how engines are built. You know, roll up your sleeves and get your hands dirty."

"I think I would like that." Avery never thought of school as something he could enjoy. He had always associated learning with tedium.

"I have an idea Avery." Rand stepped in. "I have a mechanic here who takes care of these cars. I'm building him a garage in the back. What would you think if I built in another garage next to it and brought in a professional mechanic who would be your mentor.

"There's no better way to learn than one-on-one with a pro. You wouldn't have any of the pressure that comes with a school. Start with an old tractor or a car and just have fun. Your mentor's job would be to teach you and answer your questions while you restored it. We could find someone who could even certify you so it would count towards a degree."

Avery's eyes were filled with wonder but his face showed concern. "But how much would that cost?"

"Don't worry about it Avery. I have so much money I don't know what to do with it all. Investing in a young engineer is more than worth it. When you get good at it, maybe you could help me out and keep my collection here up and running. What do you say? You and Megan could live right here in Malibu, on the estate if you like."

"I'll talk it over with Megan, but I think it's a swell idea!"

They headed back to the house where Rand told Elsie about his offer to Avery and Megan.

"Rand that's genius. They can stay in one of the guest cottages while their house is being built here on the estate. I'll go and talk to Megan."

Later that evening Avery and Megan announced that they would be staying in Malibu. Avery would start training as soon as they found the right teacher. In the meantime, the mechanic at Rand's garage would help set Avery up with anything and everything he needed. Megan was already busy picking a spot and planning their new house.

Rand took that afternoon to spend time with each of the Vampires and talk to them about what they wanted to do once they retired from duty. Johnson wanted to do research and development in the field of firearms. Baker was trying to save his family's farm after losing two brothers to the war and Rhodes just wanted the simple life. Wiley wanted to complete his doctorate in medicine and Rand asked him if he would consider becoming the General Practitioner for everyone on the estate. Wiley agreed with the caveat that even if his career eventually took him other places he would ensure that medical facilities on the estate would rival the best in the world.

Similar arrangements were made with all of the Vampires. They all had dreams and aspirations, Rand and Elsie made them all come true. The men would be taken care of for the rest of their lives. Some of them felt too strongly about accepting help and politely declined. Rand even went so far as to show them, on paper, the staggering amounts of money he and Elsie had. Still, a few of the men stubbornly refused to accept their gifts. In the end Elsie, just as stubbornly, set up accounts and portfolios in their names anyway.

"They're our boys and I'm going to take care of them even if they're too proud for their own good. Someday they'll need it and so will their families."

Rand and Elsie's activities had teams of lawyers and accountants streaming in and out of the estate for days. Carl was working for Hughes, but Rand and Elsie set him up with his own accounts. One of the houses was being built specifically with him and his eventual family in mind, which proved serendipitous. On his star-studded evening out in

New York, he had met a girl and for the first time in his life, he was interested in settling down.

There was one thing left for them to take care of. At the end of the week, they took David Talbot down to the beach by the secret path that led along the cliff face, talking as they went. Talbot marvelled at the clandestine excavations.

By the time they made it to the hidden hangar his head was spinning. Rand began to explain about the other excavations under the house, the complex security and weapons systems, armoured walls, sonar array off the beach and radar station embedded in the cliff face.

They showed Talbot all the secrets of the estate; bookshelves that rolled back into stairs and secret passages that led to weapons caches and communications rooms. It was an extensive tour. Finally, they took a passageway that led from an armoured communications bunker to the back of a closet in their bedroom.

Passing through the bedroom, they entered a door through another closet that led down a long path to another section of the house. It was newly built and practically a house unto itself. They emerged in another spacious bedroom that joined, by way of a secret door, to a master control room.

The radar, sonar and communications could all be run from the one room.

The house was built to such a size and quality as to suit a large and wealthy family. They sat down in the main living area, tired from the trek. French doors slid back to allow wide access to the patio and pool area. Beyond the pool deck was a half acre of landscaped lawn that looked out over the cliffs to the sea. Elsie leaned over and put a set of keys into Talbot's hand. Then, closing her hand over his she looked at him earnestly.

"We need you David. Please live here, raise your family here, be the master of our estate and take care of our people. We will be leaving soon, but you will know exactly when we'll return. You'll be an old man in your late eighties, but with any luck we'll make it back in time to see you again."

David nodded slowly, tears welling up. "I am so honoured. It will be my life's work."

"I've left a full accounting of the finances and we've written down everything we would like done over the years. Anything else that is there is yours to use as you see fit. You have power of attorney in all our affairs and access to all our accounts. Tonight we throw a party and say goodbye. Tomorrow Carl will fly us to Montauk."

The party was relaxed and blessed with a beautiful sunset. Rand used the iPad discreetly to take photos of everyone. Avery and Megan wanted to know what it was, but Talbot just told them that he would explain it to them later. After dinner and a round of drinks Rand rolled out a wheelbarrow full of cement. With the help of Pau and Wiley he stood up a prefabricated hollow cement pillar that had been brought in earlier that day. They wrestled it over to a spot at the edge of the patio closest to the cliff edge. Then, when he had cemented it in place, he pulled out a document.

"This hollow pillar is a time capsule. This paper will go in it and we would like you all to sign it as witness. It will go into the capsule and be removed when we return."

It was the first that they had made mention that they were leaving.

Megan scowled, "Where are you going?"

"We have to go away, but we will be back one day. David will explain it after we've gone. Tonight is our last night." Elsie explained.

The announcement caused a commotion, but all questions and protests were put aside as gently as possible. Their staff and friends had grown accustomed to their eccentric secrecy so the issue wasn't pressed.

They all signed the document which was added to a stack of other papers including the congressional declaration of their unusual status and accomplishments, a thumb drive, locks of Rand and Elsie's hair, sealed vials of their blood and photos of them with the Vampires in the jungle that had been taken with Jeter's camera.

Rand put it all into a black, rubbery plastic bag that was rolled closed and clamped with a steel security strip that stamped the time and date into the metal. They put it all inside the pedestal and sealed the top of it with a large round flagstone. Then they framed the edges with wood and filled in several inches of cement on top. Rand and Elsie made impressions of their handprints then etched the date and time into it. When it was finished there was another round of questions from everyone but again, they were put aside.

"All will be told in its proper time, but for now Elsie and I want you all to know how much we love you all. Your faces are etched into our minds and your spirits into our hearts. We will carry you with us always, and always our hearts will be bent on returning to you here."

"Very touching old man." Hughes had arrived in the midst of Rand's speech. He was grateful for the big man's impeccable timing. "Now, if I could borrow you two for a moment," Hughes said, leading them away across the lawn, "I have some important business to discuss."

The final glow of the sunset drenched them in a dim red light. It made Howard's sad expression even more grim.

"It's been quite an interesting journey since you first showed up on my doorstep. I never thought that the dashing young couple I met at the Waldorf in New York would become the star around which my world would orbit."

"I think it's a mutual orbit Howard."

"I want to come with you. You see I have a painful affliction which, I suspect in the future they will probably be able to treat. I think it has something to do with my nerves, but it's been getting worse and it's about to drive me crazy. I experience a horrible pain whenever I touch something or am touched." The confession was a crack. Underneath his expression it became apparent that Hughes was putting up an incredible effort to mask his pain.

"Rand, please let me come with you."

"Howard you don't need my permission. You are your own man, it's your call to make. For our part, we are your friends and will do anything and everything in our power to help you in any time or place."

"Thank you. I fear that if I had to cope with this for a lifetime I would lose my mind."

Elsie quickly left them and trotted into the house. "I'll be right back."

Rand sat down with Howard on the bench overlooking the sea.

"I have left instructions with Carl." Hughes continued, "I have also been in contact with General Dodson. He is up for retirement soon and would be an excellent man to run my personal business. Carl has recommended another man, I believe you call him 'Chief'. He will be taking over my engineering department."

"Excellent choice. Chief is an amazing talent and one of Skunk Work's best. I'm sure they will hate to lose him."

Elsie returned with a glass of water and a bottle of pills.

"Howard, let me give you something for your discomfort. It's not much, but it should help a little."

Hughes looked skeptical. "What is it?"

"It's a strong analgesic called Paracetamol, I keep it in my medical pack. Take these and tell me if it helps at all. It should take about twenty minutes for them to kick in."

"Will I feel dizzy? The doctors have been trying to prescribe opiates, but I refused to take them. I don't want to be a drug addict."

"No, these don't have any opiates and they're not addictive. I don't know if they will do anything to help you, but they can't do any harm. It's worth a try."

Hughes downed the pills with water. "I just told Rand that I had already made plans to have various people take over duties in my business and personal matters."

"Of course you did Howard. When have you ever left any stone unturned? You knew you were coming with us and that was that. Asking us was only a formality." She laughed.

"Do you see through all men so easily?"

"Imagine how I feel." Rand joked.

They went over the details for Hughes transfer of power and double checked each other on things they might have missed. After about twenty minutes Hughes rubbed his arm and a smile grew across his face. "Hey, I think those things actually did the trick." The excitement in Howard's voice was uncharacteristic. He was usually so deadpan.

"Yes, I'm sure of it, the pain is receding, it's bearable now."

He stood and hugged Elsie. "I couldn't do that before, it hurt too much. Those things really work. Are there more in twenty-fourteen?"

"Yes, as much as you need. I don't know if they can cure what you have, but at least they'll be able to treat it." She handed him the bottle. "Take two every four hours and make sure you have something in your stomach."

They returned to the party that had gathered around the large fire pit by the pool. Candles and flowers floated in the water, the smell of vanilla and rose drifted together with the scents of the cedar wood fire and the sea. They spent the evening with their friends leaving nothing unsaid as the stars winked in the clear sky of the Indian summer. Finally they went to bed, leaving the stragglers to finish off the last of the wine.

The morning mist was thick as Rand and Elsie dressed in their 1949 clothes for the last time. Rand wore a tan suit and fedora, Elsie a practical business dress. The only thing that was out of place was the black nylon backpack that Spang would ride in. Elsie carried Spang this time while Rand packed all of their modern hardware into the other pack. The weight of it all was more than a hundred and forty pounds. He would have to put on the pack at the last minute and hope he didn't have to walk far with it once they arrived.

They loaded the Cadillac Ranch Wagon and said goodbye in the driveway. Everyone was there. They met the staff first with small parting heirloom gifts. Rolex watches for the men, diamond lockets for the women. The Vampires were next, many of them with new tattoos of the Vampires insignia. With the base in Montauk as a headquarters, the Vampires would be operating as an independent special forces unit. The C-123 Spook and XCG-20A would be stationed at a nearby airbase waiting to ferry them to anywhere in the world. Tearfully they worked their way down the line, shaking hands and giving hugs. At the end, Talbot brought them all to attention. Rand and Elsie gave their final salute, saying, 'In cruor unus.'

Avery and Megan were next. Rand gave Avery a stainless Patek Philippe Ref. 1518 watch and Elsie presented Megan a diamond locket from Tiffany's with a picture of Rand, Elsie and Spang on the inside. 'Friends Forever' was engraved on the back. Finally they waved and piled into the Caddy with Talbot at the wheel.

"You know, we're the ones getting the raw end of this deal." Talbot said as they pulled away. "You'll see us later today, for us it will be around sixty years."

They drove to Hughes airport in Culver where the XCG-20A waited on the tarmac, Howard and Carl sat at the base of the stair-truck having coffee at a little table complete with flowers and cakes.

"Its about time you showed up." Hughes laughed.

"Comfortable are we?" Elsie chided. She couldn't remember seeing him this relaxed.

Crewmen loaded Rand's heavy backpack onto the plane and they all boarded. Hughes paused at the top step and looked over his empire one last time.

"If it weren't for this damned condition I could stay and keep it flying."

"That's what I'm here for boss. I won't let you down." Carl assured him. Hughes just nodded and found his seat.

With all of the journeys the plane had been making, Carl had big comfortable seats installed that could be removed or reconfigured for missions. The interior, though still utilitarian, had been quieted significantly. They all strapped in for the five-hour trip to Montauk and all took turns copiloting.

"After this," Hughes remarked, "I imagine I won't have the chance to fly a plane from this era that's still in new, working order."

"What are you talking about?" Rand consoled him, "In a very short time you could be flying this very plane, albeit sixty years older." And with Carl and David looking after everything, this plane should be like new."

As they came into New Jersey airspace, they were picked up by a small spotter plane that escorted them in. Under tight but discreet security the XCG-20A was quickly rolled into a large hangar. They climbed into a big Buick and waited for several minutes as two plain cars and a farm truck with security men in them headed out to secure the route. There were no signs of trouble on the short trip from the airport. The spotter plane continued to shadow them to Montauk point.

"Not sure how much use that little plane is." Hughes muttered.

"Oh that's just the spotter sir." The driver replied. "If there was any trouble he would call it in and the two P-51s patrolling at twenty-thousand feet would respond quick as a flash.

Besides, there are men stationed all over this road. Heck, we even have a couple of tanks."

"I see. That makes me feel much better." Hughes said appreciatively.

When they arrived they made their way into the lighthouse like tourists. The old keeper greeted them and lowered the stairs.

"How's that young Tennessee gentleman I shot?" He inquired.

"He's just fine." Elsie took out a pen and jotted down an address. "Here, you can write him if you like, I know he would love to hear from you."

Talbot and Carl carried Rand's heavy bag. It took two trips on the tiny elevator to get them all down. They met Lieutenant Gerard and the newly promoted Sergeant Sato at the first checkpoint.

"The sergeant and I want to thank for our new posting.' He said shaking their hands. 'We can't thank you enough."

"It's you that we should be thanking, for your service.' Rand told the young officer. 'Now, I'm afraid it's time for us to leave."

They worked their way down into the base and took the golf carts through the tunnels. The facility was unusually quiet, all work having been stopped with the order that the facility was to be destroyed.

The Second String

They rode up the cliff face in the elevator and went back through the observation room until finally they stood at the door to the main TSS control.

"I've been instructed to keep anyone from observing you as you operate the TSS." Sergeant Sato told them.

"I guess that makes sense." Elsie agreed. "Well, we say goodbye here then. It has to be short, my heart can't take it."

She hugged Talbot and Carl quickly then went into the control room, wiping her eyes. Rand gripped Talbot's hand. Talbot's eyes were red and his face showed the effort it took to keep some semblance of composure.

"We will never forget you. We will tell your story so our children will know who you are and what you did. They will keep the secret but at home... your home, there will be no secrets."

All Rand could do was nod appreciatively. Carl could say nothing, he just shook his head like he couldn't believe what was happening. Then with one last look in their eyes, Rand turned and went into the TSS. They waited a few moments before Howard came in after them and shut the door. The small room was quiet except for the constant humming of the facility.

"Well, here we are at last."

"Step up here Howard, help me get this pack onto him."

Rand shrugged into the weighty pack then Howard tucked Spang into place.

"We all have to be touching and we all have to touch the TSS control cabinet at the same time."

"Ready?" Rand glanced around at them then hit the black button on the top of the cabinet. Slowly the thrumming started. Soon the colours flashed and separated and the sound reached a fevered pitch. Rand left the main dials where Remmel had last set them and just let the machine wind up. Then he tuned the frequencies slightly back with one of the smaller controls and gave Elsie a thumbs up.

"Okay," She said calmly, "It's going to be black and you will have no sense of your physical body, then a slight disorientation and hopefully, we'll be there. Ready?"

"Good Lord." Howard squinted and held on to Rand's arm.

"Three, two, one, mar—"

Peace and stillness. No light, no golden cord, just a wisp of a dream.

Noise and dust.

The Second String

"Just stay where you are! No one move!" A commanding voice grew in their consciousness.

Spang barked and ran out of the backpack and jumped up on the soldier's leg for some attention.

"Holy…"

They were in a pile on the floor at the foot of the control console. A soldier had his sidearm pointed at them.

"Easy Corporal, we're not the enemy." Elsie was standing slowly, shaking slightly and holding her hands up. "Spang, come here." Spang went back to Elsie.

The soldier kept the weapon on them, eyes wide and clearly in a state of shock.

"Calm down son." Hughes spoke softly, "This is a time machine. We've just come from nineteen-forty nine. We need to talk to your CO."

Rand lay on his back, the weight of the pack held him to the ground. Suddenly a rattle of weaponry filled the door as six more soldiers brought odd looking weapons to bear. Rand noticed that on their shoulders was the insignia of the Vampires.

"Woah, c'mon you guys! In cruor unus, we're on the same team!" Rand was starting to get irritated. The soldiers flinched at their motto being thrown at them. They looked at one another in confusion. A commotion split through the back of the group.

"All right let's see what we have h... Lord almighty." A one star general pushed through. The man was of Japanese descent, greying and oddly familiar. A smile broke across his face.

"Stand down and clear this room."

The soldiers all retreated except for the one still holding his pistol and staring wide-eyed.

"Corporal, it's alright these folks are VIPs. Help him with that backpack. Now soldier."

The General stepped down into the room as the Corporal went over to Rand.

"After all these years. Here I am on the verge of retirement and you come popping in looking like it was yesterday." He shook his head.

"It was actually about five minutes ago." Elsie eased and returned the smile. "General Sato I presume?"

"You presume correctly." The man stepped up and shook their hands vigorously. "I'll be... it worked even though we destroyed it."

"We brought the functional one with us. You'll have to destroy it again for the last time."

"Yes, I figured as much. We had no way of knowing when you would show up."

The Second String

"To tell you the truth General, neither did we." Rand shrugged off the pack and put Spang on his leash. "When are we exactly?"

"December twelfth, two-thousand thirteen."

"Rand you did it!" Elsie jumped on him and Rand fell to his knees.

"Oh thank God! We're back, we made it back in time!"

"Yes, quite literally I believe." Hughes quipped.

"Corporal get an escort detachment assembled for Mr. Hughes and the Carters."

"Hughes... as in... is he...?"

"Yes he is son, now get moving."

The young Corporal bolted from the room barking orders. The General gave them all a moment. Rand and Elsie stood and composed themselves but there was nothing that could wipe the smile from their faces.

"Now let's get you out into the world. I'm sure you have a lot to do." He looked them over suddenly realising that they were in nineteen forty-nine clothing. "Let's see if we can round up some more current attire for you."

Several of the men donated clothing to them and Elsie fit into one of the smaller soldier's jeans and t-shirt. Spang received lots of attention and the men begged the General to let them have a mascot dog in the base. Rand and Howard had to wash out all of the pomade in their hair. Then, with the help of a couple of the younger soldiers, they restyled it to a more modern look.

"I feel like an idiot." Hughes grumbled. "Is this really how they look?"

"New times Howard." Rand grinned at him. "There's gonna be a lot more changes to come so you're going to have to deal."

"What, cards? What do you mean?"

"Deal, as in 'deal with it'. It's the new American English language and it's comprised mostly of slang. You'll have to learn that too. You'll get the hang of it."

Hughes sighed and they made their way up the lighthouse elevator and outside. Immediately Rand and Elsie could tell the difference.

"Do you smell that hon?" Elsie closed her eyes and breathed in.

"Yeah, it smells more like nineteen forty-nine than twenty fourteen."

"The air...I think they took our recommendations to heart."

"General has there ever been an air pollution problem in New York city?"

The general looked at them puzzled. "No. Why?"

Rand and Elsie just looked at each other and giggled.

"Here's your ride." The General said as an unusually vehicle quietly rolled up to them. The black and olive green body was wide and low but it had the ground clearance of an SUV. Tires were extremely large and seemed to be made of a series of flexible arms that spiralled out from a central hub. The arms flattened out to form the outer surface of the wheel, which was covered in a series of interlocking plates of some kind of rubber material. The majority of the vehicle was comprised of a glass canopy that formed the roof, front, back and most of the sides. The sides slid up to reveal a spacious interior that had to have been inspired by water flowing smoothly over rocks.

The general watched their expressions in amusement. "Priceless." He chuckled. "I will remember those looks for the rest of my life."

"Kind of like the look you had when we parked our plane that day long ago."

"Is that what I looked like? Yeah, probably so." He opened the door for them. "It's quite a far cry from what cars used to be like, hmm?"

They climbed into the sleek glass vehicle. Hughes kept quiet, but his eyes absorbed everything. Elsie nudged Rand and whispered quietly, "No driver."

"It runs on Hydrogen fuel cells." The General broke the silence then changed the subject. "I knew this day would come. You guys changed my life. I wasn't planning on being a career military man until I got that promotion and posting to Montauk. The clearance alone made me a commodity. So, where do you want to go? How do you want to handle this?"

Elsie looked at Rand. "We would like to go home if that's okay with you."

Rand took a crack at the last part of the question. "Is it possible to keep this under wraps? I mean, nobody knows we were gone."

"Hey, you guys are the professional time travellers here. I have no idea how it works and frankly, I don't want to know. As far as I'm concerned, I'm just giving some old friends a ride. No one needs to know, but let me be the first to say welcome home."

With Sato's help it didn't take long for Rand to get Talbot's number from the onboard computer. The phone rang and a voice answered that sounded like David. "Hello?"

"Dave? Is that you?"

"I'm sorry this is the Talbot residence, you must have the wrong number."

"No, wait, Talbot, that's who I'm trying to reach - David Talbot."

"That's my father, but he passed away a year ago." The voice was skeptical.

"Oh, I'm so sorry." Rand choked up, next to him Elsie's hand went to her face as she doubled over. "He was a dear friend to us." He managed to say.

"I'm sorry, who are you again?"

"Rand and Elsie Carter."

"Oh my God…" The phone rattled. Then in the background they heard "Honey, it's them! It's Rand and Elsie!" The phone rattled again, "Did you just… arrive?"

"Yes we did, I'm sorry what's your name?"

There was some giggling, "My name is Rand. I think I was named after you."

"What did your father tell you about us?"

The man was now half crying and half laughing, "Everything!"

Rand couldn't take any more and broke down in tears. Howard took over, awkwardly talking into the air. "Hello, this is Howard."

The laughter and hoots in the background made it hard to hear. "I know! You made it! Come home! We're all here!"

Howard relayed the message even though everyone could hear it clearly. "They say to come home."

Rand and Elsie doubled over in another wave of happy tears.

"Oh, one more thing," Hughes leaned over to Rand, "What's the password?"

Rand looked up and rubbed his eyes, 'The Dude abides.'

"The Dude abides." Howard repeated the phrase stoically. Screams and laughter erupted on the other end. "They seem to be very happy about that."

Sato interrupted, "Okay, we're here. It's your plane. Where do you want to go?"

"Is Hughes airport still running?'

"You mean Hughes Industries International? The one in Chicago or the one in Culver or the one in Beijing, Rome, London or any of the other million gajillion locations?"

Howard cracked a wry smile. "Capaldi you old… Culver, definitely."

"It's private, but I'll call through. I'm sure they'll have no problem granting you access."

Hughes looked disappointed. He was used to having doors opened for him, not asking permission. "I guess things are going to be a bit different from now on."

The plane that waited on the runway resembled a bulbous knife blade with the wings incorporated into the tail piece. The belly and edge sections were white with a black canopy glass that ran over seventy of the eighty-five foot fuselage. The three of them stopped short and gawked at the plane.

"Jeepers."

"Looks fast."

"Only one way to find out." Elsie strode to the stairs.

Inside were luxury accommodations. The Cessna Citation X wound up, taxied and quietly rocketed down the runway. Soon they were cruising through the afternoon sky at six hundred and fifty miles-per-hour. Hughes admired the interior.

"Not bad, but if they shed some of this weight it would be faster. What's really amazing is the size of those engines. They're tiny."

"There are going to be a lot of those kinds of discoveries for you Howard, just remember to keep them to yourself. As soon as we let Carl know you're here, I'm sure we'll get you settled in." Spang was enjoying his own private pillow on the couch.

The jet landed an hour later. A man in jeans and a polo shirt was there to meet them. They would have recognised him anywhere.

"Good Lord you are the spitting image of your father!" Rand shook Talbot's hand. "How much do you know?"

"Like I said on the phone, everything. You just came in from the TSS at the secret base in Montauk from nineteen forty-nine after saying goodbye to my father and Carl. We have all been waiting for this day for a long time, ever since I was born. I can't believe you're the same age as me, I feel like you should be older."

"Nope, finally we're back in our own time." Elsie didn't want to reveal that they were actually six months before their time.

"Mr. Hughes it is such an honour to meet you." He shook Howard's hand carefully.

He bent down, "Hello Spang! You've had quite a trip huh?"

Spang liked this human, he anticipated lots of morsels.

They walked across the runway towards Rand and Elsie's de Havilland Beaver.

The Second String

"Hey there she is, she looks just like she did yesterday."

"Oh, we've taken great care of everything, you'll see. Now, I'd like to introduce you to Elsie Capaldi."

A stunning blonde woman stepped out from behind the airplane. She was in her thirties and unmistakably Carl's daughter. She stood, shaking like a leaf, looking at Rand and Elsie. "My father told me so much about you. It's like looking at a legend coming back to life!" She ran to Elsie and hugged her. "I'm named after you!"

"I'm so honoured to meet you! Is Carl…"

"He passed away twenty years ago. Cancer unfortunately, just before we had the cure. He went quickly, but before he passed he gave me this to give to you." She took out a picture of Carl, Rand and Elsie standing together in the Argentine jungle. "He never doubted for a minute that you would return. That is how we were raised, knowing that you would be here."

"I don't know what to say. I wanted so much to see him again." More tears fell as they mourned their departed friends.

"But we know the greatest secret of all don't we baby?" Rand pulled Elsie to him, "They are still here, and they are closer than you think."

Elsie Capaldi stepped up to Howard and took his hand cautiously. It is my greatest honour to meet you Mr. Hughes, and welcome you home. I am happy to report that Hughes Industries thrives and continues to be a global leader in not only aviation but engineering, industrial design, electronics, and in the film and entertainment industries. I am currently the acting CEO, having taken over for my father when he got ill. I am happy to hand the reins over to you as soon as you wish."

"You are my… Carl's successor? Outstanding. I couldn't be more pleased. We'll talk about all of that soon, for now let's just enjoy the moment."

They piled into the Beaver. There was an awkward moment when Talbot tried to get into the pilot's seat just as Rand went for it.

"Of course, what am I thinking?" He gestured for Rand to go ahead. Rand laughed and climbed in with Elsie in the copilot's chair.

"This is going to be weird. Two Rand and Elsie's, both around the same age."

"Just call us the Carters."

The two in the back seat looked at each other and laughed. "We have to tell them."

"Yeah, we were going to wait, but it's just not going to work. Call us the Talbots."

The Second String

Elsie screamed, "You're married?" she screamed again.

"It's a good thing we've got headsets on." Rand teased as he started down the runway.

The estate was just as they had left it. The grounds and houses had been looked after like an egg. The Talbots walked with Rand and Elsie through the secret hallways to their bedroom. Some things had been upgraded including the wiring and windows, but everything was as close to perfect as possible. The large bed faced a dark wood floor-to-ceiling wall of french glass doors that opened accordion style to the outside patio. The edge of the pool was visible through the wide opening and a sea breeze blew in.

Elsie said quietly "This is where we woke up this morning."

Rand Talbot looked at his wife, wide eyed. "Incredible. I was raised in the Talbot house, the section you built for my dad. Our main occupation was taking care of your house." As Rand Talbot spoke, people began arriving quietly to listen. They each carried a candle. "On Sundays we all prayed as a family, ate as a family and played as a family. It has become like our motto." Laughter peppered the room and more people arrived, children and old, teenagers and parents.

"We all live here. We are the descendants of the Talbots, the Capaldi's, the Wilsons, the Wileys, the staff and the Vampires."

Elsie and Rand looked around them as more people stepped onto the porch with candles. "We are the community you started and nurtured through your generosity. We were told that you would come someday. No one knew when because it was not known how accurately you could control the TSS. So, like our parents we lived our lives, took on their responsibilities and waited."

When they all arrived there were over fifty people standing around them silently, joy bursting from their eyes.

"My father promised you he would be the caretaker and he did his job admirably. It was passed to me and now I have the privilege and overwhelming joy of saying to you, at long last, welcome home!"

The audience cheered and applauded. One by one they turned and placed their candles in the sand next to the weathered pillar of the time capsule that Rand had made the day before. Then they came to meet and speak with them. They were all very patient as each person got a turn, first was Avery and Megan. They were in their early eighties, but were still fit and healthy.

The Second String

"You took long enough." Avery joked with Rand. His eyes still had their sparkle. He was missing a finger on his left hand. "I caught it in the lathe, oh… must have been about ten years after you left. Megan was very pregnant with Jamie at the time. She still didn't know how to drive and she had to take me to the hospital. I still can't say what was worse, the finger or the car ride. Anyway, we'll have time to catch up later Mr. Carter, I know you have important things still to do." He shook hands and went to find a warm chair with Megan.

"He still calls me Mr. Carter." Rand laughed back his emotions as Elsie took his hand.

Of the twelve staff, there were only four who were still living. They and their families had lived on the estate and raised their children. Now most of them were grown and moved away. All of them had gone to college and a few had even got their degrees specifically to take over the jobs that their parents did as curator, chef, aviation mechanics – all of them still in the family.

They learned that Nickelson had went back to Argentina to visit Gerardo, Luis and Diego after Perón was ousted for harbouring the Nazis. He met a woman and stayed there for the rest of his life. Carl flew down with various members of the team many times over the years and Elsie and Rand were promised stacks of picture books, movies and stories about their adventures.

A skinny young man came up and vigorously shook Rand's hand, then leaned in to him with a gleam in his eye and said, "I'm the donut captain. I'm here for the monkey."

"You must be related to someone who went to pick up the Delahaye!" Rand laughed.

The young man nodded, "My grandfather. He was the first curator, hired by the California Academy of Sciences to manage your collection. He constantly told that story."

"And how is the collection doing?" Rand was anxious to know.

The gleam in the young man's eye got even brighter. "Oh, you'll just have to come and see that for yourself Mr. Carter."

Rand got the distinct feeling he would like what he found. "Soon, I promise. Who is the curator now?"

"I am of course. I fell in love with the museum as a child and worked by my grandfather's side. Of course Mr. Wilson was always there too. The collection is like his child practically. When my grandfather retired the Academy replaced him with several different people over the years, but the position always seemed transitory. You know, a place for budding curators to cut their teeth. Of course Mr. Wilson always taught them well. In retrospect, it was the best thing that could have happened for both the collection and me.

"The collection became a proving ground, and therefore people worked very hard to maintain the highest standard of perfection. After I finished school, I went to Cairo for several years, and then New York where I worked for the Natural History Museum. When the position opened to curate the collection it was perfect timing. Serendipity I still say though I'm sure that Mr. Wilson had something to do with it."

"By the sound of it I would have to agree with you. It's so wonderful to have it in the family. I am looking forward to a full report."

There were many such conversations as they met with everyone. A large buffet was served inside as the evening air grew chilly and the house was packed with people. Howard was distracted by virtually everything he saw, from light switches to kitchen appliances. Around six in the evening, Talbot politely herded everyone off.

"We'll need to get you set up with phones and clothes and all…"

"Yes, we'll take care of all that, but we have other priorities. We'll be leaving tomorrow at first light. First to Belfast, then Houston, Texas. We can pick up things—"

"Sorry, don't mean to interrupt. I'll send someone out for clothes right now. The shops close at nine. I'll have the Citation XR ready to go whenever you like."

"That's the private jet right? How long will it take to get us to Belfast do you think?"

"It's a long flight, about two hours, you flew in on the X but the XR makes it seem faster. It will go six hundred until you reach forty thousand feet and enter the sonic stream, then you're mach six to Europe."

"The sonic stream?"

Talbot looked confused. "I'm sorry, I thought because you were pilots.."

"The twenty fourteen we left is not the twenty fourteen we came back to."

"Technically it's still two thousand and thirteen, December twelfth."

"Right, well we shared technology back in forty nine and it must have made a big difference because supersonic air transportation didn't exist after Concorde was cancelled and certainly never privately."

The Second String

"Well," He shrugged. "Concorde is in it's fourth generation and there are specific routes that planes can exceed the sound barrier in. The sonic boom upset people so much that an international consortium assigned designated air lanes that keep the traffic away from populated areas. Granted there are people still living under the airspace, but they know before moving there that it is something they have to put up with. It's a very thin line by the Canadian border, Montana and the Dakotas and... well, you get the idea."

"Put us down for departure at six please."

The Talbots wrote down their clothing sizes and said goodnight. They took Howard to his own private house as he tailed them with a barrage of questions. Just after ten o'clock two of the staff showed up with complete wardrobes for each of them. When the women left, they took Rand and Elsie's nineteen forty-nine clothes to have them cleaned and preserved. Once they were alone again, they tried to relax by the fire. Rand poured a brandy to try and calm his nerves. They both knew that what lay ahead the next day might prove the most difficult event of their lives.

"I get off easy compared to you." Elsie took Rand's hand. "It's easier to leave someone who has been unfaithful, and I can't wait to see Marty and Megan!"

"Elsie you know that my heart belongs to you. I just hate the thought of blindsiding her. There's no explanation, she won't understand. It's going to be bad."

The next morning one of Avery and Megan's grandchildren was waiting for them next to a long, off white Bentley. Rand and Elsie chuckled to each other. The last time they had rode in a Bentley Rand had taken it on a dirt track and jumped it. The heavy machine held up very well until the axle snapped.

Rand wasn't fond of being chauffeured around, but until they got oriented with their surroundings, they decided it was best. The young man sat up front and directed the car where to go.

"I'm Owen. Dad wanted me to help show you how things work." Owen explained how all of the vehicles were autonomous but could be taken over manually at any time. The planet was universally networked with an array of satellites that provided high speed data transfer from even the remotest of locations. The service was free, just like water or air; both of which were clean and in abundant supply globally. Rand and Elsie fired questions at the young man who kept pace with informative and articulate replies. Owen had the same gift of gab as his grandfather at that age.

The plane waiting for them on the tarmac looked similar to the plane from the day before but even more sleek. It was wide and long and covered in a black glass canopy that ran the length of the knife edged fuselage. The body widened into wings at the very back where, in place of a tail a sleek second wing was joined at the wing tips and arched over two vertical supports. The engines were housed underneath the rear body and seemed to form the thickest part of the plane.

"The plane operates the same as the car, though if you want to take manual control you have to have a special license." Owen informed them. "Otherwise, just tell it where you want to go and it will take you to the closest airport to your destination."

The interior was white, with wide chairs and a combination of some kind of plastics and fabric that seemed more natural than plastic. The domed canopy formed the entire ceiling and part of the wall in one uninterrupted piece of white material that matched the interior. Glass surfaces didn't take smudges and held onto the bottom of Rand's orange juice glass like it was sticky rubber. Rand was trying to determine the nature of the glass when a young woman walked back through the plane to introduce herself. The girl couldn't have been more than twenty.

"Good morning, my name is Mandy, I'm your concierge. Mr. Talbot told me that this is the first time aboard your plane. If you like I can show you some of the features that will make your journey more comfortable."

Mandy went on like this for several minutes. Though annoying, she was informative. The canopy could shift to any colour or opacity they wanted and could even go completely clear. Every glass surface, including the canopy, was a touch-screen computer monitor. When Rand touched it with his thumb and finger a small square appeared with a tiny set of digital controls. The controls allowed him to designate the opacity of the glass and access to computer functions. He could widen the square with his fingers to the size he desired and drag the window to any location on the glass, even jump it across to the table or any other glass surface. The same technique was used to designate part of the canopy as a personal window.

"Just tell the plane your destination." Mandy concluded her well-rehearsed presentation. It was obvious she was nervous.

"Okay," Elsie took a stab at it. "Plane, take us to Omagh, Northern Ireland."

"Oh, I'm sorry.' Mandy interrupted. 'The plane isn't called 'plane'."

"Well what is it called?"

"Nothing yet, it's brand new and you are the owners. You have to give it a name."

"I name you Zippy!" Rand said with authority. "You are Zippy and Zippy is what you shall be henceforth and forthwith!" He sat back down. "Something like that?"

Elsie just snickered and put her face in her hand.

"Sure Mr. Carter. Let me help you set that up. Computer, establish voice recognition for owners plural, two."

Thank you. Will the first owner speak their name please?' Replied the pleasantly computerised voice.

Once they had coded in the voices Elsie tried again.

"Zippy, take us as close as you can get to Omagh in Northern Ireland."

"I have no destination known as Northern Ireland. Would you like to go to Belfast in Ireland?"

"Yes, that will do."

With a soft thump, the engines started and the plane began to taxi.

"Departing for Belfast, Ireland. Would you like me to arrange air transportation to Omagh upon your arrival?"

"Yes please."

The acceleration was the smoothest Elsie had ever felt. Over the next thirty minutes, they climbed to forty thousand feet and began picking up speed. Rand and Elsie made the whole canopy transparent and giggled like children as they broke the sound barrier. The cabin was as quiet as the inside of the Bentley and they discovered that while Mandy's demeanour was impersonal and overly pleasant at first, she warmed up to them over breakfast and became more relaxed.

The sensation of speed at mach six under the clear canopy was unbelievable. Clouds appeared and disappeared in a flash. Mandy stayed seated most of the time and went a bit pale. They learned that most people didn't have the courage to 'trans the canopy' in flight. To Rand and Elsie it was the experience of a lifetime. They couldn't wait to get back and talk shop with Elsie Talbot. In two hours, they were landing in Belfast.

Rand looked down as Ireland stretched out like a green watercolour carpet at his feet. "The last time I saw Belfast from the air, I was sitting on a parachute in the pilot's seat of a little Cessna. There was smoke, just there," He pointed, "from where a supertanker full of natural gas had driven into the pier. Now look at it."

The city of Belfast shone like a crystal in the sun. Buildings of every size and shape created an artistic landscape of sculpture and nature. 'Zippy' landed vertically. The touchdown was so smooth they could barely tell they were on the ground. A helicopter stood by to take them to Omagh where a taxi would be waiting for them. Mandy offered to hire them a limo but Rand felt that it would be too conspicuous. A shuttle vehicle took them from their hangar to the helicopter which began spinning up as they approached. The machine was a sleek, dome covered design with two small counter-rotating rotors and a rear propeller instead of a tail rotor. In seventeen minutes they were touching down at a small airport outside of Omagh. The taxi was self-driven and like everything, required a card for payment. They used the card Rand Talbot had given them and the car drove them into Omagh. They decided to wait for evening so they checked into a hotel in the city center.

"It's not like it used to be at all. There were lines of old buildings down this street here and pubs over here." He explained to Elsie. "Taxi, go down John's Street please."

"John's Street. Is this correct?" The automated voice said a bit too loudly. It was obviously not of the same quality as the AI in the plane.

"Yes."

Rand could make out the street system as it used to be, but it was much wider now and lined with trees and gardens.

"Sally's Pub should be here on the right." Rand tried to peer through the trees.

"There it is Rand!"

"It's still there." He took a deep breath. "Okay. That's where I'm going to be on a Friday night, guaranteed. Taxi, find a nice hotel close to here."

The taxi suddenly pulled over. "Sally O'Brien's Inn. We have reached your destination." Information about the Inn was displayed on the screen.

"Well that's handy, we'll just stay here until it gets dark."

"What if they recognise me?"

"Was it a hotel before?"

"No, but —"

The Second String

"So then the people who work on the hotel side won't know who you are. Just stay out of the pub and you'll be okay."

They paid for the cab and went into the lobby. Rand immediately recognised the night bartender who was talking to the girl behind the desk.

"Uh oh, I know him. I'm just gonna go hide in the bathroom."

"Right. I'll get the room."

The bathroom was very different from what he remembered. The wall-to-wall mirror showed a Gaelic football match, Tyrone vs. Donegal. Tyrone was up 2-12 to 1-14. A man came out of the stall and washed his hands quickly. Rand thought, *That's what I used to do that to preserve my calluses before playing.*

The man turned and smiled at him and stopped cold as he looked at himself. But it wasn't himself, not the man he saw in the mirror. This man was heavier and puffy, his eyes weren't as bright or sharp. He carried himself slightly bent and seemed somehow diminished. They only had a second to be surprised before they shimmered into colours and merged into one.

Montgomery Thompson

Chapter 14

The God String

*'The only pathway to achieve a love of God
is by understanding the works of his hand,
which is the natural universe.'*
~Maimonides 1135-1204

For a moment Rand fought with his previous self for dominance, but his will, honed by everything he had been through, was much stronger and he won out. Suddenly a host of memories he never had came flooding into his mind; Moira on top of him that morning, he needed strings for tonight that's why he was out now, but he stopped in at Sally's to remind them that Kieran wasn't going to be in. He wanted to see if Colin would sit in when he got off his shift – *NO!* He struggled. *Elsie is in the lobby, his wife, he had to tell her that she didn't need to get a room.* He had merged, he wouldn't forget. Spang, Talbot, Carl, Remmel he threw names and faces into his mind until he was sure he was himself, the new Rand. An intense heat flashed all over his body but didn't burn him. He knew he had won out. The old Rand would fade, but for now he had to keep on guard. Maybe it would be better if they did get a room. He dried his hands and went out to the lobby.

"What took you so long? We've... Rand, what's wrong, you look different."

"I am Elsie, I was in the bathroom, we merged."

"Oh..." Her hand went to her mouth.

"Did you get a room?"

She nodded. "Are you okay?"

"We need to get to the room please hon. Be calm." He took her by the arm and they made their way down the hall following the signs to their room. They quickly locked the door behind them.

"Oh my God, Rand are you okay? You're still Rand right?"

"Yes, Elsie I'm me, but it wasn't easy. It was like we thought, there's a struggle for who gets control. Fortunately the old Rand was a bit soft and I've hardened up a lot. I think you may have a tougher time of it though. After all, you're going up against Commander Elsie Clay."

"Don't worry, Elsie Carter's heart is much stronger than Commander Clay's. Our love won't lose Rand. It has kept us together through battle, through survival and through time. One stubborn little astronaut isn't going to break it."

He pulled her into his arms. More than ever he needed to erase the recent memories of Moira. Holding Elsie close was the best thing for it. She sensed his need and slowly undressed him and laid him down. Hungry and heedless of the sweat and slick sweetness that fused them they immersed into each others embrace, breathing together in grateful and joyous rhythm.

As he held her he knew that the time had come for him to resolve the last thing that lay between them. After a quick shower he left Elsie at the hotel and walked the half a block to his old flat.

Moira always had Fridays off and would usually spend them sleeping in late, relaxing around the place and getting ready to come to his gig that night. The modern streets were so altered that he hardly recognised the place. It occurred to him that it was possible that in this reality he may have never met Moira. Maybe he was with someone else, maybe they had broken up. The apartment building was very different. He stood in front of the half stone, half steel structure feeling slightly disoriented. An atrium courtyard led him up a set of stairs to a mezzanine level. His apartment door was a strange semi-ovular shape. He recognised all of these things with old Rand's memory, but they were oddly new to him. He went to knock but old Rand's memory told him to put his hand on a spot on the doorframe. It opened on its own. *DNA key.*

Inside he recognised very little. The furniture, curtains and even the coats hanging on the wall were different. Moira's voice came from the kitchen.

"There you are, didja get your strings?"

A thought he had had a thousand times flashed through his mind: all of the amazing new technology in the world and they still hadn't managed to invent guitar strings that didn't break. The thought was a distraction from the fact that he had forgotten how much he liked her accent. He flushed with guilt.

"No Moira, I didn't get my strings."

She came out of the kitchen wiping her hands on a towel. "Why? What…" Then she saw him.

"Rand? What's wrong, what happened? You look different."

"Yes, I suppose I am Moira. Listen, we need to talk…"

"Sit down baby, let me get you some tea…"

"No. Moira, sit please, and listen."

His voice carried an authority she didn't recognise. Her mouth clamped shut and she sat.

"I have been doing a lot of thinking lately and I have to confess something." He let that sink in as she braced herself. "I don't love you Moira. Not the way you deserve. Not the way we both deserve."

Her mouth dropped open and tears started like they had just been waiting for the chance. She tried to mouth the word '*I…I…*' over and over but no sound came out.

The news had a sudden violence that cracked her heart in two. He was sick to his stomach. The old memories cried out - *it wasn't love, but it was something! It was good even if it wasn't the real thing. There was caring, compassion, respect and an acceptable level of happiness that very few, it seemed, had.* Now the new Rand, the intruder was saying that it wasn't good enough. *Greedy bastard.* With great effort Rand hauled up his emotions for Elsie and let swing at the old self.

There was no contest, real love blazed through the excuses of the good enough. He wasn't going back. He was going to be better for himself, for Elsie and even for Moira.

"There is more for you and I cannot stay any longer. You were always good, always kind, but we were only half-living, getting by on our kindness and good times. There is much more to it than that, but we have to break the dam to let the water flow. It's been too scary to do, but now I'm doing it. I will leave in a moment and you won't see me again."

Moira finally found her voice. "I... I thought you were going to propose to me. Oh my God! What kind of fool am I?"

"I'm sorry Moira, I'm so sorry."

"How can you stand there looking all hurt? Who is it? One of those tarts down at Sally's?"

"No Moira. If you can't see the truth in what I'm saying then you need to think about it. In time you'll realize that what we had was not love, no matter how many times we said so."

"Go! Just go." She slumped onto the couch and buried her head in the pillow. In the end there was nothing he could do, so he left. Outside the sunlight dappled through the branches in the cool December day. As he walked up the street, the darkness drafted off his back and disappeared. She would heal, she would be okay and maybe she would grow. If she did, then she would find something greater. It was up to her.

As he came back into the hotel room the sight of Elsie struck him like a hammer. He ran to her and swept her up, crying into her dark hair. She held him until he stopped. Then they freshened up and went down to the street. The taxi took them back to the Omagh airport and the waiting helicopter. In seventeen minutes, they were touching down in Belfast. Mandy welcomed them aboard Zippy. In another ten minutes, they were accelerating to mach six across the Atlantic on the way to Houston. Mandy sensed their need for privacy and retired to 'do some chores' in the rear cabin. Elsie had Rand tell her everything that happened.

"She knows you fell in love with someone. It shows Rand, there's no hiding it."

"She thought it was one of the waitresses at Sally's."

"What did you say?"

"I didn't say it wasn't. She'll find out that it wasn't of course. I've always said that Ireland is a small town."

"That's a good thing most of the time."

"Yes it is, wonderful really. But if you're trying to keep a secret it's sometimes not so easy."

"It must have been really painful for you."

"It's always a terrible thing to hurt someone, but whatever I felt is insignificant to what she's going through. I could literally hear her heart break. She thought I was sitting her down to propose to her. Talk about a worse case scenario." Rand put his head in his hands.

"God, that poor woman. Well, maybe it will make her mad enough to make some big changes. Maybe it's just what she needs to get her to where she needs to be to be happy."

"That's what I'm praying for. Just know that there is not an ounce of regret or doubt in my heart for how I feel about you. My heart is yours, everything that I am."

The mood was somber as the plane slowed to cross over Florida, then it picked up speed and traversed the Gulf of Mexico and touched down at Ellington Field Airport in Clear Lake, just outside of Houston.

"You realize hon that you could go on your ISS mission all over again, without the tragedy this time of course."

"I thought about that. I think I've had enough of space for one lifetime. Besides, I was at the height of readiness when I went. I'm out of training now for over two years, it wouldn't be fair to the crew. And the minute they do a bone density scan on me they will pull me from the mission. Hey, maybe that will work in my favour."

"What do you mean?"

"Well I've been wondering what excuse to use when I suddenly quit the program."

"Why can't you just quit?"

"Rand, you don't work your whole life to become an astronaut just to walk out at the last minute for no reason."

"Oh, right."

"Failing a bone density scan is the best way I can think of to leave quietly."

"There will be a lot of people sorry to see you go."

"I'm sure there are plenty of people who will happily take my place. Besides, who knows what the space program even looks like now? I mean, just look at the difference in air travel. What do you think it looks like on technology's sharpest edge?"

"You're right. You probably won't even recognise the NASA of today."

They got a taxi as before, arriving just after six in the evening at the Hilton hotel in Clear Lake only yards from NASA's headquarters. Elsie lived in one of the subdivisions of the town.

"She's... I'm going to be making the kid's dinner in a half hour. Bob will be on the couch watching TV. The couch faces away from the kitchen separated by a half wall, at least it used to. I'll approach through the sliding glass door so the kids can see me. I want them to see us merge, it will be much easier to explain everything that way."

"Won't it be a bit much for them? Megan is twelve, so that should be okay, but Marty is only eight."

"I know how old my children are Rand. Remember, their mom is a special forces pilot and an astronaut. I'm pretty sure that heady concepts are easier for them to grasp."

"What if they think you're an alien or something?"

"That's why I want them to see me, especially my eyes. They'll know it's me and not something supernatural."

He stood and held her. "I'm afraid I'll lose you. Even more than going through the TSS."

She kissed him deeply and looked into his eyes for a long minute. "I'll be back with Marty and Megan in about an hour. I promise." Then she turned and went out the door. All Rand could do was prepare for the kids' arrival.

Surprisingly there weren't that many changes to the neighbourhood. The streetlights were different as were most of the cars along with some architectural changes to the houses. Her house was modest. Astronauts and military pilots didn't do the job for the pay. Elsie left the taxi and walked around the back. Dexter, their small black and white shepherd met her at the gate. She quietly said hello and calmed the dog then went to the sliding glass doors that opened into the kitchen.

The scene was almost exactly as she had told Rand. She paused a second and watched herself, keenly aware that this was an opportunity no one had ever possessed in the history of the world. She was making dinner at the stove with her back turned to the kids who were doing their homework seated at the island unit.

Elsie wanted to run to them, but she knew she had to time everything perfectly. The top of Bob's head could be seen over the back of the short wall that ran behind the couch. The TV, a large piece of glass, was running several shows at once.

There it was, her life. She had thought she had it all, but looking at it now from the outside it made her sad. That perspective was all the motivation she needed. Elsie slid the door open and came into the kitchen.

The kids immediately turned their head and made eye contact. Surprise and confusion ran across their little faces. Elsie put her finger to her lips and Megan clamped her hand over Marty's mouth. Elsie held out her hands to them and made an excited face that said she was so glad to see them. Then she pointed her fingers at her eyes 'watch'.

She walked up behind herself and tapped her on the shoulder as the kids held their breath. Her old self turned and froze as she came face to face with Elsie. Elsie thought she looked sad. Her features were too sharp and she seemed frail. In a brief flash of colour they merged. Elsie braced her will for a battle, but all she heard was '*Thank God!*' and the old Elsie relinquished. As old Elsie's memories flooded into her mind she realised how unhappy she had been.

"No way!" Marty burst out.

Elsie came to him and looked him in the eye, "I love you." Then she hugged them both.

"Mom?" Megan said, looking at her closely. "What just…what…"

"I'll tell you in a bit. Right now I want you to go upstairs and pack some things for an overnight."

"Cool! Are we going to Disneyland?" Marty asked.

"Better." Elsie promised.

'Was our old mom an alien?'

"No Marty."

"Well, I'm glad you're back." Marty hugged her and Elsie marvelled at the child's perceptive abilities.

"Get moving cowboy." It was something she said to him everyday when he was getting ready for school. He jumped off the stool and ran upstairs. Megan paused and looked at her closely again.

"It's me sugarplum. I'll explain everything. Right now I have to talk to your dad."

"He's not coming with us is he?"

"No baby, but you will see him soon I promise."

"I know. It's because of Monica isn't it?"

"Yeah, some of it. Go on now and help Marty pack. I'll call you down in a little bit okay?"

She nodded and trotted upstairs after stopping to kiss her dad on the cheek.

"What was that for?" He asked from the couch.

For Elsie, the next part was easy. "That was goodbye Bob."

He swivelled around on the couch. "What's that hon?"

"You're going to have to stay with Monica now. Get an attorney, you're going to need it. You now have five minutes to pack and say goodbye to the kids. Time and…" She looked at her watch. "… counting."

"Wait, wait, let me explain!"

"There are no explanations. I know everything. You don't have to feel bad, you don't have to do anything. Just go and live your life, be happy. In the future if you feel the need to stray just have a spine and end the relationship you're in first. That is all. Time for you to go."

"But."

"I'm not asking Bob. Out, now."

He went upstairs and packed quickly. Elsie waited and listened. Bob began telling the children that he had a business meeting to go to.

"No you don't Bob, tell them the truth!" She yelled up the stairs.

"Elsie, that's not…" She heard him huff. How dare he, she thought. She marched up the stairs. "You tell them Bob. They deserve the truth, they'll learn that no matter how difficult it is that it must be faced."

Bob sighed. "I've been having an affair, seeing another woman. You know Monica? Well, I think I'm going to go live with her. But we'll see each other all the time." He looked back at Elsie who nodded in confirmation. 'And we'll have lots of fun. I know things will be different from now on, but it doesn't mean I love you any less. You two are the most important things in the world to me."

"It's true. He loves you very much. So, daddy's going to go and we're going to go on an adventure. Are you ready? Say goodbye to daddy and finish packing, we'll be gone for awhile."

The kids didn't know what to think, but they seemed excited to get going. Elsie and Bob went downstairs.

"Elsie, I'm sorry…"

"I'm sorry too Bob. I was too focused on my career and never enough on you. You did well considering the circumstances. Just the Monica thing, but I suspect that happened after you realised that the love was gone. Don't sweat it. The kids and I are going to have a lot of fun."

"What about the station?"

"Not your concern. Bye Bob." She opened the door.

"Yeah, but what about—"

"Not your concern. Go on, you'll need these." She handed him the car keys.

"You're giving me the car? Thanks!" Bob threw his luggage into the backseat and drove off, confused and relieved.

Elsie came back in as the kids came down. "Ready? Let's go." She closed the door and went to the waiting taxi.

"Where's the car mom?"

"Daddy has it. Don't worry, I have many others." She began explaining everything to the kids as they drove. She plowed through question after question until they arrived at the hotel.

"…and the man who saved me is who I have been with for the last two years. His name is Rand and he's really cool. Oh yeah, we're really rich too."

"Really? How rich?" Marty said excitedly.

"Really, really rich." She paid the taxi and took the elevator to the top floor.

Rand heard them approaching, he couldn't remember being more nervous. The door opened and Elsie came in first followed by Megan then Marty.

"Wow, you guys look so much like your mom!" Rand blurted. Megan laughed, Marty hid behind Elsie.

"Rand meet Megan and Marty."

"Hey you guys, I've heard so much about you. Did your mom tell you what happened?"

They nodded.

"Pretty crazy huh? But she never stopped trying to get back to you, which probably sounds weird since, to you, she was here the whole time."

Elsie looked at Rand with a shrug. Rand came over to them and knelt down. "Here's the thing, I have proof of what she told you if you want to see."

Both kids nodded.

"Here. These were taken in nineteen forty nine, that was the time we got sent back to." He showed the pictures on the iPad. "I managed to take along the iPad and shoot some pictures. This is us next to the planes, and us with in the jungles of Argentina, see? There's your mom. She was really brave and helped a lot of people. I also have video on my iPhone."

"Why did you use an old computer?" Megan asked.

"What do you mean?"

"this is one of those old computers from like the seventies. If you went back from two thousand fourteen, that's next year. Why didn't you bring a modern computer?"

"he iPad is from the seventies?" Rand looked at Elsie. "Megan, you are one sharp cookie. Twenty fourteen used to look a lot differently, but we shared some of our technology with the people in nineteen forty-nine. By the time we got back here, everything was much more modern than it was when we were here last time. It's like going back to the caveman days and showing them what underwear is."

Marty laughed, "Pretty soon you have cavemen all running around wearing underwear!"

"Yeah, then they figure out that they need clothes, cuz they don't want to run around in underwear!" Megan squealed.

Rand looked at Elsie. "Yeah, something like that."

She kissed him and whispered, "Good job hon, you broke the ice." Then she turned to the kids. "Hey guys, you wanna go on a really cool plane? Let's get outta here."

They left the hotel and took a cab to the plane. The children were fascinated and it turned out that Mandy was very good with kids so the flight went well. Soon they were fed and sleeping on the bed in the forward stateroom.

"Are they going to be okay? This is a lot for a kid to take on."

"Yes, they'll be fine. They'll be surrounded by love and truth and we'll make sure they see Bob and Monica on a regular basis."

"Monica huh? I wouldn't count on that lasting. You might want to ask him to leave her out of the picture for a while. It's tough enough watching your parents break up and meeting the new step-dad after watching your mom walk through the door and merge with your old mom."

Zippy, the Citation XR had to maintain subsonic speeds across Texas, Mexico and the Gulf of California after which the sleek plane jumped back up to mach six. It rocketed north off the coast of Baja and California and touched down smoothly at Hughes airport in Culver City. The Bentley waited at the hangar for them and they all piled into the big car. It was eleven at night and the kids were still rubbing their eyes.

"We'll be there in about twenty minutes then we'll get you snuggled into your beds." Elsie cradled both of them in her lap. To Rand she was as happy as he had ever seen her.

"Mom?"

"Are you and Rand going to get married?"

"That's a good question pumpkin. We got married back in nineteen forty nine."

Meagan thought about that for a second. "Wait, doesn't that mean you were already married to Rand when you married dad?"

"Yes, I guess it would."

"You guys should get married again for reals, I mean, in this time just to make sure."

Rand, not for the last time, marvelled at Megan's insightfulness. "That is an excellent idea Megan. How would you like to help plan it? A fairy tale wedding, we'll spare no expense!"

Megan giggled with excitement and curled up against Elsie tighter.

"Sir," The driver leaned back to Rand quietly. "There is a blanket in the under seat storage. Right under the young lady sir."

Rand pulled out the cedar drawer from under the seat and tucked the soft blanket around Megan and Marty. "Hey kiddo, I'm really glad we're all together. Everything is going to be great from here on out, I promise."

It was a relief to finally see the gates of the estate close behind them. Over the next couple of days there were many details that kept them busy.

The Second String

First on the list was treatment for Howard. Though he masked it very well, they knew he was in pain.

They took him to a team of leading doctors the very next day. Howard's pain symptoms were diagnosed as Complex Regional Pain Syndrome. Fortunately, there was a long-term cure for the disease and they began treating him immediately.

Elsie and Rand saw the effects of the treatment right away. The doctors told them that the pain that Howard dealt with every moment of his life had increased to unbearable levels. He scored a forty-two out of a possible fifty on the McGill pain scale, even higher than such events as amputation and childbirth. How he had contained it and functioned normally was a feat that defied comprehension.

Next were all of the legal necessities. Driver's licenses, pilot's licenses and taxes all needed to be updated. Rand studied for his private pilot test and continued for more advanced certifications. Howard was another matter altogether.

Elsie Talbot began to build a case to prove the truth of what had happened and bring it to the attention of the President and Congress. She used the Hughes Corporation's significant contacts to track down and subpoena secret congressional, CIA, Air Force and Army records.

While this was going on Hughes kept a low profile, but he found it difficult not to fly or drive anywhere. He desperately wanted to explore the incredible new world he lived in.

In the meantime Elsie had her divorce finalised then she and Rand began to arrange for the wedding. Megan and Marty took to life at the estate quite well. They had many other children to play with and countless things to do. Christmas came and the estate sparkled with seasonal magic.

Rand and Elsie opened the coffers with bonuses, parties and decorations. They spent money hand over fist not only on their own needs, but throughout the community. No matter what they spent, it never seemed to make a dent in the available funds.

In mid December they had a meeting with Rand Talbot along with their accountants and financial advisors to get the big picture on their holdings and net worth. The news was shocking. Their net worth was over the two hundred trillion mark. This made them singly the wealthiest people in the world by quite a margin. An entire accounting firm of over fifty employees existed just to keep track of their affairs. The scope of it was too much for either of them and they elected to begin selling off over half of it.

They decided that over fifty percent of their business should be dedicated to philanthropic pursuits. A think tank was set up to develop the most efficient non-profit business model for charitable organisations that would channel the highest possible amount of money directly to the causes that needed it the most.

It was a large-scale undertaking and included input from independent sources as well as several university and governmental agencies. There were still people in need in the world and they became dedicated to getting aid to them damn the red tape, post-haste.

It wasn't until late February that enough evidence was gathered to submit an appeal to Congress regarding Howard. It didn't help that the entire affair had to be kept top secret. A special panel reviewed the appeal initially and the evidence was so solid and startling that the panel immediately elevated the issue to a secret Senate subcommittee.

Witnesses were brought in, including General Sato and eventually Rand, Elsie and Howard. The time capsule was carefully opened and the contents were used as evidence in the case. A transcript of the secret congressional meeting of nineteen forty-nine was read aloud which proved to be, as Rand put it, the nail in the coffin of any doubt that their experience or Howard's identity was not authentic. A New Jersey congresswoman headed the subcommittee and read their findings as Rand, Elsie and Howard stood before them.

"By the evidence we have heard today it appears that the three of you are responsible not only for bringing to justice the world's most evil villain, but also for the avoidance of numerous catastrophes over the years which could have seriously affected the ability for mankind to survive on this planet. And that, my esteemed colleagues, is an understatement. It is unfortunately a thing which must remain secret, for the entire affair is to do with a device of unthinkably dangerous capabilities. One, if revealed to exist and reconstructed, could throw the world into upheaval and lead to our annihilation as a species."

So the speeches went on until at last it was put to a vote, which passed unanimously, to once again take pains to insure the TSS remained secure. Howard was given a new identity from scratch. He was Howard Hughes, grandson of Howard Hughes who had worked behind the scenes at Hughes Industries and would now sit on the board while Elsie Talbot continued to head up the company.

"Jeepers, all of that just to make me Howard again." He laughed.

"Howard, you have to stop saying 'jeepers'." Elsie teased him.

Hughes, Rand and Elsie hired instructors to get them up to speed with the rules and procedures of modern aviation. By April, they were flying on a regular basis. Whenever possible they took the kids up too. Spring was in the air in Malibu and wedding preparations began to take over the estate. Rand learned that his museum collection had grown to over seven hundred cars, one hundred and eighty planes and countless other assorted collectibles. He decided to finally make the collection public and sold over fifty percent of the vehicles at charity auctions, but he kept the Bugatti type 40 for the wedding. On May tenth, Miracle Day they gathered their closest around them and told the story of Miracle Day. Summer passed in a flash as they worked through the myriad of things they had to take care of to finally get settled. As September passed they made final plans for the wedding. At last it was October tenth.

They woke early and got ready. Marty and Megan were rounded up at 10:00 and they went to the time capsule by the cliff edge. Everyone on the estate made sure to leave them alone as they sat and looked out over the sea.

Rand looked at his watch, 10:05.

"It was in five minutes the TSS fired and stopped time. Rand and I didn't stop. We continued for a fraction of a second into the future." Elsie explained to the children who wondered what they were doing there. "We think it was because we were in a deep sleep that night, a sleep that took us out of our bodies. Some people call it astral travel, some people try to attain that state through meditation. For whatever reason, Rand and I were in it when the TSS went off. When time in the world stopped for that split second we were astral travelling and not in this world, so we continued. When we moved forward we had to have someplace to go. What we found out was that all of creation came with us, minus the living human beings. It's a phenomenon known as the God String. God looks after each soul. No one is forgotten and they can never get lost. He makes sure that we have a world to live in. So the world and everything in it moved forward just to accommodate us."

"What about Spang?" Marty asked as he held Spang in his lap.

"Well honey we think that it's because animals are always living in the present just as God is, but that's just theory, we don't know for sure." She continued, "So when we woke up the next morning there was no one around. We were completely alone."

"That sounds scary." Megan shivered.

"It was. I thought I was alone, stuck on the International Space Station with no way of getting back down. I didn't know Rand was experiencing the same thing down on Earth, but what was amazing is that we were in the future. Granted it was less than a second into the future, but it might as well have been a million years."

"We called that future FirstTime," Rand explained, "because no other humans had ever been there. A far as we know it was the first time that particular time had happened. But FirstTime only lasts as long as there are people in it. FirstTime waited for us when we left it, but Doctor Remmel and his mad wife were the ones to return to it. We believe they died by Erna's own hand. When they arrived in FirstTime a deadly grenade blast destroyed them and the TSS control station. It was at that moment, FirstTime ceased to exist." *We think.* He thought.

Elsie continued, "Now, we are here on October the Tenth at ten minutes after ten o'clock on the morning when the TSS was activated and sent us into the future. The second we live past this moment will erase the event and RealTime will write over FirstTime. It will take a little over two years, but RealTime will once again become FirstTime."

"So this is a very special moment in the history of mankind. We don't actually know what will happen. Are you ready?" Rand looked at them both. Their little faces were filled with wonder and determination.

"What do we do?" Marty asked.

"It's going to be hard. It's one of the hardest, most challenging things in the world to do."

"What is it?"

"We wait. Are you ready?"

They both closed eyes tightly.

"Oh no, you must always face uncertainty with your eyes wide open, hope on your tongue and prayers in your heart. Ready?"

"Okay, here we go."

They waited. A small breeze blew in off the sea. A wind chime tinkled from the bough of a tree. Megan sniffed.

The Second String

"I think we did it." Elsie grinned. "Did you guys feel anything?"

"Yeah, cold!" Marty complained. Elsie laughed and scooped him up. Well, that means it's time for a hot breakfast, and then you know what?'

"The wedding!" Marty giggled and squirmed as Elsie tickled him. The early fall sun burned away the morning mist, lavishing them in golden light. As they all walked back to the house Megan trotted up behind Rand, and reaching out, took hold of his finger.

ABOUT THE AUTHOR

Musician, kayak guide, renaissance swashbuckler…Montgomery Thompson like to do fun stuff. Born in Maryland, raised in Colorado, Monte claims Sandpoint, Idaho as his hometown but most of the time he can be found in the hills of Northern Ireland.

Also from Montgomery Thompson

The God String
The first book in The God String series.

Augmentia
The first book in Augmentia series featuring a subtle but crucial cross-plot- tie-in with The God String series

His works for kids include:

The Christmas Wish Tree
A Celtic faery Christmas tale for middle grade and up.

The Shielding of Mortimer Townes
A middle-grade science fiction adventure!

Online
For more information and links go to:
https://montejthompson.wixsite.com/books

Link to Monte on Facebook at:
https://www.facebook.com/MonteJThompson

The author welcomes exploration of the conspiracies,
theoretical physics and research of people, places, equipment,
vehicles, technology, and events relating to the accounts in this story
which may or may not be partially, or wholly true.

Printed by Amazon Italia Logistica S.r.l.
Torrazza Piemonte (TO), Italy